COURT OF MAGICKERS

THE STARS AND GREEN MAGICS
BOOK 4

NOVAE CAELUM

Robot Dinosaur Press

https://robotdinosaurpress.com

Robot Dinosaur Press is a trademark of Chipped Cup Collective.

Court of Magickers

Ebook ISBN 978-1-958696-12-5

Paperback ISBN 978-1-958696-13-2

Cover art and book design by Novae Caelum

Author photo credit Novae Caelum

https://novaecaelum.com

AUTHOR'S NOTE

Court of Magickers was originally published as season three of the ongoing serial *The Stars and Green Magics,* covering episodes 94-150. (It's now called Book 4 in the series, with *A Bid to Rule* becoming Book 3 to give the best reading order.)

I made some minor editing changes from the original serial version, most notably that Rhys's last name is now Delor.

This book features several characters who use gender neutral pronouns (they/them/their, fae/faer/faerself, e/em/eir, or other neopronouns).

This book, barring the occasional and inspired burst of strong language, is a solid PG-13.

For detailed content notes, please see:
https://novaecaelum.com/content-notes

1

DOCKING

> *I formally request that more magickers be trained in the support and strengthening of our warships. If we had more magickers on hand, our fleets would be drastically more maneuverable.*

— REAR ADMIRAL I.L. NTRANT IN A REQUEST
TO VALON NAVY HEADQUARTERS

Rhys tapped their heel nervously on the deck of the cargo shuttle, rubbing the fingers of one hand together in the same rhythm. Out the starboard porthole, they watched the tiny dot of the *V.N.S. Occam's Storm* drift closer. Well, or they were drifting closer to the *Storm*.

Out here, just before the hazy border with Kidaa space, no one made any fast moves. One of the few things the Valoran Navy definitely knew about the Kidaa was that Kidaa ships always came when there were quick maneuvers near their space, drawn like moths to the light. No one wanted much to deal with the Kidaa on most days.

"Will you stop that?"

Rhys turned to Misha, who had taken out her earbuds and was glaring at Rhys's bobbing knee.

They pressed their feet flat to the deck. "You were doing it a few minutes ago."

"I'm listening to music. You're just...doing that."

So in the week and change that had come *after* meeting Misha, Rhys wasn't having to restrain themself from wanting to kiss her. They would be very happy, exceedingly happy, if Misha would be out of their sight for a solid ten minutes.

Ten minutes being exactly how long the shower had given hot water in that first lumbering freighter, which had gone off course and added a few days into its travel time because it had blown some engine part or other. Rhys swore the racket the engines had made would haunt their dreams for years.

Misha rolled her eyes. "Oh, grow up."

"You grow up."

It was a tired argument.

They both settled back against their seats, not looking at each other.

Rhys glanced up at the carefully neutral body language of the pilot in front of them, who was doing his best to ignore them both. The shuttle was all one compartment.

Oh, Adeius. They'd been too lost in their own thoughts. They'd absolutely been too undisciplined in this last week or so—they should have been all Lt. Rhys Petrava, junior ops lieutenant, in space. They were technically on duty any time they were in space, but it hadn't felt real again yet, not after leaving the palace and its glittering, familiar world. They'd been struggling more than usual to separate themself from the worries of what was happening at the capital, and Misha's informality had been a welcome diversion. Misha had— mostly—been a welcome diversion.

This pilot, borrowed from the second freighter they'd

taken to reach the border, was a civilian, but that didn't mean the dignity of the Navy wasn't at stake. And Rhys was acting like a child, they knew it.

Rhys was minutes away from boarding their ship, resuming their life in the Navy. They had to pull themself together.

It was just... Misha was driving them absolutely insane. If she wasn't humming some random song—and *yes,* oh Adeius, she'd gotten "Off-hours Haunt" stuck in Rhys's head *again*—she was making random comments on random things that didn't have to do with anything else, or trying to think up random games to pass the time, and well, those were sometimes okay, but she was just—ugh.

And the way she kept flipping her green bangs out of her eyes. The way her just-barely-lipglossed pink lips puckered when she was thinking hard about anything. The dimples, Adeius, the dimples.

They closed their eyes and leaned back, pretending to settle in to rest, fooling absolutely no one.

Misha nudged their arm. They heard crinkly things.

"Want one?"

A peace offering. One of the last of the chocolates she'd bought when the first freighter had docked to pick up the engine parts, and they'd decided to try to continue on without it. They wouldn't have been able to take it all the way to the border anyway.

Rhys took the chocolate without comment and popped it into their mouth.

The phosphorescent green dye was dimming from Misha's hair, and so was Rhys's white phosphorescent dye, though theirs was still a little brighter. Her dimming phosphorescence, though, made Misha's green aura more apparent.

And the most infuriating thing about Misha? They'd been

with her for most of two weeks, and they still knew little more about her than that she liked phosphorescent hair, was a magicker and apparently kept a folded up portrait of First Magicker Mariyit Broden in her pocket at all times, and had a bad taste in partners.

They'd hit an impasse, neither of them wanting to share more about their private selves. Misha was obviously a magicker, and she knew Rhys knew the semi-forbidden royal art of evaku, able to read nuances in and subtly manipulate the people around them. Able to lie *really* well, while Misha was able to read the truth.

And so they danced around anything actually interesting and ended up learning a lot about their favorite songs and what shows they each liked, but it had been more frustrating than anything else.

Rhys's favorites hadn't truly been their favorites, at least not all of their favorites, and as a magicker, Misha knew that. They had their standard set of favorite music and shows all lined up for Navy life, but they hadn't wanted to share the things they'd held dear during their life at the palace. The dramas that they'd binged when they were younger, watching every nuance and appreciating that the directors must have had a healthy knowledge of evaku to pack so much meaning into various eye twitches and sneezes. Yes, Misha knew they knew evaku, and she hadn't pressed any further than that, but that life wasn't a life that could overlap with their life on ships, or their life in uniform.

And they hadn't told her who their siblings were. Or who their mother was. That they could talk to Truthspoken without having to bow. That the back wall of their apartment in the residence wing of Palace Rhialden adjoined the Seritarchus's own.

Misha, for her part, hadn't wanted to talk about her

family, either, or her life as a magicker. She only wanted to talk about her exes, of which there were many.

Rhys's obsession with researching the puzzle of the unknowable Kidaa had only given them two days' worth of something to do before Misha had grown bored with it.

So they both had things they didn't want to talk about, they weren't overly compatible in their interests, and they both couldn't start a relationship anyway, if they were going to serve on the same ship together. So...maybe there was no problem.

Some time later, the shuttle gave a shudder as the docking clamps mated with those on the *Storm*. The freighter's shuttle was meant to carry heavy cargo and hadn't been small enough to fit safely into the *Storm's* docking bay, which was meant for two person scouts and small atmospheric craft.

When their first freighter had diverted, Rhys had been a little frantic to find someone who could get them to the border fast. Their leave was already up, and while military leave usually allowed for the vagaries of long travel, it wasn't infinitely elastic. To get to Arianna's engagement in time, Rhys's captain on the *Storm* had pulled rank and gotten them a transport back to Valon at military speeds—and that was still mortifying and something Rhys didn't want to have to face coming back. But Rhys hadn't been able to manage the same for the trip back, which doubled the time in transit.

There had been another freighter at that station where they'd docked for parts, though, a freighter already going near the Kidaa border. Rhys had, at least, managed to convince that captain to take them all the way back to the *Storm*, with the help of a far too generous donation from Rhys's private bank account, and a lot of begging.

The freighter captain had looked hopeful that Misha might help shift the strength within the freighter's structure and hull so that it could travel faster in Below Space than it was rated for, if not quite military speeds, but she hadn't offered. Rhys wasn't sure about the protocol with Green Magickers serving on Navy ships—she'd be the first on the *Storm* since they'd been stationed there—and hadn't pressed her.

Still, the money had been enough to get them here. And Rhys was quite a bit poorer. At least the account had been only in their Petrava surname, and not their mother's Delor.

Rhys touched the front of their uniform jacket. They couldn't feel the tiny data chips tucked inside the front pocket, but they knew they were there. Iata, the Seritarchus's bloodservant, had given them those chips—one, when activated, bore the seal of the Seritarchus.

Which was another reason they wanted to keep that life separate from Misha, and they *hated* that particular reason.

"There you go," the pilot said as the docking lights on their displays turned green. "Thanks for flying with us."

There was absolutely no sincerity in that statement. But Rhys nodded and thanked him back because it was polite.

Rhys, as the ranking officer, went first through the airlock into *Occam's Storm*. The air was cool and dry, slightly metallic, and much better smelling than the variations of stale sweat and grease that had permeated the two freighters. The bulkheads here were clean, gray and soft white, the light in a soft spectrum of daylight on the day shift.

Home, they told themself. This was home.

They straightened, hand to their heart as the ensign on airlock watch straightened.

"Lt. Rhys Petrava requesting permission to board."

Ensign Neri Wawuda was a compact woman with brown skin a few shades lighter than Rhys, her hair tied up in a tight knot, her mouth, as ever, barely repressing a smile. And she was a welcome sight, too, someone Rhys was coming to call a friend.

"Permission to board granted. You'd better go see the captain right away, she's not happy at all that we had to divert to pick you up. Or that you're a week late. Those are not her exact words."

Yeah, Rhys bet.

They grimaced, formally nodded to Neri, and stepped aside as Misha entered.

"Ensign Misha Moratu requesting permission to board."

"Granted. Best go see the captain, too, though I think she'll be much happier to see you, Ser Magicker."

Rhys blinked. Yes, they'd known Misha was coming to be the ship's magicker, and that she was the new ensign their captain had requested before they'd left, but knowing that and seeing it in context were apparently different things.

Misha's aura, which Rhys had begun to take for granted as just a part of Misha, flared bright green around her. Her bearing hadn't changed, but her composure had. Not quite somber, but not as openly...Misha.

She'd be responsible for the structure and safety of the entire ship when the ship traveled through Below Space at military speeds, which it could do now that she was on board. During quick maneuvers. During battle, if they ever saw battle, and Rhys secretly hoped they never would.

Misha gave them a look, all smiles and teeth, and they sighed. Okay, still definitely Misha.

"I'm going that way anyway," Rhys said, and started off. They called back over their shoulder, "Did the captain specify immediately? I'd like to drop my duffel off at my quarters."

"Yes, sir, there was definitely an 'immediately.'"

2

THE CAPTAIN

The captain? Of course they're an excellent person, they're the captain!

— NURA IN THE FAMILY VID COMEDY *THE GREAT GALAXY SHIP GALACTIC!*

Rhys shifted the weight of their duffel on their shoulder and eyed Misha straining under the weight of hers. Her pale face was pinched, her brows drawn tight.

She'd dumped most of her ex's junk on that last station, but then had picked up a few sets of Navy uniforms that mostly fit—thank Adeius the last station had them among the supply shops, as Rhys was tired of lending her their workout clothes. She'd accidentally grabbed her ex's duffel, not her own.

Misha had also picked up various wood and metal trinkets that she said would help her with her magics. All of this combined was obviously heavy.

But Misha's body language was very much, "don't ask me if you can carry this, nope," so Rhys kept their mouth shut.

Misha glanced aside at them, drawing closer, and lowered her voice.

"So...the captain. Anything I should know?"

And she hadn't thought to ask that on the whole trip here? Maybe they could have avoided a whole lot of grief and boredom if she'd just asked Rhys to give her a crash course in all things *Occam's Storm*. Or if Rhys had thought to offer. But time with Misha on the way here had seemed to hold its own sacred bubble of separateness, too.

Rhys shrugged. "She's the captain. Stern, mostly, but fair. If you need anything, you're better off asking Commander Gian, or whoever you'll be assigned to for your department head—uh, do you know who that is? Or how your department fits into all of this?"

But Misha was giving them a weird look. Like they'd suddenly sprouted horns or something.

"What?" they asked, and couldn't stop the testiness in their voice.

She made a wavery motion with one hand.

"You're different here."

"I'm on duty. So are you. Just—just listen, follow orders, be nice, you'll be fine. Okay? You can track me down if you need anything, I'm in ops, but I'll be busy." They didn't know with what, exactly, but they were absolutely sure their commanding officer wouldn't be happy with Rhys being a week late.

Misha eyed them with a speculative look they didn't like, and they kept their eyes ahead. She was a magicker. Maybe that hadn't been so big a deal when they were on their way, but it was now. She'd be in an entirely different class of everything here. And they couldn't, in their fragile career—which was even more fragile now that the captain knew who their mother and siblings were—do anything that would make them stand apart as someone not to be trusted. Not especially after a magicker had attacked the Heir at the capital.

At the captain's office near the bridge, at the forward heart of the ship, Rhys pressed the hatch panel, waited for the chime to sound inside, and tensed when the hatch opened.

Captain Ira Nantrayan was a tall woman with dark brown skin and hair cut sensibly short and absolutely not dyed. Definitely not phosphorescent. She tapped a blunt fingertip on her desk, looking up to study Rhys with a gaze that had always made them want to squirm. And they did let themself squirm, just a little. It wasn't good to show how much control of themself they could truly wield.

"Lt. Petrava. Did you have a good time on Valon?"

Rhys opened their mouth, hesitated. Was that a trick question? She would have seen the news about Arianna being attacked by the rogue magicker, and then her abdication and Dressa's stepping up to be the Heir. "Good time" wasn't how Rhys would frame any of that.

"An interesting time, sir. Thank you for asking."

Her mouth twitched. She and the ship's physician were the only ones on the *Storm* who knew Rhys's full name. They'd had to disclose it to the doctor when first boarding because it was attached to their medical records, though that was protected by privacy policies. And they'd had to disclose it to their captain when they'd needed to ask for leave to Valon in a hurry to get there before Arianna's engagement, because there'd been no other way to get there in time but to take a transport at military speeds. And no way a junior lieutenant could manage that on their own.

They hadn't *had* to go, but...but it was their sister. Yes, they had. And despite Valon being its own set of stressers, they'd also needed a break from their life here. Just a few weeks. Just a few weeks of being able to be themself, and not worrying about having to say the right things to keep them squarely in their shipmates' minds as ordinary. Well, or at least an acceptable kind of weird. They'd still occasionally get harassed because of their father, the general, but at least their father wasn't an admiral and in the Navy.

The captain tapped her desk again. "Well. Welcome back aboard." Rhys expected her to say more, to chew them out for being late, but instead, she turned to Misha.

"Ensign Moratu, I'm glad to see you're here in good health. Lt. Petrava will see you to your berth assignment, and I'm glad to see you're already acquainted. Your duty roster will be posted to your comm, and see Commander Gian with any questions you might have." She smiled, and managed to make it look painful. "Dismissed."

Rhys saluted and left quickly, just in case her not chewing them out was a mistake and she might remember to do it now.

Only when they were in the corridor did they remember that she hadn't told them where Misha was bunking, so Rhys could take her there.

Well, okay. They had their comms. Berth assignments would be posted on the ship-wide feed.

Misha had strode a few paces down the corridor, and Rhys stepped quickly to catch up.

"The captain seems nice."

Rhys slanted her a look. Was she military, truly? She had shown little signs of military discipline at all, or that she even really understood the concept. They knew that magickers were often fast-tracked through officer training because they were too needed to be otherwise, and too few were inclined to serve on ships that were built for the purpose of violence, even if that wasn't a magicker's purpose onboard.

Misha's job would be to tend to the ship's hydroponic garden, using it as a reservoir of strength when she needed to feed that strength into the metal of the ship's support beams, or the metal of the hull. She could detect, too, when the hull came under pressure from Below Space, and shift the ship's strengths around to compensate, or else direct where repairs were needed.

Smaller ships tended to handle the faster layers of Below Space well enough, but ships that held a crew of over ten generally had risk of random buckles during travel in Below Space at military speeds, and you couldn't travel through it while shielded. And even with all the precautions, accidents in Below Space were very rare, but not impossible.

"The captain is fair," Rhys said, repeating their earlier tutorial. And mostly, she was. Rhys's problem was that they'd grown up in an environment that tilted fairness heavily in their own favor, and they knew that. They were still stinging that she hadn't listened to their theories about the Kidaa, though. Iata and the Seritarchus had listened.

Which, Rhys sighed, was saying *something*, but not necessarily what they wanted. Couldn't they just make a career of things on their own?

Misha was holding up her comm. "Looks like I'm in... deck eight, section B—"

Oh, no.

Rhys knew. They knew what she was going to say before she said it. "Cabin four."

And there, right there, was the reason why they hadn't been chewed out. Punishment came in many different forms.

Misha looked up, her brows drawing together. "How did you..." Her eyes went wide. "That's your cabin, isn't it? Oh, gods, Rhys, I didn't know."

Well, how could she have? And maybe it hadn't been punishment, other than the basic punishment of having to give up your privacy to the newest member of the ship. It was even practical—Rhys had been the newest officer onboard until Misha boarded. As a lieutenant, Rhys had a possibility of a cabin to themselves, but not a guarantee. They'd thought—well, they'd assumed—well.

Well, and there was their Valon upbringing again.

Rhys shut their mouth into a tight line.

Fine. Fine, well, they wouldn't be in their cabin much anyway with their duties, and they'd take over the ship's tiny library to conduct their research. The database connections were faster there anyway, and they'd been planning some simulations of Kidaa infrastructure in the spare moments when they'd had time to think this last week.

It would be okay. It would have to be okay.

Misha looked over to them, bit her lip, and they read the consternation in her posture well enough.

Rhys forced themself to relax, their smile to grow genuine. And, it wasn't that they didn't like her. They truly did. But she had the potential to know far too much. And they just really didn't want their two worlds to collide here.

And they just really didn't want any issues with self-restraint, either. Because despite everything, despite the bickering they'd fallen into for the last few days, Rhys was absolutely sure not sleeping with each other was killing them both.

"It's okay," Rhys said.

But she was a magicker. And that was a lie.

Adeius, this was going to be a long tour.

3

AURAS

Change happens slowly. Change can happen in an instant. Change might not happen at all. All of these things are true about change.

— ARIANNA RHIALDEN, MELESORIE X IN *THE CHANGE DIALOGUES*

Ari slowly opened her eyes. She blinked in the dim light, looking across the small cabin at the other stacked bunk. Eti lay on the bottom bunk, and she couldn't tell if he was asleep or not. His aura was a murky green in the shadows of the bunk, mostly seen with senses other than sight.

"Eti?" she whispered, fighting to fully wake up.

Nothing.

He was solid again. That was important. And she shuddered as more of where she was came back to her. And why she was here, and how she'd gotten onto this ship.

Adeius. Oh, Adeius.

She pulled her hands from the blanket she only vaguely

remembered curling up in. She looked down at the bright forest green flaring around her, sharp and obvious, though it cast no actual light of its own.

Ari sat up, her heart pounding.

She remembered the ship taking off from Hestia with her strapped into the co-pilot's seat and Eti the observer's seat, while Doryan got them out of atmosphere. And then, as soon as they were clear enough of the gravity well, into Below Space.

She remembered barely holding her attention together, and Doryan guiding her and Eti to this cabin, apologizing that the ship had been built for speed and corporate courier duty, not accommodations.

She remembered Doryan taking Eti's hand before they left and saying he would be okay. He had survived this, and he would survive this. He was strong, so strong, and courageous to have done what he did.

Then Doryan had looked to her, smiled with their kind, crinkling eyes in their broad tan face, and said they'd all get through this.

Ari's throat closed.

And her stomach growled—how long had she been asleep? She had no comm, but the cabin did have a comm display beside the hatch. Would the door be locked? They were prisoners, no matter how kind Doryan, their magicker captor, was determined to be.

She got out of bed, pausing to stretch out her stiff muscles and carefully test her throbbing joints. Not as bad as they could be, but everything she'd done the day before hadn't been kind to her body.

She made her way stiffly to the hatch, bracing against the wall as she peered at the display. The main screen showed Valon City Standard Time, early in the morning. Which had no real meaning to her now, since she didn't know what VCST time it had been when she'd boarded the ship.

She touched the time controls and fiddled until she brought up a second window with Hestian local time, city of Racha.

Had she really slept for half a day?

"Eti," she said, "are you awake? Do you want to eat?"

Anxiety rose as she thought of trying the hatch and finding it locked. That they might not, in fact, be able to eat. That Doryan might not be as kind as they'd shown themself to be before, or that they'd have orders not to feed their prisoners.

She couldn't defend herself now, not easily. Not with the Bruising Sleep weighing her down, slowing her down, and not with—

She looked at the green aura around her hands again, sighed. Not with *that*, certainly. Magickers couldn't do violence—at least, not without great harm to themselves.

And maybe not all of her anxieties made sense, she was fairly sure her mind was not moving in the same proportions as her reality, but her reality was bad enough. And she couldn't bring herself to touch the hatch release yet to test it all out.

"Eti?" she asked again. He didn't say anything. Didn't move.

He was breathing, she could sense that, with her...other senses. Was his aura a little less dark than the day before? Or maybe that was just the darkness throwing it into relief.

Her bladder was becoming insistent, though, and she didn't see a hatch to an adjoining washroom, so she went back to the hatch controls and—

Adeius, the hatch opened.

"Eti, I'm going out. I'll be—out here."

The rhythm of his breathing changed. He had heard her.

"Yeah," he finally said, just a small word, just a breath.

"Do you want anything?"

"No."

She waited another moment, then left him and ventured out to find the washroom.

The ship truly was small, and she didn't have any problems navigating the tight central corridor. Another hatch was to her left when she came out—Doryan's cabin? A hatch with the universal sign for a washroom was across from it, and a hatch at the fore end of the short corridor opened, she remembered, into a common area, and after that, the cockpit. To her right, toward the back of the ship, a ladder led down to what looked like a low compartment. Engine access, or maybe a small cargo area. She could only see what was beneath the ladder, and wasn't about to try and climb down just now.

In the washroom, bladder taken care of, she splashed water on her face, finding a clean wash cloth under the sink to wash off some of the dust and sweat from the day before. And her cosmetics, though the waterproof ones weren't keen to come off.

She looked for cosmetic remover, but didn't find any. And then had another short panic about what if the ship didn't have cosmetic supplies, and she looked even more Rhialden without the cosmetic mask to cover it all up?

The small swallow holo tattoo beside her eye fluttered, and she squeezed the cool edge of the sink in exasperation. Her face, angular and too lean, skin a little lighter than it had been as Arianna, her brows a little thicker, the hair on her upper lip more visible, was still far too Rhialden. Too close to her own. And the deep bruising under her eyes from the Bruising Sleep was far too obvious.

Well, no fixing any of that at the moment.

She touched all of her piercings—mostly not sore

anymore, and they'd all weathered everything that had happened the day before.

The washroom had a cramped shower, but she'd have to work up to that. She'd need to eat first, if she could, refill what strength she could. She needed to better assess her situation.

But she did manage to tame down the spiking indigo mess of her undercut hair.

She really did need to eat, but she lingered by the sink, studying the truly shocking new addition to her reflection in the holo mirror.

Green was all around her.

She remembered asking, as a child, if Green Magickers only saw the world through a haze of green. It made sense—if this was actual light and not some property of the magics themselves, she would certainly see green with it surrounding her completely. But her father had said no, the aura wasn't visible to the magicker themself unless they looked at their body directly.

She could confirm this was true. She could see her green aura in the mirror, or when she looked down at herself, but the world didn't look that different around her.

And it looked vastly different, it felt different, she could sense varying strengths—of, what, lingering life essence?—in every object around her. In the walls. In the deck beneath her feet. Her clothes. The metal of her piercings—which, ironically, *were* all still intact though she'd crumbled a car yesterday.

A knock came at the hatch.

"Imorie?" Doryan's muffled voice. "Are you all right?"

What a ridiculous question.

But she forced herself to think it through because was she, truly? Right now—not later, just now. She was in pain, but that wasn't related to these magics. She was in the most disastrous of messes, but though her anxieties had all spiked, she still heard genuine concern in Doryan's voice. She felt their sincerity in her bones, though sincerity and safety were certainly not the same thing.

And they weren't at Valon yet. She didn't have to think about what would happen when they got to Valon yet. Not right at this moment.

Ari glared at the aura around her hands and shook her hands out, knowing full well that it wasn't going to shake the aura off. She had tried that the day before, and it hadn't worked then, either.

She still had the med patches on her upper arm, the medicines good for another day yet, she thought. She certainly wouldn't be getting more from Dr. Lin.

Her stomach churned as her thoughts brushed the doctor and—all of that.

Ari swallowed hard and thumbed open the hatch.

Doryan stood there, dark brows knitted, wide face pinched with concern.

Adeius, they truly were sincere. They wanted to help. They were distressed that she was in distress.

She had to fight hard not to crumple and remind herself, again, that Doryan was still her captor. Even if she knew they had to be.

"I'm fine," she said. And then a belated, "Thank you."

4

CONCERN

> *Medically, a Green Magicker's seal implant is neutral. It bonds with the skin of a person's cheek and can't safely be removed without the release of the First Magicker. But beyond that, it neither helps nor harms the patient. It is a purely societal device—on a physical level. On a psychological level, I feel it is much more damaging.*
>
> — DR. M. OYALA, IN XIR ADDRESS TO THE
> GENERAL ASSEMBLY

"Are you hungry?" Doryan asked. "Let's get you something to eat. Do you need anything?"

Ari let them guide her, not quite touching her, into the common area. She sat at a table that could seat four while Doryan pulled pre-packaged food containers from a cooling unit.

"Something light, if you have it," she said.

They looked at the labels. "This is too spicy. This—this

might do. Vegetables and rice with chunks of protein. Optional sauce."

They handed the container to her, and she scanned the ingredients, then popped the thermal seal. The meal quickly heated up.

Doryan grabbed one for themself and settled across from her. And for a moment, they ate in a silence that wasn't completely uncomfortable.

She studied them, as she hadn't truly had the time or ability to the day before. Maybe in their thirties, she thought. Heavy-set. Clean and well-kept, dressed in loose gray knits they hadn't been wearing the day before. Their face was handsome, youthful even, the fine lines beside their eyes looking to owe more to smiling than stress.

They looked up, caught her studying, and smiled.

And because she had to know, truly, she asked, "Do you know my name?"

Doryan nodded. "You were thinking it a bit too hard yesterday. I'm sorry—that happens, sometimes. If someone is trying very hard not to reveal something, it often blares like a loudspeaker at the front of their thoughts."

She knew that. She had been trained to be careful with her thoughts around magickers. But she hadn't been in any state to rearrange her mind into proper order yesterday.

"What will you do with that information?"

Doryan shrugged. "Nothing. It's my duty to bring you to the First Magicker, as this whole mess is above my authority to handle. First Magicker Mariyit Broden—and the Seritarchus, because this case is so high-profile, and I'm sorry about that—will decide what to do from there."

They hesitated, watching her closely. "Are you concerned about the Seritarchus?"

Her head snapped back. Were they asking her if she was

afraid her father would do—what? Punish her for this mess? Uphold the various charges against her? Abandon her to the magickers?

"No," she said. Though she wasn't, with everything in her, looking forward to seeing her father again like this.

Failure whispered in her thoughts, and she shoved it aside.

"My father won't be happy," she said. "But—"

But would he stand by her? He'd already replaced her with Dressa, and that had only been when she'd allowed herself to show weakness at her engagement ball, not when she was—was, Adeius, a Green Magicker. Not when she'd messed up this badly, and this publicly. He'd be within all his rights to let the charges stand against her, if that was for the good of the kingdom. To stand against Imorie, at least, and at the moment, she couldn't be anyone other than Imorie.

She braced herself for that possibility. Because it was a very real possibility. She might meet no kindness at all at home.

This was not how she'd expected to come back to Valon, not even a little.

And she'd left her own people behind. She'd left Bettea, but maybe that was best, maybe Bettea could run before fae was trapped into this mess, too.

"All right," Doryan said. "If you feel unsafe at any time, let me know immediately. Because of who you are, the Seritarchus will have top say in what happens from here, certainly. But because you are a magicker now, the law allows us to protect our own against hostile family members."

"My father's not hostile to magickers," she said. She at least knew he wanted to bring them into better social parity with everyone else. They'd helped him at the start of his rule, and did he think he owed them for that? Maybe he did.

"But I'm not sure," she added, "what he'll do with a publicly accused murderer."

Doryan made a sharp gesture. "No. You aren't a murderer. Neither is Eti. But we'll discuss that later, as that conversation won't be easy. Please, please be gentle with yourself just now. The effects of holding yourself invisible will take days to wear off, or longer. Your life is safe, and I promise you that. No one among the magickers will allow harm to come to you when harm was done to you."

She believed their sincerity, but wasn't sure she could trust they had the authority to make that promise. She knew too well how the political wheels of Valoris turned.

Doryan sat back. "As for myself, who you are won't ever leak from me. We, as magickers, have the highest standards of discretion. Much like the Truthspoken, I suspect."

She looked back down at her meal. Her stomach churned, both needing and not wanting the food.

She swiped an errant strand of hair out of her eyes. She needed Bettea. Adeius, she *needed* Bettea with a suddenness that hurt. And she had left faer on Hestia. At Windvale. Captive to those criminals.

Her breath caught, and her spoon froze on its way to her mouth.

How could she have left Bettea behind? She'd had no choice that she could see, but still, she could have protested further, insisted that Doryan send some sort of help. No matter if it might have made the situation worse.

"What name would you like me to call you by here? There are security systems in place on this ship—we are being monitored—but only the First Magicker's office will have those recordings. Well, and the Seritarchus. That's the deal—all high security magicker dealings are also relayed to the office of the Seritarchus, and I coded this with the highest

level security, for his eyes and the First Magicker's alone. No
system, however, is without its potential flaws."

Ari stiffened, trying to run back through the conversation. She hadn't tried to dance around the fact that the
Seritarchus was her father. She should have thought of
surveillance—it was ingrained that everywhere, barring a
few safe places like her bedroom suite at the palace, could be
monitored. So why had she thought she could leave her
guard down here? Would her father, when he heard these
recordings—and he no doubt would—count this against
her, too?

"Imorie's fine."

Even talking about this now left her feeling exposed. "Do
you have a sound dampener? Or a signal scrambler, so we
can talk more freely?"

"No, I'm sorry. Again, we are required to be monitored."

She grimaced. "Are you always under surveillance, then?
Never allowed any chance at privacy?"

"We have our privacy," Doryan said calmly, as if that
hadn't been a loaded question. "But in high-stakes, high-risk
situations, yes. This ship is designed specifically for those
situations. We're traveling to Valon at military speeds—this
ship's small enough for there to be little danger in Below
Space at those speeds, but I'm still monitoring the ship's hull
strengths with my magics so we're safe. Only two days to go
until we reach Valon."

Ari took a breath, nodded.

"Can you teach me to hide my aura?"

Eti had hidden his. She hadn't at all known that he was a
magicker. Maybe, if she could hide her aura, she'd have a way
out if she needed it. If she herself had to run. Somehow.

Doryan hesitated. "No. We must show our auras at all
times. As well as our seals." They waved at her bare cheek.
"Which I must take care of now, by the way. It won't hurt,

though it might be a little sore for a few hours after, as your body integrates the implant."

Adeius, the seal. She gripped the edge of her seat beneath the table, the room slowly spinning. "Can't we wait until Valon?"

"No, I'm sorry. News of what happened will reach Valon ahead of us. Even military speeds can't outrun an un-crewed comm drone. You must be sealed before we arrive. It's the law, and it's protection, too—to show you're in compliance with the law, and to keep you safe from being exploited, as I gather Eti was."

Anger flared within her, but Ari could hardly argue against the law. A week ago, two weeks, she would have absolutely stood by its necessity. Sealing magickers kept everyone safe—people's privacy was intact if magickers couldn't read anyone unawares.

But what about the magickers themselves? Did they feel safer when they were sealed? She certainly didn't feel that now.

How could she have thought this was a good thing for the magickers? She hadn't, truly, thought much about magickers at all. She'd asked her father, when he'd taken on the persona of a magicker, how he could stoop so low.

Ari studied the table, lips pressed tight.

"Are you okay if we do that now?" Doryan asked. "I have sealed many people, and usually if it's done quickly, there's less angst in the anticipation of it. I promise you, there is relief in having it over, and you'll have time to get accustomed to having it before we land on Valon."

She didn't want to have it over. She didn't want to get accustomed to it. She wanted none of this to have happened at all, and wanted this green aura around herself gone.

She made a noise as pain stabbed at her gut, that same not-quite-physical pain she'd felt before whenever she'd thought of violence. Her mind—her soul, whatever—apparently didn't like the idea of her not wanting to be a magicker.

"Every magicker goes through this," Doryan said gently. "The shock of the manifestation, the fear for what's ahead, the denial and grieving a life that is now behind you. But you have a wonderful life ahead of you—"

"You don't know that," she snapped, glaring up. "You can't say that at all. I'm—"

She clamped her mouth shut. She was too emotional to trust herself not to say something compromising. *More* compromising.

She tapped her low heel on the deck, looked away.

"Fine. Do it."

Everything in her screamed for her to take that back. To push this off. To hope that maybe these magics would go away, and not burden herself with an act of such crushing permanence as a magicker rank seal implanted in her cheek. She could never hide it—not, especially, if she couldn't Change.

But she knew when she was deceiving herself. Adeius, so much more so now that she could literally sense the truth or not in her own thoughts.

She was a magicker. That wasn't going to go away, like the Bruising Sleep wasn't going to go away, either. Whatever happened from here, both of those things were a part of her life now.

"We do have time," Doryan said, going back on their earlier statement that doing it quickly would help. What did they read in her that they were backpedaling?

Time would be good. All the time in the universe would be good—never would be better.

But she knew, she absolutely knew she couldn't get through this if she was dreading this moment ahead. She needed it behind her.

Doryan nodded and stood, going to a palm-locked cabinet on the starboard wall. They came back with a black case, which they set on the table.

She couldn't stop her accelerating heart-rate. She couldn't control anything at all.

"This won't take long."

5

THE SEAL

> *Often, as Truthspoken, we must do that which we are not personally inclined to do.*
>
> — ARIANNA RHIALDEN, MELESORIE X IN *THE CHANGE DIALOGUES*

Ari studied the holographic rank seal shimmering on Doryan's cheek as they opened their case. It was the size of a large coin, roughly centered in the hollow of their right cheek. The fractal patterns seemed to shift as Doryan moved, the light catching different depths in the metallic material.

This was the law. Adeius. Yes, until she was faced with wearing this seal herself, she had upheld that law. Would have said it was for the highest good of the kingdom. Could she still believe that? Could she set aside her own emotions and find that solid logic again?

As Truthspoken, it was her duty to uphold the law, and could she do her duty?

She didn't feel very Truthspoken just now.

Doryan pulled out two palm-sized boxes from the case, one black, one silver. And a small device with a few buttons and a tiny screen.

"This is wrong," she said, her throat closing. She couldn't stop the words from coming out, though she shouldn't have said them. She was usually so much more controlled than that.

But the words were true.

Doryan looked up. "Maybe."

"How many people have you sealed against their will? Isn't that a violence?"

They met her eyes.

They didn't need to answer that one.

The meal she'd just eaten churned in her stomach.

Ari touched the smooth skin on her cheek. She had a tattoo now. She had piercings, and though she wasn't particularly partial to either of those things, they were just modifications. She'd done them before, too, and then erased them when she was finished with a role. Couldn't this just be like that? When she was better, when she could Change again— maybe she could get a seal like her father had used to play the magicker. Temporary, and removable if needed. Of course, that depended on if she could ever learn to hide her aura.

That depended on a lot of things.

She was Truthspoken. She'd been born to rule this kingdom, shouldn't she *want* to uphold the law?

Okay, so and if Eti had been sealed, would Badem's people at Windvale have been able to use him against her and so many others—and, Adeius, Badem had said the Javieris were using him, too, and she'd have to think hard about that later.

How many people's secrets had he been forced to take and hand over because they had over him that he was an unsealed magicker? And he could take those secrets because he *was* an unsealed magicker. People wouldn't suspect the shy and awkward gardener.

So was that small bit of protection against exploitation enough to make this right? Was that protection for society's secrets enough to make this right? Enough to let her accept its necessity?

She had to believe it helped society. Yes, most magickers couldn't hide their auras, she suspected, but still, some could. Eti could. There had to be more unsealed magickers out there being used like he had been, and that thought wrenched at her insides.

And sealed magickers were always welcome on ships during travel, as they could offer extra protection and sometimes extra speed. That was a benefit, wasn't it?

And magickers were highly respected for their ability to read truths in disputes and trials. Their witness of someone's truth was as binding as the Truthspeaker's. Would that witness have the same weight if they weren't sealed? If their position wasn't so official and state sanctioned? It added credibility. It added stability to society.

All of these things, on some level, were true. And many of them were also lies, or at least not the full truth. They weren't the reason magickers were sealed. Everything, always, came back to control.

Doryan removed a coin-sized crystal disk from the silver box and a blank holographic rank seal from the black box.

"Hold out your hand, please. The crystal will record both your DNA and your base strength to determine your rank and seal pattern..."

Doryan's gaze flicked back up to her face, and she understood their hesitation. Whatever else she was now, she was still Truthspoken, and just now, she wasn't her own genetic self. Had there ever been a situation like this before, where a

Truthspoken had manifested Green Magics? She certainly hadn't heard of it, and she would know.

If she was sealed now, her seal pattern wouldn't be true to her own preferred default DNA—which, that in itself was a relief. She'd be sealed as Imorie, not Arianna. It wouldn't, truly, be her own seal.

But that, her new senses told her sharply, was still mostly a lie. She was Imorie—Imorie was her. And right now, with everything happening, she might need to be Imorie for...well. Maybe indefinitely. She certainly couldn't be Arianna again as a magicker. It was bad enough that Imorie was a contract Rhialden.

She wanted to scream at these magicker senses to stop— please, stop showing her what she didn't want to see.

Ari held out her hand, and Doryan placed the crystal in her palm.

"We periodically re-assess strength and re-adjust the seal pattern as needed," they said. "So we can adjust this later, if you..." They made a vague waving motion.

If she Changed, they meant. If she was allowed to be herself again, or if she was even able.

With their hand brushing hers to place the crystal, she could feel the sharpness of their discomfort. At her being Truthspoken? At this seal, in part, being a lie? Or the whole sealing process in general?

They felt no triumph, at least, in sealing her, a Rhialden Truthspoken. She knew that.

Ari looked down at the polished crystal. She'd studied how Green Magickers were sealed as a passing part of her training, but she hadn't seen the process itself before, as that was typically private. She'd seen diagrams. Images and holos. In person, in this context...this was so very different.

The crystal was smooth, the material heavy and dense, so clear it seemed to hold the essence of water, or maybe sky, not the earth it came from. It didn't have strength in it like she imagined most rocks would have, or like metal had felt, even, but rather...purpose.

Doryan laid the blank rank seal on top of the crystal in her palm, shining face down.

"This will take a minute."

Ari waited for something to happen, but she could only see the back of the implant, matte gray with its nano circuitries. Nothing changed on that side.

And this...this part itself was actually interesting. If she'd been given a choice, if this was rank like the military wore rank on their lapels, if this was a mark of honor, or if she could remove it, this would actually be useful.

Doryan carefully pulled up the rank seal from the crystal and turned it over, peering at the design.

They made a soft, "Ha."

"What? What's wrong?"

She craned to see.

Doryan turned the seal to face her, holding it by the edges. "Fifth rank. That's your *base* strength. You'll likely reach sixth rank, maybe even seventh, with time and training."

Doryan, she remembered them saying, was fourth rank, and they were high enough in the magicker hierarchy to be trusted with this ship and its secrets. Seventh rank was what First Magicker Mariyit Broden was. She didn't think there was a higher rank than seventh, and only a very few sevenths at that.

Was she giving up a life as the Truthspoken Heir to maybe become the First Magicker someday?

6

RANK

The seven ranks used by Green Magickers correspond to points along a graph rather than any marked skill difference between one rank and another, though there are skill differences as ranks progress. By far, the lower ranks are the most widely represented among magickers, with the highest held only by a comparative few.

— DR. LORD PIXI VIYALOROKKA IN "THE SOCIAL STRUCTURE OF GREEN MAGICKERS"

That her rank was high was...interesting. And of fucking course Ari's rank was high at the baseline. Rhialdens didn't do anything in half measures, even when it was out of their own control.

She turned her hand with the crystal and set it back down on the table, where Doryan scooped it up, stared at it a moment, then set it back in its box.

"All right," they said. "This is the part that's a little uncomfortable, though it won't hurt, just might feel odd."

Ari's stomach tightened.

Doryan pulled something else from the case and waggled it. "Holomirror. I can position the seal, or you can do it yourself. Sometimes it's easier, though, if you don't see yourself until it's finished."

Ari took the mirror and turned it on, projecting a shallow holographic panel in front of her, which moved with her as she turned her head from side to side. She tried not to wince at her own ragged state. The bruising under her eyes was much worse in this lighting, and without her cosmetics, than it had been in the washroom.

She touched her cheek again, trying to capture a memory of what it felt like—not as smooth as it should be, or had been, when she'd been Arianna. But it would still be smooth after. The rank seal would mimic the texture of her skin. Would meld with it, truly inset.

She took the seal from Doryan, holding it, as they had, by the edges. "Will it stick on the first try?"

"No, it won't bond until I tell it to." They tapped the small device they'd pulled out earlier. "Take all the time you need to position it. You know where it goes—reference mine if you need to."

Ari nodded and carefully pressed the cool metallic seal to her cheek. She kept herself from shivering, barely. She shifted her positioning a little to one side, a little down. Right in the hollow of her cheek.

"There? That looks good. Hold still. This part will feel like a small pinch, but the local anesthetic will kick in. Ready?"

"Yes—"

There was a pinch and Ari jumped, but the seal stayed when her hand flinched away. Her cheek felt warm, but it wasn't painful. She watched in the holomirror, horrified and fascinated, as the edge of the seal sunk into her skin, bonding with it.

She reached to touch it.

"Not yet," Doryan said. "Give it an hour to fully set."

She poked her tongue at her cheek on the inside, but that felt no different.

"It might be a little sore for the next few hours, but after that, you won't notice it's there."

"Yes, I will," she said.

Doryan sighed, pulling their instruments back into the case. "This is our life, Imorie. There are parts of being a magicker that are *wonderful*. I'm sure you haven't had the chance to fully explore your new senses, but you will see the world in a way that most people never will. You'll see beauty that most can't even fathom, and that's yours. You will always have that beauty. You will always know who to trust, and who not to. You can take a ship, when trained—and at your strength you'll certainly be able to—into Below Space at military speeds, no matter the size or how many are onboard. And more, and we can talk about that, all the possibilities of what you can do now. Who you are now. And every magicker has their own specialties and gifts as well—I am a healer. You might be that, or might have other skills."

She watched them through this speech, heard the sincerity of it, and also felt the very faint taint of bullshit at its edges.

Doryan stopped, caught her look, and grinned a little wistfully, looking down. "It's not a bad life."

"It's not the life I wanted. It's not the life I was promised."

"No," they agreed. They shrugged. "And how many of us truly have that?"

Her hand strayed again toward her cheek, but she stopped herself from touching it.

She'd already been off-track in her life. And had she, truly, been deluding herself that she would ever be the Heir again? Dressa was already engaged to Lesander. That engagement wouldn't bear going back to Arianna again, and she didn't want it to. She wanted it even less now that she knew the Javieris had a hand in Eti's abuse and what had happened at Windvale. And she didn't know if she'd ever fully recover from the Bruising Sleep. There was no cure.

All of those thoughts—all of those thoughts were true.

So what was there for her now? Remain Imorie, train however the magickers trained to eventually become the First Magicker? Would even the magickers let her do that, knowing her parentage?

She waved off the mirror.

Doryan had put their sealing case away, and was coming back now with another case.

"Cosmetics," they said, sliding it across to her. "On the theory that most people come on this ship in a rush, without their own supplies. There's changes of clothing, too, in that wall cabinet over there—all in neutral tones, like what I'm wearing now. It's a simple cut, I'm afraid, but it's quality stuff. I'm sure you'll find something in your size. You can wash your clothes you have on in that unit over there—or dispose of them. You're welcome to keep the clothes you take from the ship stores."

Ari opened the cosmetics case and felt a dizzying amount of relief at the powders, vials, and brushes inside. No, she wasn't the expert at cosmetics that Bettea was, but she was Truthspoken. Her training still rivaled the top cosmetic schools. She could still obscure her features, push back closer to Imorie's again.

"We have a good two days yet to go until we're at Valon. You're welcome to anything in the common room here, though I ask that you not enter the cockpit—the hatch is locked—or go in the back engine area, and the hatch leading into there from the cargo space is locked, too." They shrugged. "I wouldn't blame an escape attempt, I truly do understand, but I do ask you not to try it. It wouldn't, in your case, help the situation."

No, it wouldn't. As much as she itched to be anywhere but here. Doryan's words weren't a threat, but simply fact. She was a Rhialden, and she did have a responsibility to see this through.

She was also certain that her face, by now, was spreading across the systems of Valoris as a magicker accused of murder, which was monumental enough that she'd be recognized anywhere. And she couldn't Change. And she was now sealed, and couldn't hide her aura, either.

Ari escaped instead with new clothes and her cosmetics to the washroom.

7

FOCUS

I wonder sometimes, though, should Change be as natural to me as breathing? Because it is. I don't know what I'd do with myself without Change.

— HOMAJ RHIALDEN, SERITARCHUS IX IN A
PRIVATE LETTER, NEVER SENT; PUBLISHED IN
THE CHANGE DIALOGUES

He Changed. He Changed because he had to. One last time, he told himself, just one more time in this role he'd spent a lifetime perfecting, and an equal lifetime letting it consume him.

Homaj slipped out of his trance, lying in a bed that was no longer his. Feeling the familiar confines of a body he wasn't sure he wanted.

He groaned and pushed himself up, tasting sour Change mouth, shoving long black hair out of his eyes. He'd left a cup of water by the bed—he drank it all now.

Homaj eyed the closed door to Iata's bedroom. Iata would be up again shortly.

In the meantime, he needed food, and Iata would need it, too. The Change had been faster than either of them would have liked, but they'd both wanted to beat the social uproar that would happen when the regular comm drone from Hestia came into Valon System. That first emergency drone had given them a short margin of time to prepare. Had they been fast enough?

He looked at his comm—which had become Iata's comm —on the bedside table. And he decided the news and his inbox could wait the time it took him to settle his system after a fast Change, because he would be good to no one if he was in both emotional and physical distress.

Homaj pulled on the robe he'd set out at the end of the bed and padded out through the prep room to the door into the apartment beyond. Outside the door was a cooler sent up from the kitchens, as Iata had asked.

He brought it back into the prep room and sat at one of the vanity tables, pulling out various containers and utensils.

The door to the bedroom swung wider, and Iata came out, looking haggard, but himself. Taller than Homaj now, the planes of his face a little sharper, more severe. His own long hair clipped in a loose, uncharacteristic bun. He was still carrying most of Homaj's mannerisms, though.

It wasn't always the time during a long role that was the hardest, but after. They both knew, from when Iata had been him for weeks at a time before, that the aftermath could be rough. The reshuffling of paradigms and personal spaces.

Iata stopped and stared at him, and Homaj saw his conscious effort to make the subtle shifts to get all of Homaj's body language out of his own.

Iata's aura flared, and he sighed, reaching into the cooler without looking and opening the first thing he'd grabbed. Homaj picked up one for himself—a meat pastry, steaming as he broke the thermal seal on the packaging.

Iata sat down at the other vanity with a grunt.

They both waited until they'd finished their first package before they spoke.

Iata drew out his comm, which he'd grabbed from the bedside table, and thumbed it on. Or at least, he tried to. "Shit. I can't unlock it now." The comm would be looking for Homaj's DNA, and just now, he didn't have that.

Homaj held out his hand, and Iata handed it over.

"My own is still in my room," Iata said, and reached for another container of food.

Iata's eyes were puffy from the fast Change, but the food was helping. Homaj didn't think he looked much better. He pulled the thermal seal on his next container with one hand while he held his comm with the other.

He set it to projection mode and placed it on the vanity— a flood of windows came up, and Homaj's tension spiked.

Adeius. He did not miss this constant noise.

"Turn it toward me?" Iata said around a bite of food.

Homaj shifted it so Iata could see it better. Iata couldn't interact with it as himself, either.

Homaj pulled up the news feeds first, eyeing the many, *many* blinking indicators in several inboxes. The regular comm drone from Hestia must have come in, bringing the news.

"Fuck," Iata said, and got up, striding back toward the bedrooms. He came out a moment later with his own comm, wiping dust off the screen. "Fuck, it's dead." He set it down harder than he should have on the far side of his vanity table, and it chimed and began to charge.

Homaj sighed and expanded the holos on his comm, telling himself it was okay to sort through this mess of the ruler's information interface one more time. It would only be one more time, and Iata would decide what to do with this information, not him.

They both leaned forward as he pulled up an array of the top headlines. All had the same theme, summarized best by the top trending article:

Imorie Rhialden méron Quevedo, Arrested on Charges of Murder and Practicing Unsealed Magics

When had the comm drone come in?

About ten minutes ago. So this was new. Very new. And it was already causing an uproar.

Homaj's throat tightened as he touched a vid holo, a five-second loop. It had to have been taken by a civilian comm because the footage was shaky, but zoomed in enough that he could clearly see his daughter. And he had no doubt it was his daughter, she visibly resembled the Rhialdens and was projecting not a few of her own tells. Green glowed around her as she looked frantically around, her mouth pulled tight. A local guard held her upper arms on either side of her, and was she cuffed? Yes. Yes, she was.

Rage flared at this treatment, but—but. He didn't know the situation. There had been deaths. He couldn't afford to assume that she hadn't been involved—

"She must be terrified," Iata said softly.

Homaj shook himself. What was he thinking? This was his *daughter*. He would not stand by and let her fall. This body he'd Changed back to, this persona he knew he'd have to inhabit again and was already halfway into now, was messing with him.

His heart slammed into a fury in his chest, and he reached for the edge of the vanity to steady himself.

"Maja?" Iata said sharply. "Maja—breathe."

He was having a very hard time getting air and couldn't concentrate enough to tell his body to calm down.

"Adeius." Iata knelt down until their eyes were almost level. "Look at me. Their ship won't come in for at least a few hours yet, I think. We can Change back. You won't do her any good if you're falling apart."

He closed his eyes, focused on his breath. *Focused.* And slowly, slowly, it calmed.

He shook his head.

There was a noise from the bedroom, and Iata whipped around, heading for it.

Homaj, too, sat up, alert, trying to pull the rest of himself back together. Had that been a knock? His guard captain, Zhang, coming in through the back corridors, instead of how she'd left by the main corridor? She'd left when they'd locked down to Change, headed to go over details with Jalava for coordinating security when Ari's ship arrived.

But no, not Zhang. Iata came back, trailing a rumpled Dressa.

8

SLIPPING

> *Since a Truthspoken ruler's reign is deeply dependent on the nobility's belief that they are both inhumanly competent and inhumanly omniscient, they must, therefore, at all times maintain that illusion of inhumanity.*
>
> — DR. IGNI CHANG IN "DISCOURSE ON THE
> HUMANITY OF OUR RULERS"

Dressa looked between them, took a breath. "You've seen the news."

"Yes," Homaj said, straightening. Finding himself sliding into his role more fully, now that he had an audience. "We had a little advance warning from the First Magicker, and he had it from a fast drone specially commissioned by the magickers on Hestia. Her ship's traveling at military speeds—it will be here in a few hours."

"You should have told me," Dressa said, glaring first at him, then Iata. Lingering on Iata. "You need to tell me when anything like this happens."

Iata bowed his head, also slipping back into his bloodservant role.

This was wrong. This was all wrong, but they did need to hold these roles for the next...however long. The next few hours? The next day? Until Ari was settled enough that they could switch back again, surely. He ached for that moment.

Dressa looked like she was fighting for control. But, her features smoothed. Her body language calmed.

"Father. What the hell are you going to do? Are you the Seritarchus again now? Did you take back your abdication?"

"No." He stood, and found himself staring up just a little higher at her eye-level than he had before. He had a disorienting moment, wondering if he'd gotten his own height wrong, before remembering that Dressa had been subtly shifting her baseline these last few days. She must have increased her height by a few centimeters. To be on eye-level with Lesander? She had Changed her hair, too, to a halo of curls around her round copper brown face, which just now looked a little less Rhialden—or at least, a little less close to her sister's—than it had a few days ago.

With effort, Maja shook Homaj and all of his calculations out of his thoughts, out of his mannerisms. He saw Iata shift his posture, too. They didn't have to fully play these roles yet.

"No, just for when she arrives," Maja said, settling back into his private self, his private name. "I didn't think—we didn't think—it would be a good idea for Ari to have to face Iata as Homaj first off."

"Yeah," Dressa said, sighing as she pulled over a chair to flop into. "Yeah, that's probably smart. Adeius, do you know how this happened? The articles said she killed—but Green Magickers can't kill—can they?"

She looked to Iata, who'd suppressed his aura going back into the bedroom, but let it out again now, the deep forest green flowing around him.

"It's possible," Iata said. "I've seen it happen before. I hope to Adeius I never see it again. The magicker doesn't usually survive it. Which is why I think she didn't kill."

Iata and Maja shared a look. And the gnawing fears that Maja was trying to hold at bay were screaming again. But what if she had killed as a magicker? It wasn't likely, if she was still here, still breathing, but...what if she had?

"Adeius," Dressa said. "So what do we do? What are you planning? Are you going to release a statement?"

This addressed to him, but he waved back to Iata, and said, "We didn't get much past the need to Change. There will be...upset. Certainly."

"That's already happening." Dressa nodded at his open comm windows, displaying the news articles. "My inbox is bursting with people wanting to know what's going on." She pulled out her own comm, flicking up holo screens, then paused.

"Oh, no. They're already speculating it's Ari. Not just some random contract Rhialden no one's heard of who happens to look a *lot* like Ari—what was she thinking, not Changing more than that?"

"She might not have been able to," Maja said.

Dressa shook her head, still waving through her comm interface. "Well, it's not that big of a leap, especially with the magicker attack at the ball, to think this is Ari. I mean, people might think Green Magics are contagious, or can be deliberately given. Oh, this is such a disaster."

"Ceorre can verify her truth when she states she's Imorie," Iata said.

"No, not everyone will believe Ceorre if she says Imorie's not Ari," Dressa said, waving her comm for emphasis. "They know she's partial to us, to the Rhialdens, and would try to protect us. With everything happening with the Kidaa, too, people are scared. We're already losing public confidence—

we've been losing it since Arianna's ball. They're going to pin this on us, on negligence, or maybe tie it all together with the Kidaa, make something stupidly religious about it—they're people! Panic isn't rational, and people thinking that a Truth-spoken—who they're already a little afraid of—has mani-fested magics, so not only can she be anyone around them, but also hear all their secret thoughts, and now has the ability to kill—"

Iata flinched, enough that it caught Dressa's eye, and she swallowed.

"Then First Magicker Broden will verify," he said evenly. "And then others in the Council of Magickers will verify for his truth, too. Every one of them will know the importance of keeping Ari's identity out of this."

Dressa was shaking her head again. "This is going to have to be independent. She's a magicker now? People will want to touch her and verify for themselves. If they touch her, they'll know if she's lying." She looked up, her eyes widening. "Oh fuck, Iata. People are going to want to touch you—well, you as the Seritarchus—too. To verify that this isn't genetic."

Maja sat back down as his knees went weak. The only way they could absolutely ironclad prove that Homaj Rhialden was not a magicker was for *him*, as Homaj Rhialden, to prove he wasn't a magicker, because he wasn't. They'd have to do that publicly, with multiple witnesses. Another thing he'd have to do before he could Change away from this all again.

Or would it end there? Was what Dressa said true, that people would be trying to out the Seritarchus as well?

Of course they would be. This was the Rhialden Court. Any weakness drew the sharks.

Dressa watched him, assessing, and it was a strange thing to be on this end of a glare when they were both these people.

Finally, she said, "I could...Change to be Arianna."

"No," Iata said, before Maja could point out the futility in that. "If you as Dressa aren't publicly seen around all of this, that's not a far leap that we're trying to enact a cover up. We'll proceed—and we won't address these rumors directly. We can't. And we won't know for sure how to deal with this until we see Ari herself. Then we can proceed."

Dressa's body language shifted more tentative. "Could... Lesander Change to Arianna?"

Maja shared another look with Iata. Then Dressa had figured out that Lesander was Truthspoken-trained. But that was a particular hornet's nest that none of them could afford to poke right now. If Lesander did that for them, Changed for them to protect the Rhialden rule, they would be beholden to her, a Javieri. Maja—Homaj—didn't want that for the kingdom. Not now. Not in the midst of this other disaster.

And, he really did have to be Homaj just now. He couldn't be in the midst of these decisions that had to be made, all of this mess, and not give this role his all, for the kingdom. For his daughter—his *daughters*.

One last time.

"Lesander knows it's Ari," Dressa said. "She woke me up. She saw the news first."

Well—well. Then that particular snarl couldn't be helped, but he wasn't going to place the kingdom in the hands of a Javieri.

And the only other person in reach who could Change was Pria, Dressa's bloodservant, who'd never been quick at Change. She'd taken nearly two days trying to Change into Bettea, only having to Change right back again. That had been its own minor disaster.

He hadn't been here at the time, but Iata as Homaj had been, and he was adept at slotting Iata's running daily summaries into his memories as if they were his own. As he knew Iata was, too. Whatever happened today, whatever he did today, would become a part of Iata's ongoing performance as Homaj Rhialden. He'd better not screw this up.

Homaj grabbed his comm from the vanity, shrank the windows down to manageable, and pulled up his public-facing court inbox. It was auto-filtered, but there wouldn't have been time for the Human staff to wade through the worst of it yet. It didn't take him more than a few seconds to find several vaguely threatening messages from various higher nobility either in residence at the palace or in the city. The I-know-what-you-know-but-I'm-not-going-to-say-it sort of threats.

He also found several messages from the military—two from Admiral of the Fleet Dassan Laguaya at the top, and the next from Municipal Guard Commander Evallin in Valon City—asking if they should go on alert for unrest or riots, both in the city and in space. Laguaya stated quite emphatically that they believed they should, knowing the magicker ship was coming in and space traffic might want to veer away from it. Or possibly shoot it down.

Adeius. He hit reply on Laguaya's first message: protect the magicker ship, but not obviously more than you'd protect any other civilian ship. Watch the situation. Use your discretion. Don't escalate by acting first, absolutely not.

He copied his reply and decided it mostly applied to Valon City as well. He changed a few words and sent that.

The room had gone quiet.

Homaj looked up to Dressa and Iata both watching him. He drew a sharp breath and sat back. He shouldn't be making these decisions—this was Iata's job now.

But Iata held up a hand. For today, just today, it had to be Homaj's job again.

"So," Dressa said, breaking the silence, "what do we plan to do for now? Are they landing at the palace?"

"Green Hall," Iata said. "We'll direct them to Green Hall in the city."

"Should I be there?" Dressa asked. "I assume you—at least, Father—will be, but I promise you, she will not be happy to see me."

Iata's lips twitched up in a humorless smile. "Hold tight here. Like I said, we won't know for sure what to do until we know the situation from Ari. That's the top priority—finding out the damages."

"And keeping her safe," Homaj ground out. "That is the top priority." Even though he'd just ordered the Admiral of the Fleet to not protect her ship more than strictly necessary. Because of how it might look.

"Of course," Dressa said. "Father, or, Iata—you won't put her in prison? I mean, I know that might even be the best move, to show that she's not Arianna, but—I know that practicing unsealed magics can come with—uh—"

With a death penalty. That, at least, wouldn't happen.

"No," Iata said, at the same time as Homaj.

"No, whatever else—we'll find another way than that," Homaj said. He glanced at his comm. It was past midnight, pushing toward early morning. The early hour, when she came in, would blunt some of the public uproar, but it certainly hadn't stopped the nobility's response to this. It wouldn't dull the panic much.

He looked up. "Lesander is still awake?"

"Yes, she's waiting in my apartment."

"And"—he looked to Iata—"you gave her a job to find information for you, right?"

Iata nodded. "To keep her busy. And it has been helpful."

Dressa's face pinched in the briefest show of anger, but it was quickly hidden again.

Iata, he saw, marked her response, but didn't pursue it.

"Yes," Homaj said, "tell Lesander to dig up everything on

Imorie Rhialden méron Quevedo. Dressa, use your access, find any holes in her backstory, do what you can. I'm sure, between Ari and Bettea, that her identity is as solid as they could make it, but make it more so."

Dressa nodded. "Her ship will be here soon? Early morning?"

"We don't know their exact speeds," Iata said, "but I would guess then, yes. But it could be sooner."

"Okay," Dressa said. "We'll do what we can."

She headed for the bedroom and the door into the back passages, but then stopped.

"Please. Both of you, whoever of you, keep me informed."

9

SHARED QUARTERS

All you need to do to see how compatible two people are is shut them in a cabin for a week or so. It worked for my ex-spouse and I on our shakedown cruise.

— ITO BREAK, COMEDIAN, IN A VIDCAST
INTERVIEW

In the quarters that they now *both* shared, Misha wasted no time in hanging up the three things she'd had taped to the walls on the freighters. In the center over her bunk was her dog-eared holo portrait of a younger Mariyit Broden—Rhys had met the First Magicker before, he was nice enough, but not someone they'd feel the need to put on their wall, and not even that handsome. But they guessed it was a magicker thing. To the right was her scribbled list of what looked like meditation steps, and to the left that other thin holo sheet that was hand drawn, geometric, and... maddening. Rhys couldn't look at it without feeling strangely out of balance, even now. She'd never said what that one meant, only that it was magicker business—and Rhys could believe that. It was *very* weird. And still weirdly familiar.

"The shared washroom's down the corridor," Rhys said, "and I have the cabin alarm set to 06:30, an hour before my duty shift starts." They touched the bare wall between their side of the cabin on the right, with their single bunk, and Misha's on the left. Rhys had been using that second bunk as a sofa.

The wall lit with large block letters in red, showing the time—just past 09:30 now—and the basic room controls. They knew she liked the temperature warmer than they did, but it was always cool on the ship no matter what you set the cabin temp to, so she'd have to learn to deal.

"We're on the same shift, at least," Misha said, peering at her comm. "So our sleep cycles should be synced."

Rhys stifled a groan. They'd been hoping for more away time than that. Did they dare ask their duty commander to put them on a different shift? The ship ran on a Valon twenty-six hour day, on Valon Standard Time, broken into three shifts that didn't quite match up on the hours. Rhys had been on the first shift since they'd arrived on the *Storm*, and they didn't particularly want that to change now, even if they could.

"I need to report to my duty commander," they said, and knew it was too clipped, and knew that at the moment, they'd run out of space to care. "If you need anything, see Commander Gian."

"Yes, yes, the first officer. I know." She looked around at her scattering of half-unpacked belongings, wiping back her hair from her eyes. "Hydroponics is on deck two—I know I'm not reporting to a commanding officer there, I'll be in command there, right? Do you know who runs hydroponics when there isn't a magicker on board?"

Wasn't that in her duty orders? Rhys took a breath, let it out slowly.

Misha turned suddenly, meeting their eyes. "Are you okay?"

The question made them step back, their mind freezing. She was a magicker, yes. And that hadn't bothered them overly much on the way to the *Storm*, but here—and that comment she'd made earlier, about them being different here —they didn't like that.

They didn't like that she could see through what they were doing, trying to tamp themself down, line themself up with all the neat boxes they *had* to exist in to continue their life here. They wanted this life. They needed this life away from the palace, where they'd only ever be the person other people used to get to the Truthspoken.

Misha's brows drew down, and she took a hesitant step closer. "Rhys," she said. "I know we didn't talk about this. I know you don't want to—"

"I really have to go."

"Rhys, I see your aura tangling up all over the place. The only other people I've seen that happen to are vid actors— which, I dated one once, someone not really famous—and, well. Some of the nobility. I've been around a few nobles. Not all have it, and not usually in a high concentration of what- ever it is, but...you do."

"I'm not Truthspoken."

Her brows twitched. "I didn't say you were. But—I know you're trying not to be noble here, I can see that. I get that. I've got...things I don't necessarily want people to be thinking about me here, too. But if it helps, it's okay to relax around me."

It didn't help. They didn't know if they could swing between realities like that. They couldn't be the Rhys who was the child of a general to the rest of the ship—enthusiastic, a little clumsy, overall on the high end of average. And then in their off-hours, be the Rhys whose siblings were Truthspoken. That Rhys could think through so many layers—and they didn't want to even think about that Rhys now. That Rhys had no place on this ship.

Had Misha looked them up? She had to have looked them up, and they'd both sort of skirted on Rhys's connections to nobility before, so—well, they would have, in her place. They had looked *her* up on their comm at the last station, but hadn't found more than a basic public social feed. A couple of pictures with people Rhys supposed were now exes. There'd been nothing more than that important enough to have been copied and redistributed around the kingdom by comm drone.

They still felt a little bit guilty about looking her up.

They felt...unmoored, with her looking at them so earnestly.

Rhys didn't have a personal feed. They couldn't. Not with the circles they moved in. But their name was...around. People did know who they were. And maybe they were totally fooling themself thinking that no one on the ship had guessed. They weren't, by any means, a rock star, but...well.

And it was kind of cringey in this light, but they'd been at enough parties with rock stars. They'd set enough trends on their own. They were desirable as a subject of gossip just because their social life was so elusive, their view of society so rare. How many people were siblings to Truthspoken? How many people had grown up in the residence wing of Palace Rhialden?

They'd hoped being at the Academy and on ship would change that, and they'd looked themself up on the way back from Valon, too. Gossip around them *had* tamped down a bit since the last time they'd checked, but now they'd been in the middle of this whole mess with the Green Magicker, and it had jumped up again.

So Misha would find out sooner or later. No, they couldn't share quarters with a magicker indefinitely and her not see, even if she wasn't trying to, some of what was going on. And it would make the tension near unbearable, wouldn't it, if she knew they were keeping something as basic as that from her?

Rhys did want to have one place on this ship where they didn't have to dull themself down, be a little less sure. Where they could relax enough to be themself.

And wouldn't it be nice if they had someone they could actually talk to?

They eyed Misha. She was a magicker. She certainly wouldn't share secrets. They bit their lip, shifted their stance, shifted it back, not quite finding comfortable.

"Rhys Petrava méron Delor," they finally said. "But I only use Rhys Petrava in the Navy. It's not exactly top secret or anything, just...my preference. So, please keep that to yourself."

She blinked. Frowned. Then got it.

They braced themself as her eyes widened and flicked between theirs, and she bit her own lip.

She stepped closer again, extending her hand. Not quite sure where this was going, Rhys took it.

"You have my word, Rhys, that doesn't go beyond me."

They felt—it was strange. They could actually see the truth in her words, like truth was a color, and her words were made of that color.

"Thank you—" Their voice went hoarse, and they touched their throat, cleared it. "Sorry. Thank you. Um. I really must be going now, to my duty commander."

She snorted, but it was gentler, not laced with her usual sarcasm. She watched them a little more closely, and Rhys didn't like that. But maybe she sensed that, too, because she turned back to her duffel.

"Okay—see you at lunch? In the mess?"

"I—yes. I think so. If Commander Hamid lets me off for lunch, because I started late."

They tripped over their duffel on their slow backing toward the hatch, cursed, and caught themself on the wall.

There was a beat of silence, but Misha didn't laugh. When they turned back she was smirking, though, and they couldn't quite stop their own sheepish grin.

Rhys swiveled, turning the near-fall into something useful as they touched the wall near the hatch, bringing up controls to activate a mirror. They quick-checked their appearance, straightened what needed straightened, and artfully let a little askew what they needed to as well. Smoothed back their hair just enough.

They caught Misha's gaze in the mirror.

She turned away again, and they hastily slipped out before the air could get any more awkward.

10

ON DUTY

It's a cycle of three
He left me again
The world and the ground and the sea
It's a cycle of three
All over again
The spin of the galaxy

— THE RINGS OF VIETOR IN THEIR
POPULAR SONG, "CYCLE OF THREE"

The familiar path from their quarters to the operations center, far aft and deep in the heart of the ship, grounded Rhys. They found their steps settling again into the rhythm of Rhys Petrava, their thoughts flowing in the right directions again. Part of them was absolutely galled that they'd just told Misha what they had. The other part...

Was it so wrong to want a safe port to come back to every night? Even if that port also involved Misha?

She wasn't who she'd first appeared to be, either, Rhys

knew that. They'd looked her up, sure, but they'd never pried more than that. Public knowledge was still the surface.

Their thoughts drifted, from the shape of her lips, to—to how they might hang up a curtain across the room, or at least rig up some sort of opaque holo-something, they'd have to see if they could check out a large-scale projector from ship's stores, and what in the world would they put on that requisition request for the reason? "I desperately don't want to sleep with my roommate, because it would complicate everything, so please help?"

Misha irritated them. Every single impulse, everything she did lately, irritated them. Could they just focus on that?

It wasn't cooling, though. Oh Adeius, it was not cooling.

They picked up the edges of their mind and set it firmly back on duty.

If the bridge was the fore heart of the ship, then ops was aft, on deck three above the engine room. The ambient noise was always a little louder here than in other places on the ship, with the sound dampeners over the engines not quite enough to filter every hum and rattle.

As Rhys approached the double-wide hatch, touched the scan plate, and was let through, they found themself a bouncing mix of nerves and eagerness to get back to work. *This* was their home. This was where their purpose was secure, as Lt. Rhys Petrava, analyzing whatever their duty commander set to them, which was a job that suited them well. It wasn't monotonous. The information needs of the captain and the extended border fleet changed often, and Rhys was not so vain as to think they had an integral part in all of that, but still, it was a part. It was useful. It was theirs.

As usual, ops was a flurry of muted activity, with crewers and officers both sitting their usual stations. Rhys waved to Ensign Lima, who they worked out with sometimes, and nodded to Warrant Officer Eam, currently standing in a holographic map on the simulator, who smiled and nodded back.

Rhys stuttered a step as the head of ops, Lt. Commander Friesa Hamid, looked up. She'd been checking over a crewer's shoulder near the far end of the room, and Commander Hamid often roamed the ops deck, so that wasn't unusual. But the sharp look she gave them was.

Not that it was unexpected. The captain might have skipped the reaming out, but they didn't think Commander Hamid would. Junior Ops Lieutenant Rhys Petrava had learned very quickly when they first came on the *Storm* that showing up a few minutes late to duty was not how they could safely blend in with Hamid's ops crew.

Commander Hamid patted the crewer's chair and headed toward Rhys. She pointed aft.

"Petrava. Welcome back. My office, please."

Rhys tensed, but of course they followed.

Lt. Commander Hamid was short, brawny, and always in motion. Her dark brown hair was cropped close, with the pale outline of a holo tattoo just visible above the collar on the right side of her neck. She was one of the smartest people Rhys knew.

She held the hatch for Rhys to enter, then let it slide shut behind them.

"Commander Hamid," they said, straightening to attention. "Reporting for duty—"

"Yes, yes," she waved them at ease, moving behind her desk, but not sitting yet. Instead, she leaned on the desktop, considering them with dark gray eyes.

Rhys allowed themself to fidget, just a little.

"Lieutenant—" the commander sighed. She leaned back, releasing the desk, and glanced at the closed hatch.

She lowered her voice. "I lived in Valon City, worked in operations on Valon until I shipped out here a few years ago.

I've been known to read the social feeds from time to time. I'm not unaware that Petrava isn't your only surname."

Rhys stiffened. Did *everyone* know who they were here and just weren't saying? Well, not fair, Misha hadn't known.

Should they deny it? But, to what point, if Commander Hamid already knew? How long had she known? This whole time, the whole last six months they'd been on the *Storm?*

They rubbed at their face, nodded, and shrugged. "I don't call attention to it here."

"Which is probably for the best. However. If you do need to talk about...all of that...with someone who isn't going to freak out about it, you know where to find me."

Which was...slightly mortifying. And not at all the conversation Rhys had expected to have here.

"Uh...yes, sir. Thank you, sir."

She nodded, then shifted back to business.

"I have a task for you—what's to be your sole task for the foreseeable future."

Adeius, no. Please, please don't let them be sidelined now because of their family.

The chips Iata had given them, snug in their front inner shirt pocket, and the Seritarchus's command to report any new information on the Kidaa, snapped back into their awareness as well. Would they even have a chance to report anything if their commander kept them busy with this new task, whatever it would be? Would they have a chance at all to continue their work with researching the Kidaa?

They'd been itching to get back to it. They'd come to the end of what they'd been able to do with the information they already had, loaded into the secure section of their comm. Some of it was proprietary information to the Navy but not top secret—and anyhow, they did have top clearances because of who they were—but their observations weren't fit for the public yet, certainly.

Rhys stood still, except for their fidgeting, bracing for what would come.

"This is command level knowledge," the commander said. "The captain's had word that there have been a number of...incidents...involving defacement to property and land on several worlds, and some human casualties. There are Kidaa runes carved into every area of attack." She watched them. "Did you hear about this when you were on Valon?"

"No." Rhys straightened. "I—uh, wasn't there long. Kidaa runes?"

She nodded, and their thoughts raced. Attacks? Kidaa didn't attack. At least, they'd never shown any signs or inclinations toward violence or aggression. Except...the strings that they'd been pulling on, the patterns they'd been trying to bring into focus in their spare time, had sat uneasily for a while. They'd told Dressa as much.

The captain hadn't wanted to listen to their unease on that before. Was she listening now?

Rhys's chest tightened. They'd wanted Captain Nantrayan to acknowledge their work, sure. They'd wanted that badly. But they'd never wanted their work to be put to practical use so soon. Not this kind of practical, scrambling behind a curve of events that were already happening.

"We don't know that these incidents are caused by the Kidaa," Hamid said. "From the information the captain's received, there's so far no evidence of Kidaa ships being near the scenes, or in-system for these systems at all. We have no evidence that I know of the Kidaa crossing the border, beyond the occasional flit over and flit back, and that's always been that way. And since you're our resident expert on all things Kidaa, the captain has decided to put that to good use."

The commander waved toward the wall, and the unseen floor of ops beyond it. "You'll use the main sim console. Eam will shift to the secondary console. You have resource priority. I want you to review all the data we've gathered from our ship, from the others along the border, from what we know about what's happening with these attacks. I want pattern analysis, Petrava, detailed and complete."

Rhys hesitated only a moment. They shouldn't have done even that. Adeius, had three weeks off their ship made them so complacent? "Yes, sir."

Hamid's smile turned a little sour. "Because I know, Petrava, doesn't change anything. And you are late in coming back. We've work to do."

They felt their face heat. "Sir. I didn't—I couldn't access travel at military speeds, and the freighter we were on had engine difficulties—"

Hamid held up a hand. Leaned forward. "Go to work, Petrava. Captain will want a preliminary plan of study by end of shift."

Rhys stiffened, saluted. Which was more than was strictly required under the ship's more relaxed standards, but Hamid acknowledged it all the same.

Work. This was to be their work. Their obsession, their need to understand the Kidaa, was being taken seriously.

Rhys kept themself from touching their shirt pocket, and the two chips inside, on their way out.

11

BORROWED CLOTHES

> *What a Truthspoken wears is as important as their mannerisms and appearance. Clothing is performance.*
>
> — ARIANNA RHIALDEN, MELESORIE X IN *THE CHANGE DIALOGUES*

She was coming home in borrowed clothes. Gray, shapeless things that she wouldn't have worn even casually, not even to sleep in, as Arianna. She had to roll up the cuffs on the gray knit pants, because she was three centimeters too short for the shortest pair.

She'd washed the clothes she'd worn off of Hestia, party clothes and infinitely more suitable for landing on Valon. Most of the stains had come out, but the memories hadn't. So, she was wearing ship clothes.

And maybe that was better. Her Hestian clothes would already be on the holos people had taken of her. They'd already be locked into the minds of whoever saw them, forever associated with a rogue magicker, a Rhialden magicker, a supposed killer.

An actual killer—and that particular thought still hurt like hell, an aching spike through her soul.

Best to incinerate those clothes the first chance she had.

Ari took a ragged breath, braced against the sink in the washroom, taking final stock. It wasn't hard now to look in the mirror and not see herself, but Imorie. She'd done her cosmetics as best she could, echoing what Bettea had done before. Still, the bruising under her eyes showed dark, her mouth tight with worry and pain. Her hair was passable, combed and gelled to one side. She couldn't show too much elegance, no. Not too much competence in her appearance.

She couldn't do anything about the seal on her cheek, though. Or the deep green surrounding her.

Ari bared her teeth at the mirror, viciously suppressing the urge to pound on it. It was ship glass—it wouldn't break.

Adeius, she felt like a prisoner being brought to trial.

Exactly because she *was* a prisoner being brought to trial, or whatever would be awaiting her. Doryan had been a kind and infinitely patient jailer, but they were still her jailer.

She let herself feel Imorie's terror, because it was her own. And Imorie's determination to get through this, because it was her own. Whatever she faced, whatever her father would do—whether he would even acknowledge her, even in private—

She grimaced at the tightness in her gut and stumbled out of the washroom, correcting her fatigue-numbed steps as best she could on the way back to the cabin she shared with Eti.

There was no way out of this than through it, was there? Imorie Rhialden méron Quevedo was about to be seen, again, and publicly documented, *again*, as a magicker. And Imorie and Ari were increasingly becoming one and the same. Her two hours of straining to bring about even the smallest Change the night before had been met with only vast fatigue. She *was* Imorie Rhialden méron Quevedo. She couldn't Change that. She might be Imorie and Imorie alone from here out.

The ship's comm chimed as she reached the cabin hatch, and she paused.

"Imorie, Eti, please come to the cockpit to strap in for landing."

They wouldn't be making a leisurely landing, then. But no, that would be too chancy on a ship many would know carried the rogue magickers that would have just hit the news, if her estimates of timing were anything close to true. The public would already be afraid of her, and she hadn't even landed yet.

Ari hit the hatch panel, and the hatch slid open.

Eti was still lying in his bunk, back toward her, curled up.

Doryan had been trying to talk with him, she knew, when Eti had let them. But Eti had spent most of the last two days not responding to anyone.

Ari drew up short, checked her growing temper, her roiling fears, and tried to will herself to calm.

"Hey," she said. "Eti. We need to go to—"

"I heard."

Eti rolled over, staring at the bunk above him. His own newly implanted rank seal glinted in the dim light. He'd kept that side of his face hidden from her, and she hadn't yet been able to see what rank he was.

"I'll strap in here," he said.

"We'll have to get out at Valon. Eti." She stepped further into the room. Should she have tried to drag him out sooner? Do his own cosmetics, to try and make him less haggard? "Please. Just come with me to the cockpit."

He hadn't been out of the cabin except to use the washroom. She didn't think he'd even showered, though she was fairly certain he'd at least changed clothes, and Doryan had brought his meals here.

His eyes glittered in the cabin's dimmed light—he hadn't been able to tolerate anything brighter, so she'd just reset the cabin defaults to dim. She felt more than saw him studying her. Maybe looking at her own rank seal.

And she felt, too, the roiling, inward-focused darkness that was still clouding his aura.

Eti sighed and pushed himself up with what looked like enormous effort. Ari would have helped him up, but—well. She was conserving her own strength. Doryan had given her platinum bangles, three for each arm—plain metal and heavy, but she could pull on their strength if she needed to. She was almost certain she would need to.

Eti's hair was...everywhere, and the wrong side of greasy. He needed a shave, but that would take more time than they had. But she should at least get him to wet his hair down. Or maybe do it herself—she wasn't sure he'd even try on his own.

If he looked disreputable, he wouldn't help her case or his. So she grabbed his shirt sleeve and tugged him toward the washroom, wetting a comb to run through his matted hair.

Touching him took its own effort. He wasn't as actively repelling her attention as he had been before, but he was still in his own spiral, his own darkness.

Ari surveyed her quick work of his hair, but there wasn't anything she could do about the pallor of his face in the time they had, or his own bloodshot and puffy eyes.

A fine pair they made.

She met his gaze in the mirror, and her eyes flicked down to his seal.

Oh. The spirals on his rank seal were intensely dense.

More than hers, certainly. Was he sixth rank? Adeius, was he possibly even seventh? Doryan hadn't said anything—but then, maybe they'd considered this a private thing for Eti to talk about if he wished?

Eti's gaze returned to the deck.

The comm crackled again. "We're about to head into atmosphere. Both of you to the cockpit, please."

Ari hit the comm panel beside the washroom hatch. "We're coming."

12

GREEN HALL

> *A lot of it's rampant speculation, to be sure, but I agree some of it is on point. If you look at all the unanswered details surrounding the magicker attack on Truthspoken Arianna Rhialden, and her odd abdication and disappearance from court, and then the details around this contract Rhialden's manifestation and alleged murder on Hestia—and there really aren't enough details, I'm just saying—it's all too weirdly coincidental.*

— ANONYMOUS17732-R1 IN THE CHATSPHERE
VALON CITY LIFE

Doryan glanced up as Ari herded Eti into the cockpit, surveying them both before they nodded. "All right, strap in. This should be smooth enough, and we'll be landing at Green Hall in Valon City shortly."

Ari slipped into the co-pilot's seat, making sure Eti strapped in to one of the observer seats behind them and clicked the locks shut before she pulled her own harness down. The lights in the cockpit were already dimmed, and Eti was only squinting a little.

"We're not landing at the palace?" she asked.

"No—we'll be met at the pads behind Green Hall and escorted inside, where the First Magicker and the Seritarchus will be waiting. And I have to warn you both, there are people outside around the Green Hall complex, and they may not be kind. They are not there for you. They are there because of their own fears—ignore them. I will do so myself."

As if it would be that simple.

It would have been safer, surely, for her father to meet them at the palace, but not politically safer. Right now, distance between the royal Rhialdens and a magicker contract Rhialden could only help.

As the ship descended smoothly through the atmosphere, Ari's stomach knotted further and further until she had to start pulling lightly from one of the metal bangles to keep her last meal down. It wasn't motion sickness, she was sure. This magicker ship wasn't a backwater port freighter.

And then they were over Valon City, the clouds of a bright dawn sky parting to the spread of skyscrapers below. To the south and east, the height of the towers tapered into the sprawl of suburbs. To the north, the river set apart the massive compound of Palace Rhialden, glittering on the river-bank. Ari swallowed tightly at the distant sight of the palace, the long, ornate front facing the river, its wings and outbuildings and the jutting peak of the Adeium behind it. She'd find out soon if she'd even be allowed on its grounds again.

Doryan banked sharply then gave the ship over to autopilot as the ship's systems coordinated with the city grid. It wasn't often that an interstellar ship landed outside the bounds of the spaceport, and the city wasn't taking chances with this one. Ari didn't doubt regular city traffic had been diverted from their path.

Then they were low over the buildings, slowing further. Doryan hovered their hands over the controls as the ship turned in place, then gracefully set down.

Eti took in a small breath, and Ari glanced back. His hands were clutched tightly around his stomach, and she didn't think that was motion sickness, either.

Doryan stood, stretching a moment. Ari heard a soft thump and the whine of the ramp machinery in the common area.

"Both of you, follow my lead. Don't speak unless necessary, don't respond to any threats or questions. Don't meet the eyes of anyone outside the compound. We'll be through soon enough, and there will be quiet inside."

The ramp machinery stopped, and they followed Doryan back to the outer hatch in the center of the common area, Ari still herding a reluctant Eti. Outside, a mixed contingent of guards in the green livery of Green Hall and the maroon and silver of the Palace Guard waited.

Commander Jalava themself was there, looking stern as always, their pale face grim, and short silver hair fluffing in the breeze. Jalava met her eyes, just a quick look, before moving on. Which might not have been wise, but was meant, she was sure, to reassure.

And it did ease some of the tension in Ari's chest, even while she tried her best not to listen to the shouts, the jeers, the curses raining down around them from people arrayed outside the perimeter fence. The fence was by no means solid, and built that way on purpose—people didn't want to think the magickers inside did anything worth hiding.

Beside her on the ramp, Eti stiffened, head down. She was already close to him but moved closer.

He gave her a small smile, more response than she'd seen from him most of the last two days.

She reached for his hand, and despite his self-repellent

aura, she held on tightly when he took hers. She held on tight for both of them as they walked down the ramp behind Doryan, borrowed boots thumping on the metal. No one should have to face this kind of crowd alone.

Imorie Rhialden méron Quevedo kept her gaze low, but she didn't let her bearing speak defeat. She was a Rhialden, even if a contract Rhialden.

The guards formed up around them in a solid barrier, and Jalava, not looking at them again, was still near.

Inside Green Hall, the corridors had been cleared of any magicker bystanders. Jalava barked a few orders, and some of the guards went ahead of them while the rest of the group split to fit into two lift cars. Ari's group, which included her, Eti, Doryan, Jalava, and three more of the Palace Guard, took the first lift up to the top floor where the First Magicker kept his office.

She'd been in First Magicker Mariyit Broden's office twice before, shadowing her father in one of his meetings with the Green Magickers. Past a reception area, double doors opened into a large, sprawling space with high ceilings, crowned with high, horizontal windows.

It was more greenhouse than office, every corner and spare surface covered in potted plants, the air humid and soil-rich. There were even some trees, one reaching up to bend its branches to the ceiling above. The desk at the near end wasn't particularly tidy, and the cluster of overstuffed chairs and couches on the far side owed more to comfort than fashion.

They were waiting in the sitting area, all standing poised, as if they'd just left their chairs. Captain Zhang, Iata, Mariyit Broden. And her father.

Ari's gaze stuck on her father, taking in the deeply multiple sense of soul essence—whatever it was called—within him. Truthspoken.

Oh. So that's what it looked like. She'd only hazily been able to sense that in herself, but she saw it sharply in him now. And Iata—her breath caught. Iata's soul essence was even denser than her father's. More solid. Clearer, more vibrant, like the soul energy within Doryan. Like the soul energy she could see blazing from the First Magicker, though certainly not that bright.

Iata. Was Iata...could she possibly be reading that wrong? Was that energy the essence of a magicker?

Why was Iata even here? He seldom left the palace as himself. He was a bloodservant, by nature meant to stay in the background. Was he here to support her father, or—for some other reason?

The First Magicker stepped forward. "Thank you, Commander Jalava, for bringing up our guests. Ser Seritarchus, do you wish the commander to stay?"

Her father, whose clothes and demeanor today were more subdued than usual, neutral in presentation, glanced at Jalava. "Commander, please guard the corridor outside. Zhang is with me. We are adequately safe."

"Of course, Seritarchus," Jalava said, dipping their head in acknowledgment before they sharply turned and strode out with the other guards.

Ari's arms prickled. She'd assumed the guards had been there for her protection, but of course they'd also been meant to publicly reassure that the rogue magickers wouldn't harm the Seritarchus.

Eti's hand twitched in hers. Should she let go, here in this company? She could feel Eti's sharpening fear, cutting through the dullness of his thoughts.

She didn't let go. As much for Eti's protection as her own. She would not let her father pin all of this on Eti. And Eti, for all he himself was struggling, was someone solid to hold on to.

The doors to the office shut. It was her and Eti and Doryan, facing those across the room. Everyone here knew who she was.

Her father came toward her, and he seemed almost... tentative. Ari kept her chin up but didn't quite look into his eyes. She didn't know what she'd see, and she couldn't face the raw strength of his emotions, if she'd be able to see them through his eyes, as some magickers could.

His steps slowed, and something rippled across his face. Dismay? Disgust? Adeius, was she that repellent to him now? Well of course she was—

He strode the last few steps, stopped with his hands up, just shy of touching her.

"No," he said, and his voice sounded torn. "None of that."

She shivered, gripping Eti's hand harder, and felt herself solidify again. She'd just been flickering.

His gaze twitched to take her in, survey Eti, note their locked hands. Looked back to her.

"Ari," he said, his voice tight, and thick enough it made her own throat close. He stepped even closer now, and stopped again, hands up like he wanted to, what, embrace her?

"May I?" he asked.

She didn't know what he wanted, but she gave a small nod. And found herself wrapped in his arms, nearly crushed. Her hand holding Eti's spasmed, but she didn't let go even still.

She shook as the force of his emotions hit her. She didn't fully know how to parse them yet, but she clearly felt the blaze of—of—what? A rumble of concern and relief and grief and pride and so, so much warmth. It warmed her to her chilled bones.

She choked on a sob before she could help herself. Oh,

Adeius. He wasn't turning away from her. He wasn't angry with her.

She held him tight with her free arm, and felt him shudder, too. Was he also feeling her emotions?

"I failed you," she rasped.

"No. No, the other way around, Daughter. You are safe. You are safe here."

Her father never embraced her. And she was heading into panic now, because she didn't know what to do with this, or the sense of him, which was so different from what she'd expected.

"Father," she managed, and he pulled back.

She took him in fully now. His face, light with cosmetics for once, was hardly composed. So open. But she checked his tells—yes, it was him. She looked past him to Iata, who was watching, but his own face showed nothing.

"Are you well?" her father asked. One hand was back on her shoulder, as if he feared to let her go. She sensed the sharpness of his concern.

And still, the question was so ridiculous she couldn't help herself saying, "Of course I'm not well." And it came out more forceful, more bitter than she'd intended.

He nodded, as if that was what he'd expected. Was that good? Was that bad? She should be able to read her father, or at least get the general shape of his mood, especially through his touch on her shoulder. But though she still felt his concern and not a small amount of something she recognized as self-recrimination, and though she saw the tightness around the edges of his expression, the slight furrow to his brow, she didn't understand the other cues he was giving off just now. Why was he being so understanding at all? Homaj Rhialden was hardly known for being kind.

He turned to Eti.

"You are Etienne Tanaka?"

Eti looked up briefly, and Ari knew the strain it took him to do even that. She squeezed his hand.

"Yes, Ser Seritarchus."

"All right. Ari, Etienne, please come sit. We have a lot to discuss."

13

ALL THE LITTLE TRUTHS

We tell ourselves we're in control, we've been trained, we can navigate any situation with efficiency and style. We are so adept we can also lie to ourselves with ease.

— HOMAJ RHIALDEN, SERITARCHUS IX IN A PRIVATE LETTER, NEVER SENT; PUBLISHED IN *THE CHANGE DIALOGUES*

As he saw Ari and Etienne to a leather couch facing the other chairs, it was all Homaj could do to keep his emotions in check. Adeius. In the morning light from the high windows, she looked ragged. There was spark in her eyes, yes, but also a wariness he'd never seen before. His daughter had always been so sure of herself. So very much in control.

He marked the bare metal bangles on her wrists and knew what they were for. He noted her hand tightly gripping Etienne's and...wasn't sure how that had come about. The body language between both of them was mutually protective, as if each was holding the other together. Not romantic, not at all, but certainly a tighter bond than she shared with her own siblings.

He hid a grimace as he resumed his own seat, at corners to both the couch and the row of a loveseat and chairs facing it. He knew a bit about the bonds forged in trauma.

Anger flared at whoever had done this to her—not the magics, that was the maddening randomness of the universe —but whoever had steered the events that resulted in three deaths at Windvale. He'd thought the estate was safe, a place of recovery. He never would have sent her there if he'd thought there was even a hint of danger. What had happened?

To his left, Zhang glanced over at him. Her own face was guard-impassive, but he knew her well enough to see her dismay even as she was trying to gauge his reaction. He wished he was sitting directly beside her, but he had absolutely not wanted to position himself as an interrogator here, with all of those who desperately wanted to know what had happened facing those who would have to tell it. He did not think it would be an easy telling.

Beside Zhang on the loveseat, Iata folded his hands in his lap, a centering tell. His body language was tightly contained, not quite relaxed but not taking up the sense of physical space he usually did as the Seritarchus.

Homaj caught Ari's eyes straying to Iata and lingering. Iata's aura was tightly contained as well and not visible to him, but could Ari see it with her magicker senses? Newly manifested as she was, would she know what she was seeing? When Iata had first manifested, some things had come to him immediately, like understanding emotions in a touch. Others had taken time and careful training.

Beyond Iata in his own chair, the First Magicker rubbed

at his graying blonde beard, surveying everyone, then held up his hands.

"First off," Mariyit Broden said, "whatever has happened, we are none of us here to judge the necessities involved. We will listen to everything. We will, if you allow us, verify your truth as you are speaking. And we will do our best to right any wrongs done. This is not an inquisition but a debriefing."

"I would like, first, to verify the truth of Magicker Azer," Iata said, nodding at the magicker who'd escorted Ari from Hestia.

Doryan Azer, a large, handsome person with prominent laugh lines in a bronze face and shrewd dark eyes, had settled themself stiffly in a chair on the far side of Ari's couch. Homaj didn't think their tension was from the shock-and-awe some people got when first meeting the Seritarchus, but rather a protectiveness toward their charges.

That, at least, boded well. Homaj hadn't been able to tell much more from Doryan's record on Hestia than that they'd often dealt with the nobility who'd manifested there, and that couldn't be an easy task.

"I assume you know the identity of the charge you picked up?" Iata asked them.

"I—yes. And I have been as discreet as possible." Doryan spread their arms, turning to bow in their chair to Homaj. "Whatever you need of me, Seritarchus, and First Magicker, I am ready to serve. Of course you may verify my truth." They held out their hand to the First Magicker. Their chairs were close enough that Mariyit could have taken it.

But it was Iata who got off his chair to kneel beside Doryan. He held out his own hand, and a deep forest green flared around him.

Homaj—hadn't been expecting that. They hadn't directly discussed whether Iata should reveal his magics to Ari, and that wasn't Homaj's call anymore. He'd assumed Iata would want to keep that close, unless Ari herself brought it up. There would be others here—there *were* others here—who were unknown quantities to be entrusting with such a charged secret.

He watched Ari still, her attention riveting to Iata's aura. She didn't seem as surprised as she might. So she had seen, or maybe suspected, that Iata was a magicker.

Her gaze flicked to his—verifying, he thought, that he himself wasn't disturbed by Iata's aura, even if he was surprised and not entirely pleased that Iata had shown it. But it was Iata's call, and he'd already made it.

Doryan Azer didn't seem surprised, though, so they must have seen the same signs Ari had, and likely known how to interpret them better. They clasped Iata's hand readily.

"Do you have any intentions beyond service to the Green Magickers and service to the Seritarcracy?" Iata asked.

"I have a duty to the safety and wellbeing of my charges." Interesting distinction, that, because personal safety and service to an organization weren't always the same thing. Doryan continued to rise in Homaj's view.

"And I have a duty to those I serve on Hestia," Doryan continued. "People I'm currently training, and I help seal those who manifest on Hestia. And I tend the gardens at Green Hall in Racha. But beyond that, uh...no. As I said before, I'm here to serve and help however I can. I deal with the nobility fairly often on Hestia—with such a high concentration of nobility on a resort world, it makes some of their manifestations inevitable." They gave a tight shrug. "I know how to be discreet and secure."

Iata stayed still a moment, likely reading what he could from Doryan's emotions. Then he nodded. "Does anyone else besides you, and besides those of us in this room, know what you know about Ari?"

Doryan shook their head. "Not to my knowledge, no. We

talked a bit around it on the ship"—they glanced at Ari—
"but I coded all of the ship's security feeds since takeoff for
the First Magicker's eyes only."

"Good. Thank you. And would you be amenable, if we
require it, to stay on with Ari and train her? As someone who
already knows the particulars and sensitivities of this
situation?"

Doryan shifted. "I do have people who depend on me on
Hestia, people I'm training."

"I'll give you your pick of replacements, Doryan," Mariyit
broke in. "But this is too important. I'm sorry, but you were
caught up in this whirlwind the same as everyone else."

For one tense moment, Doryan seemed to still, to hesitate.
Would they actually try to refuse? But then they relaxed,
nodding, and smiled at Ari. There was genuine kindness in
that smile. "Of course I would stay. If Ari would have me."

Homaj watched something flicker across Ari's face, not
quite relief. Did she think Doryan would continue to be her
jailer? That dynamic would have to be quickly sorted out,
though Homaj didn't disagree with Iata's assessment of the
situation. Iata certainly couldn't spend the time needed to
train her if he was being the Seritarchus, and Doryan already
seemed invested in Ari's wellbeing.

"Thank you," Iata said and pulled back, resuming his
chair. Ari's eyes trailed him now, narrowing, flicking back to
Homaj. And just what was she seeing in the subtle power
dynamics at play here? Did she note that Homaj was, though
not overtly, deferring to Iata's judgment here instead of the
other way around?

On her wrist, one of the bangles she was wearing flaked
into dust, a second following shortly after. She had four left,
and he had no idea how much strength those had in
them yet.

Ari's focus sharpened on Iata, and Homaj marked the

moment she understood, if Iata was a magicker, just what that had meant at her engagement ball. Who she'd actually been facing.

Adeius, would that night never stop haunting him?

Ari stiffened, but she didn't call it out, and that was, for the moment, good. He'd better divert her from that line of thought for now and bring her attention back to the matters at hand.

"Ari," he said, leaning forward—and almost leaned back again as the full weight of her attention pinned him. She was seeing far too much in him too, he was sure. Her rank seal was not low—Adeius, not at all, and nearing Iata's rank, even, despite being newly manifested. How much more could she read in him now than when she'd been merely Truthspoken?

He knew his performance as Homaj wasn't quite what it should be. At least, what it had been with her until now. He'd been working hard to shed that caustic edge these last weeks, and he did not want it to intrude on this meeting now. Not when she was so fragile. Not when he was, too.

Whatever she saw in him, he watched her shrink in on herself again. No—no, what had she seen? Was she putting this all on herself again? But he'd trained her to do that, hadn't he? It was what he did himself.

Beside her, Etienne, who was himself trying his best to blend in with the furniture without actually disappearing, stirred. Naked terror flickered across his face. The two of them shared a look, and both settled a little.

He was afraid to ask. He was dreading these next moments, because though he wanted to know, and needed to know what had happened on Hestia, he was absolutely certain it would be horrifying.

"Ari," he said, taking care to keep his voice neutral, if not exactly gentle. "Can you tell me what happened, every relevant detail, from the beginning?"

14

YOU

Among the greater spirit essences that make up the broad pantheon of the Green Magicker religion, She Who Wakes is invoked more often than most, but They Who Breathe is invoked in times of deepest hardship.

— R. TYTRI IN *SPIRIT ESSENCES OF THE GREEN MAGICKERS*

The numbness that had been like a smothering blanket over Eti these last few days was slowly giving way to panic. And thoughts that he knew should have come much, much sooner were breaking through.

That man who'd hugged Ari was the Seritarchus. Gods, he was sitting right next to her now. Not a person in the holos, distant and aloof. Her *father*.

And on the other side of the room sat the first Magicker.

Ari squeezed Eti's hand. Could she feel his panic? Of

course she could feel his panic, as he felt her own at her father asking her to tell what happened.

The seal implanted in Eti's cheek burned, even though he was sure that was in his head. It hadn't hurt since the day before. He hadn't looked at it, hadn't let himself, though Doryan had already told him he was high sixth rank. Doryan had tried to be calm about it, and comforting, but what the hell was Eti supposed to do with that knowledge, when he was still struggling to keep the inner walls of his soul from collapsing?

Was his mother high rank? Was his sibling? His mother had taught him all she'd known. About how not to demand strength of plants but to weave his own essence into theirs, gently sharing. Respecting the sanctity of souls to their own lives and privacy. Not that the Javieris had let him keep any sanctity at all.

Gods, he missed his mother—he tried not to think about his family much, but he hadn't been able to help it these last few days. His mother had never been the kind of person who would tell him it would all be okay, because untruths, even well-meant untruths, didn't soothe a magicker's soul. Instead, she'd told him he was strong. She was strong. Their lives were vibrant and whole, even as she was the caretaker for the gardens of various merchant families who weren't rich enough to hire full-time gardeners on their own.

He missed his sibling fiercely. And how much had Geyl grown, how much had Eti missed while he was away? He hadn't been away that long, just a little over a year, but Geyl was nine years younger than him. They were heading into their teenage years, and those years could be a *disaster* for a magicker hopped up on hormones, picking up the other hormonal thoughts of every other kid their age around them. Eti wished with everything he had that he could be there. That he was there. That he'd never had to leave.

Those thoughts hurt, but they didn't tear him apart.

There were thoughts he could not think, and newer memories he could not look at. His thoughts churned as if through a maze, and every time he encountered a mirror, he had to turn back, find another way around. Except everywhere he looked were mirrors.

Vaguely, still clutching Ari's hand, he felt the intensity and careful control of her emotions as she told her father how she and Jis—well, Bettea—had arrived on Hestia. She wound through the story of how Eti had picked her up and had later defended her to Duke Kyran Koldari. She specifically emphasized that part.

He knew she was trying to defend him now. Eti wasn't sure it would do any good, or that it should. He'd done everything he could to help her, but his soul, his heart, was tired. He'd held himself together, kept himself solid, just kept going through the drive to Racha and then the journey here on the ship. But how much longer could he hold on? The pressure was so intense. The pressure to implode. Would he have to brace against this pressure forever?

He was so tired. His *soul* hurt.

He felt Ari's breath catch and looked up.

No. Her thought, echoing with force back to him. She'd caught his last thought, and stared him down. Words drifted through their tangle of emotions: *Stay solid.*

He had to hold on. Just a bit more. And gods, his family. He could hold on for his family. He was on a world again now, a planet with plants and life, not the cold metal of space. He just needed to find a quiet place, with plants and earth, sunlight to warm his chilled bones. He just needed that.

Or maybe he should find a way to leave again. No, not maybe, he would *have* to leave, and why did this not feel as important as it should? His family was in danger because of what had happened, that had to be true. He would make himself invisible, get away somehow, steal a ship? Could his sentence, whatever it would be, possibly get any worse for already being an unsealed magicker? Stealing a ship would be minor compared to that, wouldn't it?

If he did that, he'd have to let go of Ari's hand. And right now, he didn't think he could do that.

Ari went on, but he felt more than a little of her attention still focused on him.

She was holding his hand like an anchor to the world. He didn't want to use hers as an anchor in return, though he knew he already was—but what if he only dragged her into his implosion? He'd been trying so hard not to do that the entire trip, to pull his imploding energy into himself and himself only, and it had exhausted him. It was harder now when she was actually touching him.

Outside his thoughts, Ari told of her medical treatment, her slight improvement, and submerging herself as Imorie in truth. Befriending Eti, and their day in the garden. The gardener, Ryam, and how he'd seemed to have it out for Eti.

She hardly knew the whole of it, and he didn't want to tell her. Telling her his pain would be its own violence, wouldn't it? Asking her to share it with him?

Then she ran out of breath. He watched, through his lashes, as she looked down to where the bangles had been on her arms but were now flakes of rust in her lap.

The stern magicker who'd been suppressing his aura when they'd all come in stood and quietly made their way to the First Magicker's desk, bending down beside it and coming back with two short, squared metal rods in each hand. They handed two of them to Ari.

Eti watched them, trying to understand their place in all of this. No one had made any introductions that he could remember, no names, no pronouns, though the person was very firmly masc. Should he know who this person was, sitting beside the Seritarchus's guard? This magicker was themself unsealed, though no one in the room had seemed to mind that fact. So would all of them mind, as much, if Eti had been unsealed, too?

But the person's features lightly resembled the Seritarchus's, and Ari's. They had to be related. Eti knew more about the political ties between nobles than he really cared to, but he wasn't aware of the politics of the Rhialdens more than the broad strokes, and the things that nobles had griped about on Hestia. And what little, too, he'd picked up from Ari. He wouldn't know how to place this person in Ari's greater family.

Ari's breaths steadied, and Eti's attention drew back to her.

She spoke of going to that last party as herself, not Imorie. Her wanting—and he felt her attention sharpening on him again—wanting to better map the political landscape of Windvale Estate so that she could find a way to help him out of whatever bind he was in.

He swallowed, jolted by this thought, and the sincerity behind it. She'd truly wanted to help him? The truth of her words and emotions was there, but he struggled to match it to his own tangled darkness.

But she'd truly tried to help? It had gone horribly wrong, and he'd been what had made it go horribly wrong, but... truly? She'd tried?

"Etienne," the Seritarchus said, and Eti's whole body went rigid.

And oh, no, he'd never bowed to the Seritarchus. He'd been too tuned to the tumult of Ari's emotions from the start, and she'd been very braced not to bow. He couldn't see a way to do it now, either, without showing that he hadn't before, and this was her father. This was the most powerful person in the kingdom.

And here the judgment came, and it was only what was due. He had given Ari over to Ryam and Badem, though he'd tried not to. He was the one who, in the garage's basement, had—

He drifted a moment back into his own darkness, the world around him becoming distant again.

"Eti," Ari corrected sharply. And he couldn't help a flicker of warmth at that.

The Seritarchus nodded. "Eti, what was your situation at Windvale Estate?"

The darkness swirled back up into panic. The urge to just let go now, let himself disperse, was overwhelming. Spare them any more pain. Spare himself.

But...his family. And his hand, tightly gripping Ari's, still wasn't willing to let go.

She had tried to help him. That, for the moment, was something to cling to.

"It's okay," she said, turning to face him. "You're not going to get a higher authority to plead your case to, ever."

He hadn't told her about his family. She knew about Ryam and that he'd been coerced, and she'd already forgiven him for that, though his heart ached that she had. Badem had told her the Javieris were involved, but what lever did they have over him?

Could he possibly tell her now? He'd been trying to protect her, and protect his family. But did he have to protect her here, when the Seritarchus was here? And what about his family? Would the Seritarchus only transfer Eti and his family into service to the Rhialdens, not the Javieris, trade one bad situation for another? Or worse, if he said that his family were all unsealed magickers, would they be brought up on charges, too?

His sibling. He couldn't think of his sibling being used

like he'd been. That was why he'd gone with the Javieris. To protect his family.

Eti didn't think Ari knew exactly what he was thinking, but he felt her growing concern.

She'd held his hand all the way past the shouting crowds outside the fence, through Green Hall, and was still holding it now. She cared what happened to him. He knew that, even if little else felt certain.

Her father was the Seritarchus. And she, no matter what else she was, was his daughter.

Eti swallowed hard, the sound squelching too loud in his throat.

"Arianna," he said, and she inhaled sharply. But it was her name. Truer, even, than Ari. He knew that. And he didn't want to forget that again, like she didn't want to, either.

He forced himself to meet and hold her gaze. "Can I tell this to you? You as...you?"

15

A MAGICKER'S WITNESS

> *A Green Magicker's formal witness of a person's truth is legally admissible and certified to be that person's truth. Just because a person believes something to be true, however, doesn't mean that it is.*

— CAPTAIN ONUA VEN LARÚ IN A TRAINING
VID FOR THE VALON CITY MUNICIPAL GUARD

Eti sensed Ari's uncertainty at his question—and maybe, maybe he shouldn't have asked it. Maybe it was too much to ask.

She glanced back at her father, tensing. And Eti's tension was rising, too. He hadn't meant to throw her own fears wide open.

Yes, this was her father, and this world was her home, but she wasn't here as herself, not as Arianna. How could he ask her to be the one to listen—and maybe decide—for what he was terrified to talk about if she wasn't even sure she could speak for herself?

Ice ran through her, a deep shard of fear.

No, no, that's not what he'd wanted to happen. But he didn't know how to take it back. And what if he'd insulted the Seritarchus by asking Ari, not him, to hear what he had to say? He shouldn't have done that.

His edges were fraying again. His thoughts losing cohesion, and he couldn't have that happen now. Not when he'd gathered what courage he had and was holding it with both fists.

Eti reached, because he had to, for the calming essence of the plants around him. Something he hadn't yet dared to do, not here, in the First Magicker's own domain. But green wrapped around him, the soothing warmth of living things. He didn't take strength, only noticed it.

And so noticed his own.

It wasn't Ari's father who answered her fears, but the Rhialden magicker. They nodded solemnly to Ari. "Magicker. Witness his truth."

Ari drew in a sharp breath, and Eti felt her ripple of surprise. That wasn't what he'd asked of her. He'd wanted her as Truthspoken to witness.

Her mouth tightened, her soul essence regathering into a state of determination. She turned back to Eti with far more purpose.

"I witness the truth of Etienne Tanaka," she said, her voice tight.

Eti nodded, and something inside him eased. And maybe this was what he'd wanted. He'd needed someone to understand, and he hoped, oh by the breath of They Who Breathe, he hoped she would understand and not condemn. She would feel what he felt about this.

He could feel her sincerity. But what of the Seritarchus's? What of the First Magicker's? If he was wrong to trust her now, to trust anyone in this room, he'd only be putting his family in more danger.

But his family was already in great danger, if the Javieris hadn't taken what he'd done out on them already. Oh gods. His stomach twisted, but he held himself as steady as he could.

"My family," he said, and paused. Ari's gaze was like lasers, and he struggled to meet it. But her grip tightened on his hand, and he shuddered in relief at the impression that flowed with it. He didn't have to meet her eyes. She knew this was important.

"My mother and my younger sibling are—they're also magickers. Unsealed. The Javieris wanted my mother to use her magics for them, in secret. I knew she was needed to help my sibling, so I went instead. They brought me to Hestia and put me in the care of—"

If thoughts of Badem and Ryam and Windvale had shuddered him back into his darkness before, saying it out loud, declaring it as real, folded him in pain.

Gods, so much pain. And the urge to dissipate was tearing him apart.

Ari braced his shoulder, and he knew he was squeezing her hand too tightly. He carefully eased the pressure.

"In the care of Count Badem," she said, and he nodded. "And in the care of Ryam, the gardener."

Yes. He nodded again.

The Seritarchus asked, "Do you know which Javieri, specifically, required this service of you?"

Eti found a way to shake his head. His ears were ringing as his heart drummed in his throat. "No. They only ever sent their handlers and guards. I—I—Ser Seritarchus, I knew Imorie was Truthspoken when I saw her. I'm sorry. When I picked her up in the house car. And her servant, Jis. And I—made myself forget. I think a few times." He looked back to Ari, his gaze settling just beside her. "I'm sorry. I didn't have time to forget again before Ryam found me."

His brow prickled in a cold sweat. "Ryam would come every night, to the shed where I stayed in the loft. He'd make me hold his hand while I told him every secret I'd picked up during the day."

He heard a soft hiss and jerked around to see the mounting fury on the First Magicker's face, the blotching of his pale cheeks.

Gods. Gods, he shouldn't have said that. Even if they'd be able to figure it out, and he thought Ari probably already knew as much, he still shouldn't have said that. And what if they took that out on his family? Yes, the Seritarchus was known to be partial to magickers, but could he really be that different than the Javieris? Than Count Badem and everyone she worked with and sold her information to? The Seritarchus was all about information, wasn't he?

Ari was different, he was sure of that, but she was a magicker now, too.

He pleaded with her—with his eyes now, daring to look—and with his emotions running between them, for her to understand. But even if she did, he wasn't sure that would be enough.

He'd come this far.

"I saw your name again, at the party. I had no time to forget it. Ryam knew I'd been trying to hide something about you, and he was waiting for me outside. He picked up what I knew when I went outside. I didn't have time to hide it."

His eyes stung, more emotion than he'd felt in days squeezing at his chest.

Ari tightened her other hand on the metal rod in her lap. It was laced through with rust now, the edges already crumbling. She'd soon need the other. She eyed the two more bars that the Rhialden magicker was balancing in their own lap.

Iata. The name floated up from Ari, along with pronouns

and a sense of gender, a sense of calculation—Ari's calculation? Or her impression of Iata?

"Duke Koldari, at the party, was jealous of Eti's being near me, I think," she said. "At least, he'd tried to warn me off of Eti before. Eti—does he know you're a magicker? Did he know what Badem was doing there?"

"I—don't know." He didn't know. Koldari had always been aloof and apart.

"With how tight the Koldaris and the Javieris are," the Seritarchus said in a low, dangerously mild voice, "I'd be very surprised if he didn't know something. Why was he there? Does he have the Bruising Sleep?"

"I don't know," Eti said, dropping his gaze again. He didn't know, he only knew a thousand deeply private secrets from everyone *else*, not anything useful here. He knew it wasn't enough to outweigh everything else.

He closed his eyes, trying to dwell again in the neutral state of the plants. To share in their taste of sunshine.

He'd told Ari about his family. And then he'd muddied it all up with everything that had happened at the estate. Should he have told them that, among other threats, the Javieris had threatened to take his sibling from his mother if she hadn't agreed to work for them? That they'd raise his sibling, a hostage. And that—gods. He couldn't let that happen. To his sibling, or to her. Or to himself.

But it had happened—the hostage part, anyway. His family were hostages to him working for the Javieris.

Ari's hand in his jerked, and she stared at him, eyes shining. "I saw that," she said quietly, while the Seritarchus and the Rhialden magicker were talking about Ryam again, and Jis. Trying to decide what had happened, because he'd missed it, but Ari must have said fae'd been taken prisoner.

Eti's eyes widened. "Oh. Ryam shot Jis."

Ari sat back as if slapped. "Shot—"

"Stunned! I meant stunned. Sorry." Oh gods, how had he not said that before? Hadn't she known that her servant had been shot? But, no, she'd only known her servant had been a prisoner at Windvale, he vaguely remembered that, and even Eti didn't know if fae was still alive.

Another sound behind him, this time from the Rhialden magicker, Iata. His face had gone gray.

"We'll find out what happened," the Seritarchus said firmly. "Ari, continue."

"So," Ari said. Her fear roiled within her, aching and unbalanced as his own. And somehow, they'd gone from her witnessing his truth back to everyone witnessing hers.

No one had yet condemned his family for being unsealed magickers. Or reacted to his own betrayal.

"So, Badem came in," Ari said, "saying there was a message for me in her office, and I could listen to it there. But when I went out into the corridor, Ryam was also there. He clamped a hand over my mouth and a—a gun to my side, and walked me, with Badem, to the garage. And then into a room hidden underneath it."

Eti's dread was mounting again, and so was Ari's.

Ari swallowed, looked around. "Is there water—"

It was the First Magicker who stood this time and came back with a handful of water bottles, taking one for himself as well.

Ari let go of the metal in her lap, the mostly crumbled second bar, to take two waters, handing one to Eti. He didn't want it, didn't want to interrupt, but his throat was burning, his body straining from the stress. His hands shook as he pried the lid and took a sip. So, he saw, did Ari's, as she spilled a little water down her shirt.

She met his eyes again, just a brief touch and away again, but the shared memory of that afternoon in the garage basement room froze him. His heart rocketed back into his throat and stayed there, and Ari's face went sickly even beneath her makeup. Her whole body started to tremble.

A chair scraped.

"Ari," Doryan said, moving cautiously, stepping closer, "both of you, may I help? I can help soften the edges."

Her father sat forward, too. "Is that wise—"

"My specialty is healing. In particular, psychological healing."

Doryan knelt down in front of Ari, offering one of their hands each to Ari and Eti. Ari carefully took Doryan's hand, but Eti held back. He didn't know if he could handle two conduits to Ari's emotions through what was coming. He didn't know if he could handle any.

Doryan nodded. "I should be able to send ease through your link as well, Eti, if you keep hold of each other's hands."

16

CALM

> *It's a common belief that because Truthspoken have outward control over their emotions, they themselves do not feel, or feel as strongly as the rest of humanity. The act of concealing pain or joy, however, does not mean it's not there.*

— DR. IGNI CHANG IN "FURTHER DISCOURSE ON THE HUMANITY OF OUR RULERS"

Iata knew that outwardly, he was calm. But if anyone would touch him, or look into his eyes, they would feel the volcano inside. How fucking *dare* this conflagration of Javieris and lesser nobility shoot Bettea, his *child*. He would end them. He would absolutely destroy them, and he was determined not to pay attention to the agony of fire that thought sent throughout his nervous system.

And they'd held a gun to his niece, who they *knew* was Truthspoken. They'd figured that out through a magicker's coercion.

And how fucking dare the Javieris do that to a magicker?

And not just a magicker, but a family of magickers? This young man who barely looked of age with Ari, and who was so obviously struggling to hold himself together and in existence—and Iata didn't know how he'd managed so far, seeing in his aura what he'd done—this young man had been so poorly used. Eti looked terrified now that he'd continue to be poorly used, and Iata had no intention of letting that happen.

Ari had all the marks of trauma as well, so tightly coiled, hesitant where she had never been before. She'd held on to that young man since the moment she'd come in and not let go.

He would end the Javieris. He would absolutely end them for this. For all of this.

He drew in a calming breath, let it out again. Repeated that once more. Beside him, he felt Mariyit's attention on him, saw Mariyit's hand twitch toward him. Wanting to test how volatile his emotions were? To give him calm?

He had to calm down, or he was liable to do violence, not just *think* about doing violence.

Maybe he wasn't Homaj just now, with all the powers that being Homaj entailed, but he was still the ruler of Valoris. Even if so very few people knew that.

And he was a magicker.

He couldn't end the Javieris, not overtly. The only course available to him was to fight with the only weapon they'd never use: kindness.

"In that basement room," Ari said slowly, her voice flat, but with no quaver to it, and Iata could guess at the effort that was costing her, "they cuffed me to a chair. It was Count Badem, Ryam the gardener, and Dr. Lin was there as well. The physician who'd been treating me."

Iata saw Homaj tense, his eyes lighting fire.

Doryan tensed as well, and they'd be feeling exactly what Ari was feeling. Should Iata have offered to help soothe her?

He should have. And also, he was sure he would not have been able to offer any calm.

"Badem and the doctor wanted to know who I was, and who had sent me. They knew I was Truthspoken. Then Ryam came back with Eti and forced him to take my hand and read my truth."

Eti's hand in Ari's jerked, and for the first time since entering the room, they broke apart.

Was that a good thing? Would Ari's emotions have amplified Eti's in this, if they were getting to the crux of the matter? But he was certain Ari was one of the only things anchoring Eti to this world, keeping him holding on and not fading. After a magicker killed, sometimes they faded immediately. Sometimes they held on for a time, and it looked like Eti was doing so, but if this sent him right back to that moment when he had killed, there was a danger he could still fade.

Iata opened his mouth to say he should take Eti out of the room for this, but the young man's attention was still locked on Ari, his whole body braced as if shielding her from a storm. Whatever else had happened, Eti had made Ari his purpose, and Iata didn't want to break that now.

So he did the next best thing he could think of and rose, crossing the short space to sit beside Eti on the end of the couch. When Eti cringed back—oh, Adeius—he held out his hands. He should have remembered to smooth over his movements. This man was dealing with massive and ongoing trauma.

"I'm not as skilled at soothing as Magicker Azer," he said, softening his tone as best he could, "but I can provide an anchor. If you will allow me, Eti."

The young man squeezed his eyes shut. But nodded once, letting Iata take his hand.

"So," Ari went on, her throat tight, "so, I submerged myself. As Imorie in truth. But Ryam had Eti's other hand,

and he sensed that Eti could sense my recall trigger. So he had Eti recall me. I told Badem that I wouldn't tell her anything. So the doctor got out his...his surgical instruments—"

Eti's touch was ice. Iata sat very still, setting everything he himself was feeling aside just to deal with Eti's emotions. If his had been a roiling mass of lava, Eti's were like a hurricane on a gas giant. They were a black hole.

Eti tried to pull away—not, he sensed, because of anything he felt from Iata, but because he didn't want Iata to feel his own maelstrom.

"No," Iata said softly. "No, this is well." He sorted enough of the weight and breadth and tangle of this darkness, and began to do what he could. Giving warmth, giving calm, shining what light he could on the dark spikes swirling through Eti's thoughts. Dissipating those he dared. But mostly, letting himself be there.

He felt Eti latch onto him, not pulling from his strength, but desperate to find a hold on a wall he was falling down. Iata did everything he could to catch him.

"You're doing well," Doryan said to Ari. "Very well. I'm right here. Stop whenever you need to."

"Ryam saw Eti knew who I was. When Eti wouldn't tell him, he started hurting him. So, I had to tell them—"

Ari's eyes were bright with tears, the look she gave Homaj naked and raw. Iata had the briefest panic that Homaj, still wavering in his personality of the Seritarchus, might say something deeply regrettable. But his face was hard, chipped in stone.

"You did well. You did what you had to. Go on."

Eti's emotions were rising, the pace of his own hurricane picking up. And Iata had to tune out what Ari was saying, and pull Eti's attention from it, too. He would have the rest of it later. Right now—*right now.*

Will you let me hold you? Shield you? It was more impressions and intentions than words. He almost didn't catch Eti's hesitation, and then barely felt Eti's physical nod.

He wrapped Eti within his arms, abandoning his attempts to soothe, which were like trying to patch a hole in a storm, and opening himself up to Eti. His own truths, his own knowing that all of this had been wrong, and none of it had been Eti's fault. The knowing echoed from him to Eti, found resonance as true there, and back to Iata again, building up enough resonance to form a shield against the storm.

Distantly, Iata heard Homaj say, with fervor, "I would never have sent you there if I'd known. Believe me in that."

And then Ari must truly be to the heart of it, because Eti's whole body seized up. Iata shifted and clamped his hands over Eti's ears, and after a moment, Eti's muscles relaxed, just a bit.

He heard Ari cry out and saw a flurry of movement—but he was fully occupied with pouring enough truth into Eti that Eti remained there, remained present. It had been a mistake to stay in this room—he should have taken Eti out. Ari shouldn't have had to recount this, either. Even though what had happened should be known, needed to be known, Iata knew the pain and intensity of the telling.

For now, though, he hung on.

ARI PUT her fist to her mouth, her whole body, her whole soul clenching up. She couldn't say it. Couldn't think about it, that moment of magicker violence in the basement room. That moment when Eti had killed.

She just could not go forward, but she had to try. "And then Eti—*ah!*"

Her father was off his chair, perching on the arm of the

couch, wrapping her up like she was a child. She was trembling, or was he trembling?

"Don't say it," her father said. "We know enough. I don't need to hear more."

She was distantly aware of Doryan letting go of her hand, backing off to their own chair.

She was shuddering so hard she couldn't speak. And that was horrible, because she was here, with so much visible weakness, and her father—

He reared back as if he'd heard the thought, and maybe he had. "This is not weakness, Arianna Rhialden. You are not weak. You have never been weak, and all the more my fault for letting you think control equals strength."

But it did. She could hardly face the public like she was now, even as Imorie. She could never face the public like this as Arianna.

Her father pulled her tighter, and she couldn't help, just could not help the tears, though she didn't allow them to be sobs.

And then a wave of calm warmed her, like sunlight after a storm. Not from her father—her father was still a roiling mass of rage and guilt and concern.

Ari looked up, looked around. Mariyit Broden's arms were outstretched where he still sat on his chair, his eyes closed, face still. Was he projecting this calm?

But it seemed to come from all around her. From the air. From the plants that crowded every spare centimeter of this room.

She shuddered again, but this time it was more of a whole body sigh. She let go of her father, who sniffed loudly, wiping at his own eyes, and settled back hard into his chair. He perched at the nearest end of it to her, though, as if he might reach for her again at any moment.

Iata was fairly wrapped around Eti, and Eti seemed to be

clinging back just as hard. With the calm, though, they eased back until they also broke apart.

Eti flickered, and her heart jumped into her throat. Oh, no. Her hand twitched to reach for him, but she didn't know if she could touch his roiling darkness just now.

But the flickering slowed, then stopped, and he became solid again, collapsing back against the couch cushion. Iata's hand braced his shoulder. Iata himself looked pale, eyes sunken and haunted. His own aura, though, was still clear, and did Eti's look a little clearer than it had been?

"Peace," Mariyit said, and the word resonated out with its own wave.

Ari sighed and sank back against the cushions herself, feeling the weight of her fatigue. There was more to tell. So much more to tell.

Mariyit opened his eyes. "I haven't heard it all, but I have heard enough. I have felt the truths involved. I have gathered enough, I think, of what is yet unsaid—and I have Doryan's report from what happened in Racha. So as First Magicker of the Kingdom of Valoris, this is my judgment: Harm has most certainly been done, but it was not by Imorie Rhialden méron Quevedo or Etienne Tanaka. I will not enact more harm by making them recount this further, and I do ask forgiveness for what has already been done. Further, I judge their actions as self-defense and necessary, though I regret the pain involved on all sides.

"As both magickers are now sealed, they are considered members of Green Hall and will have access to all comfort, care, and treatment of their selves and their wounds, for as long as they need, for recovery. They will also have assessment and training, to be determined by the assessors. I'll issue a public statement with all the above—leaving out, certainly, the details about just how Eti was coerced into working for the Javieris, as I have no desire for anyone else to think that's a good idea. We will need to say, however, that he was coerced."

He grimaced and lowered his hands, the strength of the calm in the room ebbing, but not fading completely. "Homaj. Is that acceptable? We'll go out there, we'll witness the truth of our testimony and judgements, and hope to They Who Heal that the rabble calms the fuck down."

17

SUBTLE DYNAMICS

For Truthspoken, subtleties are everything.

— ARIANNA RHIALDEN, MELESORIE X IN *THE CHANGE DIALOGUES*

The First Magicker's pronouncement, and his question, hung in the air, waiting on her father's answer.

Oh, Adeius, she wasn't being charged by Green Hall. Mariyit had ruled that what had happened on Hestia was self-defense, and Ari was struggling to realign her possibilities. Would her father contradict that ruling? He could, or amend it.

Her shoulders tightened back up again.

Beside her, her father looked wrung out. All the little signs Ari had seen before of his exhaustion visibly clung to him now, and he ran a hand over his hair—a tell he seldom let show except in private company. He was doing little to hide the distress in his expression, but when he caught her looking, his face cleared, bottling up again.

That eased her a little. She wasn't sure how to handle his emotions being so exposed.

"That sounds good to me, yes," he said, though his eyes sought Iata's. As if for...permission?

She had noticed that subtle dynamic, too. As if her father wasn't actually in charge here. What, truly, had happened while she was away?

His voice was softer than usual, his posture...odd. Still with that note of tentativeness, less fully inhabited within himself. Had he been on a mission just before she'd arrived, was he still trying to bleed out of another role? But he'd never had issues with that before.

She knew that he and Iata sometimes switched places— well, Iata standing in for her father, at least. She'd seen that in them before, and that was their business, not hers. However her father saw fit to rule the kingdom was not hers to question. Except, was he actually ruling the kingdom just now? Iata, though himself, still had a bit of her father's mannerisms, a little more charismatic bearing than he usually had as himself. As if he'd had to Change quickly, too, and his time as Homaj had been long.

Iata didn't nod, but something passed between him and her father all the same, and her father sat back again, looking utterly drained but not upset. Then, his decision held. The First Magicker's decision held.

Ari felt lightheaded at her own sudden release of tension. She wasn't being charged. That, at least...that was something. She glanced at Eti, and he looked back, eyes shining. Had he caught any of that exchange, or was he still reacting to the First Magicker's statement? The latter, most likely.

Ari straightened, or at least tried to. So she wasn't being charged, but her life still wasn't her own. Was she, in fact, still Truthspoken? Would she be allowed at any point to rejoin the Rhialden Court? With Iata being a magicker—oh, Adeius, she was still trying to understand that—it gave her that smallest bit of hope. She could learn to hide her aura. She could learn to blend in again. Could she possibly reclaim her life here?

Before she could say anything, though, Iata asked, "Eti, where is your family now?"

Eti stirred, hesitated, then said quietly, "Kalistré."

"A Javieri world." Her father sighed. "Eti, we will do what we can to get them to safety. That is my word, and a high priority."

Eti froze. His eyes filled, and his face shone with so much naked shock and hope that Ari bit her lip to stifle her own sting of tears. The Javieris had done this to him? And there was a Javieri—the Javieri heir—in the palace now, engaged to her sister? Would this be enough to break that alliance? Had Lesander known anything about using unsealed magickers to gain information?

But the First Magicker had said the method of coercion couldn't be public. And her father hadn't been wrong when he'd chosen Lesander to be the Heir Consort—the alliance with the Javieris had been sorely needed. Maybe was needed even more now, with their grasping for power overreaching so far.

This was still all a tangled mess.

"Mariyit," her father said, "will there be any penalty for Eti's being active and unsealed?"

"No, because he was coerced. Same for his family—I don't see any need for charges there. I do see a need, as you said, for extraction and care."

Her father nodded.

"Bettea," Ari said. "Can you send someone to help—"

"Yes. And for you, Ari—"

Her father stopped, looked between her and Eti, frowned. "Forgive me, Mariyit, but I'm not confident that her safety is assured if she remains at Green Hall, although that is the logical course."

Mariyit sighed, rubbing at his bearded cheek. "The crowds were ugly all morning, and I can't imagine they'll grow less so when we announce our leniency. Yes, that might be for the best."

"Then, Ari, you'll stay in the palace. In the residence wing, in one of the spare apartments. Rhialdens take care of their own, contract or not."

"Eti stays with me," Ari said. If he wanted to? But he nodded, shifting closer again. She was his only point of familiarity here, and he...well. He was more hers than she wanted to admit just now.

Her father made a gesture of assent, as if he'd already assumed as much.

Then he took a breath, held up his hands, pulling the attention of the room. On the other side of him, Captain Zhang straightened, her own attention sharp on him. That she was deeply protective of her father was hardly a secret, but Zhang's eyes were wary, her mouth tight.

It was several heartbeats before he spoke again, but Ari's pulse kicked into yet another aching adrenaline rush her body could scarcely handle. Spots danced in her vision, but she breathed through them. It was something, at least, that he could look at her like she was now, with her green aura, and still see his daughter.

But she didn't know what was coming next. He could do anything from here. He'd said she'd stay in the palace, but for how long? He could send her away again. Denounce her as no longer Truthspoken. She still didn't know what had happened in her absence. She didn't know where she should fit into the carefully curated world of the palace, if she fit anywhere at all.

"This is your life, Ari," he said finally. "What happens

from here—beyond the necessity of staying in the palace, which I do think is a necessity—will be your choice."

She stared back, a raw and horrifying hope swelling up inside her. She hadn't been expecting that. He'd taken that choice from her before. Apparently he wasn't going to do so again now.

"You should know," Iata said, "that there is already rampant speculation that Arianna and Imorie are one and the same. That does complicate and limit the array of choices at hand, unfortunately."

Oh, hell. She hadn't managed to Change far enough, and she was still too visibly close to herself as Arianna. She'd been hoping people wouldn't notice so quickly, but of course they had. The people were always watching for mistakes, for any sign of weakness among the Truthspoken. And the nobility—what drastic complications would this new development cause for the Seritarcracy and the kingdom at large? For the magickers, too. Not just a Rhialden magicker, but a *Truthspoken* magicker. And who would believe Mariyit's judgment of self-defense if a Truthspoken magicker was involved?

Her heart was pounding too hard. Her ears rang, and the room swam around her. She had no reserves left to deal with this.

"Can I have the other metal rods?"

Iata frowned, but sighed and retrieved them from his abandoned seat, handing one to her. "After this, you'll need to rest. Or you can learn to draw strength from the gardens—without harming the plants. I'm sure Doryan can show you. Pulling from metal so often and in such quantities is not a good idea. It unbalances your soul energy."

Yes, fine. She would do that, but she'd have to get to the palace gardens first, and for that, she needed to think now, and think fast.

Her mind cleared a little as she pulled from the strength

in the metal, her breaths easing. The tang of iron sat heavy in her mouth—from too much metal?—but she did her best to ignore it.

Ari closed her eyes. What did she want, and what could she actually have within the bounds of the situation at hand?

She wanted, with everything she was, to resume her life as Arianna the Heir, but she was almost certain that wouldn't happen. Not as the Heir, at least. Not now. She pushed that aside for now with a pang.

Could she be at court, though? Could she be active in politics in any way? If people assumed Imorie was Arianna, that would be...difficult. People would try to catch her in the lie, like sharks after blood. And if it was found out that she was, in fact, Arianna Rhialden...what then? She had to separate Arianna from Imorie if she ever wanted to resume her life as Arianna. If she'd ever, at some point in the future, be able to Change again—and she had to hope, Adeius had to hope that she'd be able.

So her immediate needs were to continue her treatment for the Bruising Sleep so she could do anything at all, learn how to suppress her aura, and separate Imorie from Arianna. If Iata was an unsealed magicker—and maybe that wasn't quite the truth of it, she was certain that the seal he'd worn as Sodan Iseban had been his own, the seal her father had shown her after—then maybe she could live like that, too. She had no idea how long Iata had been hiding his magics, but it definitely wasn't a new development. Not with how comfortable and well-informed everyone here seemed to be.

So, she could do that. Eventually. Maybe she couldn't reclaim her place as the Heir, but she could resume at least part of her life. Help support the kingdom—help Dressa, even, if Dressa would have her.

Her stomach churned and she shunted that aside. She didn't know if she was ready to face that, or willing.

Her thoughts pulled back to Iata.

He truly did have the authority in this room. Everything she'd seen today, every unsaid cue, had been pointing to that. Whatever had happened, he was, at the moment, still carrying the weight of the kingdom. Would that continue? Would her father get past whatever was happening right now?

She opened her eyes, looked to her father, who was waiting, his expression still too open. Something had changed, and it had started to change, she realized, before he'd originally arranged her marriage. She remembered the day when he'd told her she was to marry Lesander, and his implying that it might be better for that to happen sooner rather than later. She'd been afraid he'd known of assassination plans, but now she wondered if it was more than that.

If she hadn't known him better, she might have feared he had the Bruising Sleep. But she was certain he didn't. She'd felt instead the crumbled array of his emotions. The batteredness of his soul, and that was certainly not just from the shock of her being a magicker. Or even the start of her illness. That was something of his own.

Okay. Variables fell into place in her overtaxed mind, but they were there. And there was a course she could take for optimum chances of what she truly wanted, and for the good of the kingdom. She was still a Rhialden, no matter what else. She would still always want the good of the kingdom.

"Iata," she said, turning to him. "I want you to adopt me."

18

A CHANGE IN CIRCUMSTANCES

> *Many a political rivalry has been settled with a marriage or a political adoption.*

— KIR MTALOR, SOCIAL COMMENTATOR, IN A POST ON THEIR PERSONAL FEED

Iata's brows twitched.

"I want you to adopt me legally," Ari went on, "but not publicly, under the Truthspoken Seal, so that I can answer truthfully that I'm not the daughter of Homaj and Haneri, or in the direct line of succession."

A political adoption, requested by an adult, effectively made the adopted family the dominant familial relation, any other connections going dormant. She would still *have been* the daughter of Homaj and Haneri, but legally now she'd be the daughter of Iata. And that technicality she was sure she could work with.

Her father's gaze sharpened, catching what she was after. He opened his hands.

"Yes," Iata said. "Under the Truthspoken Seal, and in the

eyes of Adeius, it is done. I'll draw up the formal documents as soon as I'm able—but it is done." And that answered another question. If he could do that under the Truthspoken seal, then he was functioning as a full Truthspoken. Ceorre would uphold this legality, then. "And if this is your course, if someone touches you and asks your name?"

"I would like to legally change my name to Imorie. To be reverted at a time of my choosing. But fully legal." She glanced back to her father. "Can I do that now, under the Truthspoken Seal?"

"Also done," Iata said. "Under the Truthspoken Seal, you are now Imorie Rhialden méron Quevedo. To be reverted at a time of your choosing. But that is now, fully and legally, your name."

She drew in a shuddering breath. It was necessary, it was a necessary step, but the truth of Iata's words hit her all the same.

She was Imorie.

"And your ability to Change?" Iata asked. "If someone asks you about that?"

"I can't Change. Not right now. So if anyone asks if I am Truthspoken—no, I'm not." And *that* truth in her core was... complicated. Not fully true. Not fully not. She might need to finesse how she'd answer that question. "But I won't foreswear Change. There's still a chance I might regain that ability."

Iata nodded, considering her. His bearing had shifted subtly, far less of Iata the bloodservant, and far more of... what? Iata the Seritarchus?

It occurred to her in a sick and tilting moment that whatever had happened to shift the power in the palace, it might not have been her father's will. Had Iata found a way to push him out? Had Iata, subtly, overtaken his life?

But she looked into Iata's eyes and didn't see malice.

He was still on the other side of Eti, whose expression had grown pinched at all of this, his arms tight around himself. Eti sat back as she leaned over him, reaching toward Iata.

Iata clasped her hand, eyes still on hers.

What question could she ask out loud? What had been said, and what was carefully left unsaid?

She felt what she could of his emotions, his sense of self. Tightly contained and coiled, a control so deep—that sort of control she would have expected in her father. But this was definitely Iata, not her father.

"He's okay," Eti said.

Startled, she glanced at him, and saw that truth, too.

"Daughter," Iata said, his tone dry with irony. "I have only your best interest at heart, and the best interests of the kingdom. And of Dressa, and Maja. And Rhys and Haneri if it comes to it, and Bettea and Pria. And Eti here as well. You can rest assured on all of those points."

She let out a breath and let go, feeling the ring of truth in all of those statements.

Okay. Okay.

He was still watching her ironically, though. And had he felt that her motives in asking him to adopt her weren't... entirely about being asked questions as Imorie?

No, not *as* Imorie, she *was* Imorie.

But if Iata was acting as the ruler just now, if there was any possibility he would continue to be the ruler—was there any possibility that she could, as his daughter, be *his* Heir? And be the Truthspoken Heir once again.

It was a petty thing, a desperate thing, and even she knew it was mostly futile. Dressa was engaged to Lesander, and that political alliance would always carry the day.

But she needed small victories just now. Even small victories that she knew weren't really victories. Even if it would nullify her ability to deny that she was in the direct line of succession, which had been partly the point.

"Imorie," Iata said, "I will expect you not to interfere with the integrity of Dressa's position and authority. However it came about, she is the Heir and will continue to be the Heir. That, regardless, will not change. And when you wish, if you wish, I'll rescind the adoption, and your title and inheritance will return fully to Maja's line. This is temporary."

She felt her face burn, but she nodded. She had over-reached. She hadn't been wrong to ask for the adoption, but—yes.

"I would also like, if you're both amenable, for you to tutor with Mariyit," her father said—or, Adeius, not her only father anymore, or the one with the most say in her life. "Your rank isn't low, and while I believe that Magicker Azer can bring you up to speed on the basics in the day to day, you will need more extensive training."

Doryan, who'd mostly been staying out of the recent conversation, leaned forward in their chair. "Then you do wish me to stay with...Imorie?"

"Yes," Iata said. "Please. You will of course be compensated well for your position."

But Doryan waved a hand as if that wasn't important. "As long as you can find someone to fill my place on Hestia, and as long as this is temporary, too, I will be happy to stay."

Not all quite true, but true enough.

"Of course I will train you, Imorie—both of you," the First Magicker said. "And it might be best, for now, to do so together? Please send your comm address to my office, Imorie, and we will set up the times. I think it best I come to you, so we're not parading a company of guards back and forth from the palace to Green Hall."

And that was done. It was all set, at least for now, at least to get her through the next however many days.

Ari—Imorie—no, she would still be Ari in her heart. She would only ever answer to her legal truth, not to her heart's truth.

Would that work? Would she be able to finesse her thoughts into technicalities, if someone decided to touch her arm, or tried to dance with her, whatever, and asked her bold and intrusive questions?

It would have to work. She had no intention of being banished from court again, and every intention of making herself invaluable to the daily running of the kingdom.

Her father, Homaj, leaned forward, eyes blazing. "Fight your hardest, Daughter. We will be fighting with you."

She swallowed, her throat tight. She absolutely would fight her hardest—if that was even the right metaphor now. Green Magickers couldn't fight.

Tired as she was, the last metal bar she'd been given now also rust in her lap, she assessed her posture, her manner-isms, her accent. The first two had drifted in her time in this room, though her accent and diction had mostly stayed Imorie's. She pulled all of that together around her now, not submerging herself, but rather...embracing.

Imorie had been the parts of her that were less restrained, less tied to the responsibilities of a Truthspoken. Imorie had piercings and a fucking tattoo. Imorie wasn't *not* her—because she'd known she'd have to be Imorie for a time, she'd crafted Imorie's persona around the edges of her own. And maybe it was good to stretch those wings, and maybe she had, in some ways, reached the limits of what she could have done even as Arianna, because Arianna would absolutely not be handling everything with being a magicker this well.

She sat up straighter. Reached for Eti's hand, and when he took hers, felt his own soul energies had eased a bit as well.

Mariyit stood and stretched. "Well. Ser Seritarchus, shall

we go make a public statement?" He addressed this to Homaj, but there was little pretense left that Homaj was truly in charge here.

Homaj rose and smiled tightly, but he still watched her, worry too plain on his face.

Then from one moment to the next, he was closed off again, his bearing and mannerisms back to being the Seritarchus, fully inhabited in himself. She watched the shift happen, like a reshuffling of his soul energy. Like an armoring for battle. Every angle of himself was sharper.

This was the father she knew, and the father she'd expected, though seeing him now didn't comfort her as she'd thought it would.

"Iata, will you see them safely to the palace? I do have to make this statement—then, Imorie, we will talk further."

19

A REVELATION

> *You betrayed me, my dear prince. Not by your lies, no, because you didn't tell any. You betrayed me with your truths.*

> — OLUN SHIRALL IN THE VID DRAMA *NOVA HEARTS*, SEASON 10, EPISODE 3, "THE WAYWARD SPEAKER"

"She's going to kill me," Dressa said, pacing her prep room.

"Well, of everything she might do," Lesander said, "I think we can safely rule that one out. Magickers don't kill."

"Which fact, apparently, is in dispute." Dressa reached for her comm on her vanity, where she'd set it the last time she'd reached for it. She flicked through the headlines, checked the deluge of messages in her inbox without reading any, and set it back down again with an ever-tightening knot inside her.

Lesander came close, her perfume, not yet refreshed for

the day, still lingering around her. Ocean juniper. Sea breeze and freshness.

Dressa let Lesander take her hands. Let her wife kiss her, gently. She'd solved their height difference the last few days. Lesander was no longer taller than her.

She wanted kissing Lesander to calm her. But she'd had a revelation the night before. She'd seen it, just a small clue, when Lesander had come in to wake her up.

Dressa had been drifting, not quite asleep. Trying to sort through all she'd need to do the next day—a task list for a different crisis with the Kidaa attacks, which had hardly become irrelevant now but had been set aside to deal with this current crisis. Lesander had been agitated. She'd been upset. Ari was a magicker, and in a whole kingdom's worth of trouble. And the kingdom itself was in a bunch of trouble.

And setting *that* aside...

When Lesander had come in, she'd been flushed. And after she'd roused Dressa from her half-doze and out of bed, after she'd gotten Dressa worked up with the news, Lesander had taken a small breath. Just one breath. A calming breath. And the flush on her face had rapidly retreated.

Just that one thing. It was possible, maybe, for the blood to have rushed from her face again, but the right cues hadn't been there for that. Truthspoken. Only someone Truthspoken trained would try to reset their body to default stress levels in a time of crisis. She didn't think Lesander had even noticed she'd done it—she really had been agitated. She still was now, if Dressa was reading all the little signals right. And she was.

Her wife, her Javieri wife, was Truthspoken trained. Her wife could Change.

She'd suspected that. Ceorre had, at least, and had pointed her in that direction. Iata had been wary, too. Iata had given Lesander useful but time-consuming work to do to keep her from having time enough to do anything else.

Lesander tasted like the red wine they'd had at dinner the night before. Lesander smelled, just a little bit, like fear.

Why was Lesander so terrified of Ari manifesting Green Magics? It was terrifying to Dressa, oh Adeius, it was a mess, but why would it affect Lesander this way specifically? Was she thinking that she might have married Ari and then been stuck with a magicker spouse? Was she afraid Dressa might manifest Green Magics?

Knowing Iata was a magicker, and now Ari...Dressa couldn't say she wasn't afraid of that herself. Not that Green Magics worked that way, only passing to children after manifestation. Except, well, what if sometimes they did work that way?

Dressa bit her lip, pulling back from Lesander, smiling at her, grateful for her help through the long vigil of the night.

They'd found every possible gap they could in Imorie Rhialden méron Quevedo's public identity and worked out ways to fill those gaps. Some, they'd implemented already. Some, like hiring someone—or, more likely, using either Pria or Iata, and Adeius they were running out of people who could Change—to play the part of one of Imorie's parents if necessary. Or maybe she would have to do it herself.

Or maybe she would ask Lesander. And see what that question brought about.

No. She couldn't ask yet. Not when everything else was in chaos.

"It will be all right," Lesander said. "Truly. Ari didn't strike me as someone who'd be recklessly vindictive."

"No, Ari will only plot to undermine your personal staff for months until they do a sloppy job because they think you're secretly sabotaging their wages. True story."

Lesander's nose crinkled. "Seriously? So—but she's a

magicker now. Wouldn't something like that be considered violence?"

Dressa fluttered her hands. "I don't know. I don't know much of anything about being a magicker." Which had been true until a few days ago, after which she'd been cramming everything she could learn into her spare moments.

She pressed the heels of her hands to her eyes, made a growl, let go. "Okay, so, assuming she doesn't kill me. How in the world do I approach her?"

"Will you even have to, though? They're at Green Hall right now. They might stay at Green Hall."

"No, my father will want her to stay in the palace. That, I know. It's not safe at Green Hall, not with all the uproar around all of this." And there had been uproar. So, so much uproar, and the loudest of it had fallen into cries for the magickers to be banished from the kingdom as public safety hazards—or calling for worse—and high speculation and conspiracy theories about the Rhialdens all being magickers. That—*that* was going to be a problem. It already was a problem. And the fervor had only increased since Ari's ship had landed, broadcast in very public spectacle, just under two hours ago. Whatever was happening over at Green Hall, she hoped it included solid plans for the future.

Dressa's insides were jittering. Dammit, she was just getting used to the idea of being the Heir, settling into her duties and the rhythms of it all, and now...this?

"Part of being a ruler, I know," she said, taking a moment to close her eyes and stretch, "is dealing with the shit that comes up." She paused. "Most of it, I suspect. It's just not *fun*."

Lesander snorted, but took a step back, giving her space. Lesander felt up at her hair, still in its messy bun from the night before. Dressa was properly dressed now, but Lesander had been chasing a branching data trail for the last few hours. Whether Iata had meant for Lesander to have busy work or not, Lesander *was* good at it.

"Right," Dressa said, and shoed Lesander toward her—well, it was becoming their—closet. Two whole racks among the admittedly dozen or so racks were now devoted to Lesander's clothes, and Lesander's scent hung in and mixed with her own. There was no scent of Arianna here anymore.

Dressa pressed a hand to her tightening stomach, edging into a shallow trance to still it.

She would deal with seeing Ari when it came to it. She could try to script out the scenarios, sure, but she didn't know what was going on over there. She hoped she could snag a conversation with Iata or even her father before seeing Ari, but that might not happen.

Dressa was the Heir. She knew that wasn't changing. Lesander was her wife. Her secret Truthspoken secret wife.

Dressa leaned in the closet doorway and watched Lesander's attention flit between several outfits before she effortlessly pulled out one that would be most suited for both her position and the solemnity of the day, without being too dramatically dark.

She loved this woman. She was certain of that now. There hadn't been much time to properly fall in love, but—she knew. When she was with Lesander, she felt a calm, an anchor in her rapidly accelerating life. She felt seen, not just as the persona she presented to the worlds, but as herself.

They would be publicly married soon, and they would start their children in the incubators. They would raise their children together, and those children would one day be Truthspoken, too. Trained from childhood in the fine arts of control, manipulation, and Change so they could one day rule the kingdom.

She'd wanted to change that system, but how could she think about that now, with the kingdom on the edge?

And with Lesander—knowing who and what she was, how would that change her plans? Would Lesander play the long game, slowly turning her own children against her? Teach them Change techniques on her own?

Would Lesander make her move sooner than that? The Javieris wouldn't go through the enormous amount of effort to illicitly train a Truthspoken not to use her.

Why *had* Lesander been rattled enough that she'd let a Truthspoken calming technique slip? And then not notice she'd done so?

Dressa's heart was pounding so fast she couldn't catch enough presence of mind to stop it.

She had three crises to think about now.

Lesander paused, looked back at her, brows drawing together. "It will be okay."

"I know," Dressa said. Her voice, at least, was composed.

20

PEOPLE OF VALON CITY

   The problem with ruling by fear is that fear becomes normal.

> — DR. NDARI HADI ESYN IN "A SOCIETAL
> MORPHOLOGY: TRUTHSPOKEN IN THE
> MODERN AGE"

Homaj Rhialden, Seritarchus IX stepped out onto the broad entry platform in front of Green Hall, squinting in the mid-morning sunlight. Concrete steps descended to several meters of lush grass below, and beyond that, the tall iron fence, and beyond that—the people. So many people, with their shouts, and their holo signs and icons bobbing above their heads, trying to get his attention. Jostling to see, to be heard.

He surveyed the people, only vaguely noting the guards spaced closely around the perimeter, much more closely than usual. Both the guards from Green Hall and Jalava's Palace Guard, and outside the gates, the Municipal Guard doing their best to hold back the crowd.

This crowd wasn't afraid of him. Or at least, they were defiant in their fear. Did that mean the power of the Seritarcracy was waning?

He glanced at the holo signs. There were variations of "Truthspoken, Tell Us the Truth!" and "No Rhialden Killer Magickers!" One sign, he saw with dismay, said "Free Arianna!" At least that person was on Arianna's side.

To his right, Zhang rested her hand on her holstered pistol, and he didn't doubt she also had a finger on the switch that would flip it from stun rounds to lethal. Two more of his personal guards were behind him, and a good half dozen of Mariyit's top guard contingent, too. Mariyit, to his left, had his usual faintly pleasant smile, though it didn't take a Truthspoken to see it was strained.

Homaj held up his hands. For a moment, the roar of the crowd increased, but slowly, slowly, it died down to an uneasy sort of quiet. At least they wanted to hear what he had to say.

He touched the amplifier on his throat. Made sure there were more than a few camera drones focused on him before he said, "People of Valon City. I recognize that you care about this city and this kingdom, and that's why you are here. I hear you. I, Homaj Rhialden, hear you."

The crowd roared, frantically waving their arms and their holos. He held up his hands again, but the noise didn't die down.

He wasn't going to try to shout over them—that would be a mistake, a lack of control. So he folded his hands in front of him and waited, posture relaxed and assured, as if he had planned the pause.

Mariyit stood patiently as well, as if this sort of crowd was a daily occurrence. And it had been of late, if in much smaller measures than it was today.

Homaj suppressed a grimace. His fault. That part was certainly his fault.

He tried to signal the crowds to calm again, and again it took some minutes before the voices died down, but they finally did.

"I have this to say to you today." He turned to Mariyit and extended his hand. The First Magicker took it firmly, meeting his eyes. "First Magicker, witness my truth, with all the legal surety a witness by a Green Magicker entails."

"Of course, Ser Seritarchus. I witness the truth of Homaj Rhialden."

"Thank you. I, Homaj Rhialden, am not a Green Magicker."

"True."

And now the crowd had gone truly silent, so much that he could hear the soft clicks and whirs of the camera drones repositioning for the best shots. He decided not to think about if any of those camera drones might hold a weapon. Such things had happened before, though he had to trust the guards around Green Hall had checked each one before they'd allowed the drones to hover, and were tracking their movements.

"And I, Homaj Rhialden, do not fear Green Magickers. We have nothing to fear from the Green Magickers."

"True," Mariyit said, his posture bracing under the statement.

He had one more statement to say, one more he'd planned, but he stopped himself. He could not say his daughter was not a Green Magicker. At the moment, this exact moment, it was true. His daughter—his only legal daughter—was not.

But that statement, though useful, felt like a betrayal. Of himself, and of Ari.

Well, Imorie. She had chosen that name, so it was hers.

He had, at least, answered one of the questions that had grown rampant in the last hours: that if Arianna was possibly

Imorie and a magicker, was it inherited? Were the Truth-spoken all magickers, not only able to be anywhere and anyone now but also to steal secrets with a touch and a glance?

The people should have a healthy fear and respect of the Truthspoken, but not this panic. Adeius, not this.

Mariyit looked a question at him, but it had been barely a breath's hesitation, and Homaj nodded his thanks, pulled back his hand.

Stating his truth like this, witnessed by a magicker—maybe it wouldn't be enough. Maybe the people wouldn't trust a witness from a Green Magicker, even the First Magicker, if they were determined to see...well, what was actually true. That their current ruler and the former Heir were, in fact, both magickers.

He raised both hands again before the crowd could get itself fully worked back into its frenzy.

"And if I had been a Green Magicker, hear me, I would be no less fit to rule this kingdom than I am now. Green Magickers are, first and foremost, people. Like you, like me. And anyone, absolutely anyone, can manifest the ability to use Green Magics. It could be you. It could be me. It could be your children or your neighbor or a high house prince. But we are all, first and only, people.

"People can do good, and they can do harm. In the case of the magickers, in most cases their magics prevent them from doing harm. But they are still people—any of you could do harm, too, and there is nothing but your own morals and judgment preventing you from doing that, too."

The crowd was riling up again, so he raised his hands and his voice higher. "And if any of you were in a situation where your life was threatened, you would wish for the ability to defend yourself. As Adeius is my witness, as you are my witness, and through the witness of multiple Green

Magickers, what happened on Hestia was done in self-defense. Nothing more. As a Human, as a person, I cannot deny anyone in my kingdom the right to defend themselves—"

He stopped as the crowd roared over top of him. Had they heard what he was saying? Had any of them heard him?

The speech hadn't, truly, been for those who'd already worked themselves up outside the gates, but those who would be watching on their comms or their vid consoles. It was for those who'd watch it in the days to come, who'd scrutinize Imorie, and who would be faced with Iata when he made his bid to rule. It was for the magickers, too, to let them know he hadn't lost any faith in them. For whatever that was worth now.

Homaj hoped to everything that this fervor of the people would be diverted to other pursuits by the time of Dressa's wedding. Iata and Dressa and even Imorie, if she could manage it, would be busy in the weeks to come.

The First Magicker raised his hands now. They'd had a short argument in the corridor on the way toward the front doors—Homaj had wanted to make all the pronouncements so that any hatred or blame from this incident would fall on him and not as strongly on the Green Magickers. But Mariyit had been adamant against staying silent or in the background.

Homaj still didn't know that was a good idea in this situation, but the crowd quieted again to hear what the First Magicker had to say, and roared as Mariyit finished a version of the same speech he'd given in his office earlier. A pronouncement of leniency and aid for those who had been wronged—Imorie and Eti, who these people had mostly decided were the enemy.

Homaj raised his own hands one more time, pouring every bit of his own charisma into his stance and bearing, but the crowd had little interest in paying attention to him now, and zero interest in calming down.

Zhang touched his arm, and he nodded. They had done what they had to, and what they could. He'd laid what seeds he could to help Imorie and Iata. Mariyit had taken his public stance of mercy, for good or ill, and now...now, they'd best go inside.

21

UNSTEADY

> We have only our non-evaku trained senses to rely on when determining if a Truthspoken is under strain. Truthspoken almost never show it, and if they do, it is with purpose. The idea that they never feel strain, however, is obviously false.

— DR. IGNI CHANG IN "DISCOURSE ON THE HUMANITY OF OUR RULERS"

Inside Green Hall again, the roar of the crowds only a distant background in the quiet of the entry hall, Homaj's mouth went dry, his ears ringing, the floor tilting. He managed to keep himself steady, because he *had* to maintain control, but his guards certainly saw the lapse, all of them on the alert for an attack, and so did Mariyit.

Homaj shook his head to forestall any notion that this was an attack, and let his annoyance at the situation outside Green Hall show. There were no camera drones in here, but that didn't mean no one was watching, or that information couldn't still get out. Anyone could be motivated if enough money was on the line, and he was sure it would be. Let his distress be seen as aggravation—that was a far more acceptable lapse in control.

Mariyit leaned to one of his own guards, said something quietly, and the majority of his guards broke away.

"Ser Seritarchus," Mariyit said, "if we may adjourn to a sitting room or my office to discuss this further?"

He didn't think he'd make it to Mariyit's office without needing to sit. His legs felt weak as it was, and he couldn't pull enough concentration to smooth away the adrenaline.

"A sitting room, yes. Zhang—with me. The rest of you, wait outside. Mariyit—a room with no windows, if you please."

It still wouldn't be as safe from listening ears as the First Magicker's office, but it was his best current option.

Mariyit gave a half-nod, half-bow, and strode swiftly toward the left, down a wide corridor. He pushed in the second door to the right, looked around, then held the door open for them to enter.

Homaj's guards spilled in, also did a quick look around, then went back out to the corridor, as ordered.

Only Zhang remained, and Mariyit, and himself.

Mariyit looked up at the ceiling with its soft recessed lighting, held up his hand, and then sighed. "Those cameras will cost more than the budget can afford to replace. But the cameras and microphones in this room are now disabled."

"I'll pay for them," Homaj said, and collapsed into the nearest chair, shivering. Zhang pulled a chair beside him and sat as well, and Mariyit crouched down, offering a hand.

Homaj smiled wryly, but took it, and leaned his face against Zhang's shoulder as he struggled to take even breaths. Mariyit's calming helped, but it didn't take away the emotions that were all fighting to the surface now.

He'd held himself together for twenty-three years. More,

if he counted his years in court before his rule. He was no longer, officially, the Seritarchus—barring what he'd just done today—but he shouldn't suddenly forget his years of training. He should be in much better control of himself than this.

"You just lost a daughter," Mariyit said softly.

Homaj reared back. "No, I didn't—"

But still holding Mariyit's hand, he felt the falsehood in that statement.

He had lost a daughter. Officially, and he knew Ari's reasons for doing what she'd done, and he understood the logic and the need. It didn't make it less of a knife to the gut. Iata was gaining his kingdom, and his daughter—

No. No, he had *given* Iata his kingdom, and Iata had said the adoption was temporary.

Homaj wiped at his eyes, tried to hold back more tears, then sighed and gave up, sitting back.

He held up his hand still holding Mariyit's. "Thank you, but I'm just...tired. I will be fine in a minute."

Mariyit sighed at those blatant untruths, but he let go, found his own chair, sat back.

"That did not go particularly well out there, did it?" Mariyit asked. "I still believe I was right to speak up. If we allow only the Seritarchus to speak for us, then we have no voice at all."

Homaj—Maja—closed his eyes and allowed himself, for this time in this room, to not be the Seritarchus. It was like surfacing from a deep lake to frozen air.

He had lost a daughter. Not in any kind of permanence... or maybe it would be. He didn't know. He didn't know where anything would go from here.

Maja pinched the bridge of his nose, sniffed too loudly.

His daughter had been through hell. He still didn't know

exactly what had happened, but he damn well knew enough to want the Javieris to rot in fresh graves.

"I'm going to Hestia," he said, his thoughts racing ahead as he spoke. He knew Iata would agree with that—he would investigate exactly what had been going on at Windvale, and extract Bettea, if fae was still there. And they might not be, they might have already fled the estate and the planet. Fae was resourceful, he well knew—he'd helped to train faer as he had his own children. Adeius, and the Javieri had just shot faer. Stunned, at least. Oh, that stomach-dropping moment before Eti had clarified what "shot" meant.

He looked up. "If you're sending a replacement for Doryan, can you send them now, on a fast ship—or, take back the ship they came in on, even. It'll get me"—he looked at Zhang—"*us* there faster. I want to get there before whoever's at Windvale now has enough time to cover things up. It will be over five days from when it happened until we get there, even at military speeds. I want to leave tonight."

Mariyit pursed his lips, nodded. "Do you wish to go as a magicker?"

"I—" He rapidly thought it through. "No. I'll officially go, I think, as part of an investigatory team. Zhang, will you take point on this one? As yourself? That follows reasonably—the Seritarchus would send his best people to investigate an attack on any Rhialden as a security threat. We'll be watched, and I don't think we'll have time to get any other arrangements, not with all we need to do yet. I'll Change shortly—I'll be Shiera Keralan, I think, I'm tilting female in any case, that will be fine for a few days. She's well known, an administrator, would be well able to help manage a task like this."

Zhang studied him. "No, you're heading into this shift fast, you'll likely head out of it fast. It's emotion-based, I'll set it up so two different identities could work. Another guard, I think—Captain Temir, perhaps?"

He sighed. "I—we'll see. Yes, please, manage the details. I will need to talk to Iata, and Ari—Imorie—at very least. We should get back to the palace. I'm not sure how long it will take Iata to Change, if he'll even have the chance, if more crises aren't already happening just now."

He glanced at Mariyit, felt his face heat, and didn't try to hide it. Iata knew the First Magicker better than he did, though he knew Mariyit well enough. Mariyit knew every one of the most potent secrets in his life, and Iata's, so he'd never held much reserve around him. And yet. Here and now, the circumstances, their relative positions, were changed. He wasn't the Seritarchus anymore. And Mariyit wasn't exactly even a friend.

Mariyit resettled himself, bemused. "You really are going through with this?" he asked quietly. He didn't mean going to Hestia, Maja knew. He meant...everything else.

Maja felt his face heat again. Though Mariyit had disabled the room's security systems, and though any room where conversations could be held in Green Hall had rigorous sound proofing—magickers being who they were and called on often to witness people's truths—Mariyit wasn't wrong to still be cautious, speak quietly. Homaj had been too reckless by far in detailing his plans for Hestia.

He was struggling to know where his boundaries were in his new reality, struggling to parse out what to hold close and what to share and with whom and in what way. As Homaj— he knew how to be Homaj. He was still very unsure of how to be Maja.

He nodded. Gave a tight smile, and, less shaky now, the panic subsiding, he pushed up.

"Thank you. Please—comm details of the ship, your magicker replacement, and anything else to me."

Mariyit rose as well, also looking a little uncertain on how to relate to him now. "To you, or to—" He waved in the generally wrong direction for where the palace would be, but Maja got the point.

"To me," he said firmly. Which would go to Iata shortly. They had to switch back as quickly as possible—crises didn't wait for Change. "And I can be the pilot, if that helps in your selection of replacements. You won't need to qualify if anyone can fly the ship. Zhang is qualified to fly interstellar as well."

"Good. That—yes. That will help."

Mariyit took a step toward the door, stopped. "Be careful. This business with the Javieris, and—gods—using magickers like that. That is bad business all around. Eti found out Ari, and you can be found out, too. Just because we found one Javieri-coerced magicker doesn't mean there aren't more. So, be careful. I really should detail you a magicker to help with the investigation, someone high enough to be able to tell if someone else is concealing their magics."

"Then make sure Doryan's replacement is such a person, and that they help us first before settling into their new position."

Mariyit's brows knit, but he sighed. "Whoever travels with you will be able to tell you're Truthspoken in any case. That can't be helped. I'll choose someone with infinite discretion —I think I'll need someone like that on Hestia, anyway. Gods. Fleecing information from the sick."

He opened the door, and Maja stiffened himself back into Homaj again. And as Homaj, he gave Mariyit a tight smile.

"See that it's done."

22

THE CORRIDOR

If you're Truthspoken, you can never be a stranger.

— COLLOQUIAL SAYING THOUGHT TO HAVE
ORIGINATED IN VALON CITY, USED TO
DESCRIBE THE IRONY OF MEETING COMM
FRIENDS FOR THE FIRST TIME IN PERSON

She walked the corridors of Palace Rhialden as a stranger. Jalava had wanted to clear the staff corridors and take those on the way into the palace, but Iata had said no—they would be going in publicly. The people in the palace, the various courtiers, needed to see Imorie. They needed to see she was a person, not an image in a vid feed. They needed to see she had Rhialden support.

Ari still felt like a prisoner on display as they walked across the courtyard from the landing pads behind the guest wing. They hadn't landed at the Seritarchus's private landing pad behind the residence wing, and that was probably the right move. She had Rhialden support, yes, but she wasn't a royal Rhialden.

She would, however, be staying in the residence wing.

Ari kept close to Eti throughout this walk, but she didn't hold his hand. His aura was a little less murky than it had been. Would it ever clear?

A profound silence followed them like a spreading plague. People she knew, faces she recognized from court and among the staff—people stared at her as if she was a pariah. As if she herself was the plague. There were no whispers, no movements as they passed, as if their very presence rooted the people in place.

How many of these people were wondering if she was Arianna? Most, she was sure. She was exhausted, but she fully inhabited her role as Imorie—her posture, her walk, her carriage. But they, living and working here at Palace Rhialden, knew Truthspoken could be convincingly anyone.

One thing that startled her was the number among the courtiers whose souls had visible density. Not as dense as her father's or Iata's, but a layering all the same. Were those the courtiers who knew evaku well? Did they have any illicit Truthspoken training? She would have to ask Iata later. He couldn't have been a magicker here for however long he'd been a magicker and not have seen this too.

Iata walked at the head of their small procession, his aura gone again, stoic, just a little more forceful in his presence than he usually was as himself. But it had the intended effect, and maybe that was part of the hush, too. Iata, even as a bloodservant, explicitly represented Rhialden power. Jalava brought up the rear behind Doryan, and guards surrounded all of them, strengthening the effect. No one dared to stop them, no one dared to interrupt as they passed.

Ari had walked these corridors as different people before, yes. She'd been servants and guards and various palace staff. Various nobles.

But this was different.

This time, she wasn't Ari at all. She had no claim to that name except in her deepest core, and no persona to return to.

Yet. Yet, she told herself, she would bide her time. She would make a way. But the way people looked at her, stares in various shades of scared, hostile, or speculative, told her she'd have a monumental task ahead of her.

Eti's shoulder brushed hers as they ascended the grand staircase, and she did take his hand then. Maybe he could hear her straining to breathe. She didn't dare try to pull strength from anything around her. But Eti, like he had before, like she'd tried to do with him once, too, gave her just a little bit of his own strength. Enough to get up the stairs and keep walking.

The long mirrored corridor was its own challenge. She did not expect how much it would wrench her to glance to the side and see herself fully outlined in green. To see the whole picture—the borrowed clothes, the dense holographic seal on her cheek, her aura. Here, in this place that had been her home.

Eti squeezed her hand. He hadn't said anything—they'd all kept their silence, too, after the shuttle had landed. Everything else had been decided beforehand, and only the guards barking the occasional order broke the hush. Only the sounds of their shoes on the stone tile floor. And then the carpet.

She found both anticipation and dread rising up as they passed the checkpoint from the administrative areas into the residential wing of the palace. Guards who might usually nod to her nodded to Iata as the ranking member of their party instead, and that bothered her *intensely.*

This familiar corridor led to a home she had been denied. To a life that was, at the moment, out of reach. This entire palace was supposed to be her inheritance—she'd known all her life that one day she'd rule over it with absolute control.

She'd sit at the center of the kingdom, administrating, directing, gathering intelligence. Acting where and when she needed for the best interest of Valoris.

A familiar door down the corridor opened. The door to her apartment.

Dressa stepped out. Her floral print jacket and pants were a little more sedate than her usual flare, but hardly sedate enough for a proper Heir. Not like Ari would have dressed at all. Dressa was taller, too. Her features a little less like they had been. Less, Ari realized, like Arianna's, more distance between them. That...was interesting. As was Dressa's expression, not quite hiding her dismay. As was the woman with flame-red hair who came out behind Dressa. Lesander.

"Truthspoken," Iata said respectfully as they neared.

Dressa nodded back. "Iata."

Did she know? Did she know how much power Iata actually held in this palace?

"Cousin," Dressa said, looking toward Ari now, and held out her hand.

Iata stopped, attentive, waiting. He didn't show any of his impatience or his annoyance, but he had to be feeling it. Dressa was taking an unnecessary risk, reaching out to her in public. Dressa was making a scene.

Dressa stepped closer, eyes locked on Ari's.

Well. Dressa was technically the ranking person in this corridor. There was nothing for it but to bow.

Ari dipped low, more clumsily than she might have, and that wasn't entirely feigned. She pulled Eti down with her.

"Ser Truthspoken," she said, the words here sounding odd in Imorie's accent.

What was Dressa hoping to accomplish here in the corridor, where the audience was limited, but it wouldn't be impossible for what was said and done here to leak. Ari caught Jalava murmuring into their comm ring—the surveillance data for this corridor, at least, would be more heavily restricted than usual.

Dressa's jacket rustled as she neared, holding out both hands now. The jeweled bangles on her wrists clinked softly together, catching the overhead lights.

Ari stiffened back upright, though kept her eyes downward. Imorie had met Dressa once before, she had decided, and so wasn't as awestruck as she might have been. Imorie was just a touch more defiant over her place in this web of Rhialden power than she probably should have been, too.

Imorie was absolutely not mortified that her sister was seeing her like this. Seeing her aura, her hand locked tightly in Eti's. The bruising her cosmetics couldn't fully cover. The stunted Change that had barely covered her heritage at all. The exhaustion shrouding her.

Why was Dressa reaching out to her? Dressa had to know that would allow Ari to read her emotions, though she could also read Ari's.

Dressa didn't seem uncomfortable at all with Ari's aura, though, and that—yes, Dressa knew Iata was a magicker. She would know Iata's place in all of this, too.

Ari let go of Eti's hand, feeling more than seeing him sway slightly from the release, though Doryan stepped up next to him, put a steadying hand on his shoulder.

Dressa glanced briefly at them but pulled her focus back to Ari.

"Cousin Imorie. Please. I wish to know you are well. I wish to show you that you're welcome here. We will protect you."

Ari reluctantly let Dressa take her hands.

23

EMOTION

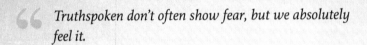 *Truthspoken don't often show fear, but we absolutely feel it.*

— ARIANNA RHIALDEN, MELESORIE X IN *THE CHANGE DIALOGUES*

E motion flooded Ari, not turbulent like her father's had been, but vibrant, loud, very much like Dressa. *Not* her sister. Dressa was not her sister.

She saw Dressa's eyes widen that tiny bit. Had Dressa heard that thought? Or maybe it was the emotions surrounding it. Ari could feel a mess of anxiety from her, a coiled guilt, a stubborn defiance. She heard, distinctly, *I did what I had to*, but those were the only actual words. Dressa might have been trying to broadcast that to her—she still didn't really know how these new senses worked.

Dressa let go, and Ari wondered if she'd sensed whatever she had been looking for. Dressa was, uncharacteristically, very hard to read just now.

Dressa turned to Iata, becoming more brisk. "Where will they be staying?"

"For the moment, in Rhys's apartment. But we're opening one of the larger guest apartments down-corridor. Magicker Rhialden méron Quevedo and Magicker Tanaka are both guests of the residence, as well as Magicker Azer."

Imorie wouldn't know the significance of being temporarily housed in Rhys's apartment, but Ari did. It was one of the safest in the wing, no windows, snugly between Haneri's large suite of rooms around the U in the corridor, and the Seritarchus's suites directly behind it. Typically reserved for an adult Truthspoken sibling until the Heir's or ruler's children came of age.

It also had social congruence: Rhys had been a member of the family drawn in from outside, and so was Imorie.

Had Iata and her father planned for her to stay in that apartment before they'd known she'd have Eti and Doryan with her? Rhys's apartment had two bedroom suites, one with a bloodservant's bedroom attached, but not three suites on their own. That, she suspected, was why Iata was mentioning the other apartment.

Dressa nodded. She'd know the significances, too. "Let them use that apartment for now. That, I think, will do."

Iata inclined his head. "Truthspoken."

Ari did her best to still her nerves. Was Dressa trying to keep her close, a rival, an enemy? Did Dressa already know about Iata's adoption of her? Would Dressa know all the angles of that as well?

Dressa met her eyes again, and Ari saw only worry.

Behind Dressa, Lesander shifted, and Ari tensed. She'd noticed Lesander's denser soul earlier, like the density in some of the nobles. Still not quite like her father's or Iata's, or Dressa's for that matter. She'd known Lesander was expert at evaku—she'd have been disappointed if her father hadn't chosen a consort who was capable of keeping up with her.

But looking at her now, looking closer, Lesander's soul density wasn't light, and there were layers, as if folded behind mirrors. On the surface, she seemed muted, open, as if Lesander was doing her best to present only one front to the world and nothing else.

Did Lesander know who Imorie really was?

Yes. Yes, that was plain from the look she sent back, steady, decidedly neutral.

This had been the woman she was supposed to marry. Now, this was the woman who would marry her sister. Who was growing close to Dressa, by their mutual body language cues. Ari hadn't wanted to marry Lesander—she hadn't wanted to marry at all. But she also hadn't wanted *Dressa* to marry her intended, either.

"We should be going," Iata said, breaking the tensing silence. "Magickers, if you will follow me, please."

STEPPING OUT INTO THE CORRIDOR, Lesander's heart wasn't pounding, but it should be. She kept it steady, though, kept herself steady as Dressa decided it was a good idea to talk to Ari right here in the corridor. Adeius, after all of Dressa's angst about this meeting, why did she think it was a good idea to make it public?

Lesander shouldn't have come out. She knew that the moment she'd stepped into the corridor after Dressa and saw the rank on Ari's cheek, and the other magicker beside her— who had to be Etienne Tanaka. His was even higher.

She was holding herself so rigidly to being *herself*. Would they still see her Truthspoken training? Her teacher had always warned her to be absolutely honest, body and soul, around magickers—and even then, there was risk, which increased with every bit of training she'd acquired.

But she couldn't step back inside now, not and not look like she had something to hide.

Dressa gripped Ari's hands.

Lesander itched to grab her shoulder and pull her back, though she knew the impulse was irrational. Her parents had never favored magickers, keeping them mostly away from the Javieri Court. But Lesander had no strong feelings about magickers either way.

Had Ari killed, though? Had Etienne? She'd just heard the Seritarchus's absolution and statement of support. But did that actually mean anything?

If she was worried the magickers might read something from Dressa about herself, though, she was fairly sure Dressa didn't know she was Truthspoken-trained. Dressa would never give her the freedom she had otherwise. The Seritarchus wouldn't, either, unless he was playing a longer game. And that was also possible.

While Dressa's attention was occupied with Ari, Lesander felt the weight of eyes on her. She looked up into the hard gaze of the bloodservant, Iata.

It was the first time she'd seen him since arriving at Palace Rhialden—Dressa had said he mostly kept to the Seritarchus's quarters and his own business. Taller than the Seritarchus, his long black hair was tied up with a gold pin with a deceptively simple design. Lesander, though, knew the cost of that particular jeweler. His clothes were fine, but almost military in their austerity, allowing only light ornamentation around the edges. His whole bearing and personality was severe, but not arrogant or cutting like the Seritarchus he served. Iata moved with economy, not flare.

She'd done her research, oh she'd done so much research. She knew as much about Iata byr Rhialden as it was possible for anyone to know who hadn't grown up here. Iata held a lot more sway in the daily running of the palace than most people assumed, and in the last few weeks, she'd learned he held even more. Bloodservants, she'd found out with Dressa and Pria, were so much more than servants. The "servant" part of their title was part of their own misdirection.

Iata's cheek twitched, and for a moment, just a moment, she thought she saw a flash of pure rage in his eyes, enough that it startled her, made her want to step back.

She braced herself, only breaking the gaze after a two-count, looking deliberately back to Ari and Dressa, who were stepping apart.

Now her heart was pounding. What had that been? Why would Iata have that much ire toward *her* specifically?

Adeius. The blood was trying to drain from her face, but she knew the physiological pre-cursors, absolutely held onto her composure with Change. Adeius, this was so dangerous.

What did he know about her? How much did he know—and if he knew and was showing it, how much did the Seritarchus know? Could they have possibly deciphered her family's signal to her, a signal only high-ranking Javieris should know?

If Pria had the capacity for Change, Iata would certainly have it. She couldn't discount that Iata could be anyone or anywhere as much as the Seritarchus. Iata had that air of control about him typical of someone with mastery over evaku—but why had he let that rage show? Had that been deliberate, or had he genuinely had enough emotion to lose control?

He wasn't shouting for her arrest, she told herself. He wasn't trying to expose her just now, if he even knew there was anything to expose. So was he under orders not to, or maybe he had a grudge against the Javieris, her family and not just her? She couldn't immediately think of a reason why, other than that the Javieris and the Rhialdens had never been friendly. Or did he have a reason to dislike her personally?

She tried to smooth over her emotions, ignore Iata's reaction as an anomaly, but her instincts were blaring that this man was a danger to her. He had a reason, some reason, to hate her. And he had power to act on that hatred.

Lesander well knew what it was like to be in the crosshairs of someone who actively disliked her. Who wanted to undercut her at every chance they could. But she'd left Palace Javieri and her mother behind, if not exactly out of their influence. She'd been hoping for something different, anything different, here.

Roiling in her own thoughts, trying her hardest not to let any of them show, her eyes connected with Ari's.

She saw little ire there. Saw calculation, and that—yes, that she'd expected. Whether Ari saw more than that from her...she didn't know. She was doing her best to let her emotions go, to be only herself as she intended to present herself at the palace, but she still didn't have her emotions in check. And she was so incredibly off-balance that she was sure she'd let something slip through somewhere.

Her family had activated her, but she still had no idea what they were planning or when, and every hour that passed was a twist in her gut. If Iata knew something, or if Ari might have sensed something and Lesander didn't act soon, didn't do something soon, she might lose any chance at movement.

More than that—she could lose her place here. She could fall from her position now, and the Javieris with her. A strike, once initiated, had to be followed through.

She didn't want bloodshed.

But she was still a Javieri.

Calm, she told herself. *Calm.* If she acted prematurely, without her family's support, it could just as easily bring everything down around her.

Lesander studied Iata out of the corner of her eye as he turned and walked away, with the rest of the group following.

She studied his walk, which she already knew well from palace footage. She studied the way he carried himself. Played back in her thoughts the exact cadences of his words, though she hadn't been paying attention to them as well as she should have been.

Lesander moved just a little closer to Dressa.

When her family made their move, she would do everything she could to protect Dressa. She *had* to protect Dressa.

Or was the signal she'd received already the signal? That thought had been running over and over in her mind all night and that morning. Was she supposed to make her own move now? To take what she knew about Ari and use it? She might be able to better control that outcome.

Why did it have to be this way? Why couldn't she have just married Dressa, raised their children, and quietly set up her Javieri children to rule? All legal, no strife. That was supposed to have been the plan, unless something changed. Unless an opportunity arose that was too good to pass up, and was Ari being a magicker and in the middle of this whole scandal just that opportunity?

She'd been prepared to do what she had to when she'd been intended for Arianna, though she'd still wanted the more peaceful option then, too. Then, the trial had been the marriage.

Now...now.

No matter her training, no matter her mother's bloodthirstiness or her family's lust for power, she wasn't a killer at heart.

She shared a look with Dressa and was afraid Dressa

might have seen too much as well, but Dressa smiled, gently squeezed Lesander's forearm before pulling back into the apartment.

Lesander cast one last glance at Ari, then Iata, before retreating herself, blood still pounding in her ears.

24

CONNECTIONS

It should probably be taken as a given, but I'll say it again for the record: not all magickers like plants.

— FIRST MAGICKER MARIYIT BRODEN,
INTERVIEWED IN THE POPULAR VID ZINE
VALON CITY SUNSHINE

There was a pattern in the Kidaa runes, and it was just out of reach. Rhys stood in the center of the large holo simulator, extremely high resolution holos of the attack areas and the runes carved into them floating around them, jiggling one foot on the deck while they rested their weight on the other—and back again. And back again. They couldn't concentrate. The pattern was pulling at their thoughts, and no memory tricks, no zoning out, nothing they tried was working to tease it out.

Or maybe it was the news they'd heard from the comm drone that had come in a few hours ago. They hadn't been paying attention—the whispers had reached them over lunch about the Rhialden magicker. That—that had snapped them out of their fugue.

Imorie Rhialden méron Quevedo. It hurt, it physically hurt to see how little she'd Changed from Arianna—should Rhys presume that she couldn't Change, or at least Change well? Ari had never been anything less than precise in all of her Truthspoken duties.

It hurt almost as much to see the holo of her, arms cuffed behind her back, looking fearfully around her. Haloed in vivid green.

And an ugly part of them, a part they didn't like at all, said that maybe, finally, this would give Ari some damned *empathy*. Let her see someone else's cares beyond her own. Well, hers and the kingdom's, which she'd always seen as her own anyhow.

But the news said she might have killed with her magics. She and another man Rhys didn't know. Was that even possible?

"Lt. Petrava."

Rhys straightened, turned to see Lt. Commander Hamid standing near a station at the back of ops, arms crossed.

"Uh, yes, sir?"

"If you're so intent on humming that song, maybe you could at least grace us with the lyrics?"

Had they been humming? Oh, hell. Yes. They'd had the tune to that Rings of Vietor song, "Cycle of Three," stuck in their head all day. But they hadn't realized they'd been humming it.

"Sorry, sir."

The commander sighed. "Go, Petrava. You've been staring at those holos for hours. Go walk it off."

"Yes, sir." Rhys took one last frustrated glance around at the runes, at the references they'd brought up and the notes they'd imported from their own comm, then touched the control to put the simulator on standby.

They hesitated. "Uh, sir, please don't let—"

"Your work will still be here when you return."

Their first day on the main simulator, the night shift duty commander had wiped all of Rhys's running programs and sent them to back memory—which was procedure, sure, but Rhys had to spend two hours getting everything arranged back into their logical visual flow, rerun one of the programs that had crashed overnight without enough power to sustain it, and, well.

"Thank you, sir."

Hamid gave them a worried look, which was more terrifying by far than any other look she could give them. She had to have seen the news from Hestia—she'd know Rhys was affected by it, though they hoped to everything she hadn't figured out how much. Imorie wasn't supposed to be their sibling. They didn't want to talk about it, either, if that's what she was thinking. Definitely did not want to talk.

So they fled.

Rhys walked a circuit of the main corridor on deck three, which took them all of five minutes, then caught the lift up to deck two, with a vague notion of visiting hydroponics to see how Misha was getting on. It was a distraction, and a little chancey for them to just be dropping in on duty hours, but Hamid had given them the direct order to "go walk it off," so this could be a part of that walk.

Hydroponics always smelled faintly of dirty socks, and today was not the exception. Rhys stepped through the heavy-seal hatch into the humid air, felt the slight artificial breeze, squinted in the sun lamps overhead. Hydroponics spanned parts of deck two and deck one, and they had always wondered why the ship designers had missed the opportunity to make the entire ceiling skylights. That would have been amazing, walking under the stars through the fruit trees and flowering berry bushes. But, well, Rhys guessed it wouldn't help much where the *Storm* typically patrolled. They tended to come out of Below Space at the edges of the border systems, not close enough to actually get tangible sunlight.

They found Misha cursing over a raised bed of what looked like carrots.

She glanced up, scowled. "What? I hate gardening."

Rhys stopped short. "But you're a Green Magicker."

"Yes, and not every magicker actually likes getting dirt under their nails that won't come out no matter how hard they scrub."

"Uh—well, can you wear gloves?" They neared the carrots, running their hand over the leafy tops.

"I hate gloves. Then I can't feel the plants as well, or anything as well. I'm a very tactile person."

Rhys waved their arms, trying to think of a comeback to that, but their mind was fraying. The runes were still eating at them, and the news about Ari—

"Sorry," Misha said, and wiped at her headbanded hair. The green was starting to fade, like their own phosphorescence.

They needed to order a kit and redo their own hair, but that would be a week or more until it could get to them all the way out here. Last time it had taken a month. Phosphorescent hair dye wasn't high priority for border scout supplies.

"Sorry. Yeah, I saw the news. You want to know how it feels to manifest? For your, uh, cousin-ish? How is she related to you? I heard the Rhialden part, do you know her?"

Rhys sat on the wide edge of the raised bed. They couldn't tell her Imorie was their sister.

"We don't really get along." That, at least, was the truth. "But I do care. And—Misha, how could a magicker possibly kill? Is it even possible?"

And what would happen to Ari when she got to Valon? Would being Truthspoken, being a Rhialden, keep her from the harshest punishment? What, by Adeius, had happened on Hestia? Rhys had only seen the sensationalized news from Hestia, the highly condensed versions that made it out all the way to the border. There wouldn't be news from the capital yet—that would come later. But most of the comm drones' payloads out this far were military documents and holos—not a lot of vid commentary made it this far out. All they had was a few scant and paranoid accounts to go on and some very damning holos.

"Accidentally," Misha said, her voice tight. "I—can't really talk about it. It hurts, physically hurts, to talk about it."

Rhys wrenched their gaze from the carrots. "Oh, sorry, no, I didn't mean to—"

She waved them off, sitting down beside them. Then held out her hand.

After a moment, they took it. She hadn't offered it often. It wasn't something that Rhys was truly comfortable with. And maybe not especially now, but—but she wouldn't ask to share with them if it wasn't important, either. They knew that by now.

"Listen," she said. "This isn't a good business all around. I can read between the lines—the other magicker wasn't sealed, and there's always a danger of an unsealed magicker being blackmailed or exploited, forced to read people, or do whatever they're told with anything else, for whoever controls them. It sucks, and it's horrible, but people suck fairly often, too. That's just how it is. It sounds like whatever happened to your cousin, she got caught in the crossfire of something else. Now, the First Magicker is a fair man— "

"Yes, I've met him."

She hesitated. The sense of calm and reassurance she'd been subtly projecting jagged into a jubilant spike of... Adeius, was she fan-girling? Over First Magicker Mariyit Broden?

"I met him *before* he was the First Magicker," Rhys clarified. "He was one of the diplomatic sorts who'd come to the" —no one was around, but they still lowered their voice— "palace now and then, and he was shadowing the old First Magicker for a while before he took over. He always had mints in his pocket. They were stale, but—" They shrugged. Candy was candy.

Misha gave him a wide-eyed stare, as if she couldn't grasp the concept of Rhys taking mints from her hero.

"But, like, besides all of that," Rhys said, "yeah, I know he's fair. He's not...not really who I'm worried about." They lowered their voice even further, and Misha leaned in. "The Seritarchus. He isn't really known for...well. Being accommodating. He won't be happy, and—"

They broke off. More than that, and they would be floating in dangerous space. They were already too far off course.

Rhys carefully tugged at their hand in Misha's, and she let go.

Her brows were drawn together, and they didn't know what she'd picked up from them, but they weren't going to volunteer anything more.

The news from the capital would come when it came. And it would come, with an event this high-profile. And this right on the heels of Arianna's attack by a magicker. There was a pattern in that, maybe—but how could there be a pattern with Ari ending up as a magicker? They'd seen that raw terror on her face, that was something they wouldn't soon forget. They'd never seen her like that before, and they absolutely knew that reaction was real. They might not be close to her anymore, but that didn't mean they didn't know her. Couldn't read her much better than she'd like.

Rhys shook themself. They couldn't do anything about Ari now. But that wasn't their only problem.

"I have this pattern," they said. "It's itching at my brain. It's like...it's like when you know three words to a song, and they're all filler words, and not enough to actually go search for the actual song it belongs to. And you don't know the key, and you got the lyrics you do know wrong. That—that is this thing with the Kidaa. Their movements near the border, their sudden abandoning or settling on various worlds, coming near our ships. The attacks, which...I still don't know what to think of them. There *is* a pattern. It's not random."

The captain might have wanted to keep that quiet, but news of the attack on Ynassi III had come in at the same time as news of Imorie. That, too, was all over the ship, making people jumpy.

Rhys shifted, eyed Misha. "Are people treating you okay?"

They almost expected, almost projected from everything they knew about her, that she'd look up, startled, and say she didn't know what they meant. She was a likable person, and they'd seen her chatting with various members of the crew, officers and crewers both. It had to help when a magicker was friendly by nature. People sometimes came to magickers for a form of therapy, too—magickers could see to the truths at the core of problems a lot more easily than the people involved in them.

But would that change for her, with this further blow to the magickers? With news that magickers had been charged with murder?

Misha shifted. "Well enough."

Well, that was a lie.

Her twisted smile showed she knew they knew that.

She shrugged. "It's not anything overt. Just...a weird look. Or someone moving just a little farther away in the corridor. As if, against centuries of evidence to the contrary, I'll suddenly start turning into a rage monster. I just...Rhys, if those magickers actually did kill, and I'll only say this once because it makes me want to throw up, but if they did kill, then their lives could be in danger. And if their lives aren't in danger, maybe they didn't kill, and it's paranoia making those charges. When a magicker kills, even by accident, it usually kills them back."

She held up her hands. "And that's like so ridiculously theoretical, because it almost never happens. But sometimes, in self-defense, or by accident when first manifesting. Sometimes it does happen. I've heard stories, and a whole lot of warnings—not that I need them, because yeah we definitely need to change this subject if I don't want to run to the trash can right now."

She clenched at her stomach, rocking, swallowing.

Rhys didn't know what to do with their hands. Try to comfort her? How? They had no calm to offer her. She was the magicker, not them.

They shouldn't have come here, shouldn't have dumped their worries on her. They were her worries, too, and amplified.

But—Ari's life could be in danger? They hadn't known to be afraid of that, other than the very real possibility of capital punishment. But the Seritarchus would never let it get that far, would he? He couldn't. He'd ordered Dressa to bend herself into Ari's life so that he could hold Ari's place for her —he loved Arianna more than anyone else in his family. But Rhys was pretty sure he loved his kingdom even more than that.

They hummed softly, trying to bring their thoughts back into line, to find a state of calm, because they couldn't be worried about this here on ship. They had their duty, and it was an important duty. Adeius, it was—

Rhys froze. Held the last note of their humming a beat too long.

25

SPIN OF THE GALAXY

> *If the Kidaa exist, and the Humans exist, what other lifeforms might exist beyond the bounds of Human-explored space? At this point, we can only speculate. We have found no evidence of other civilizations, no ruins, no monuments, beyond the Kidaa.*
>
> — DR. BLINN MENDOZA IN THE DOCUVID SERIES *WHO ELSE IS OUT THERE? (AND ARE THEY FRIENDLY?)*

"What?" Misha asked, biting her lip. Her shoulders were braced against more bad news.

Rhys held up a hand, still mid-hum, chasing the thought.

Oh, Adeius. It couldn't be. The thought was absolutely ludicrous.

They pulled out their comm, tried to look up the lyrics to the Rings of Vietor song "Cycle of Three" that they'd been humming all morning. It was an older song, one that had been re-recorded after the band had become super famous this last year, but it had never gained the traction of some of the others. It just wasn't danceable enough. A little quieter, though it clipped along. Moody, poetic.

Okay, so, the lyrics of all the songs in the known universe were also not high-priority storage on a border scout ship. Rhys's network search turned up nothing beyond a few people having the song file in their personal collections. Rhys didn't even have it in theirs.

They closed their eyes, pulled their mind into recall mode, and softly sang:

It's a cycle of three
He left me again
The world and the ground and the sea
It's a cycle of three
All over again
The spin of the galaxy

The Kidaa runes.

The first had meant a person, but it had some stylistic variations around the edges that slanted toward companion, maybe. At least, that was Rhys's take. The second was closest to "galaxy." The third was something like "life," and the fourth had been a slight variation on "life," a repeat. Like "All over again." The fifth had meant "water."

The sixth—there had just been a sixth, not far from *Occam's Storm* at the border. Chronologically, it had happened after the attack at Ynassi III, though they'd had news of it first, and news of that one wouldn't even have reached Valon yet.

That rune—that rune was one the Kidaa used often. Their rune for numbers in general was also the same rune for the number three. Which had always baffled Valoran scientists—the Kidaa had four legs and four toes on each foot and four fingers on each hand. Shouldn't their foundational number have been four or a multiple of four?

They did have a concept of zero, one, and two before three, but three was when numbers actually mattered to them—not multiples, not cubed, just...three.

It wasn't, either, that they did things in threes. It wasn't quite a pattern. But the rune cropped up in most places where they had runes. It meant something more than a number to them. It had to.

"What?" Misha asked again. "What's wrong with that song?"

A song about a companion. A repetition of life. A galaxy. Water—could be sea. And three. What did the Kidaa's version of three mean in that context?

They opened their eyes, shaking their head. It had to be a coincidence. *Had* to be. It was such a shaky pattern, it wasn't even a pattern at all. The Kidaa just didn't think like that, would they even get the poetic meaning of the lyrics, the various subtle Human psychological connections?

Could this be evidence that someone was playing a colossal prank? Or that the runes had been pulled from somewhere, just not somewhere obvious? But...why that song? Adeius, and the high houses wouldn't be so sloppy as to leave a pattern at all, not that kind of pattern, unless they'd wanted the Truthspoken to find it and chase after smoke.

How had Rhys's mind even made those connections—no, they just really badly wanted there to be a pattern, something to make it all make sense.

But it *was* something. They couldn't say it wasn't something. Tenuous. Ridiculous, even, no matter which direction you turned it. But.

Rhys stood, wiped at their eyes, sore from staring at displays the last few days. "It's nothing."

"That is definitely not true. Magicker, remember?"

Their smile was outwardly genuine.

Misha still cringed. Magicker, right.

"What?" she asked again.

Was there even anything there to take to the captain?

They rubbed at their shoulder, brushing the pocket that held the two chips Iata had given them. They'd kept them on or near them, always. Especially these last few days. Not so much a mandate as...a provision.

Rhys had a lot of time to think on the way back to the ship about why Iata had given them those chips. Well, or the Seritarchus. But Iata himself had seemed deeply concerned with Rhys's participation in this mission. Almost, but not quite, like a Truthspoken mission.

Rhys wasn't Truthspoken. But also, their mother wasn't wrong that they were halfway there. They had the highest caliber training in evaku, if a bit haphazard and by proxy. They thought in patterns, and they noticed details—they had to. You couldn't thrive around Truthspoken without that.

Their head—their rational brain—was telling them that this pattern they were seeing was probably nothing. Was chasing at clouds, the equivalent of a well-thought-out conspiracy theory. Why, of all things, would Kidaa runes have connections to the biggest rock band of the moment? And why would the high houses so blatantly use that if so? It was just...no.

But their instincts were saying that maybe it was something. That maybe it was more than something, enough that it was worth relaying. Which...was a big step, and not one they'd take lightly. They had to think on it, really had to think before they took that step. Because if the captain found out they'd added a secret message to the outgoing queue, that might be the end of their career, Seritarchus's seal or not.

Or maybe, especially *because* of that seal. The captain knew who they were—she knew they regularly socialized with Truthspoken. If she also found out they were sending information behind her back—

Was this really something worthy of that sort of risk?

Their head was telling them no.

But their instincts?

"I don't know," they finally said. But they were going to find out.

26

THE APARTMENT

Narrowing lines
of Below Space
like narrowing childhood dreams
and haunted places.

— OWAM, EXCERPT FROM THEIR POEM
"HAUNTED PLACES"

Iata unlocked the door to Rhys's apartment and stepped inside, waving for them all to enter. Ari glanced up at him as she passed him, and he gave her a tight smile.

He was, legally, her father. Which—which mental gymnastics she just had no more energy to handle today.

The air inside the entry was slightly stale, though the apartment was cleaned weekly. Everything looked tidy, though. Not filled with Rhys's usual messy sprawl.

Adeius, but the memories, the clashing of worlds that being in this apartment brought her. She swallowed on a tightening throat. This was not the home of Imorie's sibling.

It wasn't a place she'd spent hours in growing up, with Dressa and Rhys, playing various games and generally getting into more trouble than they should have. Those days were behind her in every way possible.

She had nothing with her now that was her own. She didn't even have a comm—they'd taken that from her at Windvale. Not even the clothes she wore were her own, and this wasn't a role. This was not a role. This was her life now.

She shivered as the air system kicked on.

"I'll leave you now," Iata said. "Please, rest. The Seritarchus will see you after you rest."

Ari wasn't sure it could wait until then, like nothing ever could wait in this palace, but it would have to. Her thoughts were unraveling with every moment, her breaths harder and harder to manage.

"Comm me if you need anything," Iata said.

She took a breath, just enough to speak. "I don't have—"

He pulled the comm from his pocket—his own, she knew. He pressed at the screen a few moments, then handed it over. The comm mattered less than the account it was connected to, in any case. She took it, noting the screen showing that she was logged in as Imorie, with blurred information on her current passcode that cleared when she touched it.

He'd been using his comm most of the short trip to the palace—had he been creating this account? Or had they keyed her into the palace system before Doryan's ship had even landed on Valon?

She clicked the comm off, holding it tightly. "Thank you." And it was awful, it was horribly shameful the tears that rose up with his small kindness.

Iata cleared his throat. "You're fully keyed into this apartment as well. Your biometrics will open the bedrooms and the main door. Eti and Doryan—you both have palace accounts now as well, which will allow you access to certain areas and palace systems, like service from the kitchens. Information on how to access them will be sent over."

"And a comm for Eti," Ari said.

"Yes, I will make sure another comm is sent over. Imorie —" He hesitated, a lengthening pause. "Please remember that you are family here."

She swallowed on a tight throat.

But not royal Rhialden family. Not publicly.

Even if she was legally Iata's child now—Adeius, she needed to sit.

"Thank you," she said again, and did her best to smile. By his slight brow twitch, the attempt was not convincing.

"Rest," he said firmly. "Comm me only when you have rested as long as you need to. Homaj can wait until then."

She nodded and swayed slightly, holding to Eti now more for her own support than his.

"Thank you, Ser Iata, for arranging this," Doryan said.

"Of course, Ser Magicker." Iata gave a small, perfunctory bow, which was a slip. He outranked Doryan—he outranked Imorie even as a bloodservant, and Imorie was the highest-ranking of their party.

But he left before she could think more on that slip, the door shutting softly behind him.

Not before she saw the two guards out in the corridor, though. Two of the Seritarchus's personal guards at her door. She didn't think they were waiting for Iata. There to keep her safe, or there to keep her inside?

She let the thought go.

Ari tugged Eti's hand, pulling him into the open living area with its colorful striped rug and dark gray sofa. A large dining room sat to the left, and a night kitchen beyond it. To the right would be the bedrooms. There were two suites, one for the Truthspoken who'd officially inhabit this space if it was used how it was intended, and one separate bedroom suite for a guest or lover. The Truthspoken's bedroom had the usual prep room and bloodservant's bedroom arrangement. Rhys usually kept that bloodservant's bedroom closed.

So should she take Rhys's bedroom, which was the main bedroom? Well, yes, she was still the highest-ranking. Eti would have the bloodservant's room, because she wanted him close, and sensed he wanted to stay close, too. Doryan would have the other guest suite.

One of the reasons Iata had chosen this apartment, she was sure, was that like the other Truthspoken apartments, there was no surveillance in the main bedroom or the prep room, and she couldn't say the same for the other apartments down the corridor. She knew that hadn't changed with Rhys living here, either. They could talk freely in those rooms.

She wanted so badly to just collapse right now into the nearest chair, but she pulled Eti on toward the main bedroom suite.

Ari touched the door handle, and the lock clicked open. Yes, Imorie's biometrics did open doors here. Iata or her father would have them on file from what she'd uploaded and pinged back at Hestia.

Lights yawned on in the prep room.

Rhys's sprawl wasn't in evidence here, either, though their various scattered cosmetics across the two vanities were familiar. The faint scent of their favorite products hung in the air.

She pulled Eti to a low couch in one corner. Doryan took the chair at corners to it, sighing as they sat. They didn't look so much tired as...overwhelmed. Though they were trying valiantly not to show it.

The prep room door had closed behind them, soft-locking automatically, but Ari didn't get up to throw the dead-bolt. Every locked door registered in the palace's system, and she didn't want to broadcast even to Jalava's monitoring crew that she had anything to hide.

"We can talk here," she said, leaning back into the couch's deep cushions.

27

IMORIE

It's in your most desperate times that you find who's been hiding their truths from you, and who's been sharing them all along.

— ARIANNA RHIALDEN, MELESORIE X IN *THE CHANGE DIALOGUES*

And now that they could talk, Ari's throat closed tight, everything that had happened that morning clogging her words.

She clutched the comm Iata had given her, something that weeks ago wouldn't have even seemed like a luxury.

Doryan leaned forward. "Imorie. Are you all right?"

She held up a spread hand. "Fine."

But grimaced, because she felt the untruth of that, and she was with two other magickers.

Here in the palace. In Rhys's apartment. Adeius.

She turned to Eti. "Your family. I didn't know. We will help them."

Eti, who'd pulled one of the pillows from the couch and

was hugging it to himself, made something between a nod and a shrug.

She swallowed. Lesander—he had to know Lesander was a Javieri, was engaged to Dressa. It was only on every news feed just now. Or it had been, until her own disaster.

"Lesander can't hurt you. She won't."

He glanced up at her, mouth pinched. "I don't think she knew me."

And maybe she hadn't. Maybe she didn't know what her family had been doing on Hestia—that was possible, yes. But Ari had seen her soul density, and she doubted Eti or Doryan had missed that, too. Not nearly as dense as Dressa's, no, but more than the courtiers.

"Just—be careful around her." And she was realizing now that she couldn't protect Eti, not in the way she'd like. Lesander outranked Imorie in this palace. Lesander outranked nearly everyone but Dressa and the Seritarchus. And Haneri and Ceorre. Well, and Iata. If none of them were around, Lesander could make trouble that Ari wouldn't be able to do anything about, not without burning her identity.

Would Lesander make that trouble? Ari had only one brief meeting and one night at a ball that she'd been barely making it through to judge Lesander's character. It wasn't exactly high praise, either, that Dressa seemed to have embraced Lesander fully.

She drew in a hard breath. "One more thing, and then I'll rest."

Doryan nodded. And she considered asking them and Eti to swear their secrecy, to hold their hands and witness their sincerity—because she could do that now, as a magicker—but she was just too tired. And the chance that they knew most of what she was going to say already was high. That meeting at Green Hall had been a mess of unraveling secrets. So she just forged on.

"Iata is currently ruling the kingdom, I think. He and Homaj have switched on and off for years—that goes nowhere beyond this room. But you might see him again as Homaj, and you'll see his magics, so you need to know this— it's him, though you'll need to treat him as Homaj. I know Eti and I will see his magics—could you see when he had his aura concealed, Doryan?"

"I saw the possibility, yes. And got the sense from him when he verified my sincerity that he was in charge of that meeting. Which I was a little confused about, I will admit."

Ari's smile was tight. "That is the Rhialden Court. Trust nothing and no one." She paused. "But if you do need help, I think you can trust Iata, whether he's himself or Homaj."

Doryan's features flickered through shades of dismay and bemusement, and she had to remind herself that they hadn't grown up in this world. But Eti—Eti seemed to take this in stride. Maybe because he'd formed a trust with Iata through whatever Iata had done to help him today, maybe because he was well used to layers of subterfuge.

Her gut tightened at the thought.

"Well," Doryan said, standing and stretching. "If you're going to rest, I'll go hunt down some lunch. Both of you could use a meal, too, I'm sure—where is the kitchen? I assume past that enormous dining room out there?"

"It's a night kitchen," Ari said. "I'm not sure how stocked it is. But you can use the apartment comm to call to the kitchens for food—there's a panel in the living room, and another in the night kitchen."

She stopped, struggling again for breath.

Her hand, almost of its own volition, crept toward Eti's and found it.

He gripped her hand back. He didn't give any more of his strength, and she wouldn't ask for it. But he was there.

Doryan waved on their way out the door. "I'll find it. Both of you, go rest."

She glanced at Eti—he'd drawn back in on himself again, hugging the pillow tightly with the arm that wasn't holding hers.

"I won't let the Javieris hurt you," Ari said again.

He stirred, but didn't comment. Was his aura turning murkier again? Yes, she could feel it. Could feel his soul's flow turning inward again.

The door shut behind Doryan, and for a moment, there was silence.

She and Eti, alone for the first time since the ship. Unmonitored for the first time...ever? Had Eti always been watched at Windvale? She certainly understood what it was like to be watched.

"I'm sorry," she said.

He started. "What? Why?"

"For dragging you into all of this."

He didn't look up. "Not your fault."

Adeius. He truly believed that. And the momentum of his soul delving inward was increasing. Did he look a little hazy around the edges?

She did her best to send him her own calm. Not calm she actually felt, but calm that she knew would be there if she had the ability to reach it.

He shuddered, and steadied. She saw him steady, coming fully back into the world.

"Eti..."

And how did she ask this? She knew him, she could feel his raw emotions, but she didn't know his sense of pride. She didn't know his history, and the parts she did know were horrifying.

"Eti, are you okay to sleep alone? In your own room, I mean? There's a bedroom connected to mine. But it's separate. There is a door, and a bathroom inside." They'd slept in the same cabin on the ship, and she was glad there'd only been two cabins on that ship. He hadn't been in any state to be alone.

He shrugged, tensing back up. "Yes."

Oh Adeius, had that sounded weird? She hadn't been thinking of that at all, and was too tired to tell.

"Eti, I'm ace. I just want to be sure you're okay. And that you won't..." She didn't finish that thought, seeing again Iata grabbing him up, holding him to existence. She swallowed.

"Oh," Eti said on a long sigh, and now truly did slump back. "Me too. Mostly." He nodded, looked back over, his body language turning tentative. "I don't want to be alone."

She nodded. Then with a gathering of effort, got up, pulling him up with her before she let go. She wandered to the closet, squinting as the lights came on.

Rhys wasn't Truthspoken, but that had never stopped their ability to fill a closet. The large space was nearly half used up with Rhys's regular wardrobe alone, and there were still some of the older outfits near the back that Rhys had outgrown a long time ago.

She was short and thin—too thin just now—and Eti might just fit something from Rhys's late teens.

"This is your sibling's apartment?" Eti asked, stepping inside.

"Yes. They're in the Navy, away on ship just now. At the border with the Kidaa."

She pulled a long-sleeved band shirt and a pair of lounge pants for herself—they'd be loose, but it was good enough for now—and another band shirt for Eti, having to dig a little farther for decent pants. That particular era of teenagedom had been Rhys's sequin phase. But she did find a mostly innocuous pair of black lounge pants and handed them over.

"Your sibling wouldn't mind?"

"Maybe mind me wearing their clothes. You, they'd be fine with."

Eti frowned, but took the clothes anyway.

"Uh—"

"I'll change in the prep room," she said. "You can change in here. Give me a minute."

She went out and mostly closed the closet door. Then stripped as quickly as she could out of the ship's borrowed clothes into Rhys's borrowed clothes. But it felt better, so much better to be out of the ship clothes.

"Imorie?" Eti called softly.

"Okay."

He stepped out, more tentative than before. The band shirt and loose pants were a little big, like hers, but good enough for resting.

Ari nodded and grabbed the comm from where she'd set it on a table to dress, crossed as quickly as she dared to the bedroom. She paused to let her heart-rate calm, then unlocked the door.

She stepped inside and stopped, looking up.

"What? What's wrong?"

It had been a few years since she'd been in here. The last time had been over one of Rhys's breaks from the Academy two years ago, she thought. Sometime in the last year—and it had to have been the last year, because the band had only gotten big this year—Rhys had plastered a huge poster of the lead singer of The Rings of Vietor over their bed. Shirtless. In very high detail.

Ari stepped aside to let Eti see. For a moment, he stared.

"I do like their songs," he finally offered.

She coughed a laugh, she couldn't help herself. And saw the faintest smile from him in return.

Adeius. That smile was like sunshine.

"Come on. The bed's big enough to sleep four."

Which was a weird thought. It wasn't a thought she'd ever have considered as Arianna.

She glanced at herself in the wall mirror across from the bed. And it was a wonder no one had yet dragged her to the palace physicians.

Did she still feel like Arianna? In any way that mattered?

She let herself, just for one moment, pull her bearing back into what it had once been. Back straight, chin high, eyes daring everyone around her to even try to challenge her. Fully inhabiting and emanating her own power and position.

Eti, standing on the other side of the bed, watched her.

"Ari," he said. "I can still call you that, if you'd like."

He was so attuned to that nuance of her name. He wasn't Truthspoken, but he could see right through her.

She looked back at Imorie in the mirror. At herself. Ari had never particularly fit her anyway.

"No," she said softly. "Imorie is fine."

Imorie pulled back the covers, and they each took a side —not touching, not even close, the bed truly was that big. She placed her comm carefully beside her, screen off. Then she rolled onto her side, away from Eti, wincing as the movement shot pain through joints she was trying to ignore.

"Are you okay?" Eti asked.

She must have made a sound. Or maybe he just knew. He was high sixth or possibly even seventh rank, nearly as high as the First Magicker.

She heard a shuffle behind her, felt the bed move. Felt him shifting closer, a steady light in her magicker senses.

He placed a hand on her back and she felt him doing his best to give her calm. Give her strength. He had nearly died today—she was sure he had nearly died—yet he was comforting her?

She bit her lip so hard she was sure she'd drawn blood.

She rolled onto her back, caught his hand again, held it

tightly. Looked into his dark brown eyes, red-rimmed, tired. He was exhausted. He was terrified for his mother and sibling, and it was taking everything he had to stay here, to stay with her. He wasn't in as much danger of fading as he'd been earlier, whatever Iata had done had helped, she sensed, but he was still unsteady. Still not out of danger.

He wanted to leave right now and go help his family. At least know they were okay.

"We can't get there faster than my father's people already on Kalistré," she said. "That's what will happen—the comm drone will get there fastest, and he'll send his agents to take care of your family. It's more than either of us could do on our own." Especially as magickers. She still wasn't used to the feeling of *not* being able to defend herself if necessary. Of not being able to fight—but then, that was doubly true, as a magicker and with the Bruising Sleep.

She didn't add all the things that might go wrong, either, but he absolutely knew them. Shuddered with them. The Javieris might have already harmed his family. It was a possibility, yes. And Eti's publicity in this whole mess might have caused his family harm as well—families of magickers weren't well-loved, especially if they were harboring an unsealed magicker.

Especially if that magicker had killed.

She moved closer, slipping her comm into a pants pocket, turning toward him, their foreheads close.

Calm still flowed from Eti to her. Despite everything, calm still flowed.

And she slept.

28

WHO

We have yet to find one single theory unifying all understanding. Some have pursued this notion their entire lives and never seen more than glimpses of transcendence. Some cite various religions as having solved this millennia ago, or fringe scientists, or philosophers. But the facts remain scattered, never quite adding up.

— LORD INDA KOLDARI IN THE ANTHOLOGY
NOBLE VOICES IN PHILOSOPHY, VOLUME THREE

Dressa rapped her knuckles twice on the panel door to the Seritarchus's study, and after a moment, the door clicked open. Iata was at the desk, then. She'd thought he would be.

She blinked when she saw him, though—still himself, sitting at the desk with an expression of tight concentration, holos all around him. Which was...weird. She hadn't seen him sitting there as himself before, only as her father.

Well, and she'd be seeing more of him in this position

when he made his own bid to rule, wouldn't she? She hoped to see that.

Iata glanced up. "People are tying the Kidaa attacks to the magicker accusation of violence—both of these things hit at exactly the wrong time. Both with groups that shouldn't be able to do violence, or historically haven't, in any case. Homaj hasn't denied the magicker deaths. He's only said they were in self-defense. Which...I suppose we shouldn't try to cover up evidence already out there. That would only make this worse." He brushed back a strand of hair that was creeping into his eyes.

Dressa'd had a lot of things to say when she'd stepped in. She'd had so, so many questions. One of the biggest of which was why Ari seemed to think, to utterly believe, that Dressa was no longer her sister.

But she asked, "What do you need from me?" She approached the desk. "How can I best help just now? We've made Imorie's identity as airtight as possible. I made headway into my inbox, answering people as if I'm pleased to see my cousin, who I only vaguely know. I'm not sure anyone's buying it at this point."

She didn't stop at the front of the desk as she usually did, but moved around it, glancing at the open holos.

Iata gave her an odd look, but waved at the holos, inviting her to look.

A quick glance didn't give her anything more than she already knew and what Iata had just said.

So was this the point at which Truthspoken power tipped over? It was already precarious, but was this where people assumed that the Truthspoken, far from protecting them, either no longer could do so, or were actively out to get them? The fear in so much of what she'd read today was so strong.

"Handle the matter with the Kidaa," Iata said. "It is, unfortunately, secondary just now. I need to deal with this crisis with the magickers—I need to aggressively meet with nobles and the military and the Assembly and diplomats and assure them all that the Rhialdens are as strong as ever. That this was merely an incident, an unfortunate one not involving a member of the ruling family, and it will pass."

"But you can't reassure them," Dressa said, still scanning various holo windows, but without really seeing the text. "You are a magicker—they'll absolutely be testing you about that."

Even here in his study, even here with her, who knew, he was keeping his aura hidden.

"Maja had his truth confirmed by the First Magicker—"

She finally turned to him. "Iata, that means nothing! To those who are determined to believe it, that only means further collusion with the Green Magickers. People are terrified—people believe magickers can do so many things that are just not true, see into their dreams, read their thoughts from a great distance, all of it. They're absolutely terrified that their rulers have this power over them."

Iata closed his eyes. His hands on the desk trembled, and his aura flared briefly, was tamped back down again with a growl. Adeius, if he slipped in the next few days, where would they all be?

"Can my father resume his place as Homaj for the next few days—"

"No," Iata said firmly. And she understood. Maja had barely managed through the switch this time, judging by the hints of strain around Iata's mouth. "No—I suspect he's already planning to go to Hestia, which is where I would have sent him anyway. No, I'm not going to make him be the ruler right now. That would only break him, and likely break the kingdom further. He's barely in control."

Iata glanced up, held out a hand.

Dressa hesitated, then took it.

"What do you feel from me?"

She quieted, testing out her own emotions, and trying to sense anything beyond them. When she touched a magicker, it was usually like a sense of someone else nearby, like someone was having a subtle conversation with her.

When she'd touched Ari, it had been a flood of emotions, all of them intense. Adeius. She deeply wished she hadn't wanted to sense what Ari was feeling. To know that Ari was okay, but also to sense if Ari would try to retaliate—she hadn't wanted to give Ari time to compose herself and hide those emotions.

The accusation from Ari had been strong. Dressa had, after all, taken Ari's title, and her betrothed—not that Ari had wanted to marry Lesander anyway. But the vulnerability Dressa had felt from her, oh that had been so much worse.

"I don't feel anything," she said after a moment. She couldn't sense anything now more than her own emotions. She only felt the tangible touch of his hand.

He nodded and let go. "I'm locked down so tight right now that only a higher-ranking magicker could feel anything at all. Or see that I have magics. I'm testing how long I can hold this. It is painful—I'll need to pace it. But it will get me through the next few days."

Dressa shifted. "Who knows that you're a magicker? Captain Zhang—she has to know, right? She's been functioning on and off as your guard, when she's not with my father. And she'll be going with him, yes?"

He nodded, settled back again, and his aura did flare back around him now. A release of tension so he had more strength to bottle it back up again.

"Do the rest of my father's—your—guards know? Do they know you're not Homaj?"

"Jalava knows I'm not Maja. The rest...Chadrikour has her own observations, I'm sure, but she hasn't voiced them.

Neither has Ehj. The others aren't quite as close or been with us as long."

"You have to tell them. Tell Chadrikour, at least, if she'll be functioning as captain while Zhang is away. Tell her you're both Iata and a magicker. Tell her what you told me—show her the damned book. You can't do this without people knowing your blindspots and vulnerable points. They're there to protect you."

His lips curled in an ironic smile. "Yes, Truthspoken."

Dressa checked. He was still himself, Iata the bloodservant, and she wasn't quite reconciling that with the power she knew he held. She'd been unconsciously posturing as a Truthspoken speaking to a bloodservant, not an Heir speaking to a ruler.

"Sorry." She opened her hands, took a step back. And she'd been crowding him at his desk, which she never did with her father. "Sorry."

He shrugged. Stood. "I should Change. Best that be done quickly, and Maja will be back soon to Change, too. Quickly, though—"

He summarized in terse statements what had happened at Green Hall. And those statements were bad enough— Adeius, did she even want to know the detailed version? She sensed there was much he was leaving out.

The gulf in Dressa's stomach grew wider and wider.

"So the Javieris did this to them? To Ari, and to Etienne?"

"He prefers 'Eti.' I don't think it was an attack on the Rhialdens specifically, but yes. That's what I want Maja to find out more about."

Had Lesander known this was going on? Had it been her parents carrying this out directly, or maybe a lesser branch? Could she hope it was that?

No. This was too big, the information gathered too valuable. Prince Yroikan Javieri had to be involved. And Duke Koldari was also somehow involved.

Adeius, Lesander had been acting weird after that meeting in the corridor, more contained and edgy than usual. Did she know something about all of this, more than she should know?

"And you *adopted* Ari?" Dressa asked. He'd said that quickly, with as much emphasis as anything else in his summary, but she knew that choice had been deliberate. Well there, at least, was the mystery of Ari's insistence that she wasn't Dressa's sister.

She shifted, her mind running straight through all of those implications. Ari would absolutely have thought that through from all directions—Ari had to know Iata was currently ruling the kingdom.

"You're still the Heir," Iata said firmly. "She knows that. That's not going to change."

Dressa cleared her throat, nodded.

He moved past her. "Now, if you will excuse me—"

"Iata," she said, and he stopped on his way to the door. Turned back, brows up. "Iata, her rank's not low. Like yours isn't low. Rank can run in families, yes, and magics can run in families, but higher ranks are rare, right? Her rank is one in a thousand or more magickers. Yours, what, one in five thousand, ten? If magics are random, how are both of you, high-ranking Rhialdens, also very high-ranking magickers?"

She stepped forward, waving as the patterns fell into place in her mind—not complete, not any of them complete, and it was maddening. "The Bruising Sleep, the Kidaa attacks, Lesander and her family, you both manifesting. All of these things, all of these coincidences, spread so wide that we shouldn't be able to see them as anything else, but—"

"But they're something," he said. "I know. I'm seeing it,

too. They shouldn't be able to be something. But somehow, they are."

"Who," she asked, "who has the power to make all of these things happen? Who could possibly have that kind of power? To give the Bruising Sleep. To make someone a magicker—is that even possible?"

The words hung heavy in the air.

There was someone, though, wasn't there? There was someone or something directing all of this.

Had Adeius, god of the stars, who'd guided the Valorans through the void to their new worlds millennia ago, decided the Truthspoken were no longer serving them and determined to bring them down? Dressa wasn't sure if that was a ludicrous thought or not, and it made her want to laugh hysterically.

Had someone somehow found the keys to not just a mysterious illness, but mysterious magics as well? Had that someone also found a way to control or coerce the Kidaa?

Could all of this be the Kidaa themselves—but then, why? Why would the Kidaa care about the politics of Human worlds far removed from their own? They never had before. Would they even understand all the nuances of Human politics?

"I don't know what's possible," Iata said. "But I intend to find out."

He moved again toward the door, but stopped when she didn't move.

"Dressa, I really do need to go Change—"

She held up her palms. She knew it was bad timing, but also, she needed to say what she was going to say because it *was* bad timing.

"Iata, I want to start the bloodservant for my Heir."

29

THE CHILD

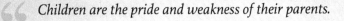

Children are the pride and weakness of their parents.

— LORD MYNIN JADIAR IN A POST ON THEIR
PERSONAL FEED

Iata's aura flared out around him, and she knew she had pushed him past his point where he could hold everything together just now. Adeius. She hadn't meant to do that.

Dressa held out her hands. "I'm sorry. I know this isn't good timing—"

"I understand your reasoning." His lips drew tight. "I assume you haven't talked to Lesander about this?"

She clasped her hands carefully in front of her. "No."

And that was the main reason right there. Why her thoughts had crystallized in the last few hours, then the last few minutes, on this point.

She knew Lesander was Truthspoken trained. She knew, too, that Lesander had been skittish ever since they'd seen Ari in the corridor, and hadn't said why. Dressa also now had

Iata's information that the Javieris were behind what had happened to Ari and the other magicker, Eti.

She didn't know the extent to which Lesander had been involved in that. She didn't know exactly why Lesander had been trained as a Truthspoken and then purposely sent into the heart of Palace Rhialden—but Prince Yroikan Javieri wasn't known for taking half measures, or for low ambition, either.

Dressa did know that last night, Lesander had been rattled enough to let her training show. Dressa couldn't assume, just couldn't, that the lapse had been over Lesander's concern for her, or for Ari.

She loved her wife. Adeius it *hurt* to have to think what she was thinking now, hurt in every bone of her body. She didn't want to think that she had married her enemy. Didn't at all want to do what she knew she must.

She wished with everything in her that she was wrong. That Lesander wasn't here to destroy everything she had vowed to protect. But she couldn't plan for that.

"I want," she said, weighing out her words as she said them, testing for her own truths, "I want this bloodservant child to be able to be my own heir, if it comes to it, but not Lesander's."

Iata nodded. "That might be a solution right now, but that child will have to live with the knowledge that they are your first child, but not your heir. Or, you will need to conceal that knowledge from them. Like my fathers did with me."

"Adeius, Iata." She pressed both palms to her forehead, began pacing around the sitting area in the center of the room. "What else can I do? If Lesander is here to, what, overtake the kingdom? I don't know? To influence me to the point that I give her and the Javieris more power? Can I even hope it's as benign as that, with everything else going on?"

Iata's lips were pressed tight, his arms crossed. "It will

break the marriage contract to start a child who is yours but not also Lesander's. You will have this secret from your wife, Dressa. A secret child. Can you carry that weight with you through that child's upbringing? Can you look them in the eyes as you train them and never call them yours? Can you face Lesander without that becoming a hidden resentment between you? And what if she finds out? It's the kind of thing that could start a war. Are you prepared for that, Truthspoken?"

Rattled at her title, rattled at hearing it from him, in this context, in all of these contexts, Dressa slowed her circuit, stopped. Smoothed out the front of her jacket.

"I understand your reasons, Dressa," Iata said, his voice quieter now. "I understand your fears. Lesander might be exactly the threat you fear—but she also might not be."

"Then—"

Adeius, her eyes were welling.

"Dressa, talk to your wife. The one thing your father never understood in his own marriage—you have to talk to get answers. Ask her what you want to know. Ask if she's Truthspoken, ask if she knew about Eti and Windvale."

"But—"

"Dressa!"

She inhaled sharply. Iata never lost his temper. *Never.* He was acerbic, yes. She'd come to see him, in his own way, as kind. She'd never heard him raise his voice in anger.

He was almost shaking. His face sheened with sweat.

She took a step closer. "What—is it your magics—"

But his aura was already visible around him.

"As a magicker, I can't do violence without consequences. But Dressa—I am not the person just now to tell you what to do about the Javieris."

Bettea. Oh Adeius, he'd said Bettea had been stunned at

Windvale, was still there, and that fact had been buried among all the other urgent details.

His child. Another victim of the Javieris.

Her stomach wrenched. Was Bettea all right? If Iata was this rattled, this angry?

His aura abruptly disappeared. His face was a mask of casual calm.

"Dressa, I must Change. You're the Heir. Go talk to Ceorre if you need help with this, but it can't be me." He paused. "But do talk to your wife."

She just managed to nod before he blew out of the room, very carefully closing the door behind him.

30

THE KIDAA

The Kidaa have no direct parallels to Human communications systems. They appear somewhat likely to use small maneuvers as a yes or no code to communicate, though the utility and accuracy of such use is often in question. When they have something to say, though, they'll overlap their ship with a Human ship and speak directly to the commander.

— ADMIRAL BRYNC QUACH IN HER REPORT
"THE STATE OF AFFAIRS WITH THE KIDAA"

R hys hadn't stopped humming for the whole last day, and wonder of wonders, Misha hadn't complained when they were in their shared cabin. Running on a hunch that was more mental itch than anything else, Rhys had drafted a proposal to the captain to access the private music collections of the crew and see if more songs fit similar patterns to the runes and "Cycle of Three," though they hadn't mentioned that song exactly, because, well. Wonder of wonders, too, the captain had approved that request without comment.

It had actually been fun sitting on their bunks, calling up song after song, listening to the lyrics and debating the various possible connections and themes. There were a *lot* of rock songs about being unlucky in love, but very few of them Rhys marked for a second look as maybe relevant to the Kidaa.

Misha's stories about her own bad luck in love were deeply entertaining, however.

"So my fifth crush that year was just mind-shatteringly gorgeous, and xe wanted a career in modeling, I'd swear xe had Truthspoken genes somewhere in there, but xe also had the ego to go with the career choice and didn't like that when xe touched me, I'd reflect back to xer all the little nasty things xe didn't want to see about xerself. I wasn't trying to, and I didn't really care about the petty stuff, either, but xe was bent on seeing xerself as perfect, so being with a magicker just wasn't going to make that happen." She shrugged, and Rhys grinned, waving a finger in the air before pulling up an older song about lost love.

Misha threw a pillow at them.

But it was itching at their mind, too, about the way the Kidaa kept getting close to ships at the border. Too close. They were known to approach on occasion, and especially if there were any kind of fast maneuvers, but there'd been reports from border ships that the Kidaa would come very close now and then linger. Like they were watching, maybe? Or maybe like they had something to say? But the Kidaa ships didn't try to communicate. After a while, they just left again, as weirdly as they'd come.

It wasn't the same pattern itching at them from the runes, but it felt like another island in the sea of this puzzle.

"What about this one?" Misha asked, tossing up another

song from the list they'd divided. "The lyrics say something about seas and worlds, and there's a phrase in there about life that repeats three times."

Rhys sat up from where they'd been staring at the ceiling, trying to let their mind collate all the data they'd taken in as a whole. They'd still been humming softly, and stopped now.

"Which song is that? I—"

Out in the corridor, sirens blared.

Rhys looked at Misha and they both scrambled off their bunks. It was evening on the ship, and they were both done with their shifts for the day, but they hadn't changed out of their uniforms. Rhys slapped closed the collar on theirs, pulled on their shoes. Misha levered into her jacket, which she'd thrown over the back of her desk chair.

"What is it?" she asked. "What does this alert mean?"

The comm clicked, and the first officer's voice blared, echoing throughout the ship. "All hands to stations. Kidaa ship on approach. Ensign Moratu and Lieutenant Petrava to the bridge."

They shared another look before they took off mostly-not-running, passing other junior officers and crew scrambling in the corridor.

Rhys was jittering as they crammed into the over-full lift, pressing the button for deck three.

"What's happening?" one of the crewers asked. "Sir, you know about the Kidaa. Why are they coming for us?"

Rhys wanted to say that they didn't know the Kidaa *were* coming for them, that the Kidaa weren't aggressive, that they didn't have anything to worry about. But their mind was too full of patterns, their thoughts too seized on what this might mean.

It might mean nothing. It might be the same thing other ships were experiencing—they had no evidence whatsoever that this would be anything different. And why in the worlds would they think their ship was special, it was just one ship at the border. Nothing would likely happen.

But Rhys had never seen a Kidaa ship up close. And the captain had called them and Misha both to the bridge. Misha, likely, to be on hand to quickly reinforce the hull if needed. Rhys, almost certainly, because of their project with the Kidaa.

They told themself again it would be nothing more than routine—or, well, at least nothing more than expected with the Kidaa.

But in their gut? Their gut was telling them a different story. Not rational, not even a little. They knew better than to ignore their gut.

The lift stopped on decks five and four, then headed to three, Rhys and Misha the last occupants remaining.

Rhys glanced to Misha. She had gone rigid, her mouth a tight grimace.

"What? What are you feeling?"

She squinted. "It's weird. It's really freaking weird, Rhys. I sense everyone on our ship—a vague sense of excitement and panic. But beyond that...density. And focus." She swallowed and took a step back from the lift wall, maybe away from the direction of the Kidaa ship's approach. Which would be fore, Rhys figured. And that...that set off different kinds of alarm bells in their mind.

Misha stepped into Rhys before they could chase the thought, though, and flinched away when they tried to steady her.

"They see me back, Rhys. Oh gods, I think they do."

"It'll be fine," Rhys said. "They have to have felt ship's magickers sensing them before, if they can sense it at all. This isn't anything new."

"Well, it's new to me."

The lift stopped, and Rhys nudged Misha into motion.

The bridge was a heavily fortified interior capsule that took up decks two and three in the center of the fore of the ship. Rhys had worked an ops duty shift on the upper deck of the bridge for a few weeks once, but they hadn't meshed well with the other crew on that shift, as much as they'd tried to, and they'd been transferred back to ops proper again.

Outside the heavy interlocking hatch doors, Rhys touched the scan plate. They were only slightly surprised when it still let them inside.

Misha, who'd been wringing her hands together all the way up, now gripped them at her sides. Rhys, too, checked their own demeanor, adjusted it to be a little less frenzied, more focused.

The lights on the bridge seemed a little brighter than they'd been before. The people more tense, the captain standing in the center of it all with her arms crossed, face impassive. If she was nervous at all, she wasn't showing it, with skill a Truthspoken might envy.

She glanced back as they entered, waved them forward. Rhys didn't know which of them she wanted, or both, but they both approached anyway.

"Magicker Moratu, please take the bracing station—"

Rhys didn't hear any more of what the captain said, because they caught a look at the forward viewscreens and their ears started ringing. Ahead of them—and, Adeius, yes, the view wasn't zoomed in—loomed the nose of a massive, blunt ship made of brown metal, an alloy Valoran scientists had never been able to replicate.

"Fuck," Rhys whispered.

"Yes, quite," the captain said.

Rhys straightened. "Sorry, sir—"

"No, it's appropriate. That ship is still on approach. I think they're going to try to overlap. Any thoughts, Lieutenant?"

Rhys felt dizzy, growing horror warring with growing excitement.

The Kidaa didn't use comms to communicate—not, at least, with Humans. They would use small maneuvers sometimes, a yes-no sort of code that had been mutually stumbled upon, and never fully agreed on what everything was supposed to mean. But if they really had something to say, they made their ships intangible in some way, came right up to a Human ship, right through it, until the Kidaa who wanted to speak lined up with the Humans on their bridge. The Kidaa did, at least, have some notion of who and where the commander was—and that itself was frightening.

But overlap happened so seldom that the instances were all heavily studied. These overlaps were, beyond archeological or scientific expeditions, the only official contact Humans had with the Kidaa. The only times they truly met face to face. And it was happening now, to the *Occam's Storm,* when Rhys was on the bridge.

The captain had asked them for thoughts. They shook themself, watching as the nose of the other ship grew ever closer. This was happening now, and happening soon.

"No—no thoughts yet, sir."

31

CLAN STARLIGHT

One of the strangest things we know about the Kidaa is how they communicate ship to ship with Humans. There's not a lot we do know about overlap, as the military isn't keen to release details. But we do know something, as it happened once to a civilian trade ship, and some details leaked out. I'm sure most of the versions seen in vid dramas, though, are wildly inaccurate.

— RASA REVAYA IN FAER VID ESSAY SERIES
THE GLORIOUS WEIRD

Rhys got a prickle up their arms, which they thought was just them until others in the bridge crew started shifting uneasily, too. The captain rubbed at the back of her neck, eyes glued to the viewscreens ahead.

"Comm, ship-wide," she said. "This is the captain. Prepare for Kidaa overlap in..."

"Three minutes, twenty seconds, sir," the woman at the helm said.

"Approximately three minutes. Do not move from your station while the overlap is occurring. You'll likely see Kidaa going about their business on their own ship—they'll appear ghostly, they can't touch you, though they can see you. Do not make any moves that could appear threatening—remember your training. We've all trained for this. Let's be professional, people. Let's make our Seritarchus proud."

Rhys swallowed hard. The nose of the Kidaa ship had completely blotted out any visible stars. It would reach the nose of the *Storm* in less than two minutes now.

And make the Seritarchus proud? Rhys knew the Seritarchus. Homaj Rhialden wouldn't particularly care how the crew of one border ship carried this off, unless something went horribly wrong.

They tore their gaze away long enough to look back at Misha. She was standing to one side of the bridge near a structural pillar, palms braced against it. She'd strapped herself with a harness to the pillar itself, so her hands would keep contact even if the ship shook or gravity cut out.

Neither of which would happen, Rhys told themself. No encounter with the Kidaa had ever ended in violence, ever. Not in two hundred years. No overlapping had ever gone badly, just...weirdly. Absolutely nerve-wracking, they'd read, and they'd read all the accounts.

"Petrava," the captain said quietly, "I'm going to do the talking. But I want you right here, telling me if there's anything off. Be subtle about it." She glanced aside at them, brows raised. "I know you can do that."

They swallowed again. And somehow, they hadn't put it together that if the captain had called them over and hadn't dismissed them, and that they were still standing next to her, they'd still be standing next to her when the Kidaa spoke to her. They'd be right there. They'd be facing the Kidaa, too.

"Overlap in three, two, one."

Rhys braced themself. They felt nothing.

"Turn the sirens off," the captain snapped.

The sirens stopped blaring and left in their wake an eery, unsettled silence. Everyone watched the viewscreen as the Kidaa ship's outline became ghostly in the *Storm's* harsh running lights. Rhys thought they could see the translucent silhouettes of individual Kidaa moving about their own ship on their four legs, their gnarled, wedge-shaped heads turning from side to side.

This was what Rhys had wanted, wasn't it? To actually get answers? To actually get to see the Kidaa and make assumptions for themself?

"Overlap with the bridge in ten, nine, eight..."

Rhys's instinct was to brace themself, but they reached past it for training they never allowed themself to use here.

They let go, for the moment, of Lt. Rhys Petrava, junior ops lieutenant, all around ordinary person, and let themself inhabit their full array of responses, senses alert and highly tuned, aware and relaxed. Their pulse still hammered—they could do nothing to smooth that away, like an actual Truth-spoken—but they knew how to center themself, to move past their body's responses, to calm them.

The outline of an oval formed in the viewscreens, then expanded outward into the nose of a ship.

There were indrawn breaths, but they had been trained for this. Training most crews never had to use, sure, and not as heavily drilled into them as fire drills and weapons drills, but still, the training was there.

Everyone stayed in place as the Kidaa ship completely overtook them, ghostly outlines like fuzzy holos showing the hazy interior of the Kidaa ship.

A Kidaa person came into view on the bridge, walking down a short corridor. They wore a loose garment over their arms and four legs, covering any runes that might have been carved into their gnarled, tough skin. Rhys studied them. Could they tell the Kidaa's clan by the way they moved? But there were hundreds of known Kidaa clans and a few more added to the known list every year.

They should have asked the clan markings for this ship, that was relevant, but they didn't want to speak now. They'd ask later. They knew at least, that this person wasn't from Clan Hydrogen or Clan Ice—this Kidaa didn't have those clans' distinctive, rolling gait. Not that ruling out two clans from hundreds would do Rhys much good.

More Kidaa came into view, who seemed to be completely ignoring the Humans, if they could see them in the same way —and they probably could. Their large, oval eyes, set high on the wedge of their heads blinked, but never connected with the Humans'.

Then three Kidaa came into view, standing in a row, facing them. This—this was it. These were the leaders of this ship or this clan who wanted to speak.

Rhys settled their posture into a relaxed alertness, waiting.

The overlapping ship slowed, then stopped, with the three Kidaa just ahead of Rhys and the captain. And how did the Kidaa *know* to stop in front of the captain? How could they have no concept of so many Human things but be able to read rank so well?

The three Kidaa became, mostly, tangible, while the rest of the Kidaa ship and crew remained translucent.

A rumble like glaciers moving came from the Kidaa to Rhys's right. An older Kidaa, Rhys thought, judging by the mottled purple pattern on their gnarled, grayish-gold skin. Kidaa in higher positions typically wore less clothing, but had more heavily carved skin. Rhys had seen scholars specu-late that clothing was seen as utility and therefore something reserved for lower members of a clan, while runes were marks of honor and earned over time. That assessment, though, could be entirely wrong.

Light fur stood up in running rows on this Kidaa, and trails of runes were etched deeply into the tough surface of the Kidaa's skin. It was also speculated that Kidaa could survive over twenty minutes in the vacuum of space without a suit, though no one had ever confirmed that theory.

The ship's translation software kicked in.

"Clan Starlight. Human ship. Goes to the center, breathes from the center, goes with intensity and *untranslatable*. Clan Starlight wishes to speak with the Humans about starlight."

Rhys blinked slowly, their mind kicking into high gear. Okay...okay. That was similar enough to other overlap greet-ings, and there were almost always a few untranslatable words, though that was getting better over time, slowly, as encounters like this happened and words could be inferred from context.

Captain Nantrayan straightened, gave a slight bow. "I'm Captain Ira Nantrayan of the border scout *V.N.S. Occam's Storm*. I am pleased to speak with Clan Starlight about matters they wish to discuss."

The center Kidaa, taller and with darker skin than the one on the right, made a gesture with one hand, something sweeping with two of their four fingers. That was odd. The Kidaa speaking usually stayed still during overlaps, moving only to speak with their mouths. Scientists had only observed Kidaa using gestural language among their settlements, the civilians.

Then—then all three Kidaa turned to Rhys.

"No. Clan Starlight wishes to speak with the one of the three. Wishes to speak about starlight. Human one, we have spun. You have spun. Human worlds *untranslatable untranslatable*."

"Petrava," the captain said in a low, unsettled voice.

Rhys hadn't, for all their training, frozen, though they wanted to. What the *fuck* did the Kidaa want with them? That had to be a mistake. One of the three? The three Truthspoken, did they mean? But Rhys wasn't Truthspoken—should they say that? It would out them to the entire ship for their parentage and connections, but did that matter here, with the Kidaa? When so much was riding on all of this. They felt that, absolutely felt in their bones that what they said next, what they did next, was *important.*

Rhys also bowed, more deeply than the captain. They needed an edge. Needed to connect on a level that just wasn't possible, but they had to get closer, had to try.

"Human ship. Clan Starlight. Goes to the center, speaks from the center." Was that right? Would that even be remotely the measure of trust they were trying to convey? Would that translate right into their rolling, rumbling language, if it had been translated into Valoran in the first place?

The three Kidaa shifted, looking at one another.

Oh Adeius, what had Rhys done?

They straightened.

"Human one, must know we have spun. You have spun. Human worlds *untranslatable untranslatable.* Clan Starlight speaks of starlight. Speaks of *untranslatable untranslatable.*"

Rhys wanted to punch their fist to their thigh in annoyance. They needed to know what those untranslatable things were, and they had the sense that the Kidaa had vastly, *vastly* simplified whatever they were trying to say to fit into the realm of what Humans would understand. Into the still limited lexicon that Humans and Kidaa had between them. Rhys was not, by any means, an expert on Kidaa body language, but could they read impatience just now in the shuffling movements? And how could they help that?

"Clan Starlight, Human one has no understanding." But how could they ask about the untranslatable bits when they couldn't remotely pronounce the Kidaa words?

"Uh—someone—can you replay the untranslatable parts?"

"Do it," the captain snapped.

The two rumbling words, or maybe phrases, came back over the comm.

"This," Rhys said. "Have no understanding. Can you, uh, make it clear?"

They were grasping at the very boundaries of all they knew, all they'd studied.

The Kidaa shifted again.

The center one made another flicking gesture, and...and music blared.

"...he left me again, the world and the ground and the sea..."

Rhys clamped their hands over their ears, the words to the song they'd been humming the last two days screaming into their eardrums.

"...it's a cycle of three, all over again..."

What the actual fuck?

The music stopped, as abruptly as it had started. Rhys stood, not two meters from the Kidaa, trying as hard as they could to suppress their body's need to shiver.

"I-I don't understand." They looked to their captain, whose eyes were uncharacteristically wide. This had never happened before. Kidaa had never even shown any signs of having Human broadcast technology, or understanding it at all. Or interest in understanding it at all.

"Human one," the center Kidaa said slowly, and Rhys had the distinct sense they were speaking as if to a child. "We have spun. You have spun. Human worlds *untranslatable untranslatable*. Human speak not with breath, not with center, with singularity. Human *untranslatable* speak."

They didn't understand. Was this a warning of some kind? A question? A plea? What was the tone, could they read anything from that? Could they read anything in the Kidaa body language at all? Could they see any patterns—of course they could see patterns, but could they decipher them?

They didn't know enough. Didn't have enough information.

"Are you—does Clan Starlight ask of Humans, does Clan Starlight warn Humans of, what, danger?"

"Clan Starlight goes to the center, breathes from the center."

"Yes, we know you are honorable. What is it you're trying to say—"

"Petrava," the captain warned, and Rhys took a breath. Pulled themself back to their own center.

"Human one, Human ship thanks Clan Starlight for speaking from their breath, their center. This Human wishes to understand if Clan Starlight warns of danger. Is—is this spinning of danger?"

"Starlight," the center Kidaa said.

Did that mean danger from Clan Starlight? Actual starlight, or stars—what, a supernova? Would that even remotely make sense? Wouldn't Valoran scientists already know about that if so? It could mean anything. Literally *anything*.

They were so out of their depth. Sooo out of their depth. They looked to the captain, but she was looking to them.

"One of the three," the Kidaa said. "We have spun. We have spoken."

Then they waited. As if waiting for Rhys's response?

Rhys wet their lips. "Human one thanks Clan Starlight for

speaking. Human one does hear, is listening, but wishes to understand."

"Starlight," the center Kidaa said again, and leaned forward, as if to punctuate this statement. As if it meant something vastly important. Their dark oval eyes fastened on Rhys, and it was entirely unnerving.

Rhys had a brief, wildly out of place flash of being stared down by the Seritarchus on one of the few occasions they and their sisters' antics had caused the Seritarchus to step in himself. There was a terrifying weight of authority in this Kidaa's eyes.

"Please, honorable Kidaa, what do you mean by Starlight?" They spread their hands, though they had no idea if the Kidaa would recognize the gesture.

The music blared on again, just a few seconds.

Okay.

The Kidaa shifted again. *Was* that impatience? Would they get impatient, and what would happen if they did?

Rhys wanted to try and understand, but the captain placed a hand on their shoulder.

"Wrap it up," she said softly.

Rhys gave a tight nod.

"We hear, Clan Starlight. Humans hear."

They didn't understand, but they did certainly hear. Rhys's ears were ringing with the faded music.

Then the three Kidaa became intangible again. The Kidaa ship slowly backed, the whole process reversing.

Rhys stood still in the center of the bridge, absolutely reeling.

"Disengaging overlap," someone called out.

Misha, palms still braced on the support pillar, gave Rhys a wide-eyed look.

"Petrava," the captain said, her voice nearly a whisper. "My office. Now."

32

CAPITAL POLITICS

My general, my prince. Shouldn't we wait to go to war until we know there will actually be one?

— OLUN SHIRALL IN THE VID DRAMA *NOVA HEARTS,* SEASON 9, EPISODE 8, "A WALK IN SURFACE PARK"

Rhys followed the captain silently to her office behind the bridge, their head spinning. What had any of that meant? There was an ominous feeling in their gut, amplified from the unease they'd been feeling about the Kidaa for months now.

Why had the Kidaa wanted to speak with Rhys specifically? How by all the worlds had the Kidaa known who they were, or that they were connected to the Truthspoken? Or even that they were on this specific ship? That—that was what was eating at them most urgently.

The captain didn't wait for the hatch automatics to shut it, but grabbed the manual handle and slammed it into place.

Rhys jumped.

"Are you Truthspoken?" the captain asked, spinning to face them.

"What? No—"

"Because the Kidaa seemed to think you are—'one of the three' they said. I can't think of any other prominent 'three' they'd specifically request to speak to—they always and only speak to the ship's captain."

Rhys was reading signs of panic around her—Adeius, she was losing her grip.

Rattled as they themself were, Rhys calmed out their features, made their body language absolutely unassuming.

"I'm not, Captain. I was raised around the Truthspoken, I know evaku. I know a lot about Change—I couldn't help but learn with my siblings—but I don't know how to Change. I'm not Truthspoken."

"Will you swear that by Adeius, or so help me, should I haul Moratu in here and have her read you?"

"She's already read me. She knows who I am. I'm not—"

The captain waved them off and seemed to deflate. She braced herself on the bulkhead beside the hatch, and this moment of vulnerability was almost more alarming than what had just happened with the Kidaa.

No, no that bit with the Kidaa was definitely top crazy of the day.

"Captain," Rhys said, "what do we do with this? Should we go back to Valon?"

The question, the reminder of duty, maybe, seemed to brace her, and she straightened. Smoothed out her uniform, walked behind her desk. But she didn't sit down, gripping the back of the chair instead.

"That's standard protocol in an overlap scenario, yes. But you think we should stay?" She shook her head. "And I should be taking protocol advice from a junior lieutenant in ops?"

Rhys sat—if she wasn't going to, they weren't about to let their own wobbly legs give out. "Captain, the Kidaa wanted to talk to me. I don't know why. I have no idea how they think I'm Truthspoken, even if I was—I'm not—but if it was Arianna or Dressa, they shouldn't even be able to tell then." A thought occurred. "Maybe they have senses like Green Magickers? Or technology that does the same thing and can see Truthspoken? Adeius, that would be terrifying. But then, how do they know who the captain is? They've always stopped with the captain, no matter if the captain's standing in the center of the bridge or not."

They looked up, their face heating. They were still too rattled to have fit themself back into the neat box of Lt. Petrava, and they were treating the captain like they would one of their sisters—a co-conspirator, not an authority figure.

The captain gave them a tight, bemused smile, and finally sat down. She touched her desk display, pulled up some holos—a near-system map, Rhys saw, which showed the Kidaa ship still moving away. And as they watched, the ship's blip disappeared. Gone back into Below Space.

Rhys breathed out a long, deeply grateful sigh.

"Sir," they said, aware that they were still overstepping bounds, but also aware that the situation was all weird all around, "they're talking to me. I don't know what they're saying or what it means, but I'll do my best to find out. But I think I need to be here. If they want to talk again."

Her brows went up. "You think they will?"

"I—don't know? But that music. Sir, that's the Rings of Vietor song that I identified yesterday as maybe having a part in the pattern of the attacks, and I guess I was right, oh Adeius I didn't truly expect to be right—" They ran their hands back across their hair, gripped briefly at the back, let go.

"That was what the request for music was about? I thought it was odd, but assumed it was important."

"It was. I don't know if any other songs fit the pattern—or should I even keep looking now?"

"I want your complete analysis of that conversation first. No, give me your first thoughts report first, then your complete analysis, as I assume that will take a few days at least. I want your first thoughts report within the hour—I'll send that in my dispatch to Valon."

Rhys shifted in their chair, feeling, again, the presence of the two chips Iata had given them in their jacket pocket. If ever there was a situation where it warranted actually using these chips, it was this one.

But the captain was already mistrustful of them. They couldn't risk sending a message with these chips and not telling her. Not now.

But...maybe they didn't have to show her both chips. It would be absolutely the wrong move to show her the Seritarchus's personal seal just now.

They reached into their pocket and pulled out the comm chip.

"Captain. The Seritarchus gave this to me, which will encode a message directly to him. If I find anything of note about the Kidaa in my research, I'm to report."

The captain was quiet a long moment. She surveyed the chip in Rhys's hand but didn't make any move to take it.

Finally, she nodded. Not quite acknowledging, not quite defeated.

Rhys quickly put the chip away again.

"Sir, I didn't have a choice. I didn't think the Seritarchus wanted it known, either—"

She held up a finger, and they stopped.

"This one's definitely going in the official comms," she

said, closing her hand again. "But if you want to send your private observations...that is acceptable."

It wasn't.

"Captain, this is about the Kidaa only. Not the ship, not the crew—"

"Not my competence as a border captain?"

Rhys met her eyes. "No, sir."

She sighed. "Lieutenant, you are entirely too composed around senior officers. If you are determined to carry out this charade that you are not, in fact, the most powerful person on this ship—"

They flushed hot, bile rising. "Captain, no—"

"Calm, Petrava. Yes, I get it. You are Lt. Petrava. But you are also the eyes and ears of the Seritarchus here. You are specifically requested by the Kidaa to speak, eschewing my own authority. What am I supposed to think? Do you have authority to give orders to me? Is that why you want the ship to stay? Was that an order, Petrava, not a suggestion?"

"No, Captain! No, it's just that the Seritarchus knows me. He trusts me, I think, and in the Seritarchus's world, you use every asset, that trust is so valuable—and I—" They shut their mouth, their eyes stinging. Adeius, how had this all gone sideways so quickly? They wished terribly that they knew how to smooth their tears away, like Dressa or Ari could. Instead, they were left with blinking hard and trying to pretend those tears didn't exist.

"Petrava," their captain said, and stopped, looking exasperated. Finally, she opened her hands. "You think we should stay, that the Kidaa might come back to talk to you again?"

"I—yes, sir. Maybe. If they wanted to talk to me specifically, I don't think it's a huge leap to think they might want to again. Especially if they were trying to get a specific message across, and we didn't get it. I mean, I didn't get it."

"Adeius," the captain said, and rubbed her hands

together, a wholly uncharacteristic nervous gesture. "Please don't tell me that the Kidaa approaching our ships these few lasts weeks was because they were looking for you?"

Rhys felt the blood drain from their face. Was that true? Were the Kidaa looking for someone, at least, who they'd identify as Truthspoken, even if they'd been wrong about Rhys? Were the Kidaa expecting Rhys to speak for all of Valoris?

"Well," the captain said. "Did you understand anything they were trying to say?"

"Um. Sir, I need to think about it. I need to look at my notes and the patterns."

The captain held up her hands. "So help me, Petrava—yes, we'll stay. You will include with your statement to the Seritarchus why you, specifically, thought that was a good idea, understood? I am breaking about a dozen protocols in keeping us here."

"But...do you agree, Captain?"

"I myself want solid answers, and for whatever reason, the Kidaa have singled out the *Storm* to give us...something. I want you to find what that something is, Petrava, and that is absolutely an order. And—do whatever you do to put that noble air aside again. Find a way to write off what happened as a mistake—the very last thing I need right now is a crew spooked about a Truthspoken among them, and I'm sure some of them will make that connection if I did and rumor will get around. It always does. Find a way to curb it. I'll speak to Commander Hamid and the senior staff—they will know what's going on. But to everyone else, you're Lt. Petrava."

Rhys swallowed. They didn't like more people knowing they weren't *just* Lt. Petrava, but they couldn't argue with her on that. She was right that her staff would need to know why the Kidaa might have singled them out.

"Yes, sir."

Had that been a dismissal? But she was still studying them, her eyes narrowed.

Under that sharp gaze, Rhys itched to fold themself back into the neat box that was Lt. Rhys Petrava, junior ops officer.

But the Kidaa *had* singled them out. Maybe wrongly, but they had. It was six days' travel to Valon, even by the fastest military speeds. Five days by comm, another five back.

Rhys did, in fact, have the Seritarchus's personal seal in their jacket pocket, though they hadn't used it. Not yet.

And those thoughts were so far beyond dangerous it took their breath away. They were supposed to report, not act. They weren't qualified for this, they had no authority to make any kind of decisions here, even if the Kidaa seemed to think they did.

"Petrava. Why are you here? Why, with all of your lofty connections, are you here on my ship? At the border, far from anything relevant to the Rhialden Court?"

Rhys bridled at the repeated accusations they heard under that question: were you sent here for me? Were you sent here to spy on us? Are you, in fact, as powerless as you're trying to tell me you are?

She didn't believe them when they said that they weren't. She hadn't believed any of their denials earlier.

And with the Kidaa looking at Rhys, speaking to them instead of her...could they blame her? And with the seal in their pocket, with their connections, and their own training-by-proxy, was she that wrong?

Was the captain right that the *Storm* should pack up and head for the capital as quickly as possible?

But that wasn't what Rhys's instincts were saying. That wasn't what their pattern-sense was saying.

A lot could happen in ten days.

"Captain," Rhys said slowly, "I'm just trying to make a career in the Navy. Something that is my own." They swallowed, this very personal admission being pulled from them. "I do have a place in the palace. I know that. But it's not *mine*. Sir. And also, I like patterns. The whole thing with researching the Kidaa was an accident. I didn't set out to be anything here other than..."

They couldn't say themself. Not still under her intense stare. She knew that who they were here wasn't the whole of themself, not by far.

So they shrugged.

"Well," the captain said, and sat back. Waved at them. "Go. Get me that report. And, Petrava—please by all the holy stars, do not involve my ship in capital court politics more than you already have."

Rhys bridled. They hadn't done anything to involve the ship in politics, and were about to say so, when they saw the trap in that accusation and shut their mouth. They had that seal in their pocket. And they weren't supposed to be a noble here. They couldn't get it all out of their mannerisms, no, not in the long term, but they didn't have to rub it in.

"Yes, sir," they said quietly. They took a breath, and forcefully rearranged their thoughts back into those of Lt. Petrava, junior ops lieutenant, who'd just had a *very* weird and terrifying experience but was going to go write the report the captain needed.

The captain watched them, maybe noted the shifts in their posture, their demeanor, but she didn't say anything. Just waved them toward the hatch. And, gratefully, they slipped out.

33

THE KNOCK

Sometimes we are at war with ourselves. And that is no different with Truthspoken than it is with any other person.

— ARIANNA RHIALDEN, MELESORIE X IN *THE CHANGE DIALOGUES*

Ari jerked awake, her hand still holding Eti's. His face was inches from hers, his eyes closed, the tightness around his eyes relaxed.

His eyelids fluttered, and he let out a soft groan before pulling back.

A knock came on the bedroom door—it must have been the second time.

She was in Rhys's room. The dimmed lights around the ceiling trim showed the band posters, the fashion posters, and a few framed accolades from the Academy. No one should have been able to pass through the prep room door except Iata or her father—well, or anyone who could Change.

Or, apparently, Captain Zhang, who nudged the bedroom door open.

Zhang stopped, her gaze moving between them both, assessing. But Zhang herself was asexual. And if Ari still didn't exactly know where she herself fell on that spectrum, her father—and she had to guess Zhang by extension—knew that she hadn't wanted to marry. That she'd never shown that kind of interest in anyone. She still didn't feel it now.

Eti sat up straight, hair mussed and eyes panicked, as if just now realizing what this might look like.

"Nothing happened," he said.

Zhang's lips twitched up. "Be at peace, Magicker Tanaka. You're not on trial, and I believe you."

Eti shuddered, and Ari—

No. No, she had decided to embrace her name as Imorie. She remembered that now.

She was about to get off the bed, but she paused. Did her decision of last night still fit?

Imorie felt better, felt more her right now than Ari. There was a taste of...*something* there, something more open and freeing and wild.

Hmm.

Imorie pushed back the covers and stood. She wore Rhys's ill-fitting band shirt and older pants, which Zhang very politely didn't blink at.

"Your father would like to see you," Zhang said.

Which one, Imorie wondered?

"Have you eaten? Do you need any medication before we go? I'm sorry, we should have asked that before. We don't have any records of your treatment."

And it wouldn't look good at all, would draw far, far too much attention, if the palace on Valon sent any formal request to Windvale for records.

Imorie touched the med patches still on her arm, still

under her shirt. She was sure they had no medicine left in them. She thought about pulling them off and giving them to Zhang, but that—that was a mixing of worlds, of Windvale and Palace Rhialden. That was an intrusion she couldn't handle just now, not when she had to mentally prepare herself to see her father. One of them. And she wasn't sure how to handle Homaj or Iata just now. Wasn't sure at all where she stood anywhere in this environment, which should have been her home.

She drew a long breath, carefully not steadying herself in Arianna's mask of calm. She was Imorie, and Imorie damn well had a right to be scared about a meeting with the Seritarchus.

Imorie reached for her comm where she usually left it on the bedside table, but it wasn't there. She felt it in her pocket instead.

It was evening. She'd slept most of the day. Adeius, what had happened in that time? Her thoughts branched off into a dozen horrible paths.

Zhang pulled a comm from her uniform jacket pocket, holding it out to Eti. It was a model Imorie recognized from palace stores. "This is yours, Magicker Tanaka. It's already keyed to your biometrics and your palace account."

He leaned forward as she approached the bed, took it warily. "Does the Seritarchus want to see me?"

"No, only Imorie."

Eti hunched, and a slice of anxiety wormed through Imorie's chest. Could he be alone right now?

"Magicker Azer has food," Zhang said. "Let's go out to the prep room—Imorie, I can help you dress if you wish."

She needed a shower, but didn't have the energy for that. She did need better clothes.

Zhang headed back for the door. "I've brought clothing for you both—Doryan's moved the rack into the closet. Staff will augment the wardrobe in the next few days, but this should be enough for now. Do you need help with dressing?"

Imorie's irritation spiked, but the repeat of the question hadn't been unwarranted. And in her wobbly state, she might need help.

But her joints loosened as she walked into the prep room. Doryan wasn't there, but the prep room door was propped open—Doryan came back in with a tray of food, setting it on the low table in front of the couch. The food, whatever it was, smelled hearty but bland. Thank Adeius they'd remembered that she couldn't stomach much more right now. Was it the stress, or was it the Bruising Sleep? If she hadn't had medication the last few days, if it had all worn out, was she regressing?

Still, if the patches had anything left to give, even the tiniest traces of help, she hadn't wanted to take them off. No matter knowing who'd put them there.

Zhang followed her into the closet and hovered while she tugged out of her temporary bedclothes. Zhang handed her a pair of black silk trousers, an indigo shirt, and a deep violet jacket with a loosely ruffled collar. They were clothes she might have chosen for herself as Imorie—and which eye had picked these out, her father's, Iata's, or Dressa's?

She swallowed and checked herself in the mirror—her cosmetics were worn, though they hadn't streaked. Much.

"I can't help with that," Zhang said, waving at her face. "I never did get the hang of it." And Zhang would have had enough practice, going with her father on many Truthspoken missions.

Imorie might have had the skill, but she didn't have the strength. If she was only going to her father's study, this would have to do.

Zhang offered an arm for support, and Imorie took it, leaning on her more than she'd like.

Eti had come out and was filling a plate with rolls and what looked like a bean pastry.

Imorie hesitated.

"I have orders not to bring you back to the Seritarchus before you're ready," Zhang said. "And I also haven't had dinner." She smiled. "Eat up."

Zhang let go of Imorie to carry over one of the vanity chairs. Sitting down, she grabbed a plate for herself.

Zhang had always been a part of her life. Like Iata, or Jalava, or Ceorre. Just always there, always a constant. And what would Ceorre think of all of this, too, of Imorie's new vivid green aura? Of her new name, her new position within the family? Ceorre certainly would know Iata was her father's actual brother, of that she was sure. And that Iata also sometimes took the place of her father. And that Iata had just adopted one Imorie Rhialden méron Quevedo.

And what would Ceorre, the Truthspeaker of the Adeium, think of her heretical magics and the seal on her cheek?

Did Ceorre know about Iata's magic? Could Iata possibly hide such a thing from her—but she'd have to know. The First Magicker knew it, Homaj knew it, Zhang knew it. Dressa did, too, and now Imorie and Eti. Who else knew about a secret as explosive as that?

She touched the rings in her brow. A nervous gesture she was acquiring, and she didn't like it.

How could she ever reclaim her life with these people after what had happened? After becoming a magicker. It wouldn't ever be the same. Even if she completely healed from the Bruising Sleep, even if she could Change again, even if she learned how to conceal her aura, and if she got the First Magicker to remove her permanent seal in favor of a removable one.

These people would all still know who she was and what she was. She would still have vulnerabilities that were so wide. She might be able to Change again someday, but she'd always, always be a magicker. That would never go away.

And it hadn't sunk in yet, not fully. She knew that. She knew she'd have an internal storm to come, and she was holding that off as long as she could.

How was Iata managing? And how long had he had to manage as an unsealed magicker? His magics were certainly not new. Did she want to spend all of her life terrified that someone might touch her and accidentally pick up on her emotions?

Imorie met Eti's eyes as she carefully ate one of the rolls, still warm from the oven, or kitchen, or wherever it had come from. She hardly knew him. She'd slept inches from him.

He looked away, but she was understanding that now. She herself had needed to train hard to maintain eye contact when she was younger. It was something not all Truthspoken took to naturally.

The thought of going to see the Seritarchus without Eti with her made her insides feel cold.

Why? How had she gotten so thoroughly attached in such a short time? Was it attachment from trauma? They had been through hell together. But he'd been trying to protect her from the start. She'd thought it was a crush on his part, but she didn't think so now.

Eti was a decent person, and she'd met so very few of those. A decent person caught up in horrible things he couldn't control. He'd used what little control he had to protect her. And she was doing what she could now to protect him. Though she was doing a much poorer job of it than he was.

He looked up again, offered a small smile. Still trying to be strong, for her.

Imorie forced down a second roll, then stood. "I'm ready. And Eti's coming with me."

34

SHIERA KERALAN

> *We rule kingdoms. We make decisions for billions and trillions of people. And yet choice in our own lives is an option we don't often have.*

— HOMAJ RHIALDEN, SERITARCHUS IX IN A PRIVATE LETTER, NEVER SENT; PUBLISHED IN *THE CHANGE DIALOGUES*

Imorie drifted hand in hand with Eti, following Zhang through the Seritarchus's apartment. As a contract cousin—distant cousin—to the royal Rhialden line, it was just possible she had been here before, been to his study. Once, she decided, at the same time Imorie would have first met Dressa. It had been enough to leave an impression.

The rooms were all dimmed for the evening, showing only hints of the opulent accents on chairs and shelves and wall frames. The air smelled faintly of cleaner—the staff had been through it today. Tabletops and floors shined.

She passed familiar guards, who surveyed her and Eti with professional blandness—but she was with Zhang, their captain. Zhang wouldn't let anyone through who was a threat to the Seritarchus.

Zhang knocked on the door to the Seritarchus's study. She reached up in a lapse of her usual decorum to squeeze Imorie's shoulder, and then pushed inside.

The last time Imorie had been in this room—well. She had been a different person. She had been a person who'd been barely keeping herself awake on that couch, a person whose father had sent her away.

Homaj hadn't made any indication that he would do that this time. He'd said she *should* stay in the palace.

Because she was a different person? And what if she had come back as Arianna? What if there weren't these layers of distance between them, through identity, through a different name and an adoption?

She felt warmth from Eti. Through the haze that still sludged his emotions, a strong and steady warmth.

He was terrified, and he still sent her warmth.

She squeezed his hand, and together they stepped inside the study.

Zhang didn't announce them as she might have any other visitors. She simply nodded to both the occupants of the room and backed out again, shutting the door behind her.

Imorie's attention caught first on the person who was visibly Homaj Rhialden. His hair was tied up in an ornate knot and secured with a tapering row of razor-edged spikes. An aggressive style, that. His cosmetics were more femme than the neutral he'd worn that morning, lips a dark plum. One of his favorite shades when he was in a mood. He wore flowing royal blue trousers, a frilly cream vest over a shirt printed with soft pastel waves. His bearing, his posture, everything about him said Homaj Rhialden. When the conversation started, she knew she'd even see Homaj's tells. She'd seen him do it before.

But he wasn't Homaj.

She turned to the second person, a middle-aged woman with wavy blonde hair tied up well but not expertly, heart-shaped face pretty but not beautiful, posture straight but not elegant. An ordinary person in this exalted realm of the extraordinary that was the Rhialden Court.

This woman wasn't a member of the court, though, but a part of the Seritarchus's administrative staff. Shiera Keralan was also one of Homaj's preferred personas when her gender occasionally slipped fully female.

Shiera gave an ironic smile and made a gesture with one hand, a two-fingered swoop. Pronoun gestures weren't common these days, more something used on special occasions or in historical vid dramas—people usually just stated their pronouns or wore obvious gender cues of some sort. The gesture, though, confirmed she/her pronouns. And when she was Shiera, she preferred to be called Shiera.

Imorie nodded, turned back to...well.

The man who was, actually and legally, her father. Her adoptive father. Who she was certain was, not just in persona but in fact, ruling the kingdom just now.

They were both watching her, seeing what she would do. She read that tension humming between them, recognized it with a lurch as the sort of thing siblings would do when their long-running prank was about to be found out. She'd seen those same looks on Rhys and Dressa before.

Adeius, did they seriously think she hadn't known about them switching places?

"Did you tell Dressa about this?" she asked. "Because she'll definitely need to know."

Iata shared a look with Shiera, like they'd been doing earlier at Green Hall.

"I asked for you to come alone," Iata said, and sighed, waving at the couch. "Though, yes, if Imorie has chosen to bring you, you are welcome, Eti. I don't believe I can have many secrets from you."

Eti shifted closer to Imorie, glancing over at her.

She leaned close to him. "He's fine. If you read him, he's read you, right? He knows your own truth as well as you know his." Hadn't he been the one telling her Iata was good at Green Hall?

And then she had to lean on him as a wave of dizziness hit her. Whatever had been holding her together earlier had gone now. Could she possibly ask Iata for something else to pull strength from?

He was frowning at her now, moving toward the couch and cluster of chairs in the center of the room.

"Sit. Everyone sit, please."

Imorie didn't miss how Iata took the chair Homaj usually sat in, and Shiera seemed absolutely content to claim one of the other chairs. A lesser place here.

Her stomach tightened.

Imorie settled with Eti in the center of the couch. Both of them close, both of them also tense.

"Are you well?" Shiera asked, and more than a little of her own personality bled through her less polished presence. That was...alarming. Her mother almost never broke character when she was in another persona.

Imorie reached, almost unconsciously, for Shiera before she realized what she was doing. But Shiera took her hand, and Imorie felt the roil of her emotions. Hesitation, fear, guilt, that tang of self-loathing she'd felt that morning.

Imorie quickly let go.

Iata rolled his shoulders, his own mannerisms bleeding through. Which was also more than a little disconcerting. She wasn't used to him looking like Homaj but not actively *being* Homaj.

"You aren't surprised about us," he said. "So I can only assume that you've known. How long?"

Imorie sat back, panting. "Do you have something metal—"

His face hardened. "No. No more metal, especially when you're so new to your magics. Pulling too much strength from anything, especially eons-old minerals, can set you back far."

Her lips drew tight. "I need something. I have no strength for this conversation."

Iata and Shiera exchanged another look. And she was thoroughly sick of that.

"Then we'll keep this short," Iata said.

"And can you teach me..." she paused for breath "...to hide my aura?" She nodded at him and his aura-less state.

His gaze flicked to her seal, then to Eti, and lingered. "Later, perhaps. It's not a comfortable skill."

Eti shifted, his anxiety spiking.

Iata's aura flared out around him now, and his face held a naked relief that she was sure he wanted her to see.

"I want you to settle into your magics first. It takes time to acclimate, and you can't hide your aura at court just now anyway. If you still intend to be visible at court."

"I do." And because she knew he was still waiting on her answer to his question, and knew him well enough to know he wouldn't let it go, she waved between Iata and Shiera and said, "I think I was seven when I figured it out."

35

MISTRUST

The First Magicker isn't necessarily the highest-ranking magicker, but they will certainly be close.

— DR. LORD PIXI VIYALOROKKA IN "THE
SOCIAL STRUCTURE OF GREEN MAGICKERS"

Shiera barked a laugh, covered her mouth, but her eyes were sharp and bright. "We thought we were so good, didn't we, Yan? She was *seven.*"

Iata shrugged, looking annoyed. At Shiera, more likely, than Imorie. "You trained her well." His eyes speared Eti. "You are a man of discretion, Eti Tanaka. I am placing my trust in that. You do have my trust."

Eti nodded, daring to look up, meeting Iata's eyes if only for a moment. "Yes, Seritarchus."

Then Eti had remembered what she'd said earlier, that Iata was actually ruling the kingdom. Adeius, good. She was fairly sure he was following all of this.

"Imorie," Iata said, "I'm assuming you also know about my lineage? That was one of the other things we needed to discuss tonight." He was casual about it, but he watched her closely on that one. And she knew he'd marked her double angle in asking him to adopt her.

"Yes," she said slowly. "Bettea told me."

Iata's face blanked at the mention of Bettea, and her chest tightened.

"Are you going to—"

"I've already sent word to our people on Hestia to look out for Jis Ameer. And Shiera is going, too, once we're done here tonight." He turned to Eti. "I've sent word to our people on Kalistré as well, that's already in motion."

Eti nodded, his voice tight. "Thank you."

"You're going?" Imorie asked Shiera. That...that she hadn't expected. And she wasn't sure she wanted Shiera gone just now. For all that she'd feared seeing her again on the way into Valon. The memory of that first embrace at Green Hall made her throat ache.

Her heart lurched into a pound, her forehead breaking out in sweat.

Shiera shifted forward. "My choice. I—Imorie, Iata will be the Seritarchus for a time."

There was a lie there, she felt it ringing hot and clear. She felt Eti's unease as well.

Shiera huffed a curse, looked to Iata. And she knew she shouldn't have brought Eti. There was more they both needed to say, and despite the trust they'd put in Eti so far, because they'd mostly had to, there was no way Imorie could expect them to trust him fully. She wasn't even sure she did herself. Though she still couldn't let go of his hand.

"I'm abdicating," Shiera said, and that also didn't ring true. "I—have abdicated. Iata will, eventually, make a bid to rule as himself. After Dressa's wedding. Ari—"

"Imorie," she said, and Shiera closed her eyes.

Adeius, she hadn't meant that to wound.

Eti started to tug his hand from hers. "I'll go," he mumbled.

"No," she said, gripping his hand tight.

"Imorie, it's self-preservation," Iata said. "He's already too involved. And I'm truly sorry for that, Eti. Though I am not sorry at all that you're no longer under Javieri duress."

There was an edge to his voice that made Imorie pause. She looked between him and Shiera. Shiera eyed Iata as well.

Eti was drawing in on himself again, hunching inward. Should she have not let him come? But she felt with everything in her that he needed her right now. That she needed him.

Iata grimaced. "We will sort this later. Eti, you do have my trust. May I also have your word that you will not share what you know about me, and about Shiera," he waved at Shiera beside him, "with anyone other than ourselves or Imorie, or anyone else Imorie says is safe?"

Eti swallowed. "Yes. You have my word." And despite his earlier protest, his grip tightened on Imorie's, and he moved even closer, their shoulders pressed together. He needed to be near her. She was steadying him, as he was steadying her.

Iata nodded, and though he didn't quite relax, he made an effort to be less visibly strained. All of it, she was sure, still a part of his performance. She sensed the fear underneath, the uncertainty. With his aura flaring strong and a deep green, she could almost feel his emotions from where she sat, not just read them from his body cues, the edges of his own tells —which were still mostly Homaj's.

"What rank are you?" she asked.

A bit more of his tension returned. "High sixth. Maybe. I haven't been tested again since I manifested, which was nine years ago."

He'd been hiding this for nine years? And she hadn't at all seen any signs of that.

He was a high rank, too? As were Eti and her? Wasn't high rank supposed to be rare? And yes, she knew that magicker strength and equivalent rank often increased as much as a full rank or two over time. Was he possibly as strong as the First Magicker? Could she tell from just looking at his aura?

But the green of his aura hazed in her eyes. She desperately needed something metal to draw strength from, and she didn't want to pull from the frame of the couch she was sitting on. Her breaths were coming faster, harder than they should. And she would not pull any more strength from Eti, though she felt him offering again.

It was Iata who leaned forward and held out his hands. "I can lend you some strength, only a little, enough to get you into the city."

"The city?" she asked. She had no energy left for travel. She needed to lie down. Her whole body was numb with the need to sleep again.

"For treatment," Shiera said. "The palace physicians are good, but they don't have specialty in the Bruising Sleep."

Imorie went rigid. "You're taking me to one of the hospitals—to one of the permanent homes for—"

Shiera shook her head emphatically, her thin silver earrings jangling. "Not to stay. Only for treatment. I know one of the doctors, I've spoken to him before, and he is discreet. We'll visit him at his house."

She'd spoken to him as Shiera? Or as Homaj Rhialden? Or someone else?

Shiera had said she'd abdicated, but Imorie didn't know why. And she wasn't sure she had the energy to find out just now. She needed more of whatever Dr. Lin had given her, and she needed it badly.

How could she trust—but she needed to trust. And Eti would come with her. She knew in her soul that he would not let anyone stash her away again. He just wouldn't. And she could turn invisible if she needed to. If she absolutely had to.

"Yes," she said. "Yes, we'll go into the city."

She'd manage, somehow, to ride one of the electric bikes through the underground tunnels. And she'd manage, somehow, to walk down to the garage with the bikes. She'd come to the apartment here with only a little of Eti's help.

But what little energy she'd had on waking was gone now.

Shiera got up, moved to the fireplace side of the room to a tall cabinet and pulled out...a folded up hover chair.

Which had absolutely been stored there so she wouldn't see it until now. Shiera knew her with a clarity that left her far too exposed.

But she nodded when she saw it. She wasn't Truthspoken anymore. Not now. Did it matter if she showed weakness?

And it would get her to the treatment she needed to get on with her life. To one day, oh Adeius one day, take it back again.

There had to be some strength in that.

Shiera paused on unfolding the chair, which hovered at knee-height. She looked up, chagrined.

"Your choice. We don't have to go into the city. We can see the palace physicians. They are also discreet."

Imorie swallowed. And what did Iata want her to do? What claim would he lay over her life, like the Seritarchus always had? He was her adopted father now. And if Shiera had abdicated...she didn't know how permanent that adoption would be.

"This is your life," Iata said firmly, echoing Shiera's position. "You choose your treatment."

His words rang with his own truth. He did believe them.

But did he know if Shiera was planning to shove her aside? Would he want Shiera to? Imorie could become his heir, and he might not want that at all. He'd already said as much at Green Hall—Dressa was his heir. Dressa was still the Heir, and Imorie complicated that clarity.

His brows drew down. "Imorie. You have my word—you are free to come and go, to have whatever treatment by whatever physicians you wish. This is still your home, and it will not stop being your home. I have absolutely no wish to see you harmed. None of us do."

True. True. All true.

And could she possibly have thought otherwise?

She blinked hard, looked away, nodded.

She noticed that Iata was very carefully not sharing looks with Shiera now.

Shiera's gaze was tight, to the side. She knew what part she'd already played in Imorie's mistrust.

Iata stood, smoothed out his shirt, and with the gesture was fully back to being Homaj again. "I do have more work tonight. Imorie—if you decide not to go into the city, I'll make sure the most qualified physician sees you in your apartment within the hour."

Shiera, taking her cue, was now also firmly back to being a member of the palace administrative staff. She bowed in agreement to this statement.

Imorie looked between them, straining for every clue to motive, to mood, to safety or danger.

But she was exhausted. And she hadn't been willing to trust the palace physicians with her illness before. They were absolutely discreet. And also, they always knew too much.

She stood, with Eti's help, and moved with care toward the hover chair.

36

THE TUNNELS

Everyone knows Truthspoken have their own paths about the palace and the city. These paths are our safety. Even in our various roles, an often-used public point of entry would overexpose our patterns. We need these paths even now. Maybe especially now.

— ARIANNA RHIALDEN, MELESORIE X IN *THE CHANGE DIALOGUES*

The walk—or float, for Imorie—through the back corridors was nearly silent. She'd warned Eti against speaking in the back corridors, so he quietly walked beside her, or behind, when the corridors became too narrow for both him and the hover chair.

Eti's steps barely made a sound. And she knew, she just knew that with everything in his life, with his personality, with what had happened with his family, that he'd learned how to be silent, to be unobtrusive. It wasn't the same as being Truthspoken, not by a lightyear, but Eti also knew how to play a role.

She watched Shiera walk ahead, a different walk than she used as Homaj, but then, her mother had many, many different walks.

Her mother. No, Shiera was no longer her mother. Not legally her parent, and Imorie was less certain through these dim corridors if that had been the best idea. She desperately wanted to sort through every implication of Shiera abdicating, too, but her mind was too tired, and thoughts strayed.

They wove through the tight spaces and random up and down stairs that ran between the two levels of the royal residence, then down through the hidden places of the rest of the palace. Down into the basement, then sub-basements. Her hover chair was compact and had the give to squeeze through tight corners when necessary. Shiera had thought of that.

And Shiera, apparently, had come down beforehand to the small sub-basement garage used only by Truthspoken and bloodservants and set out a bike with a sidecar. As if the chair wasn't embarrassing enough.

But she was panting even from the exertion of working the controls—and her nerves—on the way down.

"Forgive me, Eti," Shiera said, "I didn't plan for a third." She waved at the other bikes in their racks. "Choose one. I'll key it on for you."

Imorie had the fleeting thought, as Shiera helped her up, that if Iata was currently functioning as Homaj, who was maintaining the bikes here? Or the corridors themselves? That was typically a duty shared among bloodservants, and there were two less of those at the palace just now. Unless, Adeius, Shiera had taken over Iata's bloodservant duties?

She looked up as Shiera helped her settle into the sidecar.

It wasn't totally safe to talk here. It was never totally safe to talk anywhere, but Imorie didn't have a dampener on her, and only a very, very few had access to this garage.

She said in a low voice, "Are you doing what you're doing because of—"

She swallowed hard, her body betraying her fear of the answer.

Because of her. Had Shiera abdicated her rulership because her daughter had failed her?

Shiera's grip, supporting her arm, tightened. "No. This is my own decision. It has been...a long time coming." She attempted a smile that didn't do any of the things a smile should do. She was still, in every outward way, Shiera Keralan. But Imorie saw through, saw more glimpses of the person she'd been seeing since landing on Valon earlier that day. A person who was not in control. Who was weary. Who was...not angry with her.

She gathered what strength she had left.

"Why?" she hissed. "Why did you replace me with—"

Shiera's smile became a jagged twist. "That was Dressa's solution to my error."

Eti wheeled over a bike. "Will this one work?"

His voice was small, and he knew who he was talking to. He might not know all the nuances of everything going on, but he knew enough.

"Yes, that's fine. Here."

Shiera pressed a thumb to the bike's control pad—she would have Changed the DNA in her thumb to something the bike would recognize and accept—or, she might have keyed her persona's use of the bikes and back corridors into the palace systems years ago.

Imorie watched the simple act with a jealousy she did not expect. She could no longer Change even in that way. She didn't have access to the back corridors or any of the locks that would have admitted her before.

But then, if Shiera was abdicating—had abdicated, though Imorie thought that wasn't quite the whole of it—

Change would be a thing forbidden to her as well, once that abdication was public.

There were no Truthspoken in this room.

Imorie wanted to press the issue of abdication, to find out if it really had been Shiera's choice, or if Iata had somehow pressed her into it, or—something. She was still having a hard time reconciling this person she saw today with the person she knew, the Seritarchus who ruled with rigid and absolute control.

Or, absolute illusion of control.

The bikes zipped through the tunnel, under the river and into the city. The sounds of the tires on pavement was a soft, steady drone, the air stuffy, slightly damp. Imorie rested in the sidecar, fighting to keep steady breaths.

Shiera had abdicated. So was she planning to go into exile? Would Imorie be losing the only parent who'd ever cared about her future? Or—Adeius, that moment when she'd corrected her name earlier. She'd watched that hit Shiera like a shot to the gut. Had she already lost the only parent who'd cared about her, had she ever had Shiera's regard at all if she'd been sent away?

The bike slowed, and she looked up.

"You're flickering," Shiera said, her voice tight.

Was she flickering? Had she spiraled that far?

She tried to sit up straighter, but her legs were cramped in the tight space.

Eti, who'd overshot them, slowed until he was back alongside them.

"Uh, ser, can I—" He waved at the bike Shiera was riding.

Imorie got what he was trying to ask. And silently thanked the gall it took him to ask.

"Can he take me? And you take his bike?"

Shiera came to a full stop and looked between them, then silently got off her bike, pressing the controls. The bike gave a soft chirp, and she let go, reaching as Eti got off his own bike.

They switched without another word. And Imorie seethed at just how intense a relief it was to have Eti beside her, not Shiera.

It took her the rest of a ride to work out that Eti was, at the moment, less of a stranger to her than her own parent.

37

HIDING

> *Decreed this day of Cosonay the Fourteenth, in the rule of the Third Melesorie of the Eleventh Dynasty, 2731 New Era, that Lord Emira Seyat is accused of the crime of blasphemy in attempting to become a Truthspoken. Lord Seyat is sentenced to execution, to be carried out humanely. So be it under the breath and will of Adeius.*

— OFFICIAL ANNOUNCEMENT FROM PALACE
RHIALDEN

Lesander was sure Dressa knew something. It hadn't been a feeling Lesander could pin down at first, but it was in the things that weren't there—the lack of warmth behind a passionate kiss, the lingering gaze that held depth and not just smolder. Or the things there were too much of—Dressa chattering far past when she usually would have finished dressing for the night's social gatherings.

And there would be social gatherings, even on as tense a

day as today. They would have to go out and reassure the court, the people, that all was well.

Each greeting would be another twist in the knot that was Lesander's stomach. Who among those she met might be her contact? Who might pass her a message, who might tell her it was time to act, that she would have her family's support?

Though she was still growing the horrific premise that this was solely her job now, hers alone, to act on behalf of her family.

She'd heard no word from anyone.

Dressa was wary, and Dressa shouldn't have to be wary. None of this should be happening, and everything was wrong.

"What's wrong?" Dressa asked, looking up as she applied a different color lipstick for the third time.

Lesander, who was already dressed and staring at the wall over Dressa's vanity mirror, released her hands from the back of Dressa's chair.

She was too visibly stressed, but she couldn't help it.

And Adeius, she couldn't stand this anymore.

"Everything." The truth.

She watched Dressa swallow. Heard it, even, and she didn't think Dressa had meant for her to hear it.

Lesander hated that it had come to this, both of them analyzing the other, both of them watching for signals and clues and...

"I'm Truthspoken trained," Lesander blurted. The words came out strangled, too tight, and her hands tightened again on the back of Dressa's chair as she watched her wife's face in the vanity mirror.

They weren't publicly married. An annulment might still be possible, or some quiet arrangement.

It might be the best option she could reach for, though the thought of it was wrenching her apart.

Dressa inhaled, held it, nodded. Lesander waited for her breath to come back out in an explosion, which Dressa did sometimes when she was trying to clear her thoughts, but Dressa instead held herself contained.

Dressa stood. She turned to Lesander and wrapped her in a tight embrace, which...was not at all what Lesander had expected.

"Thank you," Dressa said into Lesander's shoulder, and shuddered. "Thank you for telling me."

Now it was Lesander's turn to swallow. So Dressa had known.

How long had Dressa known? Had she known before she'd asked Lesander to marry her?

And did Iata the bloodservant know, who'd glared at her so fiercely earlier? Did the Seritarchus?

What were the parameters of her world here? What were the dangers?

Dressa pulled back from the hug, braced both of Lesander's arms, and looked fiercely into her eyes. It was a gaze Lesander almost couldn't meet.

She'd confessed only the smallest of her sins, hadn't she? Or at least, the smallest she'd been meant to carry out.

She opened her mouth to say more, to find some sort of ally, some safe shoreline as she waited, waited for the storm.

But she pressed her mouth tight again, smiling, her eyes shining with very real tears.

She hugged Dressa back. "I love you."

It was true. She hated so much that it was true, because love was weakness. She'd been taught many things, among them never, ever to let herself love, not even if it served her own purpose. Love made her immobile. Love realigned her loyalties.

Her mothers had never truly loved each other, and they'd never intended to. And she was certain her mother the prince didn't love Lesander, either. Prince Yroikan was hardly capable of it. Love did not serve her purposes at all.

Dressa nodded into her shoulder. "Yeah. Me too. You, I mean. I love you too." She looked up, but not quite at Lesander. "We're late—my fault, I know—but everything's a mess right now. We have to go down there and show our smiles. Be the Heir and the Heir Consort. We'll talk after, okay? We'll talk as long as we need to. Will you be okay until then?"

Dressa was asking if *she* would be okay? Dressa had seen her distress, then. Of course Dressa had seen her distress. Dressa was the only real Truthspoken in this room, and Lesander felt like a barely functional imitation.

Yes, Lesander could just tell her. Tell the Seritarchus. Tell them both they were in danger from her. From her family, more specifically, but also—from her.

She could tell Dressa and betray her own family and the entire purpose of her existence. She could throw away a lifetime of training, of hiding, of fear, of hope. She could give up every hope of her family ever gaining control of the kingdom.

Because they had to. The Rhialdens had no idea what was coming. Her mother had never given her specifics, because Truthspoken rulers could pry out specifics, and Lesander was to be sent into their midst. But there was something big looming, something that had even her mother scared. Yes, her mother wanted power. But also, her mother *needed* power.

And maybe Ari's becoming a magicker wasn't the trigger for the signal after all. Maybe it was the Kidaa attacks—if her parents weren't behind them—and maybe it was something else, something to do with the magickers, or the Onabrii-Kast Dynasty, or the Adeium, or...something else. She didn't know.

And should her parents have sent her to Valon, as they had, without the information she'd need to know how to act, and not just rotely obey?

She'd been trained to be a ruler. She needed information to make decisions.

Lesander relaxed and smiled. "I'll be fine."

Dressa's smile back had a knowing edge, not believing Lesander's forced levity. It wasn't the sort of smile that Dressa the socialite would give to those around her. It was a private smile, a glimpse into Dressa's true personality. Which, Lesander was coming to see, wasn't as close to her public persona as Dressa wanted everyone to believe.

Dressa was a flower. Dressa's petals had blades.

And it was screwing her up in so many ways that she found that so deeply attractive.

"Yes, you'll be fine," Dressa said. "And meanwhile, you'll be dying inside, I know. Come on. We'll get it over with, and then we can talk."

"I really am fine," Lesander insisted as Dressa capped her lipstick and hustled her to the door. "I'm surprised *you're* fine."

"Oh, I'm not fine." Dressa's smile now was far too cheerful, showing too many teeth. Out of tone even for the gatherings they'd be at tonight.

Lesander touched her arm. "Are we okay?"

She shouldn't have asked. But she held her breath, waiting for the answer.

"Yes." Dressa met her eyes. Hiding nothing.

And Lesander should have told her then.

But she didn't.

38

THE PHYSICIAN

> *The Bruising Sleep is a disease associated with poverty and so not something the nobility chooses to talk about. Those who contract it often can't afford the treatments available, which are expensive, or at least can't afford treatment and also afford to house and feed themselves. So we end up with state-run treatment homes overflowing with patients who must depend on what the state gives them, which is barely enough to put the disease into remission, and so they must stay. It is an appalling situation, and not one we can ignore because it's inconvenient. These people did nothing but contract an illness we've failed to understand.*

— A. MADRIC, FROM *THE COLLECTED SPEECHES OF THE GENERAL ASSEMBLY, FOURTH EDITION*

Normally, when taking the tunnels that ran from the palace under the city, they would park the bikes in one of the many small underground garages. They'd walk the rest of the way to the surface, coming out in one of a hundred or so pre-arranged places that would avoid suspicion. But Shiera, riding ahead of Eti and Imorie, chose one of the few routes that led to a ramp that would let them ride the bikes out into the city itself.

Imorie knew where they were and what was nearby. She knew the locations of the hospitals that treated the Bruising Sleep, and the housing facilities that long-term patients seldom left. She'd visited a few of these facilities, showing the Seritarchracy's visible support.

But Iata had promised her she would not come to harm. Whatever that meant in this context. She still had Eti.

Shiera sped them up a long ramp and slowed near the top. They entered a tunnel that ran parallel to a street in Blue District. Shiera glanced back as Eti also slowed his bike.

"It's not far from here. Around a kilometer to the south. Residential area."

Shiera had said they'd be going to the private home of one of the physicians, but Imorie was still braced for it to be otherwise.

Shiera gave her a raw look, and she knew Shiera had marked those small signs of her tension.

But Shiera said nothing as they approached a wide metal door at the end of the tunnel. She got off her bike to place her hand on the door's scanpad, and the door groaned and slid upward.

They were in an industrial neighborhood, the door part of what looked from the outside like a loading bay. The building would have just enough planned activity over the year not to be suspicious.

Shiera waited while Eti passed her, then closed the door again on the other side.

They rode into the sparsely lit streets.

The night air was unusually chill for this time of year, a fine mist of not-quite-rain in the air. Not at all like Hestia's over-saturated humidity, its fragrant tang. Here, the air hung metallic, the background noise of engines and people and businesses humming around her.

How could she possibly be missing Hestia just now? This was her home. This was a city she knew like no other.

It wasn't long before they entered a residential neighborhood, then Shiera slowed and pulled into a walkway leading up to a two-story tan brick house.

They stopped and dismounted, Shiera locking the bikes to a fence post. Imorie held onto Eti as Shiera unpacked and unfolded the hover chair again, and she tried not to let needing it make her stomach tighten.

And she tried not to be afraid, too, at the look of a neighbor through a front window. She had an aura now. She wasn't just anyone visiting, she couldn't be just anyone now.

Eti's aura wasn't as visible as it could be, and she felt his own wariness as he looked around them. He wasn't used to being in the open as a sealed magicker, either. But even if he did know how to hide his aura, and maybe she'd be able to pry that secret out of him in the next few days, there was the seal on his cheek to deal with, too. Neither of them could hide their seals.

Imorie hunched in the hover chair again, following Shiera, with Eti just behind her, up to the home's lit entrance.

The man who greeted them looked to be in his seventies or eighties, brawny, his short hair dyed a pale pink.

"Ser Keralan," he said, "I'm pleased to meet you in person. And this is..."

His eyes landed on her, then Eti, and he didn't show any

particular shock at two magickers showing up at his house, two magickers who'd been publicly accused of murder—even if they'd been absolved.

"Imorie, ser," she said, meeting his gaze.

He nodded. "Yes, come in, come in." He stepped back and let them pass, holding the door open before he shut it—and locked it—behind them.

"And Etienne Tanaka," he said, as if there'd been no pause in the introduction. "Ah. Yes. I do follow the news, much as it isn't good for my health. And thank you for calling ahead, Ser Keralan, that at least is better for my nerves. Pleased to meet you all. I'm Dr. Mateo Adewale, please come to my exam room, and we can get started. I'm sure you don't want to stay out tonight longer than necessary."

Imorie glanced at Shiera, but Shiera was fully back in character and didn't give anything away.

They crowded into a small room at the back of the house, where Imorie's exam proceeded much as it had with Dr. Lin on Hestia, with the added churn in her gut, the fear that this doctor, too, might turn out to try to kill her. Try to expose her.

The scalpel turning in the light, the doctor smiling as he anticipated using it.

Imorie blinked. No, that was over. It *was* over. And Dr. Adewale was not Dr. Lin. Whatever else she thought of Shiera, she absolutely knew Shiera wouldn't deliberately take her to a psychopath.

Dr. Adewale did the scans it took to identify the Bruising Sleep. He confirmed it, of course, and when he looked at the med patches she'd left on her arm, hoping they had at least a little residual medication left, he frowned, but nodded at the labeling and dosage.

"This one is typically effective, yes—it's expensive, so I don't use it often for my patients, unfortunately, but if you're able to afford it, I can give you some." He spun in his chair and pulled open a cabinet, coming out with a handful of med patches.

"All expenses are covered by the palace," Shiera said. "As are your own fees."

"Good, good, thank you."

Imorie's shoulders sagged in relief at the sight of the patches, identical to the ones she'd been given on Hestia. So her treatment hadn't been malicious. And it had been working.

"Has it been too long?" she asked. "Since my last dose ran out? Will it still be effective?" Would she backslide? Was her exhaustion now stress and travel lag, or was it more?

"How long has it been since the last patches were applied?" Dr. Adewale asked.

She had to think. "Five days."

"Oh, no, you're fine. This should start working again within a few hours. May I?"

She rolled up her sleeve as far as she could and let him peel off the old patches, clean the skin, and apply two new ones.

"How long does this last?" Shiera asked. "And will she need to come back often for re-assessment?"

"She's staying at the palace? I will send over all my notes and the dosage instructions to the palace physicians, if that is acceptable. Truly, I'm honored that you'd come to me, but I am so busy at the clinic. There isn't anyone adequately covering for me tonight, as it is. But your generous gift will, of course, help the clinic and those who live there."

Shiera nodded briskly. "From the Seritarchus. He sees what's happening here and is helping as he's able."

Imorie saw the bitterness crease the physician's face before it was quickly and inexpertly hidden again.

"In any case, I think we're finished. Imorie, I'll send you with the patches I have—please do not take more than the recommended dosage I'll send over, which means no more than one patch at a time, for the duration of that patch's efficacy. So, unless you have further questions—"

"Have you seen other magickers who have the Bruising Sleep?" Imorie asked, leaning forward in her hover chair.

Dr. Adewale blinked. "I have seen a few. And a very few have manifested at my clinic. But not more than statistically manifest in other hospitals. Hospitals and clinics are a place of stress for most people, and one thing we do know about Green Magics is that they often manifest in times of stress."

"Which is as we thought," Shiera said, and stood. "Thank you, Dr. Adewale. Your help is most appreciated."

And Imorie knew she shouldn't have asked, though she wasn't yet sure why. She knew the possible correlation between Green Magics and the Bruising Sleep had been researched before, and found inconclusive, with no evidence to support the theory. Green Magics weren't a disease, for one —and ah, that was why she shouldn't have asked. The theory was popular among the anti-magicker movements. She just... she hadn't been paying as much attention as she should, as the Heir, to all of this. She hadn't thought the magickers required much of her attention at all. She herself had thought...well.

Dr. Adewale paused in his cleaning up the patch wrappers and waited, expecting them to leave. Shiera was waiting on Imorie's cue, she thought, and—was she ready to leave yet?

"Dr. Adewale, I have another question. Uh"—she glanced at Shiera—"will hormone therapy interfere at all with this treatment, or with the Bruising Sleep in general?"

"Oh, no, that's fine. Though I do tend to use a different drug formulation with those who have the Bruising Sleep than not, I've found that particular one works best while managing the symptoms of the Bruising Sleep. I do have that here, do you wish that treatment as well?"

"I—yes."

Imorie swallowed on a tightening throat. She hadn't really thought it through, though the idea had been hovering in her peripheries. She couldn't Change. She needed to get farther from how she'd looked as Arianna, and cosmetics could only go so far, and—she needed to *Change*. She needed a difference, and to settle more into being Imorie. And a more pronounced androgyny felt good there. Felt like a place she could settle for a while.

Imorie wouldn't be able to just Change the effects away, she knew that. She did know that.

She looked up again at Shiera, and Shiera nodded. Eti had sharpened his attention on her as well. Was he concerned? He shouldn't be. Not about this.

Dr. Adewale turned back to his cabinets and came out with an implant applicator. "I'll key the dosage to your physiology. Would you like fast effects? Slow effects?"

"Slower, I think."

"Any particular effects? I can change the dosage mix."

"I—no. Default is fine."

"All right. This will last around six months, after which you'll need to have it replaced."

She nodded, and stood still while he rolled up the sleeve to her other arm, pressing the applicator flush. She flinched at the pinch, but the pain faded quickly, the implant's local anesthetics doing their work.

Imorie glanced down at the red mark, let out a breath as she pulled her sleeve back down.

"Uh—how long?" she asked. "Not with this, but the patches—how long until I'm well enough for...not being this sick?"

The physician shrugged. "It's different for everyone, and

so very hard to tell. But from what you described earlier, you were already making good progress. I would think in a few weeks you will feel much better than you have been, and in a few months it will all be very manageable."

She could handle that. If she could hold her own at court until then, if nothing major blew up until then, she could handle that.

Beside her, Eti flickered, twice.

Nerves spiking, she swung around, nearly sliding off the chair. "What? What's wrong?"

He flickered again, and she reached for his hand. He let her take it, but his grip was stiff. He met her eyes, though, and she could feel him gathering his courage.

"I need that, too."

Needed what? Needed her treatment?

His eyes strayed to the implant applicator the doctor had set on the table.

Oh. Oh!

She hadn't known, and if he was out of his own hormones, he should have asked—but he was asking now.

"Yes, of course. Dr. Adewale—"

"Of course," the physician said, and took Eti aside to scan him.

Shiera moved close to Imorie and said in a low voice, "I can't imagine he was able to get genetic treatment, or any other significant treatment, if he's been hiding his aura as an unsealed magicker. Offer the services of the palace physicians, if he wishes to use them. He has nothing to hide now."

Imorie nodded, glancing at Eti as the doctor pressed another implant injector to his arm.

She looked back to Shiera's body language subtly shifting. Shiera saw her attention, flicked the pronoun sign for he and him.

Imorie rolled her shoulders. And did she and her fit her anymore? Did it fit who she was becoming?

Was she becoming something different than what she had been? Or was she merely exploring the bounds of a persona?

Eti's eyes met hers. He smiled briefly, a genuine smile, and it warmed her.

Arianna Rhialden would never had cared so much for the light behind a single smile.

She wasn't Arianna Rhialden just now. Shiera—Homaj— wasn't her father. Wasn't the person she'd tried to impress her entire life, a pillar of absolute control.

She flicked her fingers in the pronoun sign for they and them.

Homaj's lips twitched. He nodded and leaned close again. "Call me Maja. Just Maja. Or if you still wish to call me Father, that's okay."

No, Imorie couldn't. Not and keep their thoughts centered in Iata being their father. Homaj—Maja—was not their father just now.

Imorie's eyes stung.

"Maja," they said softly. And were hit with a flashback of saying that to Badem, of using Maja's personal name as a way to get around naming him as their father.

Fuck.

"You will get through this," he said. "You will."

Then Eti was back, and that unholy risk of a conversation really had to be over.

Eti reached for their hand and they took it. He walked beside them back through the house and outside where they'd parked the bikes.

The bikes, of course, weren't there.

"This neighborhood," Maja growled, back to being very obviously Shiera, and pulled out his comm. "Commander

Jalava, this is Shiera Keralan. Forgive me for using your personal channel, but I'm in the city with two of your charges and our bikes—yes. Yes, we will wait inside. *Thank you,* Commander."

Imorie laughed, a wild and torn sound, too bright in the chill night air.

Maja grinned, baring almost perfect teeth.

It wasn't funny. None of it was funny. But it was ridiculous. Was all of it ridiculous?

And Imorie thought that maybe, maybe they might be okay. If they could laugh. If there was something to laugh about.

39

PASSENGER AND PILOT

Isn't it ironic that friends I've made while someone else can be truer, those fleeting moments more honest, than relationships I've forged as myself?

— HOMAJ RHIALDEN, SERITARCHUS IX IN A
PRIVATE LETTER, NEVER SENT; PUBLISHED IN
THE CHANGE DIALOGUES

Maja swept stray strands of wind-blown blonde hair out of his eyes as he walked, Zhang a few steps behind him. The landing pad behind Green Hall was dark, and that had been a security risk— people could see in, but if there was no light, it made it at least a little harder to identify who was boarding the ship. It also made it harder for Mariyit's guards to keep tabs on any potential trouble, and there was likely to be some brewing.

But Maja knew that Shiera Keralan would be identified. Shiera, at least, was well known among the palace staff—not as a persona of one Homaj Rhialden, but in her own right, and trusted enough to often be sent away on administrative duties. Which was convenient.

He'd started this afternoon as Shiera, and while it was night now and his gender had tipped further back to male, Shiera was a comfortable enough shield. He'd Change on the way. Or maybe he wouldn't. It would be more airtight if he landed on Hestia still as Shiera.

Zhang would also be identified. She had been a near constant presence with him as Homaj for his entire reign, and while she was always in the background, those who paid attention to such things knew who she was. If Zhang and Shiera were both boarding a magicker ship, along with whichever magicker Mariyit had sent to escort them on this trip, that would give rise to all kinds of speculation.

Iata would do his best to massage the facts, of that he was sure. The Seritarchus was sending his trusted guard captain to untangle whatever mess had happened on Hestia. Iata could spin that as concern for the people, not for his own family's reputation.

Maja's head hurt. His throat ached, and he needed a cool drink. He was doing his very best, when he didn't have to, to not smooth away with Change the small normal Human pains that most people took for granted—like thirst. And headaches. He wouldn't be able to do so when he foreswore Change for good. When he fully and publicly abdicated.

It was, so far, a singularly uncomfortable experience.

Zhang moved ahead of him as they neared the extended ramp to the small, sleek ship. Another risk—he would be completely exposed for a minute, no more. But everything about his body language screamed palace bureaucrat. And everyone knew that Homaj was still at the palace. Iata would make sure of that.

"Is Captain Temir inside?" he asked in a low voice as Zhang passed him.

"Yes. Already boarded."

That for whoever would be listening, and people would be listening. He spotted no drones, and Green Hall security was good, but directional mics would be aimed this way, mic gain boosted.

His other persona of Captain Kian Temir of the Palace Guard was to have boarded as well, and if people missed his boarding in the dark, well, it was dark. Workers and guards would have been going back and forth to the ship to replenish the stores, and for security checks. A boarding could be missed.

The ruse gave him more options.

He followed Zhang up the ramp, through the opening hatch, and into the cramped common room. The ship was big enough for eight, if they bunked four to a cabin and prayed no one's temper flared. But there'd only be three—officially four—on this mission.

And the ship was small enough to travel faster than commercial traffic without the need of a magicker's reinforcement of the hull in Below Space, though they would have a magicker with them to travel at military speeds. Speed right now was critical.

And where was that magicker? Zhang had said that Mariyit had said the magicker was onboard and ready. Were they in the cockpit? Back in one of the cabins?

"Hello?" he called.

He heard a noise from the cockpit, and Zhang tensed, though she didn't draw her weapons as she might if she was publicly escorting him as Homaj.

"In here," a hoarse voice called from the cockpit.

The hairs on Maja's arms rose, and he shared a look with Zhang. They both knew that voice.

Former First Magicker Onya Norren looked up from the pilot's controls as they stepped inside, looking every moment of her hundred and nine years, wispy gray hair tied back into a tight bun, smile present but weary.

"First Magicker Norren." He stopped, offering a deep bow. They were alone here, but he wasn't about to relax being Shiera until they were in Below Space. And Onya knew his persona of Shiera Keralan, she knew exactly who he was.

But why was she here? Surely—*surely*—she couldn't be the magicker Mariyit had sent?

She was of high enough rank that she, in part, sustained her life force from the ambient energy around her. Living to be a hundred and ten or even twenty wasn't unheard of among natural Humans, but it wasn't common, either. High-ranking magickers could sometimes add another twenty or thirty years to that lifespan, though that wasn't widely known. Maja was fairly sure Onya, if she wanted to, could blaze past a hundred and fifty.

But while Maja's Truthspoken genes and training kept his own default body looking youthful far past his actual age—in his mid-forties, he still looked in his late twenties—that wasn't true for magickers.

Onya took Maja's hands, smiling. "How are you, dear?"

Adeius. No one, absolutely no one but Onya could get away with that sentence. Not even with Shiera, who had a reputation for being prickly. Maja absolutely didn't look at Zhang to note the amusement she'd be carefully hiding.

"Well enough. Onya—are you coming with us?"

"Mariyit asked me, as he thought it was an assignment I'd enjoy. Retirement is restful, but also incredibly boring. I wouldn't mind keeping a city's Green Hall for a time."

Maja wasn't sure what to say to that. And Shiera wasn't as quick-tongued as Maja himself. So he just sat in the co-pilot's seat, stretching to see where Onya was in the pre-flight checks. She was nearly through them. Doing a full list, which wasn't standard. But necessary, he thought, on this particular day, in this particular political climate.

"No bombs?" he asked as he brought up his own screens and shunted some of her checklist to himself.

"No bombs," she said, and her smile widened.

"Do you want me to fly—"

The look she gave him could have withered an entire garden. And he had to wonder how that wasn't violence.

She returned to her screens. "I shouldn't have to tell you, Shiera, that using one's skills keeps the mind nimble."

"You have never been that wise, or that old," he shot back, and she grinned to show teeth.

"Are all the supplies on board?" he asked.

"Yes, restocked before you came. Your luggage was brought up, too. I assumed you'd both want the second cabin. And your other passenger, Captain Temir. I took the first cabin because it's a little closer to the washroom. They're both the same size, though."

He shrugged. "Then we're ready?"

"We are."

He flicked the ship's comm and logged a text with Green Hall that they would launch in five minutes, sending along their passenger manifest. He signed it with Shiera's ident tags, which would automatically forward the message to Iata as well.

Zhang, behind him, carefully strapped herself into the observer's seat.

Onya saw it. "Captain, I'm not planning to tear out of here. Just a nice and orderly flight."

It was Maja's turn to grin. He had flown with Onya Norren once before, a long, long time ago. So had Zhang. It wasn't the sort of flight you'd forget.

The comm pinged: Green Hall, wishing them safe travels.

The journey, he was sure, would be the easy part.

40

LATE

> Parties and balls and receptions and socials of all
> kinds aren't necessary evils, they're important fields
> of battle.
>
> — ADMIRAL OF THE FLEET DASSAN
> LAGUAYA, AS QUOTED IN *THE CHANGE
> DIALOGUES*

The socials that night had, like most nights, carried late into the night, and there was only so much Iata could do to stave off the fatigue of the day without borrowing from energy he'd need for the next few days. He wasn't expecting any of this to slow down.

If he could show his aura in public, he might be able to pull ambient energy from the world around him, but he'd never quite managed the trick of that, and he never got the chance to practice.

He was fully on display as Homaj tonight, presenting with a genderbendy mix of femme and masc, his aura locked down as tightly as he could manage and still function. Which was a large part of the fatigue.

Haneri held court beside him, a steady presence at his side. He felt buzzy with her own alertness, her coiled apprehension. It was flaring out into her conversations with her trademark boldness, though she was unusually restrained tonight.

Because of Imorie? He'd told her what he could when he'd come to her apartment two hours earlier—what she didn't already know, and she'd already known much.

He'd told her the details of Imorie's ordeal that would never be public.

Haneri hid her reaction to Imorie's ordeal well, but he'd seen with his magicker senses more than his Truthspoken training how rattled she was.

He'd told her about the adoption—citing Iata, not himself—and Imorie's change of legal name. Haneri had to know that, too.

"I don't at all like that you have to parade yourself for the sharks, Homaj, and dance around their teeth. Or that my daughter will have to do so constantly. Both of my daughters. The high houses and the nobility will never stop trying to poke holes in your performance. They will try to out her, and catch you in your own lies."

"My daughters can hold their own. If it will be too much for you—"

She'd just glared at him, then, and took his arm, a bit too tightly.

If, in the several times she'd touched him in the last few days she'd felt anything from his magics, she hadn't said. If she'd noticed at all that he wasn't her husband, she hadn't said that, either. Iata was only somewhat certain that his role was secure with her, he had occasionally been around her as Homaj before, but there had been that kiss...

And she was speaking with him far more easily than she would with Homaj. With Maja.

Maybe she did know, and had her own reasons for not saying anything. Nevertheless, he would play his role to its utmost. And she in turn seemed determined to play hers.

And now, surrounded by courtiers who had moved on from the most obvious questions—*Did you know Green Magics run in the Rhialden line? Is the Rhialden cousin settling in well? Are you sure she isn't a danger to all of us?*—with his wine glass in hand, Iata was finding it hard to keep his mind on task.

His thoughts kept straying out to Hestia. Maja would be leaving shortly, if he hadn't already lifted. Imorie would, surely, be back in her apartment by now, safe.

And his own eldest child? Was Bettea even still alive? He wished he could board that ship with Maja and push it to every limit it had in Below Space. But, he hadn't had enough training in maintaining a ship's hull integrity in Below Space, either—where was the time? Onya Norren would certainly know how.

He took a sip of wine to cover his smile as he imagined Maja's face when he saw who Mariyit had sent. No, Iata couldn't think of anyone more qualified to go on that particular mission, even if he wanted to be there himself.

He was needed here. He, and Dressa, were the only things holding this kingdom together just now. And he was scrabbling for every purchase he could find.

Across the room, Dressa and Lesander sat at a table amidst a group of younger nobles and one aging pop star. Both were also more contained than usual tonight, though they were doing well enough to hide it.

He felt a hand on his back and nearly jumped.

Haneri leaned close. "Need some time alone?"

Needing a break signaled a lack of control, she knew that. But, he wasn't Maja. He might be Homaj just now, but the persona of Homaj had enough range to not need to be in absolute control all of the time. That had been Maja's need, not his.

He twisted his Palace Guard ring comm, two times to the left, three to the right. The signal for someone to come and make it seem like he was needed elsewhere.

Lt. Chadrikour, who was standing a few paces behind him, pressed her hand to her ear, paused, then strode toward him. Her dark brown face beneath a severe gray bob was professionally blank, but her eyes assessed him.

Dressa was right that he needed to fill her in on everything that was going on. She would be the acting captain of his personal guards until Zhang returned—no. He was fairly certain Zhang would follow Maja wherever Maja decided to go from here. Chadrikour would be his captain in truth before long.

And he needed allies just now. Needed someone to help if he had to let go of his aura. Which he really did need to, even more as he focused on it, but Haneri seemed stuck to his side. He couldn't think of a graceful way to have a moment just to himself. She was the one who'd suggested he step out.

As Homaj, he could just make a sharp remark and disengage from her—he'd certainly seen Homaj do that before.

But she had stayed by his side tonight, and she hadn't had to.

Chadrikour whispered in his ear, "Ser, a secure room is waiting, if you wish it."

"Thank you, Haneri and I will follow you shortly."

He turned back to the group gathered around him, holding up his hands. "Forgive me, I must attend to this."

He expected the usual rounds of false disappointment. But he was met with grimmer looks than he would have liked.

His nerves jangled. Did they know, could they see just how much he was straining to hold himself together?

Several people had touched him that night. A flutter of the hand, a brush of the sleeve. He was used to mingling with nobility and palace guests, Truthspoken had never held themselves physically apart from their people like the rulers of some kingdoms, but he knew those touches had been deliberate. He knew.

He smiled, gave a mocking shallow bow, and pulled Haneri with him after Chadrikour.

41

PRIVILEGE

> *If I'd been someone else, if I'd been more attracted to femme people and less wary of her family's influence, I might have welcomed Haneri differently. Or maybe not. Maybe love is dangerous for Truthspoken and best avoided.*

— HOMAJ RHIALDEN, SERITARCHUS IX IN A PRIVATE LETTER, NEVER SENT; PUBLISHED IN *THE CHANGE DIALOGUES*

Iata stepped out from the North Hall into one of the adjoining antechambers, and Adeius, he could breathe better just away from all of that cloying perfume. Not that he himself hadn't added abundantly to the sheer scent ratio of that room. But tonight, with his aura held so tightly inside him, every sense was painful.

The far door to the antechamber opened, and Ceorre entered.

His senses went on alert, because she wouldn't have come here for a social call. The Truthspeaker didn't make social calls, not especially at this hour. That she was here now meant she'd tracked him down. She'd been meaning to interrupt his evening anyway.

Had someone passed Haneri a signal? Was that why she'd suggested coming out?

But Haneri's mouth was drawn. She and Ceorre had never particularly gotten along.

"Ceorre, a rare pleasure," he said, and Haneri released his arm so he could hold out his hands.

Ceorre took them briefly, then waved toward a door leading to a secure room. "Homaj, are you having a moment apart? Good. May I speak with you?"

Haneri very definitively reclaimed his arm.

He hadn't had as much chance to talk with Ceorre these last days—last weeks, really—as he would have liked. He'd been busy with the Kidaa situation, busy with training Dressa, busy with trying to put out fires in the public sentiments around magickers. And that task had just become nearly impossible.

Ceorre, he knew, had been busy with much of the same. He wasn't sure he welcomed her presence now, not with Haneri ever so watchful on his arm. He needed to talk with Ceorre alone.

Iata had sent her a terse report of what had happened at Green Hall that morning and was sure that Mariyit would have sent something similar, but he'd needed to show himself at these gatherings tonight. He'd absolutely needed to be visible and present, not sequestering himself with the Truthspeaker while the court ramped up its own paranoia.

Ceorre knew the game. She was as expert as any of them.

"I have a moment, yes," he said, waving her into the secure room. Haneri still held to his arm, and could he truly shake her off? Maja would have already done so, but if this had anything to do with Imorie, and that was a good possibility, Haneri also had a right to know.

When they were all inside, Chadrikour withdrew.

It was Ceorre who touched the controls to activate the room's dampening systems. Then she stepped back, brow ever so slightly creased.

"What is it?" he asked. He sorted rapidly through reasons she'd have for coming to him. Had something happened to Imorie? Had the anti-magicker protests in the city escalated into riots? Had the Kidaa attacked again? He knew the value of being at these social gatherings, but he needed, desperately needed, to be back at his desk. The little work he'd been able to do earlier hadn't nearly been enough, and it had been undercut by talking with Dressa, and with Maja, and then his Change, and then meeting with Imorie. Which had also all been necessary.

He needed to be two people. He needed Maja—and needed the answers Maja would bring him from Hestia. Adeius, no, but he hoped this wasn't bad news from Hestia, which Ceorre might bring herself—

He didn't know what Haneri sensed in him, because his outward reactions were controlled. His aura was controlled. But Haneri's grip on his arm became almost protective, more possessive than just her need to be here.

He reached within, calmed himself.

Ceorre glanced to Haneri, back to him. And ah—maybe Haneri's reaction had been from Ceorre. She knew Ceorre was about to ask her to leave and was readying herself for a fight. They'd had those battles early on between Homaj, Haneri, and Ceorre.

Iata frowned. He opened one hand—yes, include Haneri, though he trusted Ceorre's discretion.

Ceorre studied him a moment, then nodded. Reluctantly, he thought. Did she not trust his discretion?

"I just had a message," she said, "from one Duke Kyran Koldari, who came in-system at military speeds. He's not listed on the passenger list of the ship he came in on, which must have been a truly exorbitant bribe. He contacted me directly because, and I quote, 'I'm concerned for the safety of Imorie Rhialden méron Quevedo, up to and especially her safety with the Rhialden royal family. I'm asking you, please, to place Imorie under your own protection at the Adeium.'"

For a moment, the full implications didn't register. He was holding his aura too tightly, Haneri's perfume was finally starting to eat at his sensory control, the fatigue chipping away at the edges of everything else.

"Koldari's set himself up as a protector?" Haneri asked. "For my daughter? That crass young fool?"

"He's not that young," Ceorre said, eyeing Haneri. "And I think he's not that crass. You know the roles people play at court. In any case, Homaj, here is our word from Hestia. Your notes said he was there. If not a witness to the exact events, then certainly a witness to whatever led up to them and the general atmosphere of the estate. I know how I would like to handle this response, but how would you like to handle this?"

He finally shrugged himself out of Haneri's grip, moving to sit on one of the room's scattering of chairs. The fabric, he noticed, was more frayed than it should be. He made a mental note to have the upholstery in this secure room replaced. He would have caught it sooner if he'd merely been a bloodservant, not trying to hold down two intense positions in the palace just now.

Koldari was here. Had likely paid a fortune to take a fast, magicker-supported transport to Valon, and more of that fortune to keep himself off the passenger list. Why? And why had Koldari taken it upon himself to care for Imorie? How well did he know her?

Adeius, Iata needed the rest of that information that

Imorie hadn't been able to give earlier, and he didn't want to press for it again now. He'd seen what sharing that whole experience had done to her and to Eti. If he pressed—well, he wouldn't. That would certainly be a violence.

And so what if Koldari did feel the need to protect Imorie? It wasn't unreasonable to assume that the Seritarchus would be furious that a contract Rhialden had dragged his family name down in this way. Not that Iata saw being a magicker as a deficit—it didn't matter just now how he saw it. It was how the people would perceive he saw it.

And if Koldari had been part of the problem, was working with the Javieris, and was trying to control Imorie now? Would he threaten her?

Would Koldari have news of Bettea?

He needed to let go of his aura. Adeius, it was taking everything he had just to keep his body still, to keep from shuddering with the need to let it out.

He managed to keep his voice steady.

"She absolutely won't be moved to the Adeium," he said. "She's here under my protection at the palace. That's public knowledge now."

Ceorre nodded, folding her hands in front of her. "Agreed. He wished to speak with me upon landing and requested use of the Adeium pad. His ship is in holding right now, waiting my response."

The situation was truly urgent.

But he closed his eyes. He needed a moment, just a moment, to steady himself enough to see this through.

He opened his eyes again as he heard a swish of fabric, Haneri nearing again, her posture protective.

She didn't ask him if he was well. She just stared, maybe daring him to say he was fine.

"Turn around," he said softly.

Ceorre's finger twitched, an aborted protest.

Haneri gave him a *look,* but she slowly turned, crossing her arms as she faced away from him.

"Well?" she asked, but didn't look back.

"Wait. Please."

He waited until she nodded, then let his aura out. It flared with an intensity that burned his nerves, sent fire through every muscle and joint. Iata bared his teeth but did not let himself make a noise. He sat still, perfectly still, until the pain eased—but did not pass.

He would not be able to hold his aura this tightly tomorrow, no matter who tried to touch him. He'd just have to make sure no one was able to.

"Homaj?" Haneri asked.

"Wait," he said, and then forced himself into a light Change trance to try to smooth over the rest of the pain.

It didn't really work.

He shuddered and didn't meet Ceorre's eyes, though he felt them on him. He began the tedious process, like repacking an old wound that never healed, of folding his aura back inside himself.

It hurt. Adeius, it hurt. But he had no other choice.

Ceorre opened her mouth—he glared up at her, and she shut it again.

No, she was not going to suggest that she meet with Koldari alone. He would be there. He would know what had happened on Hestia from Koldari's mouth. He'd have his answers.

Iata stood carefully, brushed off his silk coat. Fit himself carefully back into being Homaj.

Haneri was turning now, impatient, but he was done, as done as he could be. Her gaze raked over him, inspecting.

"What was that?" she demanded. "You've been off all night."

"My daughter—our daughter—" He stopped. It was still too painful to speak.

But he forced words out anyway, turning to Ceorre. This situation with Koldari was urgent, and he'd just taken too much time.

"He can land at the Adeium, but I'll be there with you. We will both greet Kyran Koldari and assess his motives—" He bared his teeth and shuddered as fire threatened to tear through him again.

Ceorre stepped forward quickly, gripped his forearms. "Let it out. I'm not going to have both of you lost in this for your gods-damned stubbornness. Now. Let it out. Koldari can wait."

Rattled at the intensity of her emotions, his control slipped again. Green flared around him, the fire diminished from a few moments before, but still there.

Oh, Adeius.

42

NOTHING AGAINST YOU

A Green Magicker's aura is their signature and their fingerprint. It is possible, however, for a magicker to suppress their aura, given enough practice and skill.

— ONARAWUL DRINA IN *METHODS AND MATERIALS FOR MODERN LAW ENFORCEMENT*

He looked to Haneri.

And wasn't it ironic that he was ready to become a ruler in his own right, ready to show he was a magicker, too, and just now he absolutely did not want Haneri to see this? To see him.

But then, he was not himself.

She looked back, frowning, but not...not surprised.

"What's happening?" she asked. "You're in pain—why?"

"I—" His role as Homaj was slipping, too. He had never been able to be Homaj as well when his aura was fully around him. His magics knew that wasn't his true center.

Ceorre waved from him to Haneri. "Read her. Then you'll have your answers and we can get past this. Keep your aura out throughout the back corridors—no one is watching there."

She could be wrong. Someone could be watching, a mobile bug or nano-drone could have slipped past security. But the odds of that were so small, and he needed to breathe. He needed to fucking *breathe* just now, and right now, he could.

His eyes were locked on Haneri's, and her expression was becoming more defiant.

"I know you, Yan," she said, thrusting a finger at him.

He swallowed.

"I kissed you, do you think I couldn't tell the difference?"

"And this?" he asked, waving at his aura. It was jittering around him, jagged and unsettled, as he felt jagged and unsettled.

"I *kissed* you," she said again. "I *felt* your surprise. I know Homaj likes to think I'm not as intelligent or well-connected as he is—"

"He doesn't—"

She waved that aside as the blatant untruth it was.

"He doesn't want to see you as an equal, because he feels guilty for—"

"Don't make any more excuses for him. None at all."

Iata coughed. Yeah. That was fair. He loved Maja, but that didn't mean he didn't see his brother's faults. He knew them all and portrayed them as his own.

Okay.

Haneri held out her hand. He felt the flow of her emotions even through her look, her anger, her tight coil of fear. And...something else. A root entangled around every-thing else, tightly held, protected.

He braced himself and gripped her hand.

Everything he'd been feeling from her intensified, and in

his rattled state, he was having trouble sifting his own emotions from hers.

"Haneri," he said, his voice strained, "can I trust you?"

"Yes," she said, emphatically and with her entire being.

He rocked back.

"I have nothing against you, Yan. I don't want to see my children harmed. I don't know what you and Maja are doing just now, but I trust you a hell of a lot more than him. And I trust Dressa a lot more than Arianna—Maja was bent on molding Arianna into a clone of himself, and I wanted no part of that. You can trust me, Yan. Iata."

All of this was blasted with emotion in Haneri's usual high intensity.

But all of it, also, was true. Or as close to true to make little difference just now.

"You're Delor," he said, and felt that hit her like a blow. "Adeius, no, I didn't mean—"

"I know you look at me like you look at Lesander—"

"No, truly—"

She paused, nodded, her hand still clasping his. "All right, that is true. I have some cosmetic Change training, but I'm not Truthspoken. I know evaku, but so does everyone at court. Yan. Trust me."

She was sincere. He felt that, he knew that. But he also knew how quickly her mood could whip around.

"Why did you kiss me?" he asked.

She barked a laugh, and bitterness rippled between them.

"I kissed you once before. You as—" she waved at him. At his being Homaj. "I know the difference. Mainly because he never has kissed me. Not once, not where he meant it. He's always deflected."

Iata stiffened. Adeius, what? He thought—he had kissed her once, so many years ago, when he'd been Homaj, and an angry Haneri had cornered him when he wasn't expecting it, ranting about something he couldn't remember now. She'd been trying to get him to pay full attention to what she was saying—which he had been trying not to do, being Homaj. Because that's what Homaj would have done.

She'd kissed him first. More aggressive than sexual, but for a moment, he had kissed her back.

She remembered that? But he'd thought Homaj would have kissed her at least...well, and would he have? He had barely tolerated her. Anything in public was a performance. She was his opposite in every way, their personalities and needs clashing.

He remembered—yes, he did remember—Haneri looking between his eyes, just a flick, as he'd pulled back first, abashed. He'd quickly hid whatever was showing on his face, and he'd been terrified that night that she would have found him out.

He had told Homaj about the encounter, but Homaj hadn't seemed to think it was a big deal. Homaj kissed people all the time, though he'd been annoyed that it had happened, certainly. More annoyed at Haneri than Iata.

And after that first kiss, Haneri had just continued on her tirade. Albeit with a more willing audience. Iata hadn't thought it had meant anything to her other than a means to an end.

He hated those early years. He hated the person Homaj had become when faced with the weight of power and then the added intense chaos of Haneri coming into court, a force in her own right. He'd done his best to help Homaj into better paths, better habits, and he thought it had worked. Homaj had, mostly, evened into the role of a Seritarchus, if not exactly naturally. But those early years had been...rough.

He blinked, and didn't know if Haneri had just picked up any of that from him, but her face had lost some of its storm. She looked tired now, older than she should.

Even with cosmetic Change training, she didn't look nearly as young as a Truthspoken might in their mid-forties —the nobility with that sort of training tended not to want to overly advertise it, illegal as it was. Iata himself had to work to make his bloodservant appearance look older than the mid-twenties his body wanted to default to, and which Homaj's body did. But Haneri's feel of age now had less to do with her physical appearance than the emotions he felt from her.

The gems in her hair glittered too brightly in the lights.

Ceorre cleared her throat, and Iata and Haneri both jumped.

He let go of Haneri's hand and flexed his own.

His aura was still showing, but it had calmed into is usual steady green.

"I just signaled Koldari to land at the Adeium," Ceorre said. "And may I suggest we not yet inform Imorie of her protector."

Iata shook himself back into the state of mind he needed just now. Not—not whatever he'd just been in.

He glanced at Haneri again, then pulled Homaj's personality back around himself.

"Oh, agreed," he said. "I want to see for myself if he should be allowed to see her."

Ceorre glanced at her comm. "He'll be down in less than an hour. Are you well enough for this? If you don't suppress your aura until we reach the Adeium?"

He hated being that exposed, even in the rigid security of the back corridors and tunnels under the palace courtyard. But the thought of having to shove his aura back down right now sent phantom fire throughout his senses.

Not yet. He did need more time. Would an hour be enough?

The thought of not being able to question Koldari himself

hurt more. And Ceorre didn't suggest again that she talk to Koldari alone, not even silently.

"Yes," he said. "And I'm absolutely out of patience, and Koldari will do well to see that." He managed a shrug. "But, yes. Haneri—will you see that Dressa and Lesander are safely deposited back in their apartment? If Koldari's landing gets out, and it will, of course it will"—he made a dismissive wave —"I don't want people bombarding them with questions they can't answer."

He turned back to Ceorre. "Does Jalava know about Koldari?"

"Possibly, but not from me. I wanted to talk to you first."

"I'll tell them, then, on the way. You should return to the Adeium, I'll follow shortly."

Ceorre tilted her head, still eyeing him. "Take the back corridors from here." She nodded toward where the panel door was located in this room.

He strode toward it. "Then I'll open it for you, too—we don't need a procession back there, people will find out what's happening soon enough. Go. I will be fine." The tunnels would all open for Ceorre's biometrics on the other side, even if the back corridors in the palace itself would not.

Ceorre gave him another look as he opened the panel, then nodded, her body language lining up with that decision, widening, moving back into full assurance.

When the panel door clicked shut, Haneri crossed her arms again.

"I should be there. Delor is aligned—loosely, mind you, and not as closely as the Javieris—with the Koldaris. Koldari might trust that. Though he might not—he never seemed that impressed with me before."

Iata opened his hands. "I appreciate the offer, but I don't want to complicate—"

"You need me there," Haneri said, and it wasn't a question.

And he did, he'd been relying on her to steady him, to shield him socially, all night. Too much.

"How long have you been a magicker?" she asked.

"I—long."

"And you've hidden your aura all that time. What's changed? Why are you having trouble doing that now? Let me help you with that."

"I—Haneri—" he spread his arms in exasperation, his gesture, not Homaj's. "Why? I understand that you're sincere, but I don't understand why. I haven't given you any more reason to trust me than Maja—"

She held up an uncompromising hand. "You have. I know when it's you. I always know. And this is my kingdom, too. And my family. I've already told you why."

Yes, but he didn't understand. He wasn't sure how to align to this reality where Haneri knew all of his—most of his, at least—most private secrets. Where she'd known them for a while.

But then, he had suspected she might know something. He had. And he'd still invited her to be near him, even knowing that.

In this private room, in this inadequate light, and in all her rage and curves and social armor and private vulnerability, she wasn't anyone he could ignore. And he didn't want to. Adeius, he didn't want to.

He held out his arm again, and she claimed it with all the inherent privilege of the Seritarchus Consort.

Which was a good sight. He hadn't seen her draw up like that in...so long.

It was her place, truly. As the Seritarchus Consort, in a matter that directly concerned the safety of her daughter, she had a right to be there, even if she hadn't claimed that right in a very long time.

Her emotions opened to him again as they touched, and he knew his opened to her, with his aura still visible around him.

He didn't like that. He didn't like feeling open, he didn't at all like not being in a known place of safety and having the open light and the air touch his aura for anyone determined to see.

But he had to meet Koldari.

So they ducked into the back corridors, his green still flaring around him.

43

KOLDARI

The difference between the nobility and the high houses is the high houses have always seen the Rhialdens as just another one of them.

— EMRE PATEL IN *DECONSTRUCTING OUR TIMES: A PEOPLE'S PERSPECTIVE ON THE NOBILITY AND THE HIGH HOUSES*

I ata waited, posture casual and unconcerned, as the hatch opened to Koldari's shuttle. Chadrikour hadn't wanted him this close, not knowing what awaited them on the other side of that hatch. It could, of course, be assassins. It could always be assassins.

He wanted news with a need that ached, and his suppressed aura was still a low-grade pain throughout his body. He hadn't shoved it down as deeply as he had this whole day, though—he couldn't sustain that, and the time through the back corridors had hardly been enough.

He wanted to know Bettea was alive, if a person like Koldari would even have thought to inquire about the wellbeing of a single servant, even if that servant was tied to Imorie, who he claimed to wish to protect.

Iata fought the urge to move, the need to let out his aura again nearly unbearable.

Haneri, beside him, tightened her loose grip on his arm. Her face was as aggressively neutral as he knew his own to be.

Ceorre on his right held her hands loosely in front of her. She'd changed quickly into her red and violet formal robes of office, with the seal of the Truthspeaker heavy and authoritative on her chest. Iata agreed with that choice. Ceorre was always her most intimidating when being the palpable presence of the Truthspeaker.

The ramp fully extended, clicked into place, and the loudest sound for that moment was the soft pings of the small ship's engines as they began to cool. It was a high-end commercial courier, and yes, Koldari would have paid dearly for a bunk on this ship. Likely was still paying by the minute for the ship to land here and stay however long was required.

The hatch swung open, and a person with light brown skin and braided blue hair ducked out, wearing well-tailored clothes. They slung a duffel over one shoulder and sauntered down the ramp. Not Koldari.

The person looked up at those gathered to greet them, faltered halfway down the ramp, then plastered on a smile. They called back behind them, "Kyran, there's a welcoming committee!"

Who was this person? *Who?* Iata should know everyone who orbited any head of a high house, but he didn't recognize them.

The person strode toward him, and Chadrikour and his other two guards, who'd met him again at the Adeium, tensed. Ceorre's own Adeium guards tensed. None of them had weapons—no weapons were allowed within the Adeium grounds—but that didn't mean they couldn't be lethal with just their bodies.

Another person emerged—and this was Koldari, if looking more worn than the last time Iata had seen him at court.

Koldari spotted him beside Ceorre, saw Haneri and his cheek twitched. But his own face was a mask of concern, with just too much overemphasis to be truly read as genuine. His long dark hair was tied up in a messy bun today, forgoing the slickly oiled look he usually favored.

"Ser Seritarchus," he said as he stepped down onto the ground and swept a bow at *just* the appropriate depth for his station. "Ser Consort. Thank you for coming to meet me. I am, of course, very concerned for the wellbeing of your cousin."

"That's very noble of you, Kyran," Iata said.

Ceorre drew an audible breath, drew attention to herself. "Duke Koldari, I did receive your message. I assure you, you need have no fear of mistreatment on the part of Imorie Rhialden méron Quevedo. They are staying in the palace, with all amenities and privileges. Imorie is using they and them."

Iata had seen that note from Maja in his inbox in the back corridors, when he'd hastily sent a message to Jalava on his comm. Along with a message from Mariyit that Maja's ship had departed.

"Then you will have no objections to my seeing them," Koldari said. "As a close friend. I would like to support them in their time of distress."

What the hell was he playing at? This was pushing far beyond his station.

"I can escort you," Haneri said, "when Imorie is well enough to see you. You are aware that they have the Bruising Sleep? Poor child, this day has not been kind to them. I have my own staff attending to their needs as well. As they've come into my household, I will of course care for them as if they were my own."

Haneri. What was she doing?

Iata very carefully did not share a glance with Ceorre. Someone, Adeius, *someone* would have to Change to show Arianna was nearby. He couldn't do it—he needed to be seen with her. Maja was gone. He had no bloodservant, there was only Pria, who struggled with that sort of Change, who didn't particularly like Change at all, and he hated to push it on her. But someone would have to.

Koldari's small smile told that he wasn't surprised at Haneri's phrasing. That he had, in fact, caught the rumors, or maybe had his own suspicions. Or worse, confirmations, if he'd been working with the people at Windvale.

Iata's anger rose again.

"Forgive me," Koldari said, turning swiftly to the blue-haired person who was fidgeting beside him, "this is my partner, Iwan ko Antia. They came back with me, they were also concerned for Imorie's safety." His eyes met Iata's, and there was nothing soft in them.

Was Koldari openly challenging him? Did Koldari, the least among the heads of high houses, have that nerve?

A movement up the ramp caught his eye, and the breath went out of him.

A person whose ident image he'd kept open on a holo on his desk whenever he'd been alone today. Jis Ameer. Imorie's personal servant at Windvale.

Bettea.

Fae was broadcasting faer tells, eyes not quite meeting his. Fae might know it was him just now, as Imorie had known, but he couldn't be certain of that. But Bettea wouldn't dare meet his eyes if fae was still a servant and not of his household anyway.

Oh, Adeius. Bettea was here. Fae was safe. And fae would have answers.

Haneri shifted beside him, pulling his attention briefly back to her, enough to warn him to smooth over whatever he was feeling. Koldari was watching his reaction. Had he let his composure slip?

Likely, and he had to carry it through.

"Jis Ameer," he said, holding out a hand. "Imorie expressed deep concern for your wellbeing. I am glad to see you unharmed."

Keep the cool distance. Keep that slightly ironic edge. Let the delight show in his eyes as malice toward Koldari, not relief. He had a witness. Now he had a solid witness. Jis Ameer was leverage.

And his gut twisted at the violence he was currently doing to himself.

He felt his hold on his aura slipping. Oh, Adeius, no. No, not now.

He paused, leaned to whisper to Haneri, "Take faer into the palace, please. If Imorie is awake, let Jis into their apartment. If not, if you would let faer wait in your apartment—"

"Of course."

That brief break in tension, that movement toward a solution, steadied Iata enough to wrestle back control of his aura.

"Come, child," Haneri said, moving to scoop up Bettea. "You will do much to steady our Imorie's nerves, I think."

If Bettea thought it bizarre that Haneri was here, let alone offering comfort, fae made no sign of it, and for that, Iata was fiercely proud.

Safe. Bettea was safe.

He no longer had Haneri to steady him. He straightened, diving as far as he could into the steadying bounds of Homaj Rhialden without submerging entirely.

"I thank you for bringing back my cousin's servant. That wins you good will in my eyes, Koldari. Just a little."

Koldari turned back to him, frowning. "Forgive me, Ser Seritarchus, but what have I done to offend you? I am here to help one of your family. I certainly didn't have to make that trip at that speed. I chose to, because I care about their wellbeing."

Iata inclined his head. "And for that, again, you have my gratitude."

"Is Imorie your child?" Koldari asked.

Adeius. Bold and in the open.

Koldari was looking straight into his eyes, and he was unsteady, and damn Imorie's idea of adoption, this was the moment that it backfired, wasn't it?

"Yes. I have adopted them, for their protection."

Koldari drew back. He'd obviously been expecting to catch Iata in a lie, not expecting that answer.

Shit. And what complications would that little ripple cause? He would have to see the adoption redrawn and made public. Publicly adopted by Homaj Rhialden...?

No. No, that wasn't what was needed here. That would only muddy everything.

"That, however, is private," he said quietly, with absolutely no hint of danger in his tone. "They are not, of course, one of my heirs, not in the line of succession. When this whole mess blows past, they will be allowed to rescind the adoption—I tell you, they are not particularly fond of their place in the palace just now. It's not a situation they wanted, nor I, though it's the situation we are in. Is that enough to satisfy your need to see them safe, Duke Koldari? They are under my personal, familial, protection. Not publicly, but if pressed, I will uphold it behind closed legal proceedings."

Koldari studied him, openly skeptical.

Koldari's partner, Iwan, hovered behind him, seeming

unconcerned, but that was a show. The person was wound tight. They knew just how dangerous a ground Koldari walked on, even if Koldari himself didn't seem to know it. Or maybe didn't care.

"Now," Iata said, straightening. "Kyran. We have most of what happened at Windvale from Imorie and their companion, Etienne Tanaka. There are gaps, however. Come with me —I would like you to fill them in."

44

OCEAN JUNIPER

> *And I've wondered ever since if you liked me for my position, or for my smile. But why can't it be both?*
>
> — COUNT JIN HEART IN THE VID DRAMA
> *NOVA HEARTS*, SEASON 7, EPISODE 10, "WHAT
> WE ALL SAW LAST NIGHT"

Dressa closed the door to her apartment much more slowly, more quietly, than she normally would. And then she leaned against it, which felt dramatic and maybe childish, but it was good to have a solid barrier between herself and the rest of the palace. And its people.

Lesander, who'd paused in the apartment's entry hall, tilted her head in question.

"What?" Dressa asked. "I am allowed to want to hold back the ravenous, questioning hordes. 'Do you know anything about your *cousin*, Ser Truthspoken,' high emphasis on *cousin*, 'When can we meet your *cousin*, Ser Truthspoken?'"

Lesander snorted, the tightness around her mouth, her

eyes, easing. And it was good to see. Dressa wished they had been able to talk earlier, to hash out whatever they needed to and get past it. Because Lesander had trusted her enough to tell her, and that was...everything.

Maybe she'd been wrong. Maybe her panicked conversation with Iata earlier was just that—panic. And Lesander had nothing to do with what had happened to Ari, and she wasn't on the side of the Javieris and had fully realigned herself to the family she'd married into. Maybe.

Adeius, couldn't she just be a fool for an evening—no, she was pretty sure it was nearing midnight—for a night?

Dressa finally pushed off the door and waved toward the prep room. "After you, Heir Consort."

"To be," Lesander corrected. Because she was right, these parts of Dressa's apartment were still under surveillance. Highly secure surveillance, but still.

"To be," Dressa said softly, and it hurt, somewhere in her chest, to not say the truth of it. All of it.

Lesander caught her hand as she walked by and fell into step with her. And the walk had the solemn, alarming air of finality, not moving toward something better.

What did Lesander think, that Dressa would throw her out now that her being Truthspoken was in the open? Between them, at least. Yes, there were laws, but Dressa wasn't Arianna. She wasn't as in love with the laws as that. She would choose her wife over the laws if she could make it work. And she would make it work. Iata already knew—he wasn't going to put any barriers in her way.

She met Lesander's ocean blue eyes, breathed in the scent of her ocean juniper. This wouldn't be a goodbye. This would be where they learned each other's depths and grew closer.

Dressa unlocked the door to the prep room and led her wife inside.

LESANDER TURNED as Dressa shut the door to the prep room, not nearly as carefully as she'd shut the door to the apartment.

Dressa glided through toward the bedroom. "Pria? Are you in here?"

Pria had been scarce the last weeks, and Lesander had the impression that wasn't usual. And that she was the cause.

She heard soft voices in the bedroom—she didn't try to follow. Then the voices stopped. There were shuffles and a soft click, and Dressa came back out. She didn't bother to close the bedroom door—Pria was gone.

Lesander's heart pounded, and she couldn't stop it. She knew her cheeks were flushed, knew she was showing visible signs of stress. And that Dressa knew that she could stop those signs if she had more control just now, which made it all worse.

Lesander desperately wanted to ask Dressa how she'd first known, when she'd found out. But did she dare?

Dressa reached out, gripped her hands, squeezed tight. Dressa was just the tiniest bit taller than her now, and Lesander had always been tall, as was her mother, Prince Yroikan. That Dressa had purposefully made herself taller was...intimidating? Endearingly insecure?

Lesander gave Dressa's hands an involuntary squeeze back.

"You're scared," Dressa said. "You don't have to be."

Lesander noticed the social tricks at work, the steady and assured body language, the warm and reassuring tone. Did Dressa even know she was doing it?

"What I am is so illegal it could wipe out my whole family," Lesander said. She tried to keep her voice steady, she really tried.

Dressa shrugged. "You're my wife. You are a Rhialden. The last time I checked, it's not illegal for a Rhialden to be a Truthspoken."

Lesander jerked her hands out of Dressa's. "I'm serious, Dressa. If your father knows—"

"He does know." Dressa backed up, playing with the ends of her sleeves, where tiny diamonds dangled from silver threads. "I think it might have been *why* you were chosen, in part. He might have known, or at least suspected, before arranging the engagement."

Lesander opened her mouth but found no words. Okay, and okay, yes, it wasn't as if she hadn't thought of that possibility in the many, many possibilities she'd considered for her place in this palace. That the Seritarchus would bring the Javieris close, bring her into his family, to keep her from setting herself up to oppose him. Hadn't he done the same with Prince Haneri Delor, before she had become his consort? You married your enemies so they became your assets.

But had the Seritarchus truly wanted a Truthspoken-trained high house prince in his midst?

Lesander smoothed down the front of her gown. "I'm not your enemy."

She'd said it to Dressa before, that first morning together. She wasn't Dressa's enemy. That, she had decided.

But what would Dressa count as her enemy? Surely anyone who acted against her family would be an enemy, even if they spared her own life.

She had to tell Dressa. She had to. Her family was going to do *something,* or expected her to do something, and she was running out of time.

And still, she couldn't make the words rise up. Couldn't make them come out.

Dressa stepped closer again, her brows creasing. "You're

terrified. Lesander—you don't have to be. Is it the Truths-peaker you're afraid of? She knows, too. She's the one who warned me to watch for the signs. No one here is expecting you to be anything other than you are. And you don't have to use your abilities—"

"Dressa, you don't understand that—"

Dressa's comm beeped. Which it almost never did, unless it was a message from the Seritarchus. She growled a curse and pulled it from the hip pocket of her evening jacket.

Lesander shut her mouth, shut it tight, because she'd been about to make the biggest mistake of her life. She'd been about to give in. To throw out years and years of training and careful planning. To throw out all the years of torment to get to this place. This moment, now. She loved Dressa, and Dressa loved her. And maybe it wouldn't last, maybe it couldn't.

"Oh," Dressa said, reading her comm on the screen, not a holo window. "Adeius, Bettea is here. And Koldari. They came in together—my father is debriefing Koldari and wants me to meet Bettea, debrief faer after Imorie sees faer."

Lesander blinked twice, realigning how this night was going to go. It wouldn't, in fact, end in a spiral. It wouldn't end with her telling Dressa everything, and it wouldn't end with Dressa throwing her out. Not yet.

The Seritarchus had left the last gathering early, and that had been, what, a little less than two hours ago? So that was what had been so urgent. She'd wondered, because she always wondered. Because she'd been trained to wonder, and to find out.

Dressa glanced in the mirror, rearranging her hair, which she'd let loose tonight. "Sorry, we'll have to keep talking later. But—we're fine, Lesander. We'll work it out. Training doesn't mean action, okay?"

She kissed Lesander briskly and hurried out.

It was a full minute, still standing there in the middle of the prep room, before Lesander's eyes stung.

What the *fuck* was she going to do?

She pulled out her own comm to check her messages. Just for something to fill the silence, the emptiness of this room that wasn't truly hers, that had Dressa's presence and personality everywhere.

She pulled out the chair to her desk, sat, and flicked up windows.

Nothing. No more signs, no more signals.

Unless she counted the arrival of Duke Koldari, one of her mother's allies—if a begrudging one on her mother's part. The Koldaris were only just barely a high house, and not even a princedom.

Was that a sign? Would Koldari try to seek her out? But that would be dangerous in this political climate, especially if the Seritarchus was already watching her.

And if Dressa said the Seritarchus knew about Lesander, was watching her, did she dare drag this out any further? If her family was waiting for just the right moment to act, what would they do if she was the one to hinder them? Iata the bloodservant had glared at her with a personal hatred, of that she was sure. He was certainly watching, and if the Seritarchus was busy just now, Iata was the one she had to watch for.

She and her family had left the signal open—either be ready, or be ready to act on your own. Either way, to adapt—action was needed. She was to interpret the circumstances, which in the palace shifted rapidly and might hinder her family all on their own. But the signal was the signal. It was already past her time to act.

Lesander rubbed between her eyes. She had plans—of course she had plans. Plans she dreaded, but plans all the same. And with everything happening around her, with everything that had happened today, she selected one of those plans, tweaked it to the circumstances, and settled it again in her mind.

Forced her hands to still.

She'd thought, once, that Dressa might forgive her for killing her father. Might even thank her. Dressa had seemed so terrified of him at the start. So defiant.

But now?

Now, Lesander had to do her duty. To her family. To her wife.

The original plan, which she'd talked her mothers out of over endless yelling battles in strategy sessions, had been to marry Arianna, start their heir in the incubator and store an embryo for the second child, and then kill her wife. Replace her. Kill the Seritarchus shortly after in a trusting moment. Ascend.

That plan had been horrible, and horrifying, with far too much that could go wrong. The Truthspeaker, for one, was rumored to be better at evaku than the Truthspoken, since she'd helped train them. Much more prudent, then, to play the long game, to marry the Heir, raise her children, and see one of them ascend to the rulership with Javieri influence. Avoid an internal struggle, avoid an external war if she'd been discovered in the original plan, which wasn't unlikely.

But, the signal. They had agreed the signal was not to be used except in the most dire of circumstances. They would stick to the new plan unless something had drastically shifted —an opportunity, or a necessity, that couldn't be passed by. Lesander didn't know why it had been triggered now, whether it was because of Imorie, or the Kidaa attacks, or something else. It could have been decided locally by her mother's agents, empowered to act in her will, or a command only just arrived from Ynassi III after almost six days of comm travel. But the signal was the signal.

She didn't dare disobey her mother, the prince.

Tomorrow, then. Tomorrow, as she saw the opportunity arise, she would act. Better to do it her way and save Dressa. And she knew in her gut that this was her signal to carry out, anyway.

Tomorrow.

45

FREAKING OUT

Growing up on Sullana, so close to the border with the Kidaa, we didn't have a lot of the opportunities inner worlds have. So I got to relying on cycles—when the small cargo ships came in and the big freight liners with their goods and fashions from the capital, when the passenger ships went out, when a band I was obsessed with would finally get to touring our world. That didn't happen often, but it did happen. I was really young when I sang backup for the Anti-spin Connection, and I remember falling hard for the lead singer—sorry, Mim, if you're listening, ha. Then they left, but they came back again two years later, and I still had that crush.

— JERETH TOBRIN, LEAD SINGER OF THE RINGS OF VIETOR ON THE INSPIRATION FOR THEIR SONG "CYCLE OF THREE"

"This isn't freaking you out?" Misha asked. "Because it's freaking me out. It's definitely freaking me out. How are you so calm?"

Rhys looked up from their bunk with their dizzying array of holo windows spread all around them. There were so many windows that their mid-bottom-tier comm was straining to keep up. They could afford a better one, of course, but that wasn't in line with Rhys the junior lieutenant serving on a border ship.

And how much weight did that fiction hold anymore? When everyone—absolutely everyone—knew the Kidaa had singled them out to talk to *them?*

They'd been avoiding their friends among the crew, avoiding everyone as much as possible, honestly, because they didn't want to have to deal with other people avoiding *them.* Or questions. They weren't sure what to do with the questions.

If they were honest, what the captain had said to them, how the captain had related to them after that meeting with the Kidaa, had freaked them out almost as much as the Kidaa themselves. They'd had trouble eating the last two days, and they usually didn't get that nervous.

"I am freaking out," they said. "I'm just doing it productively. Here. Look at this."

Misha yawned, waving the tablet where she was watching a *Nova Hearts* episode that had just come in over the comm. "I'm almost ready to fall asleep, this one is filler. You really should go to bed, too. I know you'll just get up early and start at that all again." She waved at the various holos.

"You weren't falling asleep, and you asked me a question. If you want the answer, look."

They had gone back to sifting through every song the crew of the *Occam's Storm* had on file. They'd found five more songs that had correlations to the runes from the attacks, but none that matched as closely as "Cycle of Three" by The Rings of Vietor. So Rhys had also spent a few hours dumping out notes on everything they knew about The Rings of Vietor, which was, embarrassingly, a *lot*. They knew more about the lead singer than they knew about the actual songs, because, well, a shirtless Jereth Tobrin was hot in all the right ways. If Rhys had the poster from their bedroom at the palace here, would it have shaken loose any more clues?

Misha paused her holodrama and came over, weaving between Rhys's discarded windows further out in the room. "Gods, Rhys, can you at least keep them to your side of the room? What?"

"Jereth Tobrin—you know, the lead singer of The Rings of Vietor? He grew up on a border world, Sullana. That, I remembered. But Sullana has an institute dedicated to studying the Kidaa, and they've translated the highest number of runes from any other institute in Valoris. Three of the runes that were used in the attacks were translated by researchers from Sullana."

Misha shrugged. "Can't that just be a coincidence? It's not even a good coincidence. Did this Jereth Tobrin study at the institute? Are there any other institutes as good as theirs? Does Jereth himself have a connection with the Kidaa?"

Rhys's chest tightened. This was a connection. One among a vast, vast web on tenuous connections—but then, they'd thought their interpretation of that song had been the longest long shot. And the Kidaa had blared it from their speakers.

"I don't know. The *Storm* doesn't have access to that data, and Sullana is two comm days coreward from here." They would ask, though. They'd find a way to word it inconspicuously. Border ships sent information to the institutes frequently, and received information in return. And news of the attacks were sure to have gotten out to the civilian population by now.

Rhys pointed to one of the windows with information on Sullana. "It's a Javieri vassal world. And the Javieri Prince Consort is also from Sullana." They almost hadn't wanted to say that. But...but. That was also a connection. A Javieri world had been attacked by the Kidaa, too, their capital.

There *was* a connection there, they knew it.

Misha eyed them. Then she slowly sat on Rhys's bunk, disturbing the holo windows.

"Hey—"

"Rhys. Go to bed. This isn't all those twisty capital politics. It's the *Kidaa.* They don't think like we do. Take my word on that—it was really weird." She shuddered.

Rhys growled and waved their holo windows away from Misha. "I know that. Adeius, I know that. But they used one of our songs. They know where our captains are when they overlap ships—somehow, *somehow* Misha, they knew that I was on this ship and trained as a—"

They snapped their mouth shut. They hadn't been trained as a Truthspoken. Not deliberately.

But...yes, they had. In some ways, at least, the evaku part. Through play, through association, through the willingness of the Seritarchus not to stop it. To look away. And the Seritarchus had asked them to report on what was happening at the border with the Kidaa. Had he known something like this might happen?

Oh Adeius, had all of Rhys's life been leading to this?

Was that hubris in the extreme?

"What?" Misha asked. "You just went really blank there."

Their head snapped back to her. "Are you reading me?"

She sat back. "No! Of course not, I'm a professional, and an officer, and I'm offended that you'd think I'd—"

They held up their hands, breathed as evenly as they

could. And even that exercise, gained from their Truthspoken siblings.

"Sorry. Sorry. Misha—you know who I am. Well, who everyone in my family is. I'm not supposed to be somebody. The Kidaa aren't supposed to single me out like this. They think I'm Truthspoken—one of three, they said—but how do they know that, too?" They blinked, sitting back, pulling on a thought they'd had before. "Misha, you said in the lift that you could sense them, and they could sense you, too. Is that normal?"

"I don't know, I haven't met a Kidaa before. I told you, it was really weird."

"Well, but—okay, is that something ship's magickers usually feel when coming in contact with Kidaa? Have you heard others—"

She held up her hands. "I don't know, Rhys. I'm—I haven't been at this all that long."

"Yes, but weren't you trained—"

"Rhys!"

They stopped, taking in the tightness around her mouth, the braced, defensive posture. They immediately made their own posture softer, non-aggressive.

Whatever buttons they'd pushed, they had to border some of the things Misha just would not talk about. Like anything to do with her own family, or her home, or really anything beyond her messy love life.

"Sorry," they said again, and she nodded. But her cheeks were flushed, her aura pulsing faintly. Adeius, they'd upset her. "Sorry, Misha, truly—"

She held up her hands again, got off the bed. "I know you were aiming at a point. Can you make it without that input?"

They blinked up at her. Her aura was steadying now. She swiped back her green bangs and looked...vulnerable. Rhys wasn't sure they'd ever seen her vulnerable, and it soured their gut to think they'd done that.

"I just..." Should they even bring up the idea they'd been grasping at? "I need to think on it more."

Misha nodded, returned to her bunk, put her earbuds in. She settled down and turned her tablet back to her show, the glow of the shallow holo screen softly lighting her face.

Rhys hunched their shoulders, relaxed them again.

The idea that had leapt at them, that they'd pursued just now at her own cost, was shifting in their mind, becoming less of an epiphany, more of a horror.

They'd thought about how the Kidaa might have been able to detect Rhys as maybe-Truthspoken when they were in the captain's office. But they'd had plenty of other concerns, too, like their rapidly shifting place in the ship's hierarchy, and deciphering what in the worlds the Kidaa had been trying to say.

But Misha could tell Rhys had evaku training by just looking at them with her magics, and what if the Kidaa could do something similar? And what if they could do it across great distances? They certainly hadn't seen Rhys to be able to tell if their soul energy met the specific criteria beforehand.

Rhys had thought their ability to do this might be tech-involved, and it still might be, but what if it was more akin to magics? What if the Kidaa did no violence, because they *couldn't* do violence?

The possible connection had been explored before, and Rhys had seen some stray academic papers that posited the Kidaa as a race had something similar to Green Magics. But they'd never shown outward signs of telepathy, beyond their uncanny ability to know where the bridge of a starship was with its captain. That could have a bunch of different explanations. Ship's magickers had reported sensing the Kidaa, but only in a vague sense. It was something that tripped their own senses because they were facing minds and emotions that weren't Human, or in any way familiar, but very much alive and thinking.

The Kidaa had no auras.

The Kidaa might just have really good comm tech that no one knew about, or some weird intuitive sense that humans had no concept for. And it might not be anything like Green Magics but some other kind of magics—the universe was vast and full of too many possibilities.

None of these were completely new thoughts.

And the general consensus wasn't that the Kidaa couldn't do violence, but that they had no concept of it whatsoever. Their language didn't include violence. Any rune that translated even a little close to that had Human ideas tacked onto it, because Humans generally and historically loved violence.

But how the Kidaa had spoken to Rhys hinted at something different. And yes, how they'd known Rhys would be on board, however they'd known, was absolutely to their very bones freaking them out. That the Kidaa were even looking for Truthspoken to speak to at all.

What if the Kidaa could do violence? Rhys had already hinted to Dressa that they feared as much, because there was a ghost of a pattern that didn't quite add up without it. What if the Kidaa were just choosing not to for a long time, for whatever reason?

And Rhys still couldn't discount that the Kidaa might be afraid of something else out there.

What in the worlds depended on Rhys figuring this out, right here and now? What danger was there if they couldn't?

No pressure, right?

Rhys groaned, tossed their holo windows up to reside on the ceiling, and flopped back on their bunk, throwing their arm across their eyes to block out the glowing holos above them.

Misha snickered softly at something on her show.

This was so, so above anything Rhys could, or should, handle on their own.

They picked up their comm again and brought all the windows back down, stored their configuration, then closed them out. Rhys hesitated, then made a new message on the comm line they'd set up with the Seritarchus's chip.

They paused, thinking what they should say.

They had sent their initial report, but that had been terse, with information only. And maybe that would be enough for the Seritarchus to, what, authorize Rhys to talk? Order them back? Send Dressa, maybe? Maybe.

But Rhys doubted it, not with Ari out of play and whatever upset that had caused. They'd been afraid of what the captain might think if they made their message more personal, but...they knew Homaj Rhialden. He functioned less on facts than emotions.

They tapped off text and began to write in the air with their finger. Because context mattered. Everything mattered to Truthspoken.

This is far above me, and I think it's really, really important. They want Truthspoken, and I'm not Truthspoken. Please come, or send my sister.

-R

Rhys paused with their thumb over "send." Would the Seritarchus be angry that they asked this, that they couldn't do the task given to them—if it had been given at all?

But they knew their limits. They knew who they were, and they were *not* Truthspoken. They had neither the authority nor the training to deal with the Kidaa like this, and they hoped to everything the Kidaa wouldn't try to speak to them again or do anything else until the Seritarchus or Dressa got here themselves.

And would they come, even if Rhys asked? It could mean weeks away from Valon during a critical time. But this was also critical. This was the first time Rhys had been able to find that the Kidaa had ever asked for anyone specifically, even if not by name. But it might as well have been by name. They'd asked for a Truthspoken, and gotten...a junior ops lieutenant with a well-connected family.

Homaj wouldn't take Rhys's second note lightly, they knew that. He didn't take anything lightly and knew Rhys wouldn't ask without desperate cause. Rhys had to believe help would come, so they weren't trying to handle this alone.

They sent the message and thumbed off their comm. Then stared up at the ceiling, listening to Misha's soft show-watching sounds until the episode ended, she clicked off her tablet, and turned over to go to sleep.

Then they listened to the hum of the ship.

46

THE REUNION

> *If people think of bloodservants at all, they see them as highly trained, highly trusted servants. Maybe a household manager, but still staff. But they've never just been servants. Bloodservants are family.*

— ARIANNA RHIALDEN, MELESORIE X IN *THE CHANGE DIALOGUES*

Imorie hadn't slept as long as they should have, their nerves pushing them back into consciousness. They glanced at Eti, curled up in a ball with his back toward them, still breathing evenly.

His aura looked just a little clearer than it had the day before.

They got up and walked with silent steps to the washroom for a drink, surveyed themself in the mirror and didn't see anything different beyond the smudged makeup. But, well, there wouldn't be any changes *yet* from the hormones, it hadn't even been half a day. And they'd asked for the slower changes, anyhow. Should they have asked for faster?

They couldn't Change. They *needed* to Change. Needed it with the weight of a singularity in their heart.

Imorie heard a rustling in the bedroom and looked back. Eti was sitting up, his hair mussed, squinting toward them.

He mumbled something, which they loosely interpreted as, "Are you okay?"

"I'm fine. You can sleep. I'm going to eat."

They would be debuting to the Rhialden Court today as Imorie. Adeius, and did they feel up to that? They weren't as exhausted as the day before, no, but less than a day wasn't enough time to cover a gap of several days off medication for the Bruising Sleep.

Would the court see that Imorie was sick? Would they just think it was strain from manifesting magics?

And what if the court did see they were sick? Maja had sent Imorie from court to preserve the fiction that the Rhialdens never got sick—but that had propelled them all to this point.

Imorie closed their fists, released them again.

But their legs did feel stronger, their steps surer as they moved out into the prep room. And they were actively hungry, with an actual appetite, something they hadn't experienced since leaving Windvale.

Their stomach growled.

Eti groaned and pushed out of bed.

"What time is it?"

He grabbed his comm and followed Imorie into the prep room.

"It's after six," he mumbled. "Sorry, I shouldn't have slept so long—"

"You're not a gardener here," Imorie snapped, and paused as he drew back. "Sorry. We have terrace gardens, we can go to them later, maybe, if we're allowed."

He nodded, but his shoulders were a little tighter than they had been.

Imorie spread their hands. "I'm not a nice person, Eti. I wasn't raised to be nice. But I'm trying."

That got a small smile. He shoved back his bed-messed hair, which hardly made it less messy. "Breakfast?"

They were both in actual pajamas this time, not Rhys's cast-off clothes. Imorie briefly debated showering and dressing and discarded it in favor of food.

They dropped onto the couch and tapped the kitchen menus in their comm, ordering a breakfast to be brought up, making sure not to include more than a reasonable number of their usual picks. And then they punched for some of the more extravagant options anyway, because Imorie would do that, just to see what they could get away with.

Eti moved around the room, looking at the items on the vanities, dubiously eyeing the rack of clothes Zhang had brought in for him the day before, which hadn't fit into the already over-stuffed closet. He showed more attention, more awareness than Imorie had seen in him since Windvale. Since...before.

They tilted their head. No, more attention, period. His aura glowed around him, gently pulsing, maybe in time with his breaths. With his aura showing, he didn't seem more relaxed so much as more...present. More vibrant? More vital energy at hand for him to access. He wasn't flickering at all, and his aura was mostly green, with only a little bit of the murky black in some places.

"Is your apartment like this?" he asked. "Or, uh, was it like this?"

Imorie's stomach soured, and Eti looked up sharply, as if he'd known the moment their mood had turned. And maybe he had.

"Sorry." He ducked his head.

Had he sensed their pain even turned away like that? Neither of them were touching, they were half a large room apart.

Imorie pushed up from the couch, drifting toward him. Then they diverted, running their hand along the backs of the vanity chairs.

"A lot like this, yeah. I didn't have an extra bedroom like the one Doryan's using. This apartment is meant for an adult Truthspoken sibling to the ruler, but since there isn't one of those just now, the Seritarchus gave this apartment to Rhys. Haneri's apartment is on the other side of that wall."

Imorie had to be careful not to say their mother. Because Haneri wasn't and couldn't be just now. That stung less than not being able to claim Maja as their father—they had never been close to Haneri. Imorie didn't think *anyone*, except maybe Haneri's guard Vogret, was close to her.

Would Haneri try to see Imorie? Would she even care? That...wasn't a meeting they were sure how to handle.

There was a knock on the prep room door, and Imorie froze. They absolutely knew *that* knock. Bettea. Oh, Adeius, let that not be Dressa playing a cruel joke.

But the prep room door opened and—and Bettea faerself came in, still Jis Ameer, carrying a large tray as fae kicked the door shut behind faer with a definite *thud*.

Imorie's eyes flooded. They stared at Bettea, and Bettea stopped, taking them in. Faer gaze strayed to the seal on their cheek, the bright green aura around them.

Bettea set the tray down, took quick strides toward them, and wrapped them in a hug.

"Adeius, Imorie."

"You're here," Imorie choked into faer shoulder. "How—" They pulled back. "When—"

"Late last night. You were asleep, and Haneri said not to disturb you. So I slept on the couch—had a talk with Doryan, who filled me in on everything. They're nice. I brought up enough breakfast for four, and I made sure no one saw that some were your favorites, because you didn't put any in the order."

Imorie made a sound and pulled Bettea tight again, the relief almost physically painful.

Then they stepped back. "But—how did you get away from Windvale? You came back in our ship? The *Jade Crescent*? But it hasn't been five days—"

"No, not our ship. Koldari found me, of all people. He was livid that I'd been stunned and you'd been—" Fae drew in a sharp breath. "After we eat. Uh, hi, Eti. It's good to see you well." And the anger beneath those deceptively calm words wouldn't be hard for anyone to mistake.

"Eti is with me," Imorie said, and Bettea certainly picked up on those undertones, because fae stiffened, then nodded.

"I'll get Doryan, then, I told them I'd let them know when you're ready. Do you want to dress first?"

47

GETTING READY

> *There is almost always outward rivalry between Truthspoken siblings. It's expected, it keeps the eyes of the populace on the Truthspoken in a humanizing way, and it also reminds the people that a Truthspoken's every movement is a weapon.*

> — VINA KASSIN MÉRON ANIRAT IN "THE TRUE NATURE OF TRUTHSPOKEN SIBLINGS"

Imorie ate first, then showered, then dressed, with Bettea helping them select the right look for the day. And Adeius, they had missed faer sharp, sarcastic commentary on exactly what moods would move the court in which direction.

It was different now. They were both inhabiting different roles—and she, her current reality. They weren't in Arianna's apartment, and they weren't dressing Imorie as a future ruler.

It was only when Eti went back into the washroom for his own shower that Bettea said in a quiet voice, "I saw the Seritarchus last night."

Imorie met faer burgundy gaze, taking the black silk sleeveless waistcoat fae offered.

"Your father," they said.

Bettea's brows twitched. "And apparently yours as well? Are we actually siblings at this moment?"

"For the moment." Imorie let Bettea help them into the waistcoat. "Don't make the buttons tight."

"Of course."

"Bettea."

Bettea paused, attention sharpening.

"Maja abdicated. In favor of Iata."

Bettea let out faer breath in a slow hiss, concern plain on faer face. Fae had the training not to show it, but fae also usually ignored that training.

"Why?" fae asked.

"I'm still not sure about that, other than that he seemed exhausted."

Bettea gave a tight shrug. "Maja has been getting more intense, more controlling this last year."

Imorie frowned. "I hadn't thought—"

"You've always worshipped Homaj, so I'll forgive you if you didn't see it. But the rest of us have, I think." Bettea grimaced. "Sorry. Yeah. So, I'm guessing my father isn't naming me his Heir? Dressa's still the Heir—and has there been any issues with Lesander? Does Lesander know who you are? Did she know the Javieris were behind what happened at Windvale—Adeius. Doryan told me all they knew. I'm having trouble swallowing all of that, and I can't forgive myself for not getting back to warn you—"

Imorie gripped faer shoulder. They had much, much less to forgive than Bettea.

"I saw Lesander in the corridor with Dressa yesterday," Imorie said. "She seemed reserved, though beyond that, I'm not sure what to think. Dressa seems to be enamored with her."

Bettea nodded, shifted, faer energy becoming that tiny bit more closed. And Imorie knew what was coming before fae said it, fae hadn't brought up Dressa and Lesander idly.

"Dressa wants to do your cosmetics, officially, have you go out through the corridor and into her apartment. This will be part of your introduction to court, and seen as her patronage."

Imorie closed their eyes. They had braced themself for court. They'd even braced themself for Dressa escorting them as their sponsor. She was a better choice for that than Iata, with his position overbearing by default, and himself under intense scrutiny just now. But Imorie hadn't wanted more time alone with Dressa than was strictly necessary.

Bettea held up faer hands. "She asked, and it wasn't an option. I would do your cosmetics, of course I would, but—"

"But she asked. Yeah." They pushed their hair out of their eyes. This was their new existence, where they couldn't summon Dressa—it was the other way around.

They looked past Bettea as Eti hovered in the closet doorway, his hair still damp. He had dressed in something casual from the rack supplied for him.

But she'd planned—she'd just assumed he'd be with her today at court.

Adeius, she'd assumed, because he'd been with her since they'd landed, but was that a good idea? He was a gardener. He knew how to handle nobility as a member of staff, but not walking among them. And he didn't know evaku.

He was a magicker, though. He could read people in a different way, she'd experienced that with him even before she'd manifested her own magics.

And that was also a problem—his magics. She was high-ranking, and so was he. Usually, the only high-ranking magicker who came to the palace was the First Magicker, and maybe one or two trusted and vetted assistants, as Mariyit had once been himself. With it widely known that Eti and/or Imorie had done violence with their magics—and the Seritarchus had not denied that, only pardoned them—people would be spooked.

Or was that a good thing? Would both of them together give people more pause before trying to touch Imorie?

Was approachable better just now? Or was protecting themself and their identity? Their family? They had the buffer of their name and their adoption. But that was a slim buffer for nobles out for blood.

"Will you come with me?" Imorie asked.

Eti shifted, nervously playing with the hem of his shirt.

"Dressa might not like that," Bettea warned.

"Since when have I cared what Dressa liked?"

"Yes," Eti said, though Imorie saw his apprehension. And maybe he'd said yes because he'd seen theirs.

He moved into the closet, closer, and Bettea watched with a frown.

"Well, you can't go wearing that." Bettea nodded at Eti's choice of clothes. "Imorie, go to Dressa. I'll get Eti ready, if that's your wish."

They didn't wish to step out of the room without Eti. But —okay, yeah, whatever happened with Dressa would be a lot more awkward with someone—anyone—watching. Even Eti.

They hoped Lesander wouldn't be hovering, like she had been yesterday. Imorie was not particularly in the mood to be around that awkward reminder of their failures.

Their gut twinged with the now-familiar feeling of an untruth aimed at themself.

None of this was their failure, right. So their magics said.

They still weren't sure they believed that. Not fully.

"Come rescue me if I'm not back in two hours," Imorie said, and Bettea grinned a grin that didn't reach faer eyes.

Bettea turned back to Eti as Imorie slipped past, but caught Imorie's eyes at the closet door.

"Be nice," Imorie mouthed.

Bettea rolled faer eyes.

48

THE WARNING

I've been many, many people. Some I enjoyed being more than others. Some were more myself than others. And maybe some were more myself than myself.

— ARIANNA RHIALDEN, MELESORIE X IN *THE CHANGE DIALOGUES*

"Cousin Imorie, come in!"

Dressa gave Imorie a bracing hug in the open doorway to the apartment—*her* apartment, not Imorie's, or even Arianna's—in full view of the guards.

The residence guards didn't gossip unless they were directed to, and Imorie was certain they would be directed to for this.

Imorie smiled uncertainly, but Dressa scooped them inside, chatting about recent fashions, and didn't stop until the door to the prep room closed behind them both.

Then she stopped abruptly. She pulled back, eyeing Imorie like she might a caged predator.

Dressa had been touching them—with the hug, with guiding them through the apartment—and Imorie was sure that Dressa had felt some of what they were feeling. Coming into this private room, which had been theirs less than a month ago, theirs all their life, until now. And now it was so full of Dressa's stuff and scent and personality that it physically hurt.

Imorie looked around. Lesander wasn't there.

"Lesander went out. Pria's out. We're alone," Dressa said.

Imorie nodded, caught their reflection with their smudged cosmetics and green aura in the mirror and flinched.

"Fuck, Imorie," Dressa said, and moved closer again. Someone—Maja or Iata, it had to have been—had spread around that their name was fully and only Imorie now. Bettea hadn't used Ari once. And Bettea had used their different pronouns without prompting, too.

It was a small palace.

"Are you okay?" Dressa asked, and the question genuinely felt sincere. "Are you truly okay?"

"No."

Did Dressa want them to just gloss everything over?

Bile rose with the anger that propelled it. They met Dressa's eyes.

"He promised me he'd keep my life safe for me to return to."

Dressa's turn to flinch, visibly, and that wasn't deliberate.

"I had no choice." She made a frustrated wave. "No, and you'll know that's not true—I *made* a choice, because the one forced on me was a really bad one. Really bad, and you know just how unstable everything is right now?"

"And this had nothing to do with getting to marry Lesander?"

Imorie knew that wasn't fair. Their nerves twinged with

the violence behind the words, and that *also* wasn't fair that they could no longer lie to themself when they needed to. No longer hurt someone with those lies when they wanted to.

Fuck.

Were they truly that awful? Or was it Dressa, and being here? This apartment, this palace?

Dressa's mouth tightened, and Imorie felt the burn of nausea.

"I'm already married to Lesander," Dressa said. "We did it so our father couldn't overturn it. The Javieris know we're married—no one else does. We'll still have the wedding, officially."

The air went out of Imorie. Of course they'd known there was little chance of getting their position and title back. Their inheritance, their kingdom. But maybe they'd hoped, secretly hoped that they could get between Dressa and Lesander, disrupt something in the flow, make themself so indispensable to the kingdom's wellbeing that they could slip back into their old role, even if it had different parameters now. Somehow. Even if Iata had made them swear not to.

"I'm sorry," Dressa said, opening her hands. Looking absolutely distressed.

True.

"But I'm not sorry I married Lesander. I do love her."

True. Adeius.

Imorie moved toward the vanity chair that was always theirs—but, no.

No.

They took the other, which had been Bettea's.

Dressa followed them there. "So, you've changed pronouns. You're presenting more androgynous just now, do you want to stay there, go in a different direction? How much do you want me to change with cosmetics, and do you want anything more drastic?"

"I got a testosterone implant last night. It will go more drastic, but it's not there yet."

Dressa considered, then nodded. "Then we'll push in that direction. I assume you want any masc features to look natural? Any flair? I do like the hair." She reached to flip the ends of Imorie's blue and indigo undercut, but stopped awkwardly, pulled back.

"Is it okay if I touch you? Being a...magicker?"

"I don't know how you're going to help me otherwise."

Another pettiness. Another twinge in their gut.

"Imorie, please don't make this difficult. More difficult than it is."

They glared at Dressa in the mirror, but couldn't hold it. Not when they could read Dressa's anxiety so palpably.

They nodded.

And Dressa got to work.

Dressa's skill with cosmetics was on par with Bettea's, and Imorie watched with an envy that they were annoyed with— and were sure Dressa felt when she brushed against them— as the planes of their face slowly sharpened, the angles becoming more pronounced.

Dressa kept checking, and Imorie kept nodding, only once or twice prompting her in a different direction. Occasionally, the swallow tattoo beside their eye fluttered. Their piercings glinted in the light as Dressa had them turn their head. Brow, septum, a waterfall up one ear. The hoops they hadn't removed in days.

They vetoed Dressa's suggestion of indigo lip gloss and chose instead something more natural, though they did let her use the heavier eyeliner. It gave them a more solemn, more intense look. The aim was not to be approachable, not to be vulnerable, but also not to be anywhere close to Arianna's preferences or presentation.

And they weren't.

Dressa stepped back and studied Imorie, brow furrowed in concentration, before finally nodding. "I'll tell Bettea how I did everything, but fae should be able to replicate this. And when the hormones kick in, that will help, and we can ease off on the shading."

Dressa had even darkened the fine hair already on their upper lip. Imorie took in every careful detail, and then surveyed the whole.

Yes. Much more androgynous. Pushed a bit more masc, but not all the way.

Imorie had been a little worried Dressa would reach for a green palette, a statement of their magics, but she hadn't. She'd pushed into indigoes and blues, matching their hair, matching subtle accents in their outfit.

"Ready for court?" Dressa asked.

They were tired, but not exhausted. They were sure they would be by the end of the day, but...not yet.

"Yes. Yes, but try to divert anyone who tries to touch me."

"Oh, I will," Dressa said, narrowing her eyes. "And I have all of the guards on alert for that."

"And Eti's coming with me. With us."

Dressa's gaze lingered on them, longer than was comfortable. "Iata said he was a gardener, and on a resort world, no less. Are you sure he's ready for the Rhialden Court? After what he's been through, I'd hate for them to tear him apart."

Imorie shrugged.

"No, maybe not. But he's not a stranger to nobility, either. He's polite, and he's quiet, and he'll just be near me. And two magickers, two high-ranking magickers, feel like a better shield just now than one. They might not think I'm dangerous, if they think I'm—*well*, who I was—and I don't know why they wouldn't think I'm dangerous if they do think that —but Eti's not a known quantity."

"Mm. Okay. Lesander will be with us. She'll be back

shortly, I'm telling her we're done right now." She had out her comm, tapping a quick message.

"Imorie," Dressa said, setting her comm down again, and not looking at it as it softly buzzed. She waited until Imorie met her gaze again.

"Cousin," she said, and Imorie felt the layers, knew Dressa was talking about the adoption and what it meant. For Imorie, for Dressa. For Imorie's hopes for their own future.

"Be careful."

Imorie nodded. Taking the warning for what it was. In all its layers.

"Of course."

49

THIS DAY

> *A Truthspoken ruler doesn't just have a kingdom to rule—they have a family to supervise and protect, an Adeium to balance. It's so much. But how can it be any other way?*

— HOMAJ RHIALDEN, SERITARCHUS IX IN A PRIVATE LETTER, NEVER SENT; PUBLISHED IN *THE CHANGE DIALOGUES*

Iata had slept longer than he should have, but debriefing Kyran Koldari had gone late into the night. And now...he had information he wasn't sure what to do with. Information he wasn't sure was true.

In the debriefing, he'd locked his senses down again, painful as it was, because he knew Koldari hadn't fully bought his admission that he'd adopted Imorie. Koldari would be actively searching for any angle, any information to use against him. It was just how the high houses worked.

He still hadn't pinned down Koldari's motives, and Koldari had proved more adept at evasion than he'd assumed. Not even Ceorre had been able to maneuver him to all the corners they both wished. And that was more than troubling.

Did Koldari want to marry Imorie, was that it? See if he could secure himself and High House Koldari a place in the Rhialden line? Was he trying to usurp the Javieri influence at court? The Koldaris were allied with the Javieris, but that didn't mean they wouldn't take a chance to surpass the Javieris if it arrived.

Iata slipped through the back corridors now, through the tunnels beneath the palace courtyard toward the Adeium. Ceorre had taken part in the start of that debriefing the night before, but she'd had to step out and tend to a late-night argument that broke out among a few noble petitioners in the Adeium and the speakers on staff, which had ballooned into a minor crisis.

The noble fools had taken the position that Green Magickers should be formally declared heretical, and if the Adeium wouldn't do it, maybe the people should do it themselves. Which was bad enough, but the most dangerous step from there was to point at the Rhialden family as obviously unworthy of serving as the hands and will of Adeius, if they had at least one magicker in their midst. Let alone two.

From what he understood, the argument had been near that point. Even some of the speakers had agreed with it.

His breakfast sat heavy in his stomach as he let himself into the Adeium practice room, and trying to soothe it away did little good. The sourness sat in his soul.

He found Ceorre in her cramped office, thankfully alone.

"No more fires to put out this morning? No one coming after us with pitchforks?" He shut the inner office door behind him.

Ceorre sighed, pinching the bridge of her nose beneath her reading glasses. He'd urged her a few years ago to get surgical correction for her vision, but she'd said she wanted a reminder that she was Human. Knowing the power she held, he did understand.

"Which 'us'—the Rhialdens or the magickers?"

He opened his hands, and she sighed again, came around the desk. They both took one of the sturdy, floral print chairs in front of it.

"Both, then," she said. "The anti-magicker sentiments are shamefully strong even among the Adeium, and it doesn't help that some of the holy mandates can be interpreted as viewing any mysticism beyond our own as heretical. I don't believe that, of course, and many people do not—but it's a convenient ground from which to build a base of fear, isn't it? I will be issuing a series of statements around this over the next week, and will be sure to craft all my public discourse in support of magickers. That much is necessary."

Ceorre opened the first button of her high-collared violet jacket, a more severe and even militant cut than she usually wore. Not her typical robes of office, though she still wore the heavy seal pendant of the Truthspeaker around her neck.

"Koldari," she said.

His mouth tightened. "Koldari. I would like to think that I debriefed him last night, but I am absolutely certain he believes he debriefed me. Adeius, he has nerve, and I don't remember him having that much spine before. Was he biding his time, or has something in the balance changed that we aren't aware of? Or does he know more than we were able to see?"

He'd promised himself he would no longer use his magics for the political gain of the kingdom, but even if he hadn't had his aura locked down tight last night, he wished he'd been able to solidly read Koldari, consent or not. It would have made things a hell of a lot easier today.

But that was part of the argument, wasn't it? Part of the

fear. Truthspoken, even if they had magics, shouldn't use them politically. And absolutely never without consent.

He straightened the edges of his sleeves. Homaj's gesture. A reminder of all the reasons why he couldn't let his aura publicly show just now. "I sent you a summary before I went to bed—"

"Yes, I did read it. So Koldari is saying he knew Count Badem was up to *something*, but he's painting himself as the innocent bystander who was trying to heroically root out the villains."

"He apologized profusely that he didn't get to the bottom of it in time to spare Imorie whatever pain they went through. He doesn't know what happened when Badem interrogated them—I think he truly doesn't know. He was fishing for information from me, which again is either an admirable or alarming amount of ambition."

"Alarming," Ceorre said, and he waved agreement. "So we still don't know all of what happened."

"We have Bettea's witness, and I will absolutely get every detail from faer as soon as I can. But the rest—that will be Maja's task on Hestia.

"And more than a few things in Koldari's position are troubling. One, that he seems to think he must protect Imorie against me. Well, Homaj. He also said he knew Eti was an unsealed magicker and tried to warn Imorie off from him, but they didn't listen. He says he didn't report Eti or go to the authorities because he wanted to solve this himself, keep it all quiet and everyone free of scandal. I think, though, that he was biding his time, trying to play whichever angle was most advantageous, and I don't think for a moment he would have hesitated to use Eti for his own gain if he found a way. When Imorie showed up with their Rhialden ties, apparently his focus shifted there. Adeius, what a mess. He's still demanding to see Imorie."

Ceorre reached for her mug of tea on the desk. She uncapped the lid, and Iata caught the scent of jasmine and grapefruit. One of his favorites, not hers.

Ah, Ceorre. She'd done this for Maja, always anticipating him. But Iata didn't want to be the one who needed taking care of. That wasn't who he was.

He thought about being angry. But he had no space left in his heart to feel it just now.

She took a sip of her tea, absolutely watching him. "Do you want some?"

"No—I already had tea this morning." If a hasty cup he barely remembered.

She took another sip. And Iata was growing impatient, and yes, this meeting was important, so important, but so were so many, many other things.

He needed to be back at the palace. He needed to be talking to Imorie again, he'd only had the barest written report from Maja last night about how their treatment in the city had gone, mostly stating that Imorie had changed pronouns and leaving the rest for him to sort out. Was Maja's deciding not, for once, to be entirely thorough some sort of petty rebellion? Against him?

And that was a disorienting thought.

"Yes, fine, I'll have a cup of tea," he said. "The Ynassi black." Not what she offered, and not his preference. But he needed stimulants, the strongest at hand. Even if the brand itself was Javieri-owned.

Ceorre smiled tightly and got up. She pulled another mug and a cartridge from the cabinets behind her desk, and poured in water from a tap beneath the cabinet. She handed him the mug, and he felt it warming.

"What is your assessment of Imorie?" Ceorre asked. "Can they hold their own just now? Are they well enough to keep Koldari at arm's length if we let him see them?"

"Oh, yes. Imorie might be fatigued, but they are still absolutely as sharp as ever." He frowned into the rapidly steaming mug. "Though this attachment to Eti might be a weakness—seen as a weakness, at least—that Koldari can exploit. I won't try to break them apart, I can see they're both holding each other together. But I don't know how Koldari will use that, and I'm certain that he will try."

"And the Javieris?" Ceorre asked. "I'm assuming you didn't determine if he knew they were involved?"

"He claimed all throughout that he didn't know, that didn't change after you left. But I'm sure you saw the circular truth in that. He might not have specifically known Badem was working with the Javieris, but he also knew more than he was trying to make me believe."

Adeius, he wished he'd been able to read Koldari. He was navigating this crisis without his most valuable senses.

He tried to sip the steaming tea, but the water was too hot. And it had hardly been a minute.

He shifted in his seat.

"I know Koldari likes to play the court boar, but it's as much weapon and shield as the persona of Homaj, or Arianna. Do you agree? I will admit I didn't expect him to suddenly show this much ambition or mastery of evaku. He's been holding himself back in every way. Playing a very long game, and I think he thinks he's nearing the end of it. Whatever that end might be."

Ceorre nodded, sipping her own mug again. She grimaced down at it. "This has been sitting too long."

She set it down.

"Iata. I agree with your assessment, and add that Koldari does have one redeeming quality just now, in that he recognized that Bettea was an opportunity to ingratiate himself with Imorie and brought faer along. I don't count that as altruism, but the result of faer's safe return—"

He opened his free hand. "Yes. That much I give him. And praise whatever extra exorbitant rates he paid to bring Bettea back."

Ceorre's smile was edged, but her voice grew softer. "Iata. We are alone. Please let your aura go. It is absolutely painful to watch you hold it in just now. Rest with it while you can."

He'd been intending to do that, he truly had, but it was just habit. And his mind was in a hundred different places right now.

Iata let his aura flare around him and felt an immediate rush of relief, along with the tingles of nerve pain that were becoming all too familiar.

He was holding everything too tightly—he knew that. He hadn't absolutely needed to talk to Ceorre this morning, but also...he had. He needed to know that what he'd seen and heard last night, trying to function through locked down senses and an ever-increasing battle with control over his aura, was what he'd really seen and heard. She hadn't been there for all of it, but she'd seen enough to get her own read of Koldari.

And Ceorre knew all the scales he was currently trying to balance, she understood the necessities of those pressures. That was her function as Truthspeaker—to be his own balance.

If he'd actually been Homaj, she might try to use deep pressure, pressing down on his shoulders to ease his anxiety, but that had never worked as well for Iata. And he was calm enough, in control enough, that anxiety wasn't the problem.

The problem was trying to think and act and make decisions with his senses nearly turned off. With an internal pressure to let his body and soul resume its natural state, an internal protest to being constantly bottled up.

And the fear...the fear that in a moment of weakness, he might slip, his control might run out, and his magics would reveal themselves. It had almost happened last night—it *had* happened with Haneri—and he still wasn't ready to process what that meant. There were just too many other urgent things to think about.

"We'll move the wedding up," Ceorre said. "Maja should be back from Hestia within two weeks at most, we'll say the future of the kingdom must be secured. Then he can publicly abdicate, and you can—"

He was shaking his head. "I still won't be able to show my magics. Even if I'm myself. Not in this political climate. Not if you have to step out of an important debriefing to stop some noble fucks from starting a genocide."

She sat back. "It wasn't—"

"But it could be. You don't believe I'm heretical. But it's a lever, and people will use it. I can't see a single high house backing us right now if I go public with my magics. Not *especially* with people now drawing connections to the Kidaa attacks as well. The *timing*. Everyone's afraid, and magickers are convenient targets. Adeius, I wish—this timing—"

He gripped the chair arms hard, heard the wood creak. Let go.

Ceorre's expression pinched. She was letting him see her concern, which she almost never did.

"Do you want to let Dressa rule?"

He breathed slowly, forced his body's responses to calm.

No, he didn't. He wanted his birthright. He was finally being given the chance at something he'd never thought he would have—and now these circumstances were taking it away from him again.

Iata shifted the conversation, and knew Ceorre wouldn't press again in that other direction, not yet.

"Haneri," he said. "She said she was sincere. I do believe I can trust her."

"She's a Delor," Ceorre warned. "There's a lot of room

around what she said to you last night, you know that. Delor, Javieri, Koldari, and sometimes Xiao—none of them can be trusted. Not one."

"I'm half Xiao. My father, the Seritarchus Consort—"

She made a frustrated gesture. "You weren't raised to their political leanings. You were raised—"

"To serve. I know. I *know* Ceorre. I won't completely trust Haneri, of course I won't, but where does it end? Can I even completely trust you, despite all we've been through? Yes, I believe I can, but—there is always that doubt, isn't there?"

He didn't know how he'd ended up here. He didn't truly mean that. But he wasn't in the mood to apologize. He had no spare emotions left to apologize.

"Yes, I know I must do what's best for the kingdom," he said, "I know that. And if Dressa rules, I am not at all certain that putting a Javieri *she* loves and trusts that hair's breadth from the rulership is best for the kingdom. Not when the Javieris are knee-deep in a hundred different plots to take the Rhialdens down, this situation with Imorie and Eti only the latest among them, and one we stumbled into by accident. I'm not sure this isn't all leading back to them—the Kidaa attacks, Imorie's contracting the Bruising Sleep, Windvale—"

"I think that's an overreaction. The Javieris are ambitious, yes, but do they have the resources to give people Green Magics? Is that what you're saying? It's not possible, according to hundreds of years of research. Don't devolve into over-patterning, Iata. We can't afford it."

"I'm not." He checked himself, pushing his rising anger back down again. He carefully pulled his aura back in, painfully stuffed it back into its box deep inside him, and wondered if his soul was gaining scars—no, he was sure it was.

"I'm looking, Ceorre. I'm looking at everything. Whatever is happening right now, there are connections."

"Or it could be that many people are taking advantage of chaotic situations that we can't control." She sighed, stood, and he did, too.

"I'm not saying I don't see the patterns, too. I do. But I know the danger of a mind trained on patterns. I helped train yours. We must be careful, so very, very careful, in the days to come. And Iata—I'm not sure we're going to have a choice but to have Dressa rule, if you aren't able to keep your magics suppressed. It's not fair, I know it's not, and I'm not sure it's best, but it's better than completely destabilizing the relationship between the people and their Truthspoken ruler. There is still trust right now. Not much, but there is."

"I know—I know."

He set his barely touched mug down on Ceorre's desk. His stomach was too unsettled just now to drink any more.

"Today—today Imorie will be introduced to the court," he said. "And that will either be a disaster, or it won't be. We'll need to adapt from there."

Ceorre hesitated, then met his eyes for permission before she reached to touch his arm.

He almost sucked in a breath at the intensity of the fear that she had bottled down, just as tightly as he had his aura. Enough that he felt it through that bottled down aura.

They were all in trouble, weren't they? Deep, deep trouble.

He pushed his aura down further, so she wouldn't as keenly see his own fear. But he knew it was all over his face, his body language, anyway.

"We'll weather this," she said. "We will. I'll watch Koldari. He appealed to me initially—I'll become his best friend." Her small smile just now turned predatory. "And if he proves to actually be an ally, all the better."

"He won't," Iata said, fitting his movements back into Homaj. It should have been effortless—he'd been Homaj with little pause for over two weeks. But it took more of himself than usual to fit back into the right patterns. He would have to push deeper today, remain more firmly rooted in Homaj's personality.

"All the same," Ceorre said. "I have a feeling this day will tell much all around."

50

BELONG HERE

You're either born into nobility or you're not. People can have talents that help them rise socially, like musicians or vid stars, and they can brush against the circles the nobility move in, but that doesn't make them nobility themselves.

— KIR MTALOR, SOCIAL COMMENTATOR, IN A POST ON THEIR PERSONAL FEED

Eti didn't belong here. He *did not* belong here, and it was all he could do to keep himself visible.

He hadn't thought it would be a good idea for Imorie, publicly, to take his hand when they were introduced to the court, but Imorie had held out their hand with clear intent and need earlier, and he'd taken it. What else could he do? He was steadier when they were near, when they were touching. Imorie's surety was keeping him present. And he knew his nearness was keeping them steady.

They both walked behind the Truthspoken Heir and her betrothed. Lesander Javieri. Eti could not meet her eyes and hadn't even tried. Did she know who he was? He didn't think so. Or if she did, she was very good at hiding it.

As they neared the stairway that led down to the palace entry hall, Eti heard a din of voices. He felt the imprints of lives, hundreds of lives, around him, a focused attention on exactly where he was going to be. Well, or Imorie. They were all here to see the scandal.

Imorie's hand tightened on his. Were they feeling his apprehension, or was he feeling theirs? And then, as they descended the curving stairway behind Dressa and Lesander, and the crowd all turned to watch them, to scrutinize, Imorie did let go of Eti's hand.

It was like losing the light of the sun. He stumbled a step —Imorie caught him, and this time held on again.

They shared a look.

In the entry hall, the maroon and silver uniformed guards who'd gone down ahead of them cleared a path from the bottom of the stairs. They were headed toward the main ball-room, which Dressa had said was the only room besides the Reception Hall big enough to contain everyone, and the Reception Hall was too formal. Too obviously royal.

Eti shivered in the roar of so much attention focused on him—because a lot was now, not just on Imorie—so many people who were unconsciously trying to pull from his strength to augment their own. It wasn't magics. At least, not more than the normal Human magics of the push-pull of life energy. How had Imorie dealt with this all their life? How were they dealing with it now?

Imorie had gone strangely calm as they reached the main floor. Their jaw was set tight. They weren't out of place here in that they were beautiful, and dressed for the court, but they didn't flow like these people in the crowd— Imorie moved stiffly, eyes darting around, tensed against danger.

Was that the act? Was that real? But Imorie *had* reached a calm that was steadying Eti now, not the other way around.

They leaned to his ear. "Are you all right?"

He wasn't. He truly wasn't. He wanted to hide, to get out of the eyes of all of these people.

Eti knew he was tense. He knew he'd look shabby to these people—he looked well enough, he thought, but not glittering, not even with the fine borrowed clothes and Jis's—Bettea's—quick dash of makeup to make him look less wrung out. This wasn't his world. And he knew too many of these people's secrets.

A few of them recognized him, he was sure. Some had been at Windvale. He recognized them. One or two glared at him with the heat of stars. Most he recognized made no sign they recognized him back, and maybe they didn't. And maybe they were plotting their own silent revenge.

He shouldn't have come with Imorie. This had been a very bad idea—he should have faded into the background. He *should* have found the first chance he could to go after his family.

"No," he whispered, though Imorie had already had their answer from his emotions, and moved on in their searching the crowd.

"Imorie!"

Eti stiffened as a familiar voice rose above the rest.

Imorie spun, spotting Kyran Koldari pushing toward them through the crowd.

They'd decided how to deal with him—at least, they'd decided on a course, and how he related to them would determine the rest. Bettea had filled them in on everything from faer short trip with Koldari, so there was that. But it hadn't been much.

And now—now was the moment that would make or break everything, wasn't it? Because of anyone who might have enough pieces to bring Imorie down, to ruin their chances of ever reclaiming their life, to destabilize the kingdom just now—it would be Koldari.

His sharp eyes flicked to Eti, back to Imorie.

"Kyran," Dressa said, sweet and casual. "I'm glad to see you've landed well. My father told me he talked with you last night."

Another familiar face came up behind Koldari, pushing through the crowd. Iwan ko Antia, one of Koldari's partners. Imorie had met Iwan on the day that—well, *that* day, which Imorie really didn't wish to remember right now. They really didn't wish to see Koldari, or his partner, at all.

Koldari stopped in front of Dressa, gave the barest bow required by Dressa's station. "Truthspoken." But his eyes kept straying to Imorie.

Murmurs rose. Everyone who could see them was watching this play out. People would know by now that Koldari had rushed to Valon to, what, save Imorie? What did Koldari want them all to think?

"Yes," Koldari said to Dressa, "I am thankful the Seritarchus could see me. Imorie—are you well?" And implied in that: are they treating you well?

More murmurs rippling through the crowd. That had been an insult to the Seritarcracy. And Imorie was sure it had been calculated—but was that genuine concern in his eyes?

Imorie's breaths were coming shorter in the stress of the moment. They'd hoped they'd have much more time than this before the fatigue deepened. They needed their wits, and they didn't have any metal to crumble, not that crumbling metal would be a good move at court anyway.

Shit.

And there was Eti, lending Imorie his strength.

No, they thought at him. *No, don't do that. I'm fine.*

They didn't know, still didn't know, if magicker telepathy fully worked that way, thoughts to thoughts.

But Eti squeezed their hand, and whether he'd heard their words or sensed their intent, he stopped sending them his own body's strength and remained a steady support.

How should Imorie play this?

From Eti, as he also faced Koldari, they felt mistrust, apprehension, and fear. Koldari, in his mind, was associated with Windvale and those who'd coerced Eti into working for them. Koldari was someone he'd felt he'd had to protect Imorie against before.

But Imorie would protect him from Koldari now if it came to it.

"I'm fine, Kyran," Imorie said. Hesitated. "They and them pronouns." Best that was public and out of the way, if it hadn't fully made the gossip rounds yet.

Then they waved a frustrated hand. "Well, okay, I'm not fine, but that's not my cousins' fault."

There was a ripple of nervous laughter around them. That hadn't been meant to be funny. It raised the hairs on Imorie's arms—it was too close to the sycophancy the courtiers fell into around Arianna.

Imorie didn't like the balance in this conversation, didn't like the atmosphere around them, but they shouldn't try to change it. They were Imorie, not Arianna. They were not Truthspoken.

"Kyran," Lesander said, shifting her weight to draw attention to her, turning so the light hit her face exactly right and sparked the gems woven into her flame-red hair. It was an arresting sight, and though Imorie still was absolutely not attracted to Lesander—and Lesander was married now, anyhow—they could still appreciate her aesthetic beauty. And so could the crowd, whose center now shifted to this new and heightened promise of drama.

"Kyran, you didn't show this much care for me when I turned down your proposal," Lesander said, "and Imorie is giving off rebuff vibes that I'm sure everyone here can see. Are you truly in love with this contract Rhialden?"

Koldari didn't quite take a step back, his cheeks flushing.

Imorie *did* take a step back, bumping into Dressa, who steadied them. Had Koldari actually proposed to Lesander before? They hadn't known that. Did that mean anything now, other than being the tool Lesander was using to work this crowd? And what was Lesander's goal? She was drawing a dangerous parallel to Arianna and Imorie with her talk of betrothal.

Koldari made a terse half-bow, crudely mocking. "Lesander. If you will remember, our proposed agreement was political, not romantic. And I'm here with my partner"— he wrapped an arm around Iwan, who was looking pinched —"with only the concern of a friend who failed his friend in a time of need. Imorie did us all a service by exposing the corruption at Windvale, and paid dearly for it. No one else from this court will be in danger again from Count Badem's schemes, and for that I am deeply grateful. I am only here to pay what's due—all the aid I can give in this difficult time."

It was a pretty speech, and Imorie was sure he'd rehearsed it, or some version of it, before. It was far too perfect, hitting on points that would move the crowd, avoiding others. His eyes met theirs again.

"Please. Imorie. May I speak with you privately? I only wish to know you are well."

Imorie wanted to tell him no, they truly wanted nothing to do with him, because they weren't at all sure he didn't have anything to do with Badem's operation at Windvale.

But they were curious. And the crowd was poised, now, and how would they perceive Imorie spurning the concerned would-be rescuer instead of letting themself be fawned upon? Arianna would absolutely spurn him.

Imorie looked to Dressa. "Forgive me, Truthspoken, is there somewhere we can—"

"Of course," Dressa said, and started carving a path toward the wide central corridor, aiming for one of the bank of private rooms just off the entry hall. She opened a door, looked inside—it was empty. Of course it was empty, everyone in the palace was currently out here.

"Here. You'll need a dampener if you wish to say anything truly private—"

"Not necessary," Koldari said, stepping inside. So whatever he wanted to say, he was fine with the Seritarchus hearing? And Iata certainly would listen.

Still holding hands with Eti, Imorie started into the room.

Koldari held up his hand. "Alone, please. It will not be long, I promise." He smiled his charming smile, which did nothing for Imorie, and maybe he wasn't expecting it to.

Imorie glanced to Eti, and knew it was the wrong move socially, and knew people would be marking that they'd deferred to him, but they had to be sure he was all right. They were the one who'd dragged him into this very public spectacle.

His gaze stayed on the floor. But he squeezed their hand before he awkwardly let go.

Dressa said, "Eti will be with me. We'll be just outside."

But Imorie knew Dressa would push off again into the crowds, socializing like she did best. She couldn't wait for Imorie—that gave Imorie too much social power.

Imorie nodded, silently hoping Eti would forgive them for this, and followed Koldari into the private room.

51

CURIOSITY

> *The Koldaris are often regarded as the bastard member of the high houses. Yes, they did earn their place among the high houses, but only through raw and clawing ambition.*
>
> — THUR ELSTRAT IN HER CONTROVERSIAL BOOK *THE CRIMES OF THE NOBILITY*

Kyran Koldari watched Imorie with a mask of concern which they still didn't buy, but it was eating at them that so many of his body language cues made the concern read as genuine.

"Are you really well?" he asked.

They hunched their shoulders in a shrug, wrapped their arms in front of themself in a protective movement. Something they couldn't show to the court.

"No, I'm really not. But I didn't need a rescue just now. This isn't helping me, if that's what you were trying to do. They are my family, if distant family, and more than that, they're politically motivated to spin this"—they waved in the general arc of their own aura—"as politically acceptable."

Koldari snorted, but came closer. Imorie itched to move back, but that wasn't the image they wanted to project just now. Koldari definitely had a personal space issue.

"Why are you trying to help me?" They looked up. "Why did you actually come? Though—thank you for bringing Jis, Adeius I was so worried—but the travel here in the time it took had to have cost a fortune—"

"I have a fortune," he said, and came closer still. He held out his large, long-fingered hand. Smooth palm turned up.

Imorie's skin crawled. No. Oh, no, he was going to try to get information out of them. Going to use their new and unwanted magicker abilities against them. This was Badem all over again.

They jerked back, and he held up both hands, stepped back.

"I'm sorry. Adeius, Imorie." That rang as sincere. Why did that ring as sincere? He hadn't meant to alarm them.

He swallowed. Gripped his hands tightly in front of him. "I saw the room beneath the garage. At Windvale. I knew something was going on with Badem, I was trying to figure out what before I alerted the authorities, but I had no idea it had gone that far. Did they—"

Imorie shook their head. "No. I don't want to talk about it. I *can't* talk about it."

"Is it the Seritarchus? Because I did already talk with him about—"

"No. I can't. It's—my magics."

Koldari's manicured brows knit. "Because you manifested there?"

They hugged themself tighter, edged back toward the door, and Koldari held up his hands again.

"I'm sorry. I didn't mean—I truly wish to help you. I *could* have helped you, and the gardener, he was the issue, wasn't he? An unsealed magicker. I knew he was, and I tried to warn you off, I thought I was close to understanding—"

Lie. That was absolutely a lie, and Imorie felt it to their bones. He'd already understood what was going on there.

He must have seen the shift in their eyes, because he grimaced. "Forgive me. I am a jaded courtier. And you're a living lie detector."

Which was hardly a flattering description if he was trying to get on their good side.

He was hedging around it, and they knew he would try to reach for it, so best get it out into the open now and put their own spin on it.

"You're helping me because you think I'm her, don't you? The Truthspoken?"

Surprise showed for the barest second.

"Well, no, but if I can't tell you anything but the truth, I'll have to say that your influence as a Rhialden wasn't something I discounted in our friendship. But that's politics. That's only natural. I truly like you, Imorie."

True, they thought, though not touching him it wasn't as easy to read him. And though they were fairly certain he didn't have Change training, his soul was certainly dense enough to show his extensive evaku training.

Imorie bit their lip, then held out a hand. They might be able to know if Kyran was lying from a distance, but he wouldn't be able to read their truth with anything other than evaku unless they were touching.

"Are you sure?" he asked, and the question was almost gentle, with a hungry edge that made their gut churn.

"I don't want your help at all if you're only after whatever influence you think I have—which is very small, I promise. I'm confined to the apartment I was given except for when I'm allowed out, with approved escorts."

All technically true, if not in the context they were currently spinning it with.

He frowned, but took their hand, watching them closely.

They slowly exhaled. They were nervous. Of course they were nervous. But they were not Arianna Rhialden, and of that they were absolutely sure.

"My name is Imorie," they said.

True.

"I am not Arianna Rhialden, so put that to rest."

True.

"I'm not Truthspoken."

True, Adeius, true.

"And Ondressarie is my cousin."

True.

Koldari's frown hadn't cleared. Had he felt more than those truths? Because they were all truths. Complicated, and with tangled emotions, but they rang clear and true in Imorie's inner soul.

"I believe you," he said finally. And that was also true, with reservations. "Now please believe me that I never intended harm to come to you. And I still intend to right whatever wrong I've done you in not coming to your aid sooner."

True.

But he wasn't denying that he'd come here because he'd thought they were Arianna.

They got a flicker of emotion from him before he let go, something dark and queasy that Imorie couldn't name.

Truth, as they well knew, could have many faces and many contexts. And they were sure they didn't have all the context for the truths Koldari had just presented them.

And if he had seen the basement room, they had no way of knowing for sure that there had been no recording equipment—Badem might not have wanted her activities recorded and vulnerable to being found, but also, she might have wanted a blackmail record of confessions, too.

Imorie hoped to everything that Maja would find those recordings, if they did exist, and destroy them utterly. They hoped he'd find no recordings at all.

They ducked their head, feeling the burn of shame that Maja would see that place of their disgrace at all.

Koldari misread the gesture and reached for them again. "No, it will be okay. You've done nothing wrong, even the Seritarchus and the First Magicker have exonerated you. You have the eyes of everyone now—look at this as an opportunity to establish your place in court."

Imorie reared back. "I'm a fucking *magicker,* Ser Duke. I don't see a lot of magickers climbing the ranks in court."

His eyes flashed with something dangerous. Another one of those little glimpses into his actual soul, tiny cracks in his armor. Imorie hadn't seen them before at Windvale, not more than he usually showed, but then, this wasn't Windvale. They were aware and as alert as it was possible for them to be just now. And they knew a hell of a lot more now than when they'd last seen him.

"Then let me help you, Imorie. I can help you navigate the court, introduce you to people you should know—I can't imagine the Truthspoken have any interest in your ambitions."

"Are you sure you're not angling for me romantically? Because I'm not in a place at all for that just now."

"No. I'm not. Not now. And I meant what I said earlier— I'm here with my partner."

He had his motives for being here. He had a lot of motives that Imorie could only see glimpses of, not the full picture. And he had the power here, not them. He had the rank, the position, the political pull. Imorie had the backing of the Truthspoken, but...that was a socially dubious backing, subject to be dropped at any time in the public's mind. Because why would the Rhialdens long-term support a problematic magicker?

Kyran Koldari wanted something from them, something important enough to race to Valon to get it. Something more than even the influence he might have thought he'd gain if Imorie was really Arianna.

"All right," they said. "But—not today. Truthspoken Ondressarie wants me near her today."

He shrugged. "I intend to stay for some time, at least. Tomorrow, then. And I will stay nearby today, unless you wish otherwise."

They did. They truly did—but they were more than curious now, their sense of danger pulsing. They couldn't rebuff him. Not and also find out what he was after.

What had Iata made of Koldari? They very much wanted to know that, too.

"No, stay near," they said. "And...thank you. Thank you for coming for me."

He smiled. "Always."

They turned to the door before the revulsion and growing unease could show too clearly.

52

THE CALM BEFORE THE STORM

Trapdoor in a solitary heart
Entombed beneath ruins
Enshrouded by snow's embrace
Groping for starlight, hoping to feel again.

— OWAM, EXCERPT FROM THEIR POEM
"ELEGY FOR A LOST STAR"

Lesander had been tensed all day, trying to think of the ideal excuse she might make to be alone in Dressa's apartment that night. All the easy excuses, like being sick, weren't an option—Dressa knew she wouldn't get sick unless she intended to.

But in the end, after all the social combat in court, after they'd eaten their dinner in their own relative bubble of peaceful tension, Dressa was called to meet with the Seritarchus.

"I need to talk to Ceorre, too," Dressa said, "and likely with Imorie as well, after their debut today. Adeius, but Koldari was glued to their side. Okay, Imorie after the

Seritarchus, before they collapse for the night. I might be late
—if I'm not back before bed, well, I'll save a kiss for you for
the morning."

She smiled, but it was strained. Not, Lesander sensed,
because Dressa knew what Lesander was going to attempt
that night, but because the day had been taxing all around.
Dancing circles around Koldari—she had no idea why her
mother tolerated that man as an ally—and the rest of the
courtiers had been more than draining.

And Imorie, though they'd valiantly tried to hide it, had
been swaying after the hours of social introductions and
people's attempts to touch their hand or their sleeve—few of
which had been subtle. Dressa had resorted to blocking
these attempts by sheer charisma, repelling people from her
own personal space bubble and including Imorie firmly
inside it.

Lesander was exhausted, too, from doing everything she
could not to accidentally touch Imorie or Eti. Because she
was sure her own thoughts would be a furnace.

And so now she was alone. Pria had come in once, briefly,
but Lesander had said she'd had an exhausting day and
asked to be alone, and so Pria had gone and said she wouldn't
be back before late.

Lesander had, she had to assume, a solidly safe hour in
which to Change. If anyone came in within that hour, it
would be her life to pay.

And she had to Change here, not anywhere else, because
there was no surveillance. She could Change, slip into the
back corridors, find a nestled alcove—she'd seen a few
walking with Dressa before—and wait. Wait until there was
exhaustion all around, and no one was as fresh as they might
have been earlier in the day.

She lay down in Dressa's enormous bed, the soft rose and
orange bed curtains pulled back, the sheets and blankets

fresh. They rustled softly as she settled in, stretching before she stilled.

Her heart raced in her throat, and that wouldn't do. She slowly and carefully calmed it. It took a few minutes more than she could afford, but she couldn't successfully trance in fight or flight.

Eventually, she calmed. She told herself that no one would come in, because this was what she had to do.

Lesander slipped under.

IMORIE STARED at their reflection in the washroom mirror. Was there any difference now? Any change yet, anything at all? They couldn't tell with the heavy cosmetics, and they didn't want to wash the cosmetics off. They did actually like what Dressa had done.

Dressa had just left after a rigorous debriefing about Koldari, and Imorie felt...adrift. Their world had been tipped sideways and they weren't sure that any of the usual rules applied anywhere.

They'd needed, just a moment, alone.

Imorie spotted Eti nudging into the washroom behind them and met his eyes in the mirror. He came in slowly.

"Did you—when you talked to the Heir—did she say anything about my family?"

Dressa had specifically asked to speak with Imorie alone. And Imorie got that, had conceded this time, but their thoughts had been half on Eti shut away in the bedroom the entire time. Wondering if he was working himself into a spiral, if he'd be flickering again.

Imorie closed their eyes. So this was how he'd spiraled. He had to know there wouldn't be news yet. He had to have done the math, same as they'd done—yes, the Seritarchus had sent word to his agents on Kalistré as soon as he could. But that word wouldn't reach those agents before the Javieris on Kalistré might have word from Hestia. That might have happened before Imorie and Eti landed on Hestia. Kalistré and Hestia were close.

There was nothing they could do. Nothing any of them could do to jump past interstellar distances.

"No, Eti, I'm sorry. No word yet."

Eti's face crumpled, and Adeius, Imorie felt his grief, his distress in their core. They moved toward him, but he stepped back.

"Can we go, then?" he asked.

"Eti, there's nothing we can do. We can't even do violence, we can't protect them. We're *magickers*."

"So are they!" he gasped. His cheeks blotched red, his breaths coming hard.

Imorie reached for him, but he twitched away.

"We spent all day with everyone trying to find out who you are, all of them in bad faith, and what did we even do today? What good did we do?" He waved a hand and answered his own question. "Nothing. Today was for nothing. And my family—"

"Eti, they might already be—Kalistré is closer to Hestia in comm distance than Hestia is to Valon at military speeds. Whatever the Javieris would do was done before we set foot on Valon. I'm sorry, but there's *nothing* I can do, and we didn't accomplish nothing today, the court saw me and saw that I'm not Arianna—"

He pressed his palms to his face, turning away. Imorie watched his aura darken, go murkier than it should.

No. No they couldn't have that.

"Eti," they said. "I have to be here. I'm—we're—we're still in the public eye, both of us. You have to—"

But they caught themself. Stopped. Because it wasn't true.

And damn their own in-built lie-detector, as Koldari had so helpfully called it.

Eti didn't have to be here. He was cleared of charges, as was Imorie, but Imorie was only at the palace because of their name, their looks, their familial connections as a contract Rhialden. Eti didn't need to be here. Yes, he was better near them, they both knew that. But—Imorie wasn't otherwise keeping him here for unselfish reasons.

Should they let him go? Or at least, ask the Seritarchus to let him go to his family? Send someone with him, surely. They still didn't think he was out of danger, not with how his aura was sludging again now.

But the thought of being without him ached in their soul.

They shouldn't need anyone. They never had before. But now—they didn't even want to sleep tonight without him near.

"What do you need?" Imorie asked.

Which was something they should have asked before. But then, maybe he wouldn't have been able to answer it before. He'd only just been coming back to himself.

"I need a ship," he said, and the words tore at them.

"Okay." They took a breath. Would Iata even let them go? But he and Maja both had been adamant that Imorie's life was their own.

And did they stay at court, playing a truly exhausting game of elude-the-sharks, hoping to at some point have enough energy again to rejoin that court as...what? The second Truthspoken?

Imorie needed training in their magics, that was necessary. But maybe Doryan could go with them, too. Or Eti could teach them.

And did they best serve anyone by being at court just now? They'd interrupted everything today, had consumed all of Dressa's attention as well. They'd done their best to prove that they weren't Arianna, but could they do that every day for the next...

Well, and would the nobility ever stop trying to find them out? The fervor might slow with no results. But it would never die. Not when the court smelled weakness.

This wasn't their home, not Imorie's anyway. And it had been Dressa, not the Seritarchus, who had come to them after dinner to debrief them about Koldari. Dressa, who was fitting alarmingly well into patterns and roles she said she'd never wanted, making them her own. Dressa would be the ruler of this kingdom someday, not Imorie. Not Arianna.

"I'll go with you," Imorie said.

Eti met their eyes. He didn't question. He didn't have to, because Imorie could feel his emotions through that look, seas of fear and grief and self-recrimination. And he could feel theirs.

"I should have thought to ask Doryan," he said. "When we left Hestia, to send a message—"

Imorie reached out a hand, and this time he took it. "You couldn't have. I'm sorry I didn't."

"You didn't know—"

They shrugged. No, they hadn't known.

There were too many damned secrets all around.

"Tomorrow," they said. "I'll ask the Seritarchus. Early. And...and we'll see what we can do."

There was more to it than that. Iata certainly wouldn't let Imorie go alone with Eti into a dangerous situation without guards or backup. Not when they were a magicker and couldn't Change. They didn't know if Iata would let them go at all. But this *was* their life. And they had several weeks' worth of medication for the Bruising Sleep, more than enough to get to Kalistré and back.

And maybe the Rhialden Court didn't need a reminder of magickers in their midst right now. Imorie didn't know how long it would be until they could convince Iata or Eti to show them how to hide their aura. Or convince Mariyit Broden to give them a removable seal.

Would they disobey Iata if he ordered them not to go?

They guessed they would find that out tomorrow, wouldn't they?

"I'M ONLY SAYING," Ceorre said, "that we must prepare for the very real possibility—no, near certainty—that you will need to make your bid to rule and step up within the next week. He's crumbling, Dressa. Not in the way Homaj did, but he can't bottle himself up anymore. I don't know what kind of damage he's doing to himself, but if he loses control of his magics, it might be the end of the kingdom."

"The end of the kingdom," Dressa growled, pacing the totally inadequate space of Ceorre's office. "The kingdom was ending when Arianna collapsed, then it was ending when I abdicated for her, then it was ending when my father abdicated, and now it's ending even more with the Kidaa attacks, and everything to do with Imorie, and ending worst of all with Iata—"

She was getting hysterical. She heard it in her tone and drew up short, pressing her hand to her stomach. Forcing several slow breaths.

"I'm not ready," she rasped. "This can't all be on me. All of it. It can't all be mine to deal with."

Ceorre came around her desk, face stern, eyes bright and far too intense. "You are ready. I trained you, Dressa. Iata and Homaj have trained you. There is no one more qualified anywhere—"

"Arianna. Arianna would be more qualified."

"But Arianna isn't here, and won't be. Imorie can't rule

this kingdom. It's you, Dressa. And I'll be here. And Iata—he will be here as well. Depending on how he deals with his magics, he might be able to manage as he's done for Homaj, a co-ruler in all but name—though behind the scenes this time. You won't be doing this alone. Whatever you need, we are here."

But Dressa knew it wouldn't be that easy. She would be the ruler, and it would be *her* in meetings all day, *her* making the snap decisions that could make or break the kingdom.

Her with an illegal Javieri Truthspoken at her side.

"Lesander," she said, and looked up. "She told me. She told me she's Truthspoken."

Ceorre pressed both hands down on Dressa's shoulders, a steady, constant pressure.

"We knew the possibility of Lesander's training going in. She's here where we can watch her, not using her skills out there against us."

Dressa nodded. She was still too panicky—she drew her attention back into herself, slowed her body's processes, calmed the stress response. It did help. It did.

"Fuck," Dressa whispered, half a cry, and Ceorre squeezed her shoulders in silent acknowledgement.

THE HOLOGRAPHIC FIRE crackled in the hearth. Iata used to think it was a ridiculous affectation on the part of his father, terribly old-fashioned—why have a fire at all if the room didn't need extra heat or light? Doubly why for a simulated fire?

He sat in front of it now, feeling its very real heat. His bones ached with a marrow-deep pain he was having trouble smoothing away. The heat did help.

He hadn't planned to suppress his aura so tightly again

today, but he hadn't had a choice. No less than five courtiers had gotten through various guards to touch him that afternoon. Chadrikour was livid, and she didn't know the half of it.

Tomorrow, he told himself. Tomorrow he would tell her what she needed to know. What she really should have been trusted with for years now. She'd always been steady, quiet, solidly there. She'd been with him and Maja from the day their father had been killed.

His aura was out and visible now, in the privacy of his study, but it vibrated with a chaos he wasn't used to. Normally, he was exhausted or even in pain after suppressing his aura all day, but the depth of his suppression the last two days had bordered on violence.

But what choice did he have? They had to get through this crisis.

And was he fooling himself into thinking he could last another month and a half of this? Last until the wedding? He'd been struggling with his aura even before he'd had to bury it deeply.

He couldn't just drop the kingdom in Dressa's hands, not now, Adeius not now. Today had been a chaotic mess of people trying to use this latest disaster to maneuver him.

Iata pulled his hair loose, ran a hand through it, rubbing a spot where a hair pin had been digging for the last few hours.

He needed a shower.

He needed to go to bed. And yet one glance at the red indicator next to the floating inbox icon over his desk showed that he would not be sleeping anytime soon.

There was a soft rap at his study door.

He frowned. It was late, and he'd dismissed the staff for the night. That knock wasn't Chadrikour's, either, or any of the other guards.

His frown deepened. Was it Imorie? Had they changed their knock?

But who else would have been let through his guards?

He painstakingly pulled his aura back in, but didn't suppress it as deeply as he had all that day. He turned his chair so he could better see the door, but he didn't rise. He just didn't have the energy.

"Enter," he said.

And saw...himself enter.

Iata the bloodservant, wearing an embroidered blue coat and black trousers he knew he didn't own, but was close enough to something he would wear. Brow creased in exactly the way his would be. Hair pulled back in a no-nonsense queue.

It was everything Iata as Homaj could do to keep his shock from showing.

But he said, "Iata. What is it?"

If only to buy time to think.

53

THE IMPOSTER

> *Kindness has never been an attribute desired in a Truthspoken ruler. Nevertheless, there have been some rulers who weren't afraid to show it.*

— DR. IGNI CHANG IN "FURTHER DISCOURSE
ON THE HUMANITY OF OUR RULERS"

"Seritarchus," the person who could absolutely not be Iata—because he himself was still sitting by the fireplace—said as they quietly shut the door.

As he himself often did. And the intonation was right.

He kept his face tightly under control as he cataloged visual tells. Not Maja—and anyhow, Maja was offworld. Certainly not Dressa, and it couldn't be Imorie. Bettea or Pria? No, and why would they have any reason to impersonate him? They could see him whenever they wished to, and he'd set Bettea to sorting through some of the mountain of his inbox earlier that day. Fae had only logged off a half hour ago and wouldn't have had time to Change.

He knew. He knew who this was.

No, he was fairly sure. But Lesander might not be the only person in the palace who was illegally Truthspoken trained, he couldn't assume that.

And if it was Lesander, he couldn't assume he knew what she was here for, anyway. There were certainly easier ways to gain an audience.

Rapid risk analysis.

He had a panic button under his desk, but he wasn't at his desk. He could say the short phrase that would activate the room's panic systems, but would this person react faster than he could? He'd dumped his rings on the center table, out of reach, including his ring comm. He had no gun on him, and he couldn't shoot if he had. And his study was sound-proofed. He could yell, but it might not be heard.

This person might have the persona of "Iata" down well enough for any casual observer, but he himself was hardly a casual observer. The tells were all wrong. The posture was off. The face was even a little off, too long in the jaw. This person was hardly as well-trained as a Rhialden Truthspoken. Or at least, they wanted him to think that.

Why the hell had he just let them into his study like that? It hadn't felt right. He should have called Chadrikour. This person had been competent enough to get past his guards, maybe even fool the slight variance allowance in the genetic locks on the doors to his apartment, and they'd have to have the day's ruler's passcode for that. If that had been the case, how by Adeius had they obtained that? He, Chadrikour, and Jalava had his daily passcode, that was it. And he was the only one who could use it.

Or had this person talked their way in? Waited for an opening and come in with a guard? That was possible.

All of this—all of this in the space between breaths.

"I have news from one of our informants in the city I

thought you should see," the imposter said. They crossed the room, a confident step.

"Sit," he said, waving to the chair across from him as he took the offered tablet.

Would it have poison on the screen?

He handed it back. "Forgive me, it's late. Bring up the info, I'll look at it. Have you eaten yet?"

The imposter settled on the chair across from him, taking back the tablet.

Tells, he was looking for tells.

He calculated the odds of sprinting for the door if needed, or toward the concealed panel for the back corridors, which was closer. But the imposter was watching him closely, though they were trying to hide that fact.

No, definitely not Rhialden trained. Not that the few fully illicitly trained nobles he and Homaj had come across hadn't been skilled in their own right. No one went through all the anguish of learning how to Change and the fear of being found out without gaining something out of it, and the nobility had their own preferred illicit trainers. Could he recognize a training style here? Anything in this person's mannerisms?

The imposter glanced up and quickly back down again.

There. *There.* That was Lesander. He didn't know all of her tells, but he'd seen her do that before. She must be nervous to let such an obvious tell show.

She *should* be nervous. What the hell was she doing here? What the hell was she doing as *him?* She had hardly seen enough of him as a bloodservant since she'd arrived to impersonate him, too. This was the product of deep research, high security database infiltration, possible accomplices with the Palace Guard and staff.

Where was Chadrikour? If he had to call out through the soundproofing of his study, would he be remotely loud enough to be heard? It wasn't entirely soundproof for that reason, but he would certainly give himself away if he tried.

Carefully, he felt through his bottled up aura, reaching for the ambient feel of the room. Lesander's emotions were a tightly controlled knot in front of him, her soul energy dense and unyielding. She had purpose in being here. Intense purpose.

Lesander handed the tablet back to him.

Whatever else she had researched into his life, she obviously hadn't stumbled on the fact that Iata, just now, was the Seritarchus.

He glanced down at the tablet. A shallow holo over the screen showed a Municipal Guard report from Valon City. What?

He frowned at it. She hadn't brought him nonsense information, unless this was a fake. But it was a report of another riot around Green Magickers in the city—this one, for once, in support of magicker rights. He checked the timestamp. Less than two hours ago. This report was probably waiting in his desk queue right now.

Why was she here? Why had she brought him this information? Was it a cover for something else, or was it something she'd needed him to know, and why? Why risk impersonating someone the Seritarchus knew so well in his own apartment?

Lesander shifted, and he tracked the movement warily.

So the question now was: did he play this out, not letting her know that he knew who she was? Or did he tell her? And try, even, to co-opt her into his own service?

She was risking her life just now. She knew that. He knew that. What was happening here wasn't a game. And he could have her killed for attempting as much. He could have her killed for being trained for as much.

But Dressa loved her. That much was plain.

And she loved Dressa back. It was possible to fake love, but...not in front of him. Not with both Truthspoken and magicker senses picking up on all the cues.

His rage from the day before, at least, had faded when Bettea had come home alive. And now he was just tired. And with a few minutes to observe her now, Lesander was plainly terrified.

"Lesander," he said, and looked up.

She froze, eyes wide and locked on his.

And it was throwing him off, really throwing him off, that it was almost his own face looking back at him. Maja had been him plenty of times, but that was with permission. That was with trust. And this was not Maja.

"You're good, I'll give you that. You're not that good. But I can make you that good."

Her hands twitched. Yes, she was armed, and stifling her impulses to draw her weapons.

He didn't move. He kept his own posture relaxed and had an instinct his own stillness was co-opting hers.

"Does Dressa know you're here?"

She grimaced, still his expression, then sighed, shook her head. His own mannerisms as Iata were bleeding out of her by the second, and yes, he could see her natural body language cues now. She had done a passable job of hiding them.

"Good," he said. "Come with me."

He got up. Deliberately turned his back—and every moment it was turned he had to stifle the impulse to brace for an attack. She didn't try to kill him.

He grabbed his rings off the center table and slid them onto each finger, then stepped to the panel door, opening it into the back corridors. He waited for her to follow. And after a hesitant moment, she did.

"Where?" she asked. She gave the slightest wince as she

heard her own voice—his voice—speak her words, now that she wasn't actively trying to project Iata. So she was trained in Change, but didn't have a lot of experience in it. Or at least, didn't have a lot of experience in being male. Or, maybe, in failing in front of a Seritarchus.

"We're going into the city."

HE TOLD stories in a hushed undertone as they walked through the residence back corridors, down into the palace basement, and then into the tunnels that led out of the palace. He told of his own training in Change—well, from Homaj's point of view, which he knew well enough to fabricate. She listened, and eventually, started asking questions by the time they reached the small garage with electric bikes that would take them through the tunnel that ran under the river.

They rode in silence. The engines weren't loud, but the tires were, and talking wasn't easy.

When they stopped and parked the bikes again, he pointed to a ladder and waved for her to climb up ahead of him.

She stiffened, all her wariness coming back. Had it only just occurred to her that he might be taking her out here to kill her? Or had she just hidden it well until now?

He turned his palms up. "I have no desire to have one less daughter. And you are my daughter."

Her swallow was loud in the near-empty chamber, concrete walls not absorbing enough sound.

"Then what are you going to—"

"I'm going to train you. You came to me, and I don't know why, but you obviously need more training if I was able to identify you. That's not something a Truthspoken should allow."

She looked away, face pinched. "I'm not Truthspoken. And you can't train me. It's illegal—"

"Not in our family."

She looked up, a shine of something like hope in her eyes. He felt it, a palpable force directed at him.

Iata's gut twisted. He had her. He'd maneuvered her to this moment, and it was the best possible outcome of whatever this scenario had started out as. He'd have to find out what she'd been trying to do in the first place, who'd sent her to do it or if it had been on her own initiative, and who else was working with her. That was essential. But that would come after trust.

She looked up the ladder again. "Okay, but, where are we going?"

"To the Municipal Guard headquarters."

Understanding dawned in her eyes, and with it, trepidation.

"The pro-magicker riots," she said.

"Yes. I want to speak to Commander Evallin and observe any of the rioters she brought in—the report indicated there were at least six or seven, it was possible the seventh was a bystander caught in the fray."

"But—" She stopped, one hand on a rung, and waved at herself with the other. "Am I—are you—shouldn't we be...not this?"

"I talk to the Municipal Guard often enough as myself. Iata has on occasion as well. Are you up for carrying on that role?"

"I...yes? No? You saw through me."

He smiled. It was not a nice smile. "I know Iata well, and I'm trained to see any inconsistencies. That was not a fair test. Now. If you feel yourself faltering, or feel anyone is looking at you with suspicion, divert their attention with one gesture, movement, or speech pattern you know you have down cold."

She nodded, and he watched her gather herself and become—mostly—him again. It would be passable enough for the eyes of the Municipal Guard, and it wasn't really a question of validity since he himself would be there lending his own credibility.

"All right then. The hatch above leads into a basement service closet in the Municipal Guard building—the door is locked, and I have the code. I'll be right behind you."

54

VIOLENCE

> *A course once set can't always be altered.*
>
> — ADMIRAL NARA OKUDA IN A BRIEF TO THE
> IALORIUS DURING THE FIRST
> ONABRII-KAST WAR

He talked with Commander Evallin for a half hour and observed the rioters she'd brought in for another half hour. Then he spoke with the rioters themselves, hearing their grievances for an hour more, all while keeping a running dialogue with Lesander to point out the relevant details. She paid attention. And her composure didn't falter as much as he thought it might—she was very passably Iata byr Rhialden throughout.

When he had the information he'd come for, and had let his appearance and willingness to listen do its own work, he led Lesander back to the storage closet. Commander Evallin alone had access to that hall's security footage and would delete the other relevant parts as well. He unlocked the hatch in the floor and went down first this time into the chamber where their bikes waited.

"I don't understand," Lesander said as she retrieved her bike, "why the rioters would riot in favor of the Green Magickers if they knew they'd be arrested. And why provoke violence if they're supposed to be promoting a group that doesn't do violence?"

He pulled his own bike out of its holding rack. "People express pain in different ways. That wasn't the best way, perhaps—people were hurt, and property destroyed. But it brought me down here. We were seen tonight, publicly, to have a positive interest in the message the rioters wished to convey, even if we must still condemn the means they conveyed it. We talked to some of the rioters and heard their grievances. Those people were friends and family of magickers, ordinary people who were scared for those they love."

"And will you do anything about their grievances?" Lesander asked, her voice carefully not a challenge.

He walked his bike down the ramp that led back into the tunnels. "How do you feel about the Green Magickers? What would you do, after hearing those people tonight? Maybe those people are scared for the lives of their loved ones, but others are just as scared that the magickers will destroy their own lives."

She was silent as she walked her bike down beside him. Then, at the end of the ramp, she said, "It might not be a popular opinion, but I don't think magickers should be sealed. Or at least, they should have the choice of wearing their seal, or having it on their ident documents. Yes, it alerts us to when any of them are present so we're not sharing sensitive information without knowing it, but it also makes them targets. That's mostly what we heard tonight—yes, people scared that their family members, who are magickers, are being targeted, and they can't fight back. So maybe some magickers would use the information they gather for malicious ends, but isn't that violence, too? Aren't we a lot more scared of them than we should be?"

He stopped his bike in the middle of the tunnel. "You saw your betrothed attacked by a magicker. Doesn't that color your opinion?"

Lesander tilted her head, watching him closely again. She knew this was a test. She wasn't sure if she was passing, that was clear enough.

"That magicker was rogue, and he was suitably punished for it, wasn't he? That could as easily have been any other kind of assassin. I don't think all nobility are a threat because some nobles have tried to kill someone in the past."

"Point," he said, and got on his bike.

They rode for a while in the sound of the tires echoing off the bare tunnel walls.

When they reached an intersection where they needed to turn under the river, he asked, "How would you move toward unsealing the magickers?"

Again she thought a moment before answering. Which he appreciated. She *had* been trained well, in all levels of her training—Change, evaku, court manners. And he was increasingly sure she'd had no idea what her family was doing on Hestia, using Eti as they had.

"I would start by giving magickers the choice to carry their seals as implants or carry them in a document wallet of some kind. They'd still need to have the seals in case they were arrested, or to explain themselves in certain situations, I think. At least until people got used to the idea of them not always being visibly sealed, then maybe that could be phased out, too. And they still have their auras, in any case. But a seal —a seal is a government document. I'm sure there could be ways to conceal an aura if necessary, if a person was in danger. Holographically, maybe."

"Which, of course, would pose its own problems. Do you know any magickers, Lesander? Beyond—well. Beyond our immediate family?"

She shook her head. "No, I've only met a few. But all I've met have been reasonable people."

But there was something more in what she'd said, or rather, left unsaid. He didn't press, though. They'd already come far tonight, and her body language had greatly relaxed around him.

Had she come to him tonight to cause him harm? There was little in her body language to indicate that now. She'd had a purpose. But he didn't want to press on that just now, either. He was already planning how to integrate her training into his already packed schedule. He didn't want her running loose with Change in his palace, and wanted her focused on a purpose he could direct, not whatever she'd intended when she'd infiltrated his apartment.

They moved on again, then reached the underground garage where they stowed their bikes to recharge.

Iata kept up his careful questioning of her mindset, her beliefs, and how she'd strategize in certain scenarios all the way back into the residence wing, only quieting as they were passing in and around occupied rooms.

Back in his study again, he clasped his hands together. "Well. That was a productive night. I want to see you two times a week—in the daytime will be least obtrusive, I think. Come as yourself to Dressa's old apartment. You still have access to the prep room? Good. I'll come through the back corridors, and we can get on with your training."

She was mostly turned away from him, her posture closing in on herself again now that they were back in his study.

"Why?" she asked. The tension was back in her voice as well, and all the wariness that had left her before. She stared at a painting behind his desk, an asymmetrical abstract, though he doubted she actually saw it.

Homaj wasn't gentle. Homaj, even in this scenario, knowing the stakes and the risk of losing whatever fragile trust they'd built tonight, wouldn't be gentle.

But Iata allowed himself to go a step farther than Homaj's bounds, because he knew he needed to. And Homaj was a persona that was wholly his own now. His version of Homaj could offer a hand when he saw it was most needed.

"Yes, what you have done, training as you have trained, is illegal," he said calmly. "But I see no reason not to use every resource I have for the good of the kingdom. I can't afford to do otherwise. I don't think it would be more than a year's work to bring you up to training parity with Dressa."

She turned, and—Adeius, she was crying, tears running tracks down her cheeks.

He took a step closer, palms out. "You can talk to me, Lesander. If Dressa's made me out to be an ogre—well, I can be. But that's not my intention here."

She looked away again. Sniffed. "Did you mean it when you said I'm your daughter?"

"Of course. You're married to my daughter. That makes you also—"

She gave a strangled sob and held an arm out like she wanted to embrace him, her other hand pressed tightly to her stomach.

He hesitated. Homaj wasn't the hugging sort of person, and neither, truly, was he. But she was sobbing openly now, and he stepped forward, folding her in.

"I'm sorry," she wailed into his shoulder, and then he felt a punch to his stomach, the shuddery feel of ice on his skin.

He gasped and looked down, still holding on to her shoulder as he saw the short, square hilt of a retractable blade protruding from his stomach.

She reached for it, like she wanted to drive it in again, fingers brushing his shirt, but he knocked her hand away and stumbled back. She followed him down, catching him before he hit his head on the floor, and settled him gently.

"I'm sorry," she sobbed. "I'm sorry. I had to. They would have—Dressa—Adeius, I'm sorry!"

"What—" he gasped. And only then did he lose control of his aura.

Lesander yelped and jumped back, hand over her mouth. Her fingers were streaked with blood. His blood.

She reached toward him again, pulled back. Then scrambled up and fled.

He coughed on the floor and tried to look at his stomach. Blood was spreading around the wound, but the knife was still firmly lodged. He could pull strength from the blade and turn it to dust, but not before that dust would spread inside of him, and he didn't think he had the strength to fully filter it through a healing Change, not when he'd be busy trying to stop the inner bleeding and close up the wound.

And it wasn't just the wound. The wound was deadly enough—she'd nicked the aorta, he could feel it—but a numbness was spreading inside him, a numbness that was deadlier than the wound itself. The blade had been poisoned.

"Fuck," he gasped. He groped beside him—he'd landed on the rug, but near the edge. His hand hit bare wood, and he pulled what strength he could from the dead wood, what strength it still had, without it giving way. It was enough, at least, to give him focus so he could lightly trance enough to curb the worst of the damage, while also slowing the effects of the poison, filtering what he could, isolating the offending molecules.

But he couldn't remove the knife. He could feel the shape of the wound inside him and was holding the edges together with sheer willpower, but he couldn't heal it all fast enough once the dagger was pulled out. She'd known exactly how and where to give a mortal wound.

And then compounded it with the poison. Oh Adeius, he knew poison, he'd been poisoned before more than once, some meant for him, some for Homaj. He even knew which poison he was dealing with now, and it wasn't the easiest to deal with, wasn't the worst. But all of it—all of it together was too much.

Chadrikour. Where was Chadrikour?

His attention split between the world around him and his desperate trance, he looked toward his desk—there was no way he'd reach the panic button.

His Palace Guard ring comm. Homaj's old affectation, and he had it on this time.

He managed to bring his numbing hands together, managed to twist the ring in the right sequence. "Jalava. Chadri—Help."

He lay back again, exhausted. The floor around him was starting to get brittle, and he tried to reach farther, to spread his strength-pulling wider. It would be no good if he collapsed the floor and killed himself that way.

He waited. Gasping breaths, and black around the edges of his vision. But he held on. Held the wound together. Filtered the poison.

He should try the comm again. He was straining to pull his hands back together and not disturb the wound when the door to his study banged open.

"Chadrikour!" he gasped.

But it wasn't his guard captain.

Haneri rushed in, followed by two of his guards. She looked around intently, then one of the guards said, "There! Seritarchus!"

They all rushed at him, Haneri reaching him first, dropping down beside him. The guards slowed, hesitant, and he didn't understand that until Haneri gripped his hand. Yes, his aura. There was no hiding his forest green aura now.

"You've just manifested," Haneri said. "Pull strength from me. I give it freely, it's not a violence."

He didn't question, he didn't have the strength to. He only made absolutely sure he wouldn't siphon too much from her to harm her.

Haneri grunted as her strength flooded into him, enough to keep him from passing out, to give his body enough strength to hold himself together, to keep the poison at bay. To keep his body functioning long enough for medical intervention. He couldn't do more than that.

"Get over here, you cowards," Haneri growled to the guards. "Get the surgeons. Get an emergency team. He has a life-threatening injury."

The guards finally shuddered back to life, dropping down with their emergency kits. They were medic-trained, all of them, but they weren't surgeons.

His thoughts drifted, and he wondered where Lesander was now, and he should get up and go after her, he had to ask her...why?

Haneri slapped softly at his cheek. "Stay with me! Homaj!"

He locked eyes with her, her golden-brown eyes, same as Dressa and Arianna and Rhys. He made her his entire world until the surgeons came.

55

SHOCK

Though we have little medical data for the Truthspoken, it's reasonable to assume that since they still obviously feel emotions, Truthspoken can also go into shock.

— DR. TIYONA KIM IN "MEDICAL CONSIDERATIONS AROUND THE TRUTHSPOKEN"

Lesander knew she should flee. She should leave the palace while she still had the stolen clearance of Iata's genetics and biometrics, while she could get out. Or maybe, she should Change. Yes, she should definitely Change.

She'd followed a guard into the Seritarchus's apartment, and that had been a risk, but she hadn't been able to leave that way, not with her hands shaking like this. Not with blood on them.

But her stolen biometrics had gained her access to his prep room, and bedroom. Apparently, she'd gotten Iata's

DNA close enough. Congratulations, Lesander, you've passed this one important test.

She'd stumbled into the back corridors from the bedroom, and now she was bumping through the dim, narrow corridors, only vaguely remembering where she should go.

If she was stupid. If she wasn't going to run, which she should.

At the panel door to Dressa's bedroom, she stopped, shivering, staring at her hand. Iata's hand wouldn't open that door. Dressa's would—but she couldn't concentrate. She couldn't pull enough thoughts together, enough calm to slip into that top layer of trance and Change just her hand.

She tried. Adeius, she tried, and bit back on a sob.

She finally gave up and knocked.

It was late. Would Dressa be back by now?

She knocked again, louder this time. Pounded hard with her fist.

The door clicked and swung inward. And Dressa stood there, not yet undressed, eyes wide.

"Iata! Adeius, why are you— What happened, was it your magics—"

Magics. The Seritarchus had flared with an aura.

Dressa grabbed her shoulders, hustled her inside, sat her on a chair in the bedroom. Lesander was shivering past trying to stop it now.

She couldn't meet Dressa's eyes. For a lot of reasons. For all of the reasons. She shouldn't have come.

"Iata, is this your blood? Oh fuck, did you have to kill? Who—"

Dressa stopped. Dressa slowly froze, and it was like watching time itself stop in her eyes.

Lesander, finally, met them.

"You're not Iata." Dressa's voice clogged with dread.

"Lesander. Lesander, whose blood is this? Lesander, what did you do?"

She couldn't speak. She couldn't make her lips form words.

Dressa's comm beeped, and she whipped it out. Breath left her in a strangled huff. She looked back at Lesander, her eyes burning.

And then that fire went out. Dressa got cold. Cold in every line of her body, ice in her voice.

She pressed the comm. "Jalava. Lock down the palace. Find the culprit. Do *not* let them escape. And pull all surveillance from the residence wing for the last few hours—put it under my seal." She paused, that cold gaze not moving from Lesander. "Will he live?"

Lesander closed her eyes, wrapped her arms around herself, continued to shiver.

Dressa put the comm away. She crouched down so her eyes were below level with Lesander's. And that felt intensely wrong just now.

"I didn't...want...to hurt you," Lesander got out around the shivers.

"Are you hurt?" Dressa asked.

Lesander looked at the blood on her hands. Not a lot of it, but enough.

She would have left blood on the doors between the Seritarchus's study and here. Iata's DNA. She'd thought she could take care of both of them in one strike—use the blood-servant to kill the ruler, then have Iata put away. Never have to face that rage she'd seen in his eyes again, never be threatened by it.

Would that still happen? Dressa knew the truth. The real Iata would surely know soon, too, and Dressa could vouch for him.

Dressa would be the ruler soon. Dressa could do what she wanted.

Lesander swallowed hard, and shivered harder.

She should have run. She should have gone somewhere to Change. Come back as herself, nothing wrong. That had been the plan. Support Dressa through the pain to come. She'd been prepared for that. It would kill her, she knew it would kill her, but she'd been braced for it. Dressa had to rule—Lesander had to rule beside her. Because Lesander was not, was *not* going to kill Dressa, too. No matter what her family wanted.

"Lesander," Dressa said sharply, and Lesander's gaze snapped back to hers. "Are you hurt?"

"No."

"Then this is—is his blood?"

She didn't want to answer that.

But she nodded.

She'd known where and how to stab. She'd known how to coat the blade and with which poison. She'd been taught to kill, trained for it, just as rigorously as she'd been taught to Change.

"I had no choice," Lesander said. But she knew the lie in that, even as she said it.

He'd said he'd train her. Adeius, he'd really meant it, too, hadn't he?

All his questions in the tunnels. He'd been patient. He hadn't ridiculed her. He'd acted like her coming to him was expected, even welcomed.

Dressa didn't react.

After a moment, Dressa stood slowly. She pulled Lesander up by her unbloody forearms, pulled her to the washroom. Shoved up her sleeves and forced her hands and arms under the cold water from the sink.

"Wash," Dressa commanded. And it absolutely was a command.

Lesander was still shivering, but she grabbed soap and washed, scrubbing off the red with a sudden need for it to be gone.

She finished and stood there, dripping into the sink.

Dressa shoved a towel at her, and she dried off her hands and arms.

"Can you Change right now?" Dressa asked.

"I...don't know."

"We're going to try."

Dressa hauled her back to the bed, threw back the covers, pointed to the spot where she'd slept these last two weeks. "Lie down."

Shouldn't Dressa want Lesander away from here? Not still in her bed?

Dressa waited. So Lesander carefully, awkwardly in this body, sat on the bed, but didn't yet lay down.

Dressa sat at the foot of the bed, and her voice, if not her eyes, grew more gentle.

"I'm going to save your life. I don't owe you that, I absolutely do not, but I want to. Just to understand. But you have to do everything I say. Promise me that."

Lesander couldn't meet those eyes, which were burning again.

"Yes."

"And answer me this: was this your idea? Or your family's?"

She rocked forward where she sat. Both. It had been both, hadn't it? Her family had sent the signal, and she had carried it out. She could have stopped herself. But she'd had no choice, no good choice—her family was and had always been her life.

Until she'd come here.

Until Dressa.

"I wanted to keep you safe," she said. "I wanted—"

Dressa held up her hands, her mouth twisting into a jagged line.

"Change now. Change quickly. How fast can you—"

"Back to myself, uh, half an hour? If I really strain?" She was no stranger to quick Change. Her family had prepared her for quick Change.

"You have fifteen minutes. I'll have a quick heal patch ready if you need it."

She couldn't do that, could she? Oh Adeius, and it would be painful—was Dressa trying to punish her?

Dressa had every right.

And Lesander had just promised she'd do what Dressa said, for that one small hope. She had botched this. Botched everything about today.

She started to lay down, sat back up again.

"Will he live?" she asked.

He'd taken her into the city, as if she was actually his daughter. He had said she *was* his daughter. He wasn't going to execute her. She was sure of that.

But her family.

Her family didn't know he wasn't the monster they'd made him out to be. He knew what was happening in the kingdom. He wasn't incompetent, he wasn't—well, maybe he was a tyrant—but he wasn't a horrible tyrant. Why couldn't her mothers just have talked to him? Told him whatever they knew that they were so afraid of?

Because what they feared, whatever they feared, wasn't the point, was it? Power was the point. Her mother the prince had always wanted—needed—power.

Had that always been the point? Had that only ever been the point?

Lesander was meant to be a ruler. And to be a ruler, you had to eliminate the current ruler.

Dressa's voice cut like a knife. "You don't get to ask me that right now. Lie down and Change. I'll be here. No one will harm you, that I promise."

But that felt more like a threat than a promise.

Lesander took a long, long breath. The trembling eased, if only for a moment.

She lay down, and used every shred of her training to force her mind into calming paths, her thoughts into a tunnel that would take her under, let her body do what it needed to do.

Fifteen minutes?

Her pain threshold would be high, because she'd need every bit of energy to Change.

WHEN LESANDER OPENED HER EYES, she bared her teeth in the after-ghost of a scream. Quickly, she dipped into the top layer of a trance again, trying to make the fire in every cell of her body dim, to fade into the background.

Dressa was there, tipping a cup to her mouth, pushing up her sleeve—now too big—to slap down a quick heal patch.

Lesander shuddered as the patch warmed and pricked her with the needles to administer the nutrients and medications more quickly than the skin allowed.

She coughed and sat up, took the cup Dressa offered and sipped again. Coughed again.

Dressa set a tray down—nothing from the kitchens, there hadn't been time, and Lesander hazily remembered that the palace was on lockdown.

Because of her.

But she took the snacks from the night kitchen in Dressa's

apartment and ate with intense concentration until she felt her reserves start to replenish. Her trained body knew what to do with the calories, and smoothed over every system until her ringing ears calmed, her pounding heart eased.

"Are you well?" Dressa asked.

Lesander looked up. Dressa had said nothing these last minutes, and Lesander's heart kicked up again.

"Somewhat," she said. It was her own voice. Adeius, her *own* voice.

She shuddered all over and was afraid she'd start shivering again, but her body calmed. She'd need to eat more to fully recover and replenish her depleted reserves, but her body had to settle first. And the quick heal patch was helping.

"Good," Dressa said. "You're going to get dressed, then we're going to Imorie's apartment. Then the Truthspeaker."

Lesander stiffened all over.

She wasn't in shock now. And her clearer mind, having gone through the reset of Change, was screaming a song of panic that she didn't know how to handle.

She'd trained for what to do if she was caught, but she'd never trained for what to do if she turned herself in to her enemies.

Was Dressa her enemy?

Dressa stepped back from the bed, and Lesander slowly pushed up. She was still wearing Iata's clothes—she'd approximated his size and his wardrobe and had what she was wearing now delivered to her that morning in discreet, gift-wrapped packages. And she'd done her best to replicate his scents and the creases he usually gave his clothes from how he sat and stood. She'd been proud of that attention to detail.

Now, she just felt sick.

"How long was I—"

"Twenty minutes," Dressa said, heading for the prep room.

Lesander followed, and into the closet where Dressa thrust clothing at her, Lesander's own clothes. Ordinary day wear, nothing extravagant.

Was she to be thrown out?

Would she be imprisoned?

If the Seritarchus died—

Had she really done that? Had she thought that was a good idea at all?

But her family...

Her family could rot in hell.

56

SINCERITY

Lesander dressed, her face blank, her emotions as blank as she could make them, which was not as much as she'd like.

She followed Dressa through the back corridors to what had been Dressa's half-sibling's apartment, now being used by Imorie.

Dressa knocked three times on the panel door, waited, then opened the door and pushed inside.

Imorie was already moving for the panel door, face tight. Two duffels sat open on the floor beside the bed, a mess of clothes on the covers. Eti sat frozen on the bed, his whole posture reading guilty of *something*.

Had they been packing?

"Is he all right?" Imorie demanded, rushing them. "I don't have access to Jalava's messages, the guards outside the door wouldn't say, because they think I'm—I only got the lock-down alert and that the Seritarchus had been injured." They paused for breath.

"He's in surgery," Dressa said.

Imorie shuddered, steadying themself on Dressa's hastily offered arm.

Then they glanced past Dressa to Lesander, who was still hovering just inside the closed panel door. Doing her very best not to shudder in the continued random shocks of pain after such a drastic and dangerous Change. But she was managing. The pain, she knew from long experience, would be gone within the hour, though she'd pushed harder this time than she ever had before.

Twenty minutes for a full and drastic Change.

Imorie's gaze sharpened. "You just quick-Changed. What happened? Dressa, what happened?"

Dressa checked the closed door to the prep room, the open door to the bloodservant's bedroom.

"It's safe enough," Imorie said, going back to lean against the side of the bed. "Doryan is keyed into the bedroom locks, but they always knock. Bettea is—out."

Their gaze lingered again on Lesander, growing even more intent. Then snapped back to Dressa, then Lesander.

Lesander watched with determined numbness as Imorie put the pieces together, fire building in their eyes.

Her mother's original plan—marry Arianna the Heir, kill her, and replace her—would never have worked. The Seritarchus had known who she was immediately. And Imorie was currently picking her apart layer by layer.

Her own training, extensive as it was, had been wholly inadequate to going up against the Rhialdens. She was a fake. A total fraud.

"Imorie," Dressa said, "we need your witness. As a magicker."

"You brought her *here?*" Imorie finally managed to get out from a growing and obvious rage. They rounded on Lesander. "No one could attack the Seritarchus in his study, and that's where he'd be at this time. No one but someone he trusted. So who were you? Dressa? Pria? Me?"

The breath left Lesander. Her knees felt weak, but she viciously shored them up. Told her body to remain upright.

Dressa gave her a small nod, but no compassion along with it.

But she was here. And she had promised to do what Dressa said. She hadn't run. She did want to live.

And she wanted Dressa. If that was even possible.

"Iata," she said, her voice tight and hoarse.

Imorie barked a laugh, which startled Lesander into stepping back, rattling the closed panel door.

Dressa shifted. "Adeius, Imorie, that's not funny—"

"Oh, it is," Imorie said, still grinning, but it was a savage grin, distorting their face.

Fuck. What had she missed? Lesander had been trained to think fast in a crisis, but her thoughts were scattering in all directions.

Imorie gathered a breath, pointed to a cluster of chairs on the far side of the bed.

"Sit."

What flitted through Lesander's thoughts was that Imorie, as either the second Truthspoken or a contract Rhialden, shouldn't be ordering the Heir Consort around.

She shoved that vastly inappropriate insight down. She valued her life more than that.

Lesander followed Imorie to the other side of the room and chose a chair.

Imorie carefully lowered themself into the seat opposite from her, their mouth tight. They still wore Dressa's expertly applied cosmetics for the day, but the makeup didn't hide all the bruising under their eyes. It couldn't. The day had not been kind to them.

Imorie held out their hands.

Lesander braced herself, but took them. This was why Dressa had brought her here.

Imorie stiffened as if they'd touched lightning.

"What is it?" Dressa asked, leaning over the back of Lesander's chair.

"Just...intense. I haven't done this much." Imorie visibly forced themself to straighten. "Lesander Javieri, may I witness your truth?"

Lesander didn't want that at all. But she'd known this was coming.

"Yes," Dressa said for her. But Imorie waited for Lesander to say it herself.

Lesander nodded. "Yes."

Eti took up leaning against the wall beside Imorie, not quite looking at Lesander, not in any way menacing other than his own roiling intensity, which Lesander could almost feel. Or was she feeling that through Imorie? She was certainly feeling *something*.

Imorie said, "Did you try to kill the Seritarchus?"

She couldn't lie.

But she had no intention of doing so, painful as the truth was in this company.

"Yes," she sighed.

Imorie's anger, a distant but menacing presence in her awareness, grew teeth. But Imorie's intent expression didn't change.

"So you were Iata. You entered my father's study."

"Yes. He—he knew it was me."

Imorie's grin returned. Lesander looked away.

"He took me into the city with him. We interviewed people around a pro-magicker riot."

Imorie's hands on hers tightened, squeezing too hard.

"I think he wanted to train me," Lesander said.

Imorie said nothing, and that was almost worse than if they had. Lesander felt intensely the disgust, the contempt coming from them.

Then Imorie flickered, for a moment becoming less distinct.

Eti moved forward, placing a hand on their shoulder. "I can witness."

Imorie glared up at him, and for a moment, their auras—Imorie's vivid green and Eti's darker, denser green—eerily pulsed in sync.

Imorie released Lesander's hands—Adeius, and that was a relief—and got up. Eti took the chair instead.

Which was not a relief. Imorie was one thing—Imorie was family, for whatever value that was and however long that lasted. But Eti was a stranger. And all that day, Lesander had felt a nagging sense of déjà vu around him. A familiarity she couldn't place, though she'd set it aside for different worries.

That sense came back now, though, and was it something in his movements? The way he unfolded from his inward focus to stretch out his hands to her?

She had no choice but to take them, so she did.

Imorie barked, "Why? Why did you try to kill the Seritarchus?"

Lesander sat forward, blessedly feeling little judgment from Eti. "My family. They spent so much of our fortune to train me. They risked everything to send me here. I thought I'd convinced them to take the long road, to marry—well, you, and then Dressa, to have our children, and let that be the Javieri victory. But they sent—"

How much could she say?

Fuck it. It didn't matter. It truly didn't matter. She'd

already betrayed her family by going to Dressa right after. By promising Dressa to do what she said.

"They sent a signal," Lesander said flatly. "Right when you, Imorie, came in from Hestia. That was the signal for me to be ready, or for me to act. Either way, it was time to act against the Seritarcracy, and I couldn't let my family handle it —" She twisted around to look up at Dressa. "I couldn't let you get hurt. They would have killed you."

But she didn't know that. She wasn't sure of anything just now.

Dressa slowly came around the chair, sat in the third chair between Lesander and Eti, the third point to a triangle. She held out her hands, and Eti let go of one of Lesander's, took Dressa's. So, Lesander did the same.

Her shoulders tightened as she tried to parse the new emotions that flooded her senses, separate and distinct from either her own or Eti's. Anger, of course. But hurt, too. Hurt like she'd driven the knife into Dressa instead.

Lesander swallowed. She couldn't face that, but she didn't dare let go.

She glanced to Imorie, expecting a more reasonable sanctuary of rage, but pain was clouding their face, their aura shuddering around the edges.

Like the Seritarchus. When she'd—when she'd stepped back, and he'd burst into a halo of green. She'd made him manifest.

She blinked. But—

When Lesander had stumbled into Dressa's apartment, Dressa had asked her as Iata if it was his magics.

Imorie had laughed when Lesander said she'd Changed into Iata.

The Seritarchus had known exactly who she was, though she'd gotten the biometrics close enough to work on genetic locks.

And he'd flared an aura after she'd...

Oh. *Oh fucking hell.*

Lesander shuddered, and Dressa squeezed her hand, watching her closely. But she didn't say anything.

Dressa had been so afraid of her father when Lesander had married her, but that fear had gone away quickly.

But Lesander knew about fearing a parent. That fear didn't just go away. It wouldn't. Not unless that hadn't been her parent at all.

Had someone else already done her work for her? Killed the Seritarchus and replaced him?

"What are you thinking?" Imorie asked.

Lesander debated trying to evade the question. And then debated using this as leverage, because if she was right, they all seemed to know that the Seritarchus wasn't the Seritarchus. Even Eti was staring at her intently. How much had he seen of what she'd just been thinking? How much could he feel?

But—no. Dressa had brought her here. Dressa hadn't immediately turned her in. And the tone for a conspiracy wasn't right here. There was no guilt in the air, and what she'd seen in Eti earlier wasn't the right kind of guilt. Here, there was only worry. And anger.

"I saw his aura," she said.

"Shit," Dressa hissed. "Then the medics saw it, the guards, my mother—*shit.* Why didn't you tell me that? We have to assume Jalava didn't want to talk about it over comm, that it's not yet public knowledge. Lesander, you have *no* idea what you've done here."

She was getting an idea. From Dressa came waves of fear, of panic, even.

Dressa sat up straighter. "Okay—okay, we need to do what we came here to do, then decide what comes next. Lesander, do you love me?"

Lesander flinched. What—that was why Dressa had wanted a witness? To challenge Lesander's love? But she had done what she'd done *for* Dressa, no matter that the logic seemed absolutely pitiful now.

"Yes," Lesander said, her voice, for once, solid.

"Did your family order you to kill the Seritarchus?"

"I—yes, it was implied—"

Dressa reared back. "Implied? Fuck, Lesander, can you show me this order?"

"I—"

Lesander froze.

The signal was open-ended. It was meant to be open-ended, so she could interpret and act as needed. Her mother had emphasized, again and again, that Lesander must be trained to adapt to any situation. That she was being given autonomy in the field as a measure of her mother's trust and faith in that training.

But.

But the signal was crafted to be open-ended, wasn't it, so that she could also be blamed if something went wrong. And that Prince Yroikan wouldn't be.

There was no evidence. There were no witnesses that this had been on her family's orders. This was all hers.

And now she wondered, with a rush that was sending her straight to panic, if that had *been* the signal? Had her family found out she loved Dressa and saw her as a liability? Had they meant for her to try to act and be caught? To take this fall? And if she had succeeded, well, then they still got what they wanted.

But she hadn't.

"I don't think there are orders," Eti said, jolting Lesander from her spiral.

"No," she said, glaring at him. "The signal was pre-arranged, but...there's nothing to lead back to my mother."

"Except the testimony of a magicker," Imorie said. "Two magickers."

Dressa sucked in her lower lip. "Adeius, Lesander. That's your family?"

Lesander didn't answer that, and she probably didn't need to. She was sure Dressa could feel her own complicated roil of emotions around it all.

"I came back to you," Lesander said.

Dressa squeezed her hand, tender this time. Her mouth pulled into a tight smile. But it didn't staunch the hurt between them.

"Lesander." Dressa's voice softened. "We're married. But you haven't renounced your title yet. I know that's supposed to be a public part of the wedding ceremony, but I want you to renounce it now. Then swear your loyalty to me, as the Truthspoken Heir, and to the Rhialdens, as the family you now belong to."

Lesander slowly exhaled. This was always going to be a part of the wedding ceremony, but she knew—she'd been taught—that a higher purpose superseded any oaths she'd have to give to accomplish her goals.

She'd been taught.

But she hadn't factored on having a magicker witness such oaths. Her sincerity was on the line, and those oaths wouldn't be binding or their benefits in place, in this case, if the magicker didn't verify her sincerity.

She'd done what she'd done for her family.

But they'd sent the signal. And then they'd never followed up and left it to her to figure out. They wouldn't help her if she ended up in a public trial. They might make noisy protests, but she knew, she absolutely knew that if it came to saving face and saving their own skin, her mother and her mama would turn their backs.

Maybe they already had.

She'd been born and trained to be the perfect weapon. But weapons could also be discarded.

Did her family even see her as family at all?

She met Dressa's eyes. Those lovely, deep, golden-brown eyes. She knew this oath wouldn't be enough. And she wasn't sure at all if she could say it with the sincerity needed. But she was absolutely sure that she wouldn't be able to say the same for her own family just now.

"I swear. I renounce all ties—blood, kin, household, titles—to the Javieri line. In the eyes of Adeius, with the breath of my soul, I pledge my full self, and my soul, to the Rhialden line. To my wife. To the Truthspoken Heir."

With the breath of her soul—that was something her mama said. To her mama, who wasn't as devout a member of the Adeium as she was a practitioner of one of her own world's religions, that was as binding as any legal document.

And it felt fitting, one last piece of herself before she let it go. Let her family—and everything they'd tried to twist her into, and everything they'd tried to make her do—go.

"True," Eti said.

Lesander braced herself to feel like a failure. To feel the guilt and shame of betraying her family.

And there was some of that, yes. But not as much, not nearly as much, as there should have been.

"Okay," Dressa said softly. "Okay. Lesander—there's a lot you need to know about the man you just tried to kill."

57

WHAT PEOPLE WILL SAY

> *If I had a thousand credits for every time a courtier smiled at me, then I'd own a planet, and the last courtier who smiled at me would own it shortly after, with my own smiling memorial standing over my grave.*
>
> — LORD PIN DRAVI IN A VID INTERVIEW FOR
> *THE INTERSTELLAR FEED*

"The palace isn't safe," Koldari said, leaning over Ceorre's desk. "I should get Imorie to safety. It isn't responsible to leave them here. Not even in the city—not even on Valon."

She'd let him into her office because he'd been making a scene in the sanctum, but she was regretting that choice now. If some of these crises didn't let up, she'd be right there with Maja wanting to pack up and leave.

Ceorre removed her reading glasses and set them carefully on the desk in front of her.

She did not have time for this.

"Kyran. Duke Koldari. Please sit."

He set his jaw. But then, he did sit. Uncomfortably, and visibly agitated.

Ceorre was beginning to think the problem with Kyran Koldari wasn't that he was hiding his true feelings, but that he shifted what he felt to match his purpose and then projected it everywhere. A hundred little signs that he was agitated and concerned. That he would fight to protect what he cared about.

And did he actually care about Imorie? Had that happened, and did Imorie feel anything for him? Ceorre didn't think so. Certainly not romantically, but likely not platonically, either. But Ceorre hadn't yet had the chance to talk to Imorie herself.

She'd been putting off that meeting, if she was honest with herself. She knew it would take much from her to deal with it. Imorie had been—well, *Arianna* had been—fairly devout. And just as likely to turn their anger inward as Maja.

"The situation is under control," Ceorre said calmly.

It wasn't. The Palace Guard was saying now that Iata had tried to kill the Seritarchus.

Which.

Yes, that had been her day.

And Iata himself had shown his aura, he'd had to be taken through the open corridors to the palace infirmary, Haneri holding his hand the whole way.

"Forgive me, Truthspeaker," Koldari said, "but if the Seritarchus has also manifested Green Magics, the situation is far from under control. There might not *be* a Seritarchus in the days to come—"

She sat forward. "Koldari. Do you realize who you're speaking to? Do you truly understand that?" His words could be seen as a threat, doubly now in the midst of this crisis. And Valoris didn't have one ruler, but two.

He waved her off. And she was so beyond caring about his pettiness that she went straight past shock.

She wanted a solid minute to sit and worry about her friend, who was currently in surgery to save his life.

He tapped a finger on the desk. "I think I'm the only one in the palace who seems to give a damn about Imorie's wellbeing. I don't know why you're not letting me take them off this world while it's going to hell. What possible use could you have for them now, if the Seritarchus has manifested? They're only further proof of this Rhialden weakness."

"It's not a weakness," Ceorre snapped. "And if you think it is, *that* is why you can't take Imorie offworld."

He shrugged. "Political. I meant political weakness. I have nothing against Imorie's magics."

And that, too, might also be the problem with Koldari. He was interested in Imorie, yes, but what part of Imorie caught his interest? Was he maybe too interested in their magics, even, and for what reason?

Imorie was sealed, and they did have an aura. But ambitious nobles didn't always need a concealed magicker to abuse them.

And in any case—

"No." She didn't need to give him more reason than that, but she found herself going on, "I don't trust that you have Imorie's best interest at heart. And I have taken a personal interest in Imorie as well, they are currently the adopted child of Homaj Rhialden—"

"Who *just manifested magics*," Koldari said, all earnest concern.

Ceorre waved her hand. "We are done. I already granted you enough of my time in this crisis. Koldari—this is a *direct* order from your Truthspeaker—go to your quarters. Stay there. Wait for the palace lockdown to clear. Don't try to circumvent or bribe the Palace Guard again tonight. I will not see you."

He did stand. She'd wondered if he'd do even that. What power did this man think he held?

She was getting a cold sense that he didn't think he held it —he *knew* he held it. Was he connected to the attack on Iata, had he been a part of whatever Lesander's purpose had been? Javieri and Koldari involvement all around?

Ceorre needed to get Koldari out of here and go actually talk to the people involved, but she was fielding so many extra, smaller crises just now. She was afraid if she stepped away from her desk the kingdom would implode.

"What will the people think?" Koldari asked, pausing on his way to the door. "What will the people think, when a contract Rhialden, who may or may not actually be a contract Rhialden, and the person who, even by his own admission, is their father, both manifest Green Magics? Within days of each other? While the Kidaa are attacking our worlds—*my* world. While the nobility are steadily falling to an illness that they shouldn't have, which has no cure. While the person who the Seritarchus should most be able to trust tries to kill him in his own apartment? What will they think, Ceorre? What will they say?"

She pressed her lips thin. She hadn't given him permission to use her name. And she didn't think that speech was about Imorie anymore.

She wanted to tie Koldari down and interrogate him for all the truth he had in him—but then, Iata had as much as done that and come up with nothing conclusive.

Were the Javieris and the Delors the most powerful of the high houses? Had the Koldaris quietly slipped up the ranks without anyone knowing it?

Exactly what power did this man wield, and what did he think he was going to do about it?

Koldari gave a small bow. Perfectly measured, perfectly done. Sincere in every angle.

And what did you do about sincerity when the sincerity itself had to be a lie? A lie that was effective, because it was also true.

Koldari left. And Ceorre focused back on her messages, on the reports flooding in, on the medical scanners she'd had Jalava patch over from the infirmary.

He was still in surgery.

The wound had been bad, absolutely calculated to kill.

Adeius. Adeius, let him live.

Thanks so much for reading! I hope you enjoyed *Court of Magickers*, and if you did, please consider leaving a review! The story continues in early access in *The Nameless Storm*. To find out where to read, see:
https://novaecaelum.com/the-nameless-storm

Want to stay up to date on the latest books? Sign up for Novae Caelum's newsletter!
https://novaecaelum.com/pages/newsletter

THE CAST

Note: Because this future universe has full gender equality, binary gender characters (male, female) may be cis or may be trans. I've only stated if they're trans if it comes up within the story itself.

Imorie Rhialden méron Quevedo (formerly Ari Rhialden): Second Truthspoken heir of the Kingdom of Valoris and would really like to change that. Hates when things are out of their control. Has a chronic illness. Agender, ace/aro. they/them

Ondressarie Rhialden (Dressa): The Truthspoken Heir of the Kingdom of Valoris, coming into her own. Former court socialite. Married to Lesander Javieri. Female, lesbian. she/her

Rhys Petrava méron Delor: Lieutenant in the Valoran Navy. Half-sibling to Imorie and Dressa. Has phosphorescent hair. Likes to research the alien Kidaa. Nonbinary, pan. they/them

Maja Rhialden (Homaj): The former Seritarchus. Trying to find his way back to himself. Genderfluid, pan (mostly gay). he/him and sometimes she/her

Iata Rhialden (Yan): Former bloodservant to Homaj, now the Seritarchus in Homaj's identity. Far kinder than he has a right to be. Male, hetero. he/him

Etienne Tanaka (Eti): Former gardener on the resort world of Hestia, now adrift. Trans male, ace, pan. he/him

Lesander Javieri: Secret Heir Consort of the Kingdom of Valoris. Tall and gorgeous. Secret Truthspoken. Married to Dressa Rhialden. Has a crappy family. Female, bi. she/her

Vi Zhang: Captain of the Seritarchus's personal guard. Closest friend and sometimes lover to Maja. Female, gray ace. she/her

Misha Moratu: Ensign in the Valoran Navy. Green Magicker. Has some secrets she's doing a good job of hiding. Has phosphorescent *green* hair. Female, pan. she/her

Kyran Koldari: Duke, royal PITA. Handsome and likely up to no good. Male, pan. he/him

Bettea byr Rhialden (Jis): Bloodservant to Imorie. Takes no BS. Genderfluid, aego. fae/faer

Ceorre Gatri: The Truthspeaker, aka the only person who can boss the Seritarchus around. Religious leader of Valoris. Takes no prisoners. Female, bi. she/her

Haneri ne Delor Rhialden: Seritarchus Consort, aka Imorie's, Dressa's, and Rhys's mother. Has seen some things, will see some more. Demigirl, pan. she/her

Doryan Azer: Green Magicker. Healer. Will stand up to anyone for those in need. Nonbinary, pan. they/them

Mariyit Broden: First Magicker of the Green Magickers. Kindly, but doesn't take slack. Male, gay. he/him

Jalava: Commander of the Palace Guard. Harried, loyal, usually right. Genderqueer, pan. they/them

Onya Norren: Former First Magicker. Wise and irreverent. Flies like she has a death wish. Female, hetero. she/her

Iwan ko Antia: Partner of Kyran Koldari. Upbeat and effusive. Knows more than they let on. Nonbinary, pan. they/them

THE FACTIONS

Kingdom of Valoris: 187 worlds of theocratic goodness. Ruled by the Seritarchus. Bickered over by the high houses. Shares a border with Kidaa space.

The Kidaa: A species of quadruped sentients. Organized into clans, occupy a large portion of space. Far more technologically advanced than Humans. Hard to talk to. Pacifists (theoretically).

The Onabrii-Kast Dynasty: Former territory of Valoris, now their own empire. Also share the border with the Kidaa. Not super interested in sharing anything else.

Green Magickers: Organized sub-culture of people who manifest the ability to use Green Magics. Marginalized. Can't do violence.

The Adeium: Religion at the heart of Valoris. Genderfluid god. Oversees the Truthspeaker and the Truthspoken.

The High Houses: Fourteen families that include the Rhialden rulership, five princedoms, and 8 dukedoms that together rule the majority of the 187 worlds of the Kingdom of Valoris in an ever-shifting hierarchy.

The General Assembly: A parallel governing body to the rulership comprised of lesser nobility, business people, and common people. Has voting power, but no real teeth.

Valoran Navy: Valoris's space military organization whose purpose is to deter interstellar crime, hold a military presence against grabby neighbor nations, and monitor the border with the Kidaa.

ABOUT THE AUTHOR

Novae Caelum is an author, illustrator, and designer with a love of spaceships and a tendency to quote Monty Python. Star is the author of *The Stars and Green Magics* (a winner of the 2022 Laterpress Genre Fiction Contest Fellowship), *The Emperor of Time* (a Wattpad Featured novel), *Good King Lyr*, and *Magnificent*. Stars short fiction has appeared in *Intergalactic Medicine Show, Escape Pod, Clockwork Phoenix 5*, and Lambda Award winning *Transcendent 2: The Year's Best Transgender Speculative Fiction*. Novae is nonbinary, starfluid, and uses star/stars/starself or they/them/their pronouns. Most days you can find Novae typing furiously away at stars queer serials, with which star hopes to take over the world. At least, that's the plan. You can find star online at <u>novaecaelum.com</u>

ALSO BY NOVAE CAELUM

The Stars and Green Magics

The Truthspoken Heir

The Shadow Rule

A Bid to Rule

Court of Magickers

The Nameless Storm (early access)

Lyr and Cavere

Good King Lyr: A Genderfluid Romance

Borrowed Wings (early access)

Shattered Self (early access)

The Space Roads

The Space Roads: Volume One

The Watered Worlds

The Watered Worlds (early access)

Standalone

Magnificent: A Nonbinary Superhero Novella

The Throne of Eleven

Lives on Other Worlds

Grim Birds: Five Tales of Cosmic Horror and Wonder (early access)

Sky and Dew

~

Visit Novae Caelum's website to find out where to read these titles on your favorite retailers or direct from the author!

https://novaecaelum.com

ALSO FROM ROBOT DINOSAUR PRESS

TERRA INCOGNITA BY MATI OCHA
Hiking in the Peak District at the moment Earth is—accidentally—infused with magic and thrown into an indifferent and muddled system, Will returns to his Derbyshire village to find a ghost town.

HOLLOW KING BY DANTE O. GREENE
Barridur finds himself in Hell where he meets the fabled Hollow King. A cruel and capricious god, the Hollow King offers Barridur a chance to return alive to the living world. All Barridur has to do is defeat the Nine Champions of Hell. No pressure.

YOU FED US TO THE ROSES: SHORT STORIES BY CARLIE ST. GEORGE
Final girls who team up. Dead boys still breathing. Ghosts who whisper secrets. Angels beyond the grave, yet not of heaven. Wolves who wear human skins. Ten disturbing, visceral, stories no horror fan will want to miss.

A WRECK OF WITCHES BY NIA QUINN
When you're a witch juggling a sentient house and a magical plant nursery, you already think life is about

as crazy as it can get. But scary things start happening in my mundane neighborhood when my friend goes missing. It's up to me and my ragtag group of witches —oh, and the ghost dogs—to get things under control before the Unawares figure out magic's real.

THESE IMPERFECT REFLECTIONS: SHORT STORIES BY MERC FENN WOLFMOOR
From living trains to space stations populated with monsters, these eleven fantasy and science fiction stories from Merc Fenn Wolfmoor will take you on otherworldly adventures that are tethered to the heart.

FLOTSAM BY R J THEODORE
A scrappy group of outsiders take a job to salvage some old ring from Peridot's gravity-caught garbage layer, and land squarely in the middle of a plot to take over (and possibly destroy) what's left of the already tormented planet.

THE MIDNIGHT GAMES: SIX STORIES ABOUT GAMES YOU PLAY ONCE ED. BY RHIANNON RASMUSSEN
An anthology featuring six frightening tales illustrated by Andrey Garin await you inside, with step by step instructions for those brave—or desperate— enough to play.

SANCTUARY BY ANDI C. BUCHANAN
Morgan's home is a sanctuary for ghosts. When it is threatened they must fight for the queer, neurodivergent found-family they love and the home they've created.

A STARBOUND SOLSTICE BY JULIET KEMP
Celebrations, aliens, mistletoe, and a dangerous incident in the depths of mid-space. A sweet festive season space story with a touch of (queer) romance.

Find these great titles and more at your favorite ebook retailer!

Visit us at: www.robotdinosaurpress.com

Made in the USA
Middletown, DE
03 June 2024

55133606R00239